Totally Bound Pub.

S.
N

C000177923

NEVER RETREAT

BONNIE MCCUNE

Never Retreat
ISBN # 978-1-83943-859-2
©Copyright Bonnie McCune 2019
Cover Art by Erin Dameron-Hill ©Copyright October 2019
Interior text design by Claire Siemaszkiewicz
Totally Bound Publishing

NEVER
RETREAT

Chapter One

"I won!" Raye's handful of lottery scratch tickets, fanned out on the staff room table in front of her, glowed in a multitude of bright colors. She plucked the one nearest to her. "Forty dollars!"

Julia failed to respond. "He's gorgeous, just gorgeous." Her unfocused eyes and neglect of the bear claw pastry in one limp hand showed how absorbed she was in talking to Raye Soto about the new man striding around corporate headquarters in Denver, whom they'd both met that morning.

"Didn't you hear me? My winning ticket must be an omen that I'll get a big prize. You know how much I need it to cover Andy's college. No student loans! Whoo-ee!"

"Not necessarily. You'll have better odds at happiness if you notice a male hunk in front of your face. You haven't even had a date in years."

"I wouldn't start with a good-looking guy. He'd be the most dangerous type. Anyway, you've never won awards for your taste in men," Raye teased back. Her quick survey of the modest dining area showed no other people on break, so she geared up her joking. "Wasn't your last crush the barista over at Java Hut? The one who drew your initial with cream on the top of your cappuccino then pocketed the change you were due? And the one before rode a motorcycle and crashed at least once a month?"

"You're one to talk!" Julia returned to consciousness, leaning back in her chair and tapping her index finger — this week manicured in turquoise blue with tiny spangles — on the veneer-topped table. "Your ex, who hardly qualifies as an ex since he was only around for a few months, partied so hard and so often that he forgot to come home at night."

"Let's not get into odious comparisons. I got Andy from the experience, and that's enough for me." Raye pushed back her chrome-wire chair, stood and began wrapping the remains of her meal.

"This guy would be perfect for you...if you'd drop the attitude."

"He strikes me as someone with his own attitude. A touch of arrogance. Do you know anything about his history?" *I can't possibly be considering Julia's suggestion, can I?*

"He mentioned eight years in the service, and I know from his resume, which passed through my grubby paws when he transferred here, that he has a solid ten years in the corporate world, most recently at the highest levels."

"And he's not married?" With her free hand, Raye stuffed the winning lottery ticket into her pocket then grabbed the remainder in a jumbled fistful.

"No."

"Why not? What's wrong with him? Is he gay? Abusive?"

"Wait a minute," Julia said. "*You're* thirty-four and not married."

"But I have been." She considered the super-sized fruit yogurt she now balanced. The treat wasn't finished yet, so she covered the container to tote to the staff refrigerator. "I admit he's good-looking. Those ice-blue eyes, the casual dark curls." *In fact, he's too good-looking. I wouldn't trust him as far as I could throw him.*

"Those molded lips, the bottom one a little fuller than the upper... The brooding brow..." Julia gathered her snack leavings then walked to the refrigerator and leaned against the open door next to Raye to continue. "I think you're ticked off because he treated you like an employee, not a woman. He shouldn't be snubbed for that."

"Absolutely wrong! I learned long ago not to trust charm and good looks. Anyway, why are you pushing him on me? Don't you want to try your luck?"

Julia looked up at the ceiling tiles. "I haven't told you, but things are getting serious between me and Eric. We've been talking about marriage."

"Eeek!" Raye's shriek echoed from inside the refrigerator. She pulled her head out. "That's wonderful."

"Nothing's definite yet, so don't mention it. I'm entertaining the idea because I hate to see a guy as nice as Eric go to waste — or get picked off by a sneaky man-eater, like Krystle."

"I remember two years ago when Krystle got tipsy at the holiday party. She kept rubbing her hands all over Eric then tried to pull him into the hall for a necking session,"

Julia sniggered. "Fortunately, he refused to surrender. That's when I first guessed I could trust him."

"Yeah, and he's been hanging around you ever since," said Raye. "That's going somewhere permanent?"

"I sure hope so. The hu-u-uge barrier right now to any kind of development is that car loan my folks took out and now can't pay. I can't get married, can't even move in together because I have to help out the family. Anyway, on a more cheerful subject, I first saw the new director of security this morning before he even got in the office. I was walking down the sidewalk past the entrance to the parking garage when he buzzed by on a motorcycle, as tall and solid as a soldier."

"A motorcycle!" Raye slammed the refrigerator door closed. "You know how much I hate those. You're not building a case for my becoming besties with Mr. Desmond Emmett with that bit of information. They're smelly, noisy, dangerous machines."

A stricken look passed over Julia's face. "I'm so sorry. I totally spaced on what happened to your brother." Wrapping both arms around her friend, Julia hugged hard and Raye let her. "You still miss him, don't you?" Julia whispered.

"Like the devil. Every day, even though it's been years. Damn his infatuation with motorcycles. I hear about the Broncos winning and I think, '*Boy, that'll make Carlos happy,*' then I remember he's not here. Or the first snow... I want to run in and wake him up so we can walk in the park, until I remember there'll be no more times like that. He'll never know his nephew graduated at the top of the class or that Dad and Mom both have new romances going." Raye stepped back after a final squeeze. "Thanks for not hesitating to mention him. That helps." She wiped the dampness from her eyes. "Many people act like he never existed."

"They're afraid of doing or saying something wrong or upsetting you."

"Julia," Raye said, giving the name the Spanish pronunciation of 'whool-ya' as she customarily did when they were alone, "I'm more upset to think he might be forgotten."

"Not by me."

"Let's change the subject," said Raye, blinking her eyes rapidly. "What's all this nonsense in today's bulletin about a new approach to the corporate retreat and that it has nothing to do with layoffs? It makes me panicky. You know that as soon as management starts denying a rumor, you can be sure it's true."

"Um, I'm not a part of the gossip grapevine." Julia rewrapped her leftovers.

"Get serious," said Raye. "You're the one I ask to confirm them—one heartbeat away from the seat of power and all that."

Julia stopped all movement and spoke out of the side of her mouth. "I really shouldn't tell you this and promise you won't repeat it…to *anyone*."

"Cross my heart." Raye drew an X over her chest in the time-honored way.

"There are cuts on the line," whispered Julia.

A low moan accompanied Raye's response and she leaned her head on a clenched fist. "What are people going to do? Does management ever consider the human impact? Most of the employees here are supporting families—buying homes and cars, paying medical expenses and student loans."

"I fit several of those categories," said Julia. "My parents can't do without my contribution to the rent, and you know I cover the cost of the therapist who helps Mom with her arthritis. Plus we're behind on payments for the car, which means they'll repossess."

"There's hardly ever advance notice about layoffs in the corporate world."

Julia grimaced and bit into her sweet roll as if to remove a bad taste. "They don't want to start a stampede of exits or lose the ones they favor."

"Like whom?"

"I haven't heard. The retreat's going to be one way to consider upper management personnel, though."

Raye sucked in her lower lip. "Oh, no. What will I do? I barely got my head above water from the percentage I had to cough up for the condo reroofing. Now Andy's college expenses are unavoidable, even if he does qualify for aid. I'll have to increase the contributions to my investment plan if I have any hope of making a fortune."

"You mean your monthly stash of lottery tickets?" Julia guffawed, even as she swiveled her head to check the staff room for eavesdroppers. "Haven't you learned yet that you spend more on the lottery than you ever make?" Then she continued her furtive report. "I'm sure you won't be pink-slipped. Ivy adores you."

"Well, yes, my boss and I get along very well. She's always been in my corner, ever since I came in as a temp admin. But what if *she* gets the ax?"

"The sharpest corporate lawyer in the city? Get serious. Anyway, we can't live in fear of a catastrophe," said practical Julia. "Do the best you can, as always."

"But what if — ?"

"Am I disturbing anything?" In the double doors of the staff room stood the earlier subject of their chat, Desmond Emmett, a touch of awkwardness on his face.

"Absolutely not." Raye swung away to face the wall, running a fingertip under her eye.

He continued. "I was exploring storage space to keep water, juice and snacks. Say, I met both of you earlier at the managers' meeting."

Julia stepped between the two to shield Raye and her red eyes from his attention. "That's right. We're having lunch — and Raye was just leaving."

"Yes," she agreed, tossing a half-finished bag of chips and an apple core in the direction of the trash can like a basketball toss. "*Whool-ya* and I are done."

Des started. "What did you call her?"

"*Whool-ya*. That's the Spanish pronunciation of my name," Julia said.

"And you and Raye are both...Latinos?"

"Latinas. Yes, why?"

"Simply curious." He looked back and forth between the women.

"Anything else?" Julia said

"Yeah. Tell me about the staff room. Are there procedures I should follow?"

Now recovered, Raye broke in. "You mean like cleaning up after yourself? Covering your food in the microwave? All leftovers get thrown out once a month?"

"Yes. Like those."

"I'm impressed," Julia said. "A man who doesn't assume someone else will clean up."

"Hey, how do you think I got to my exalted position? I take initiative. Plus, my parents are equal-opportunity relatives. They believe their offspring

13

should experience the satisfaction of housekeeping." Des blew on the nails of his right hand then rubbed them on his lapel.

"Are you from a large family?" said Raye.

"No, only one sister, who is quite a bit younger." Des looked around the room and asked, "I assume I should bring my own dishes if I need them, right?"

Julia obligingly followed his lead in the subject of conversation while Raye checked her watch and murmured about returning to her desk. Looking at the lottery tickets in her fist, she pocketed the winning one then waved the rest in the air as if they didn't exist.

"What are those?" Des said.

"My investment fund," said Raye. "Something's got to pay off for me." She tossed them into the trash can and fast-stepped out of the staff room as if pursued by a fiend, but she heard their comments as she left.

"Investments?" Des said to Julia.

"Lottery tickets," Julia said without a trace of humor.

Chapter Two

Afternoon rounds at the corporate offices. *Everything's secure at Pursuit Telecom Ltd headquarters,* Des noted as he strode through the wide hallways of the top floor. Ceaseless responsibility for corporate-wide safety and protection went with his position as Director of Security. He surveyed the cameras, discreetly tucked high in corners, nearly hidden by light fixtures and artwork, functioning like ever-open eyes, noted that the key-card scanners by the elevators blinked their colored 'all-clear' functions, and no unexpected or incongruous packages or people disturbed his vision.

Des had mastered a touch of apprehension about the stability of his job. Company downsizing had caused his reassignment to Denver, and the rumors swirling around the managers' meeting early that morning, through low-pitched comments in the corridors, added to his tension. He hoped his transfer hadn't been an error in judgment. *I may be new on the job here but I have years of experience,* he assured himself. *No worries. Still, these days, can anyone be certain of continued employment? I was lucky to maintain the same salary after the transfer.*

To cope now, he used skills learned and honed during his time in the service. As if observing himself from a distance, he ran through a mental check-list — strangers, unusual noises or smells, the skyline panorama visible through windows. His thorough professionalism provided the best bulwark against errors. Still, when he recalled his first hours in the office, he had to wince. *Not the smoothest entry into the corporate culture or with my co-workers.* He thought back to his not-so-graceful company introduction.

Promptly at eight a.m., he reached the super-plush carpeting by the top executives' offices. Good thing I wore my best business uniform, so I fit in with the hordes. *He smiled inwardly at the absurdity. His gray suit, pale blue oxford shirt and highly polished shoes certainly made him interchangeable with the hundreds of men striding robot-like down the city-center streets where his office building was located. Only the blue and red tie covered with miniature Superman symbols hinted at his innate quirkiness.*

He'd learned to suppress most external signs of the unconventional streak he possessed, first under a military uniform then in the corporate mufti. His exterior might appear conservative, but his underwear blossomed with bright colors. Even more, his sharp intelligence guarded a tongue given to irony behind the camouflage of smooth manners, a wide grin and a firm handshake.

As he approached the CEO's office for the all-managers' meeting, he realized he had nearly ten minutes to wait. Only one woman sat next to the walnut reception desk in the front room of the suite. He beamed the wide, crooked smile that flashed his teeth, then stated the obvious, a customary ice-breaker. "Looks like I'm early."

"Ummm," she murmured as she thumbed through a stack of papers.

"And you must be busy," he added. She mumbled agreement again. Accurate assessment of the people around him had, at times, meant his survival, so he noted her strong profile, down to a determined chin then over to hoop earrings and dark hair glossed back into a tight bun at the nape of her neck. He couldn't tell much about her figure hidden within a conservative navy-blue suit, but it looked trim.

"Know where I can get a cup of coffee? I'd kill for some. One cream."

The woman finally looked directly at him. "I don't know what planet you're from, but in this building men don't order every woman in sight to get them coffee."

Ooops. Technical error based on assumption – woman at reception desk must be at the support level. And, jumping to conclusions – support personnel bring coffee. Great. Off on very much the wrong foot. He hoped she hadn't taken offense, but her stiff demeanor warned differently. However, he'd conveyed a request, not a command. "I apologize. Didn't mean to sound overbearing. I transferred here today and hoped you'd help out a newcomer." He thought he'd covered nicely by avoiding any mention of positions on the management chart.

The woman scooped up her papers, knocked them against the desktop to bring them into uniformity and, with a pat on top, placed the stack on the desk. As she rose, another woman entered. This one's hair was equally dark, but its long length swung down her back as she walked. "Maybe Julia can help you," the first woman offered as she grabbed a trim leather tote large enough to hold files. "Julia, can you make copies of that report now for the managers' meeting?"

"Sure thing. Say, has Andy heard from the colleges he's applied to yet?"

The woman curved her mouth in a disarming smile. "Yeah. Good news from three of them, but his favorite would break our bank. That's why winning the lottery's so important."

"I'm sure something will turn up if the lottery doesn't come through. He's such a bright kid," said the woman who'd been identified as Julia.

"Thanks. And so unlike his fast-talking, fast-moving father." Without a backward glance, she shouldered the bag and exited the room.

She appears unflappable. It might be an amusing challenge to get her to react. From her appearance, she was an intelligent, strong woman, focused on her career. No, he warned himself, you're too new here to play games.

"May I help you?" the second woman asked, interrupting his thoughts and taking a seat behind the desk.

"Julia?" he asked. She nodded, and he approached her. "I'm Des Emmett."

"Oh, yes." The sun couldn't have been brighter than the smile she revealed. "I was told to expect you today. I'm Julia Flora, Scott Van Voorst's executive assistant. You have a few minutes before the managers' meeting. Would you like some coffee?"

"I'd love some," he said as he followed her. Julia smoothed her pink-and-yellow miniskirt over her thighs and led him to a tiny side room where a coffee maker reigned supreme. "Seems I stuck my foot in my mouth back there."

"Why?" She passed him a mug of hot brew.

"I asked the woman who was sitting by your desk if she'd get me a cup."

Julia's dark eyes widened and she smothered giggles with both palms. "Oh, no. Raye must have burned your ears off with her response. She's a hardline feminist. I'm sure she'd sooner dump coffee over your head than bring you one."

Des walked back to the central room, Julia trailing him. "You're right on that. Guess I was lucky. What's her name?"

"Raye Soto. Yep, you're fortunate she didn't neuter you. She must have been distracted by the meeting and the rumor about layoffs."

I should have been alerted to her reaction by the way she scrapes her hair back, not distracted by a mouth that appears ready to smile. *"Plays by all the rules, eh?"*

"Raye's had to learn control on her way up. She's raising a son alone and supporting them both. Don't jump to conclusions, though. Deep inside that well-groomed, super-efficient exterior hides a touchie-feelie pushover who will give a friend her last dollar. Forget snap judgments."

"Sorry...." Des held up both hands in surrender, gripping the mug to avoid sloshing his coffee. *"You're right."* Like a flash of lightning, he realized his true urge had been to loosen the unfriendly woman's long hair.

"I will say she didn't seem nearly as rabid as I've seen her be with overbearing males." Julia looked him up and down as discreetly as possible from under lowered eyebrows. *"Seeing the way you look, she should soften up soon."*

This sounded promising. "Are you flirting with me?"

"That would be improper in an office setting. Anyway, I'm engaged but I'm not dead, as they say." Julia straightened the files and papers on her desk then stood and collected a heavy stack. *"I've got to distribute these reports before the meeting starts. You're welcome to come with me into the conference room."*

"Sure thing," he murmured as he obeyed her instructions.

Got to select my position carefully in this new situation so I can note personalities, *he returned to lecturing himself when he entered the CEO's sumptuous private office. No particle-board furniture with thin veneer in here. All the pieces were the finest hand finished. Throughout the room, original works of art tantalized the eye, some smears of colorful abstracts, some traditional Western horses and cattle from the corporate collection. He pulled his attention from the compelling visuals on display.* As the new director, I need to evaluate the corporate culture, not study the art. Even though the management structure isn't new to me, I still need to note subtle differences here.

He walked around the polished conference table past a wall of windows, from which the entire downtown skyline was visible, to opt for the middle seat on the long, far side. His sister would love this view, he noted. Reviving close contact with his younger sister, Claudia, who was limited in her activities by poor health, had been one of the pluses of his recent move.

Moments later other senior staff came strolling, marching or sidling in, depending on their interest in the meeting and what they thought might occur. One of the first was the woman Julia had called Raye. She'd obviously used the short break to tidy up, which in her case consisted of reapplying lipstick, since her hair and clothes were impeccable. She glanced at the empty chair next to Des then at a number of others around the conference table. She took one at the left corner next to the head.

Ah, the supportive challenger's position, *he mused, then turned his attention to introducing himself to his co-workers. A few minutes later, Scott Van Voorst, the big-boss CEO, strode in, trailed by Julia, who toted a tablet and went to a chair behind his.*

"Good morning, all," he boomed. "Agendas are in front of each of you. Any additions at this time?"

Des scanned the document. Nothing unusual, *he noted, and relaxed. As the new man on the team, most likely all he'd need to do was remain alert and look congenial.*

"I'd like to introduce the newest member of our team," said the CEO. "Des Emmett transferred from the Kansas City office to handle the Security Department."

Among murmurs of welcome and a handshake or two, Des straightened a trifle and smiled at everyone in turn. "I'm looking forward to working with each of you. I'm sure I'll have many questions, and I know your expertise and advice will help. That includes any information you have on getting good seats at the Rockies' games."

Chuckles greeted this statement, as Des knew they would – at least from the men. Women were a different matter. Some liked sports, some didn't and some pretended to like sports, as if they thought the ruse would get them ahead at work or in love, like the girlfriend he'd shed in Kansas City, along with his previous office. Although Jennifer had hinted that she'd like to accompany him to Denver, he'd ignored her insinuations. In fact, if there were one positive result from his transfer, it was his ability to free himself from her perfumed, malleable, yet admittedly completely feminine body. He'd been beginning to feel suffocated in the charms she wrapped around him.

Across the table, Raye hadn't twitched, shifted or stared, although all her attention was on him. "Mr. Emmett, in between Rockies' games, I hope you'll address the major flaws in the security of the Legal Department. We've been skirting these for several months now, ever since the new software was installed." She tapped the stack of papers she held until they lined up perfectly.

The woman seemed to possess zero pretense and about as much stereotyped feminine softness, so different from his typical choice of feminine companion. He wondered what drove her, challenged her. Des made a show of pulling out his smartphone and entering a note. "Yes, certainly, Ms. Soto. Let's schedule a meeting at your earliest convenience so you can brief me fully." He scanned the personnel at the table. *"In fact, I'll make the same offer to all of you. The sooner, the better."*

Nods up and down the room indicated agreement with his proposal, while smiles signified he'd made a favorable impression. The one exception was Ms. Soto, who appeared to remain silent and thoughtful. He relaxed in his chair as the manager beside him began a few words about the success of a new marketing slogan.

The group reached the end of the agenda and things were winding down when Van Voorst cleared his throat. *"Before we leave, ladies and gentlemen, I'd like to announce a new undertaking. Those of you who have been with the Denver office for several years may recall that we hold an annual retreat for top managers about this time. Once again, I plan to do so, but this time, we'll be maximizing our ability to focus completely on the tasks at hand. Rather than flying you all to a resort on a far-away beach or the bright lights of Las Vegas, we're moving the retreat to an isolated location in the mountains. This dovetails well with our retrenchment and economizing."* Glances circled the table, although no one actually twitched.

"No, no, folks." Van Voorst's jovial chuckle accompanied his words. *"No one here need fear layoffs. I've heard the rumors circulating. The change in retreat location will simply enable us to seclude ourselves from the demands of the workaday world, not to mention distractions such as sports, global news and the stock market."* He chuckled and people joined in a crescendo when they realized he was making a joke.

Des noted flickers between some of the managers, and he questioned if the annual retreat was unpopular. Van Voorst also picked up on this, and he chortled again. *"Don't worry. The lodge may look rustic, but it has every convenience. We won't be picking up television or cable shows, but we will have a library of books, films and video games, along with full access to one another, as well as the information we need to make changes and decisions. Julia will send you information on the location and content."*

The group was disassembling, breaking up into individuals who collected coffee cups and papers, when Krystle Tanaka, Director of Human Resources, asked, "What's the purpose of the retreat? Long-range plans? Multi-year budget projections?" Her distinctive tones, comprised of bright trills that uplifted at the end of each statement, sounded like she'd studied a treatise on How to Make Your Voice Listen-able. Not.

"Even more important. Team-building." Van Voorst raised an eyebrow. "Some surprises are in store for you. I trust you'll be pleased."

"I'm sure we will be, sir." Krystle addressed Van Voorst but kept her glance on Des. "I'm eager to learn more from our new manager of security. Perhaps we can grab a cup of coffee and discuss collaborative efforts." Stars seemed to glow in her eyes.

Des picked up on the surreptitious look Raye shot Julia, indicating distaste as much as if she'd bitten into a lemon. He should welcome Krystle's beaming reception. At least she seemed to want to know him better. Why wasn't the feeling mutual?

As group members straggled out, he caught undertones of concerned murmurs. The threat of economies that included dismissals was undoubtedly on their minds, regardless of what the CEO had said. Although Des refused to let something as nebulous as mere possibility disturb his equilibrium, he spared a thought for his younger sister and her condition. Any major financial upheaval for Des could wreak havoc in her life. No sense worrying about that right now—other battles to fight. *He pocketed his smartphone and followed the others.*

Chapter Three

"Moooommmm," Andy Soto called to Raye from the front hall, "I gotta get back to school in an hour. The seniors' counselor called a meeting of the class reps about graduation. Then my band's practicing for an hour."

"I'm in the kitchen," she answered as she stirred a bubbling container of chili, steam wafting from the brew. *With the addition of my secret ingredients – corn kernels and green beans – this batch is packed with nutrition. I can even invite Dad over.*

Andrew appeared in the doorway, all six feet two inches of him, and propped one arm on each side of the frame. "I don't think I have time for dinner."

"You most certainly do, especially if you're off to your band's rehearsal after the meeting." She switched off the stove and carried the stockpot to the kitchen table, as if the soup held an elixir of life. "Supper's ready right now. Sit."

Her son shambled to his chair. "I'm glad. I'm starving." He reached for the basket heaped with saltines.

"What's new?" she asked him. Andrew had the bottomless stomach of many teenage boys and Raye spared a thought of thanks that she didn't need to worry about her food budget any longer. *The way Andy eats, this dish might last only two meals.* She remembered the very lean early years, about ten of them following Andy's birth, when she'd often had to choose between groceries or new clothes, food or a movie. Sure, her parents would never have let her and Andy starve, but since they'd split up about then and their financial situations weren't the best, she'd tried to keep her pleas for help to a minimum.

That line of thinking forced her to recall Julia's warning about possible terminations. Every muscle in Raye's body tensed at the thought of the struggles of her twenties. Then ice seemed to swell from her belly outward as she recalled her childhood. Much as she treasured her parents — and Carlos' death had taught her how insecure and fleeting any relationship might be — her mom and dad had dealt with the financial uncertainty of many working-class Americans — low pay, layoffs, few guarantees of job stability or advancement. There had been times when the family would have gone very hungry without food-stamp assistance, and instances when bean stew stretched for almost an entire week of dinners. Shopping at thrift stores had been a given, and every family member took pride in squeezing pennies by carefully rinsing aluminum foil to re-use.

Raye shuddered, shook her head and took her seat, leaning over to smooth down the cowlick that always seemed to surface on her son's head while she ladled chili into their bowls. "I need to ask you what's coming up toward the end of the school year. I found out at work today that I'm going to be out of town for a week, and I need to make sure I don't miss any of your graduation events."

An unholy light lit Andy's eyes and she hurried to add, "I'll be asking Grandpop to stay while I'm gone, to make sure you get fed and off to school on time."

"Mooomm." The teenager's chant started, which inevitably led to a list of reasons why Andy was old enough to stay by himself, punctuated by crackers crumbled over the chili. Raye waved him to silence.

"Nope. I'll be anxious enough about you without envisioning you all on your own. Anyway, you know how much Grandpop enjoys being with you. He doesn't get much of a chance these days since you're so involved with studies and sports. He can check that you get up on time and help you fix supper. Now, tell me what's happening with commencement and the end of school."

Andy started a litany of his hopes for a summer job as a counselor at the nearby community center, supervising the preteen group. Not only would the stipend help with college expenses next fall, but he'd also be in the field he'd long hoped to make his career—psychology. "By the way," he added, "you need to put down the deposits on my short-list of colleges to reserve my status."

"And how much are those?"

"Depends. I figure several hundred for the school then some for housing."

Raye winced at the ease with which Andy referred to expenses, sparing another thought of gratitude that her son somehow avoided the complaints and negativity of so many teens. Maybe because they had come to rely on each other completely over the years, she'd never had to suspect he wasn't truthful about his whereabouts, reject requests for expensive clothes and accessories or worry he was dabbling in drugs and alcohol. Of course the situation with his father might have been responsible for that fact. Michael had always had multiple substance abuse issues, which she'd never tried to hide from Andy. Nowadays, she thought Michael's erratic and rare reappearances in their lives — each time looking more unhealthy and acting less coherent — made him a walking, talking warning to her son.

As Andy switched from conversation to chowing down, Raye told him about the retreat at work. "I'll be only a few hours from Denver, in the mountains, so, in case of an emergency, I can rush back. But I am expected to stay there at night, and we're supposed to keep phone calls and texting to a minimum."

"Sounds boooring," Andy said around a spoonful of chili.

"I've got to attend." Raye sighed and rested her spoon against the side of her bowl. "Important muckity-muck stuff for my job. In fact, everyone's on edge. There are lots of rumors about more cut-backs. I can't help but fret. What would happen to you and college if my job disappeared?"

"Then we'd be so poor I'd qualify for full financial aid," he said, spreading his arms wide in a victorious gesture. Some chili drips rolled down his spoon, and he snatched it back. "See? No worries."

No worries if you're eighteen and have all the answers, thought Raye. *He's like I was at his age, sure I'd survive, no matter what.* That idea improved her outlook. She must be doing a good job as a mom if her son was so normal. "Anyway, it means a few days in fresh air surrounded by nature."

"Cool." Andy stopped shoveling food to assume a speculative look. "The mountains in May. You can take great hikes, even do some rock climbing."

A laugh burst from Raye. "How likely is that? I may walk, possibly hike, but can you imagine me hanging onto some ropes and sticking my fingers and toes into tiny cracks on the face of a cliff?"

Andy shook his head. "No way. And I guess you can't sneak me there to stay in your room so I can go climbing on my own."

"Afraid not." The chili suddenly lost its flavor. For the thousandth time, Raye wished she had a man in her life who could do male-type things with her son—teach him to repair car engines, share insights about the mysteries of sex and, yes, scale Colorado's fourteener precipices. She knew some women did these things, but she'd become a mother at such a young age that she'd never tried them, and her father, the child of Mexican immigrants, lacked the cultural background to be interested. Her brother might have filled that role, had he lived. The thrust that always accompanied her memories of Carlos stabbed her.

As she forced herself to finish her chili, the new manager at work crossed her mind. *What was his name? Des?* She bet he scaled mountains...and forded massive rivers and ran miles and won fist fights, whether he started them or not.

Now why do my insides feel hollow when I think of him?

Chapter Four

Ever since Julia started working, Raye had stopped by for a quick coffee break in the morning. She knew the challenge of being not only new to the world of big business but also being a young Latina. Sure, the corporate culture was changing, but the existence of the glass ceiling, especially for women of color, couldn't be denied.

Raye's informal attempt to mentor Julia had kicked off when she'd pushed for Julia to enroll in college, even if only for a class or two. She'd learned the value of education from experience. After dropping out of school at sixteen to give birth to her son, Raye had earned a GED then spent several years trying on careers like a series of outfits before settling down to part-time college and full-time work. The BA in general studies—English, math, geography and business—had qualified her for promotions at the firm.

A few days after the managers' meeting, Raye stopped by Julia's office to collect her for a break, when she spotted her friend wrapped in conversation with Des. From what she could overhear, they were deep into a discussion about local Mexican restaurants. "Over on Santa Fe Avenue…" Julia was saying. "El Noa Noa has been around for years. Seems like any new restaurant employee is related to someone already there, a great big family. The happy hour is to die for, and in the summer, there's a live Mariachi band on the weekend."

Raye paused and held her breath. Julia sounded as if she were about to offer an invitation. *Bad idea.* This guy was simply too good-looking and fast-talking to be trustworthy, a big red flag in Raye's mind. In her admittedly limited experience, this type of man was infatuated with one thing — himself. Even if he didn't have Michael's substance abuse problems, Des was bound to see every woman simply as a decoration and adoring audience for himself. She inhaled and prepared to rescue her friend.

"All ready for a coffee break?" she called while she walked forward, then did a double take as if surprised to see Des perched on the corner of Julia's desk.

"I was telling Des about the best local Tex-Mex restaurants," her friend said. "The authentic and reasonably priced ones."

"Yes. And the ones with huge happy hour pitchers of margaritas," Des said.

"Don't leave out the taquerias over on the west side," Raye suggested. "Ready to go, *hijita*? Looks like you've cleared away the stack of work you had earlier." She strolled to Julia's other side, bent over the desk and used thumb and forefinger to page casually through a stack of glossy flyers advertising office supplies and equipment, a ploy to mark time until Julia prepared to leave.

The younger woman shot a look from under her eyebrows to Des, head tilted in his direction. "Time for my break. Hope you'll try one of the restaurants soon."

Des moved next to Raye and Julia as they strolled toward the door. "I'd feel a lot better with a local guide," he said. "Or two."

Raye turned toward Julia so Des couldn't see her, and rolled her eyes in the time-honored display of dissatisfaction as she mouthed "What?"

Julia managed to maintain a neutral expression. "Sounds great. Some time we'll do that...with my fiancé."

"Cool. We could all go together," Des said.

They scurried off without any appearance of desire to include him. Julia murmured all the way down the hall and to the staff-room entrance. "What's with you? How rude can you be? All he wants is advice on fun activities, great places to go."

"Baloney. He's hustling you is my guess." Raye gripped the coffee pot to hold it high in a question, then poured herself and Julia cups. They sat at a small, round table in the center of the staff room, one of a dozen mismatched pieces.

"Give the poor guy a break." Julia added two creams and three sugars to her coffee and stirred as if she were making a secret brew. "New in town, no acquaintances, nothing to do." She paused. "Or are you jealous he's paying attention to me?"

Raye managed an unladylike snort. "Get serious. He's all show and no go, except when he roars up and down the streets on his motorcycle, spewing noise and air pollution, wasting his time and money. I'm telling you, he's bad news. Stay away from him."

Julia protested. "I'm not interested. I have Eric, remember? But I'm sorry for him."

"How do you know he doesn't have any friends? For all we know, he has women beating at his door, tossing their keys in his mailbox, littering every corner of his apartment. He's in one of those luxurious swinging singles apartments in the southeast area."

"And how do you know that?" Julia licked off the plastic coffee stir stick and looked up at Raye from under her eyebrows.

"He mentioned it to me," Raye muttered.

"And when did this conversation occur?" Julia pushed.

Raye thumped her coffee mug on the table. Several drops of liquid escaped, and she immediately wiped them up with a napkin. "Yesterday in my office."

"I think he's interested in you, and you're not as unaffected as you pretend."

"Don't be ridiculous." Raye swiped at the table again, although she'd blotted all the liquid.

"He did come to see you."

"Yes. My department's been having concerns over security. Remember? I mentioned it in the staff meeting?"

Julia leaned back in her chair, sipped her coffee before responding. "You, along with a number of other people, asked for Des' attention. Funny that you were the first he responded to."

"Not funny at all. My problem's the worst and I asked for help before anyone else. It just shows he's conscientious."

"Whooaa. Are you saying something positive about him?" Julia rounded her eyes in mock surprise.

"Simply giving credit where it's due. He seems quite thorough."

"I'll bet. And how did you get on the topic of his apartment?"

"He mentioned a pool party there. Asked about other places to swim because his building's facility is more decorative than challenging."

Julia scooted her chair closer to the table and leaned toward Raye. "Did he ask you over to splash around?"

"He did not...nor did I hint. He did ask about the club scene."

"Ah!" Julia slapped her palms on the small table. "I'm sure he's interested in you."

So dignified that she out-performed a judge, Raye answered, "I told him I wasn't into that sort of thing and knew nothing about it."

Julia continued as if Raye hadn't spoken. "All it would take is one little pout, wink or word and phew!" She snapped her fingers.

"How do you know?"

"Because any normal, red-blooded man would consider himself lucky if you went out with him."

"Will you stop?" Raye flushed from irritation and embarrassment. "I don't want a man. I don't *need* a man. Shake off your cultural conditioning. A woman doesn't require someone in pants to make her complete. I'm doing fine on my own, thank you very much. I have a great job, a wonderful teenage son who requires my attention and support, a townhouse I've decorated to perfection—and no self-centered, macho jerk I'd have to pander to. Why do you keep pushing this guy at me?"

Several long, silent seconds passed before Julia answered. "I feel bad for you. I worry about you getting older, all on your own. It's not Des so much as you never want to go out with anyone. I've known you for, what? About six years now, and you've yet to show a flicker of interest in a male. Your mom talked you into seeing one a few times ages ago, and you've mentioned several others as way, way past interests. I know you're not gay. Why do guys turn you off?"

Ray replied, "I finally figured out that the wrong type attracts me, starting with my ex-husband. They drink to the point of insensibility or consume even worse substances. They can't hold down a job. They owe debts the size of a mountain. The last one tried to lecture me about raising my son and threatened to discipline him with a belt. I don't want to be involved with a loser and my son certainly doesn't deserve that type of role model."

"It's not normal for a woman to be alone."

"It's normal if you're an intelligent woman who has survived several hideous relationships, grown up and accepts her responsibilities."

Julia wouldn't stop. "What did your ex do to you to damage you like this?"

"The usual. Used various substances, ran around on me, couldn't hold down a job."

"And how long have you been on your own? Seventeen years?"

Raye frowned. "What do you think I am, a nun? I've been divorced seventeen years, but I've met men, gone out on dates, done things like go to movies and restaurants, played cards, seen concerts. Two of the men were fairly steady relationships. And, I'll have you know, I attract interest—like that guy who's trying to sell me office supplies, even though I told him to go to the purchasing department. He drops by every couple of weeks. Say, that gives me an idea." Her face lit up. "He always checks out my top and tries to sneak a look down it. Maybe I can get a huge discount on pricing if I bend over a little."

Julia whooped, spattering a mouthful of coffee down her chin. Between choked chuckles, she wiped herself off. "You'd never."

"I don't know. Remember, *somos luchadoras*. You're encouraging me to take a chance. His services may be exactly what I need," Raye joked.

"Ah, yes, our motto. 'We are fighters.' You're firmly in that category nowadays, but it's not the salesman I'm recommending. It's our new manager of security."

"Why? Why?" Raye's frustration with Julia's obsession about Des spilled over in an annoyed tone.

A dreamy glaze came to Julia's eyes. "My intuition tells me that you and he belong together. You know many people swear I have second sight."

If only, Ray thought. *If only I could believe a decent, intelligent, hard-working man is out there for me.* She swirled her coffee and decided to switch the subject so Julia would give up her fruitless line of inquiry. "Speaking of men, Eric seems different from the ones I've run into. What are your wedding plans?"

"Yes, speaking of men and my boyfriend, I say there are plenty of good candidates like him…if you look."

Enough is enough, Raye thought. She checked her wristwatch and faked a double take. "I've got to get back. Can we continue this discussion some other time? Maybe over a beer?" She carried her mug to the sink to rinse it out.

"Sure thing," Julia said.

Almost in passing, Raye followed up on the rumor that had been gathering strength recently. "So what about the gossip about layoffs? There were lots of whispers at the managers' meeting. That bothers me more than boyfriends."

"Nothing definite *yet*, as far as I know," said Julia.

"*Yet?* You're the big boss' hands," teased Raye, "so you'd be the first to know."

Julia pushed away from the table while balancing the mug containing the remainder of her coffee. "The discussion about you and men?" she called over her shoulder. "I'm going to hold you to that. See you later."

"Later," Raye replied. She paused with a soapy sponge in one hand and dish in the other. *If you only knew,* she thought. *If you only knew, you innocent little girl, the number of jerks who are out there.*

Raye didn't have tons of experience dating, but over the time since her divorce, she'd met a few men. Some had been okay as friends, polite and somewhat appealing, even not bad looking. She'd hoped for enough mutual interest to tempt her into a continued connection but there had been no such luck. The few sparks had fizzled rapidly.

Others, more physically attractive, had turned out to be nightmares. These 'bad boys', as she'd labeled them, had expected an overnight in return for buying her a burger, as if they'd done her a favor by dating her. They'd been enough like Michael to scare her stiff. She shivered as she recalled them. No, she definitely was better off alone, even if her bed was as empty as the calories from a package of Ding Dongs.

Chapter Five

Shaking her mug to rid it of drops of water, Raye grabbed a paper towel to dry it when Des came through the door. *Did he hear what Julia and I were talking about? Has he been standing outside the door eavesdropping? No, he couldn't have. I'm being paranoid.*

"Hello," she stammered with the nervous twitch of the guilty.

"Hello," replied Des and inclined his head in a slight nod before he moved to the coffee machine.

Doesn't seem as if he's aware. That's a relief. But as she started toward the exit, he turned and scrutinized her. His eyelids drooped, half-covering his eyes. She stopped, clutching the cup in front of her with both hands. *A good offense is the best defense,* she reminded herself. "May I help you with something?"

"Not really," he mumbled. "I was going to ask you for a favor, but I don't want to take a chance."

She opened then closed her mouth. He must have heard the interchange with Julia about men. Her face flamed. What response made sense? Neither a shriek nor a denial, not a snappy, nasty rejoinder, innocence and ignorance—played to their ultimate—these options occurred to her. He couldn't criticize those. Drawing herself up to her tallest, she acted with the confidence of an Oscar winner. "What do you mean?"

He had no reply as his coins rattled down in the coffee dispenser.

She allowed her irritation with him to mushroom as she re-absorbed the intimate interplay she'd interrupted between him and Julia earlier. *How dare he try to make time with my friend?* She was innocent and naïve, much like Raye had been when she'd met Michael, vulnerable as a baby kitten. Des' every word, the way he sauntered across a room rather than merely walking, the ease with which he flashed his wide grin, the effortless charm oozing from his pores, and the dark tumbling locks and ice-blue eyes labeled him as a threat to Julia's peace of mind. Raye's thoughts became vindictive, but she refused to allow them to erupt out of her as rude comments. Agitated inside, she pasted on a gracious, imperturbable air and marched from the room, head held high.

* * * *

Days later, a major deadline threatened, and Raye skipped both her coffee break and lunch in her rush to complete the project—government forms without which the company faced legal penalties. She had plenty of time but she always tried to draft documents early for chief counsel Olivia Lector's review. As manager of the legal department in charge of operations, Raye made the smooth, timely function of duties her primary responsibility.

A roll of thunder and flashes of lightning announced the arrival of a summer storm and Raye paused to scan the magnificent cityscape spread below her office, as the sudden blinking of electricity and the illumination of the storm freshened the dark, heavy wood of the massive bookcases as well as the entire office suite. The open drapes framed the scene through large windows. Being twenty floors up had some advantages, above all the view — although if the power failed, clomping up and down all those flights of stairs held no charm. As she thought this, the lights flickered again and power surged on the computer. *Eeek!* She pressed a few keys. It appeared the auto-save function had worked fine.

She heard Julia's giggles before she saw her friend. Then the young woman wobbled into the office, hands clutching her stomach. "You won't believe what I've got to tell you," she gasped. "Hysterical." She collapsed in the chair across from Raye's.

"I can't talk right now," said Raye. "I've got to finish this before I leave."

"This won't take but a second, and I guarantee you'll be so energized, you'll work at twice the speed."

"All right." She turned toward Julia. "What is it?"

"You know how you've warned me about Des several times? That he may be wild and a ladies' man? Well, he came to me after lunch and warned me about *you.*"

"Me?" So shocked she thought of nothing else to say, Raye was shaken out of her work mode. "Whatever for?"

"He said he'd overheard us talking, and it appeared to him you wouldn't hesitate to use any means to get what you want."

"No way."

"Way."

"Why'd he think that?" Raye cast her thoughts back over the recent coffee break and winced. "You don't mean the nonsense about letting a man look down my shirt?"

"Exactly." Julia cracked up again. "He said you appeared to have more experience in life than I did and people might get the wrong idea about me if I model my behavior on yours."

"Ridiculous." Despite her habit of shedding her shoes when her feet were hidden under her desk, Raye jumped up to pace back and forth across the room in her stockings, fists as well as teeth clenched. "I've never been so insulted in my life. For him to think I'd trade on my gender for an advantage at work? Unspeakable."

"That's what I told him, that you and I kid around all the time." Julia got serious. "I can't blame him completely. You've gone out of your way to build a barrier around yourself where men are concerned. He doesn't know you like I do."

Julia's statement stopped Raye short. She hated to think of herself as unfair and sexist—or the opposite of sexist. *Can women be sexist in reverse?* She supposed so, but she asked her friend.

"Sure," said Julia. "That's possible. You're sexist if you treat people based on stereotypes you have of their gender."

"Like assuming women are dumber than men?"

"Or, in your case, assuming women are smarter than men," Julia tossed back.

"Yes, but there's a difference between a stereotype and reality."

Julia laughed but continued in a serious vein. "You know how we both react to stereotypes about Latinas and Hispanics. We hate it, even though we're powerless to eliminate them."

Raye flopped into the tweed-covered chair next to Julia and dropped her head backward, rubbing her neck with two fingers. "Lord, you're right. I've been acting like those jerks, like Mason Mobley, with his snarky comments about our makeup and jewelry, even though we look like nearly every other woman in the firm. Every time I'm around him, I get itchy."

She eyed her and Julia's clothes. Today Julia was in a loose, bright yellow and orange color-block top over a black pencil skirt, paired with black ankle booties. Raye was dressed more conservatively, in plain clothes that approached a uniform, a dark suit with little decoration or pattern. This was a deliberate choice for her. She'd noticed long ago that the outfits worn by women in management positions were subdued. However, the two selected similar jewelry and scarves—large, striking necklaces, hoop earrings and long, colorful wraps around their necks.

"There is one difference." Julia held up her index finger, today polished with color blocks to match her blouse. "Neither of us is exactly petite. We don't starve ourselves. And we don't try to hide or disguise our assets."

"We shouldn't have to." Raye broke off with the abruptness of glass shattering. "Do you think that's what he thought?"

"Who thought about what?"

"Des...about me. That I'm available, because of what I said to you jokingly?"

"I don't know," said Julia. "Why don't you ask him?"

No response.

"I dare you to ask him," Julia pushed. "Then you might open yourself up to figuring out what you feel about him."

* * * *

Dozens of chores crowded the weekend before the retreat. Laundry for herself and Andy, a few hearty meals in the freezer, grocery shopping, water for houseplants, written instructions for emergency contact. She was giving the living room a quick vacuum mid-morning on Saturday when Andy tore into the condo and threw himself onto the recliner.

Still in his black and gold soccer uniform, his dark hair, damp from exertion and longer than she preferred, tangled and drooped over his forehead. He scrunched his dark eyes, looking like he was six again and had been instructed to eat his green beans. She'd soon discovered disgust, not pain, hunger or love, motivated him.

"Oh, Mom, the absolutely lamest thing," he moaned as he twisted his head back and forth against the back of the chair.

She switched off the vacuum at once. Andy wasn't the type to magnify his emotions. If he was upset, a real problem had created a calamity. "What's wrong?"

He dropped his head into his hands, propping his elbows on his knees. "After you went out grocery shopping and before I left for the soccer game, I got a call. The university phoned to say the scholarship funds dried up, and they're not going to be able to come through with the stipend. Doesn't that suck? There's no way I can go there now."

"Oh, no!" Raye sank down on the teal sectional sofa across from Andy. Her stomach bucked and twisted. *Andy's scholarship gone? What can I do? What can he do?* Frantic thoughts of her mother, her father, friends and acquaintances tumbled through her mind as she struggled to identify someone who might help.

She noticed a loose fiber on the sofa's cushion, absent-mindedly tugged at it, then smoothed the material with her fingertips. The entire piece of furniture was a thread-bare and faded hand-me-down from a friend from years ago when she'd first started working at Pursuit and was thrilled at the opportunity yet fearful about the responsibility. Starting as a temp then hired at an entry-level salary, Raye had made her trip up the corporate ladder more a slog than a flight, with raises coming in miniscule jumps. She'd had almost no household goods then — a card table and four folding chairs from her mom, the beds, of course, the brick-and-board bookcases typical of students, mismatched dishes and flatware courtesy of Goodwill. Gradually she'd upgraded most pieces, but she'd never been willing to go into debt for a couch, having higher priorities, like her own education and Andy.

A surge of sick frustration swamped her. It seemed like she'd been struggling forever to keep her head above the financial waters that threatened to swamp her and her son. Yes, she'd made plenty of mistakes in her life, beginning with keeping company with Michael and ignoring birth control, dropping out of school, chasing absurd jobs that paid nothing and gave no security then rejecting her parents' offers to help. Still, like most people, she'd learned from failure and error.

Certainly she wouldn't trade a thing in her past for her most important achievement — Andy — even though she'd had to spread her higher education over years. Material goods were items she cheerfully did without so Andy wouldn't suffer for her lack of judgment. She'd thought they'd made it over the hump, when he was given the scholarship to a state university. Now this.

And what if she were laid off? She wouldn't be able to cover food and house payments. She suppressed the incipient panic, blinked rapidly to disperse the welling tears but failed to control the choked feeling. Knowing she had to conceal any hint of her fear of unemployment, she addressed the matter of college. "What a catastrophe. How can we overcome this? Is there any chance in a few weeks they'll find more?"

"No. They said their investments bottomed out. Their only answer was to try again next year."

"Next year?!" The words came out as a wail. "What are you supposed to do until then? Work in some fast food restaurant?"

Andy straightened up. "You mean, like you did when I was a baby? If you worked at whatever job you could find to make ends meet, I can, too."

"It's not fair. It's not fair after you've worked so hard in school, participated in all those extracurricular activities and sports."

Andy leaned forward and squeezed Raye's hand. "You always tell me life's not fair, to get used to it."

"Well, I'm *not* used to it. I never expected this setback." She brushed at the sofa cushions even as she gnawed her lip.

The more upset she grew, the calmer he became, in the mysterious balance that sometimes occurred between people in a close relationship. "Mom, calm down." Andy squeezed both her hands. "Sure, this bums me out, but it's not the end of the world. I can go to a community college for a year or two then transfer. I can get all my basics out of the way. When you get back from your office retreat, we can go over the forms. What do you always tell me? *Todos somos luchadores!*"

"Okay." She had to believe the bad news was only a temporary setback, had to show Andy how adults dealt with disappointment and challenges. She squeezed his hands and gave a tremulous smile. "Keep on fighting."

Chapter Six

Talk about purple mountains' majesty, here's the real thing. Des steered his Audi Quattro smoothly around the curves and slopes of the narrow mountain road. He and Raye, along with Julia and Kabir Varma from the mobile communications division, in the back seat, had been assigned to carpool to the lodge. At a recent briefing, Van Voorst, jovial as a cheap Santa Claus at a discount store, had announced the ride-shares as the first step in their teambuilding.

This part of the country was new to Des. Although he was skeptical about the value of the upcoming retreat to staff relationships, the function presented him a chance to experience his new location to the fullest. The landscape had a subtle power that was working its magic on him, with clouds billowing so high over the pine-clad forests that they looked like cotton candy for the gods, sun glittering from the stream at the bottom of the canyon that curlicued next to the tarmac. His sister would love the panorama. *That's an idea... Bring her up here for a short vacation.*

It would be so easy to forget he was bound for a work assignment, to simply keep driving and driving, discovering a town new to him, meeting folks who didn't dress in standard business uniforms, who thought about things like books and music, politics and... He snuck a glance at Raye in the front passenger's seat but couldn't see her expression, because she was looking out of the side window. In the rear-view mirror, he saw Julia and Kabir, but she was intent on the smartphone clutched desperately in her hand while he appeared to be napping.

"How 'bout them Rockies?" Des snapped out, partly to create some kind of response, partly to distract himself from his mental escapism. The other three occupants of the car jumped in unison. Raye swiveled toward him, the surprise expressed by her mouth in dissonance with the moodiness in her eyes. He wondered what she'd been thinking. *Daydreaming? Planning a strategy for the retreat? Pulling together a budget for her fall wardrobe? Who can tell with a woman?*

"How 'bout them Rockies?" Raye nearly snorted. *Where did that come from and why?* It was likely a typical lame attempt at conversation. She, for one, didn't appreciate it. She turned to address Julia in the back seat. "Did you have a lot to do before we took off?" As the CEO's personal assistant, Julia had been stuck with the minutia for the retreat. Raye had seen her in the copy room hour after hour then trudging up and down the elevator and halls with boxes and dollies, office supplies, even snacks.

"Yeah, but I managed."

"Don't forget that we'll all help you unpack. Won't we?" Raye threw at the two male occupants. "Men have to be good for something, after all. Mowing lawns, opening jars, lifting loads." She sniggered, but when the men were silent and Julia scowled at her, she wished she hadn't tried the lame joke.

"What's with you?" Des kept his eyes on the road, which was getting narrower and steeper by the second, but Raye had no doubt he was addressing her. "Can't you say a kind word about a male? You're writing off half the population."

"Not quite half," she snapped back. "You're not as strong as women. You die off at a younger age. Women make better pals. Take Julia. We have a mutual admiration society. Right, Julia?"

"Right." Her voice drifted over the front seats. "We're only seven years apart in age. We both adore Shakira and Thalia, and we're curious about the political ambitions of young George P. Bush."

"Yep. We shared information about our families, teen rebellions and school, and we found out how much we're alike," said Raye. "Music, performers, television shows, even the way we dress. We both favor long, light-weight scarves, earrings that make a statement and knock-out beaded necklaces and bracelets."

Des said, "I'll admit most men don't wear designer accessories and jazzy jewelry. But we bring our own good qualities—physical strength, skills in space utilization… We don't mind getting our hands dirty. We often make decisions faster. So why the sour attitude? Mr. Right never came along? Or did he turn out to be Mr. Wrong?"

His remarks, made with the mildest of tone and a touch of wit, sounded curious, not judgmental. Yet Raye guessed Des was making assumptions about her and somehow sensed her failure at marriage or any kind of permanent relationship. Michael used to do that—presume he knew what she was thinking, especially when he spun a tale about where he'd disappeared to overnight. Even after seventeen years, the thought of her ex-husband Michael angered her to incoherence. She also hated that Des had hit the target with no effort, although bamboo under her fingernails wouldn't force her to admit that to him.

"Experience taught me whom to rely on and whom not to. I'd estimate that many men rank in the bottom twenty-five percent on trustworthiness. Romantic attachments seem to draw out the worst in males—possessiveness, greed, stubbornness, even violence."

Michael placed even lower, she thought, recalling his first suggestion long ago when she'd turned up pregnant. *'Get rid of it'*, had been his advice. Granted, he had stuck around long enough to marry her once her father had confronted him. The fact that she'd been underage had helped, too. Provided a choice between a charge of statutory rape and giving the baby a name, Michael had caved, then hit the road shortly thereafter.

"As do lots of women," Des responded. "They become insanely jealous and possessive at the same time as they get greedy. They value only the gifts you give them, the fancy places you take them and the amount of money you're worth. They tap into your cell phone, email, text messages—and bank accounts, if they can. Could it be," he asked with a touch of humor, "that we've both picked losers in the past?

Maybe we need to make a major change in our choices."

She wondered at his choice of female companions but didn't pursue the project. "There was one exception in my life," she said. "My brother. Ever considerate, ever kind."

Des remained focused on the road that swerved with hairpin turns. "I'd like to meet this paragon some time."

"You can't," she said. "He died years ago."

A touch of embarrassment accompanied his response to her revelation. "Sorry."

With a shrug, she blinked then turned her mind away from bad memories. She'd learned there was no benefit from dwelling on what had happened. As her father always said, *'Keep your eyes on the prize, not on what's gone before.'* "The only other exception I've run up against is my dad," she added. "He may have flaws, but he's honest and behind me one hundred percent."

Des tightened his fingers on the steering wheel before he claimed. "I'm an exception, too."

"Only time will tell," Raye said.

Des fell absolutely silent, steering with care and avoiding glances in her direction, his face empty of reaction. She guessed she'd blocked any flippant response then wondered why he brought out the worst in her. She should attempt to get along with him, if simply for good working conditions. There was no reason to snap at him because he reminded her of her ex. "We still have a way to go," she said to cover her embarrassment, as she snuggled into her seat. "I think I'll snooze."

No surprises there, thought Des. Raye's reaction fit with the rest of her interactions with him. She had a chip more the size of a huge rock on her shoulder. He didn't know why, but she presented an intriguing challenge that gave him pause. *What's her history? Single mother, so no husband, maybe an ex. Does she have legitimate reasons to distrust men? Like some of the natives in Kuwait who were hounded and harassed by drunken servicemen?*

He had to admit that while the military had taught him valuable lessons, helped and matured him, he'd also rubbed shoulders with some of the scum of the earth, not counting the kids fresh from a farm or packed in cotton wool during their childhoods, who were homesick, scared shitless and insecure about their competency or even their survival. It was common for them to play tough, go overboard when they escaped the strictures of duty. But there were those who enjoyed playing the petty dictator, who even got a kick from inflicting pain. There were even some whose dishonesty and unreliability surpassed Des' imagination.

Since leaving the service, he'd learned that type wasn't limited to the military. There seemed to be a pattern — large groups, a less-than-vigilant leader, a petty dictator somewhere in the mix and a climate for abuse and bullying was created. He didn't waste time trying to figure out what made those men tick or what, if anything, might fix them. He left that up to the mental health crowd. Instead he concentrated on neutralizing their power and removing them from his sphere, if possible.

He wondered if Raye had tangled with one of them. If so, there was no telling how damaged she'd become. Those jerks could be found at all ages, any income level. *Look at what some did to Claudia.* Saddled with Type I diabetes, his little sister had learned as a child to give herself insulin injections, but when Claudia had hit adolescence and her reactions to the medicine had started to fluctuate wildly, the results weren't pretty. Some kids mocked her bouts of confusion, the sudden sweats, even occasional loss of consciousness. Then when Claudia also developed celiac disease, which made eating in public a torture, things had gotten even worse. Des' emails, calls and letters of support hadn't provided much relief.

Des gave a sidelong glance at Raye, who was apparently napping in the seat next to him. From the smooth, undisturbed surface of her face, he wouldn't have imagined she'd suffered any torments. Women with her looks usually had men running to follow their commands. *Jumping to conclusions,* he told himself. He should know by now what trouble that bad habit got him into. Pulling up a mental list of methods to force himself into a less judgmental frame of mind, he realized he'd been around her enough during the first few weeks at work to also find she was respected by most of her co-workers for her hard work and pleasant disposition, not that he'd seen much of that.

Underdogs always called forth a protective instinct in him. His sister, some buddies in the service, the Arab natives... A sinking feeling—*or is it anticipation?*—made him wonder if he'd added Raye to the list.

* * * *

"Everybody out," Des announced as he pulled up in front of a massive log structure sprawling back and out to the sides from the circular gravel driveway. Towering spruce trees surrounded the lodge while variegated rocks anchored the structure around its entire base. Several chimneys, built with the same rocks, indicated that many of the interior rooms boasted local fieldstone touches.

Struggling out of sleep, Raye stretched and looked around. Julia and Kabir didn't hesitate. They opened the back doors and exited with the stifled moans of people who had been immobilized into paralysis from riding too long in a car. She noticed that Des took his time. In fact, he appeared to have forgotten to switch off the ignition as his bright blue eyes focused on her. "What? What?" she asked. "Have I drooled on myself? Is there a problem?"

"No."

"Then let's get going!" She hoped she sounded enthusiastic about an activity she dreaded. The idea of being on stage with other employees and the top bosses for a week made her stomach clench. She gathered her purse and coat then swung out of the car to walk to the trunk, but she had to wait for Des to release the lock. Several automobiles had already disgorged chatting passengers and luggage, and even as Des' carload joined in, more vehicles pulled up. In the general pandemonium, Pursuit staff members shook hands, stomped their feet to rid themselves of cramps, asked one another if the sunny weather might hold, strolled a few feet toward the wide overhung porch to search for water or a soda and tossed bags to their owners. Through the oversized front doors, hand-carved with figures of Colorado wildlife, Scott Van Voorst took position, crossed his flannel-clad arms over his chest and surveyed his squad.

"Oh, Lord," Julia murmured to Raye as she reached for her suitcase. "I'm supposed to direct this exercise. I'd better get inside and set up the check-in area. See you later."

Raye watched Julia mount the stairs, a bag heavy on her shoulder, halt briefly by Van Voorst to say a few words then disappear into the lodge. Des, who had paused while unloading the trunk, nudged her with the corner of a tote. "This yours?" he asked, bringing her back to the present.

"Yes. Thanks." She gathered her duffle, tote and purse then paused on the uneven ground to look over her surroundings, hoping she looked relaxed yet interested. *What am I doing here?* She'd wondered from the launch of this activity how she'd been included. As the Law Department manager, she often was deputized to act on behalf of the general counsel, but she wouldn't have thought her position lofty enough to warrant rubbing shoulders and exchanging pleasantries with the top executives. Her boss, Olivia Lector—out of town on business for several days—was slated to arrive later this evening. Maybe she'd be able to offer guidance about Raye's role here.

Rumors and reality about downsizing had spread everywhere. The new head of security was an example. Des had said he was now located in Denver specifically because of management structure changes. Raye couldn't escape a nagging sense that hidden within the design of the retreat was corporate's own agenda and that her future was at risk. Raye shouldered her duffle and marched up the stairs to check in.

Chapter Seven

I must have been exhausted. For good reason—after coming home from work, cleaning the entire house then making a pot of stew big enough to feed Andrew and Pops for several days, Raye hadn't gotten to sleep until two in the morning. She recalled collapsing on the bed in the lodge without bothering to unpack then crawling back to consciousness several hours later when the setting sun blazed on her face. She staggered to the bathroom to rub her cheeks and eyes as she paused in front of the full-wall mirror.

A few splashes of cold water wakened her before she tackled her hair, which was tangled almost beyond fixing, into something less formal than the office style but still controlled. A high ponytail wrapped with a long lock, a few curls coaxed in front of her ears, had to suffice. There was no time to spare for creating a more elaborate style. Anyway, all the events at the retreat were corporation occasions, not parties. While at work, she avoided wasting time on appearances in favor of concentrating on the business at hand, so anything less severe would seem casual to others.

She left the bathroom and its treasure trove of gleaming accessories — the huge shower boasting multiple spray and massage heads, a tub doubling as a whirlpool, a collection of herbal beauty products, even a bidet. It was quite fancy for a mountain retreat. She wasn't accustomed to such luxury. She wondered why anyone would waste money on such a lavish set-up.

The bedroom surpassed the lavatory in decadent, if rustic, opulence. Wooden furniture in the faux-frontier style looked hand-hewn but still bore a polish as reflective as a mirror, as did the brass fittings. Expensive Navajo rugs functioned as bedspreads while large, colorful, yarn God's Eyes and prints of Southwestern desert landscapes adorned the walls.

Raye made time now to explore the room, first pausing at an oversized dresser where she poked through a wicker basket holding gift items — stationery, post cards, pens, pencils, a memo pad, a packet of trail mix, health bars, a key chain, even a sleep mask and paper slippers. She continued to a massive armoire and swung it open to reveal a terrycloth guest robe and small incidentals such as a shoe polish cloth and laundry bag. A nightstand held the ever-present Gideon Bible, more writing instruments, several candies to soothe the sleepless and a carafe and glass for water. By the time she reached French doors covered by full-length plaid curtains, nothing would have surprised her, so the miniature balcony revealed as she pushed the window coverings aside was expected. She stepped out to soak in the view of conifers backed by rocky terrain and breathed in to experience air that seemed to come from a different planet than the atmosphere she absorbed in Denver.

"*Hoy!*" she exclaimed before she realized she'd spoken the Spanish word for 'today' out loud. At times like these, when effervescence bubbled up inside her due to nature or happiness or optimism, the word seemed appropriate. *This I could get used to,* she thought, *for a short while,* even though this opulence was wasteful and unmerited. As a muted buzz came from the cell phone stuffed in her pocket, she remembered she'd set the alarm to alert her about the four p.m. meeting in the lounge. By speeding up the process of dressing, she flew down the stairs in five minutes to join her colleagues gathered in the pine-and-rock-themed room.

No one was relaxing. Kabir Varma, vice president of the mobile communications division—now dressed in casual, although still pristine, clothing—was functioning as master of ceremonies, and he faced the group and summarized the rest of the day's agenda.

"Welcome, Chosen Twenty-Five, to this year's staff retreat. That's what we call you when referring to you all together. As a select group of top managers at Pursuit, you'll be participating in stimulating challenges to stretch you and prepare you for future successes. Right now, we're going to orient you to the lodge and grounds to prepare you for activities during the rest of the week.

"You'll have a short break from five-thirty to six-thirty, then we'll gather again for dinner. If the trip here left you starving, grab some trail mix, sports bars or fruit from the conference table in the middle of the room. Let's have you split into two smaller groups to make things easier." He motioned a sweeping motion with one arm. "Straight down the center of the room. Those on the left, follow Ben. Those on the right are with me."

People shuffled and milled around, some heading to collect snacks, others locating friends with whom to pair. Raye spotted Julia in deep discussion with Van Voorst, and she moved in that direction but paused to allow them privacy. When the CEO nodded and walked away, Raye approached.

"Any more news about layoffs?"

Julia shifted from foot to foot. "No, and I don't expect any here. Now hush about it."

"Is this activity something you're part of?"

Julia pulled a face. "Yeah, I can come on this tour. I need to know locations to keep schedules organized." She plopped her sunhat on her head.

Raye turned and followed as her friend led the way toward Kabir Varma's troop. "You're in the strangest position, Julia. It's like you're part of the group and, at the same time, not part of the group."

"That's how it always is for me. If you're an admin, you have this label on you. You're qualified to do this but not that. You get involved with one thing, but you're prohibited from another. You especially can't qualify for promotion to management, so no big raises."

"Oh, lord," Raye broke in. She'd spotted Des strolling toward them. "Here he comes again. We can't get rid of him."

"*You* can't get rid of him," Julia replied. "My second sight tells me you don't want to. Now, be nice."

"Hello, ladies," Des spouted with unwarranted cheer. "Ready to head out?"

He nearly smiled as he noted Julia's encouraging greeting compared to Raye's aloofness. He didn't know what her problem was, but it sure was fun to upset her equilibrium. She had a cute pout that reminded him of his sister as a baby when she didn't get her way. In fact, she flat-out tempted him. *That ponytail ought to be pulled regularly,* he thought, *if simply to run my fingers through the shining cascade.*

Still, she was too polite or professional to ignore him. He counted on that response so he could continue to dog her. Like a proud professor, Kabir called to his followers as he stepped down the stairs and across the grounds, spouting advice as he went. "Be sure to wear lots of sunblock. We're at nearly ten thousand feet and thunderstorms occur regularly." Julia, Raye and Des fell in at the back. *The three of us look like the loners in this crowd.*

Raye began chattering to Julia in Spanish. Des caught a word here and there, including an exclamation that sounded like '*Oy!*' When he discovered he could translate parts of sentences, he surmised her skill level was basic, since it didn't exceed his by much. She mentioned taking a short siesta and added that her *dormitorio* was *muy buena.* Although Julia answered briefly in Spanish, she shot short glances toward Des, her forehead furrowed.

Des picked up on her unease and intervened. "*Por favor.* My Spanish is limited. Do you mind speaking in English?"

Raye stopped, arms akimbo, to draw in a breath, as if to control herself. "My apologies. I don't get much chance to practice my skills. I hope you don't mind." The polite upturn of the corners of her mouth could hardly qualify as pleasant. Des flashed a real grin back. *She's trying her damnedest. I wonder what her problem is, although I don't really care. She's fun to tease, reacts to every jab.*

Turning back to Julia, Raye shrugged and continued. "*Un día muy ocupado.* A very busy day." She inclined her head toward Des, even while she set off in a stroll again. Julia kept up while Des stopped abruptly.

He couldn't resist another challenge, solely to provoke her into losing her temper. "Whoa, hold on." He stepped back, palms forward. "We're at a company function. We're supposed to be developing team-building skills and getting to know one another better. Then you break into your *señorita* act. Isn't English our official corporate language?"

Raye stopped short. Swinging around, she said, "Our official corporate language is any we can make money with, my *señorita* performance notwithstanding."

He shifted on his feet as he checked Raye's carefully correct expression. *She won that contest.* Then he swung toward Julia. A slight pursing of the mouth, as if stifling giggles, was her sole movement.

"Do you have any other stereotypes you'd like me to educate you about? We're slow-moving? Take siestas?" Raye wore an expression of intense sympathy, and Des marveled at her self-control.

Julia interrupted. "This discussion is getting too heated for me. You two can catch up when you're done." Swinging her windbreaker over her shoulder, she stepped away. Raye remained motionless, facing Des.

"Your stereotypes might help explain why you have a chip on your shoulder when it comes to me." He pushed again, wondering how much she'd take and truly wishing he could disarm her well-disguised hostility to reveal the dynamic, alluring woman deep below her work persona.

Evidently she'd had enough, for she said through gritted teeth, "Nope. Wrong. I have a chip on my shoulder because you assumed I wasn't a manager. As soon as you saw me, you asked me to get you coffee. And now that I've noticed you on your motorcycle pulling into the parking garage, because you ride a hog."

"So you imagine I'm a wild and crazy guy. Beat people up on my off-hours. Binge drink and do drugs and women."

"There's certainly some validity to that." She turned and walked after Julia.

He dogged her. "Then I'd say you're meeting a stereotype with a stereotype."

"I speak from experience."

"What? What?"

"My ex and my brother."

"Your ex is a biker?"

"He was. I don't know what he is now, and I don't care. It's not a topic I talk about."

"Do you think about it?"

All expression dropped from her face.

"That's none of your business. Believe what you like." She reached Julia, grabbed her hand and flung herself to march off after the rest of their group.

"Thanks for the permission," he called after her. He knew she'd purposely avoided answering his question, and he wondered what that indicated. In the case of an ex, probably that she wasn't in touch with him nowadays, which was good. Bit by bit he was learning more about this woman, so different from the ones he usually met in a business setting or in bars and clubs.

Despite her appearance of irritation—if not antagonism—toward him becoming more extreme with every encounter, she fascinated him.

At work, he'd met more than his share of hard-hitting professional females, determined to get ahead at any cost. Those women he wrote off both as friends *or* lovers. They seemed one-dimensional, more interested in success on the job than thriving as whole, living, breathing humans.

During off-hours, Des often met and enjoyed women won through flattery, expensive gifts, fine food and desire as unbridled as his. If he tired of them quickly, he reminded himself that he'd renounced well-rounded women when Gina had sent him the 'Dear John' letter years ago. The heat of the desert seemed nothing in comparison to the flush of disappointment and frustration that had surged in him when she'd dumped him, and it had hung on for months, impeding his full enjoyment of his military adventure.

So he'd learned to opt for shallow, materialistic females, who valued only the gifts they received, the fancy places he took them and the amount of money he was worth. Jennifer, far back in Kansas City and absent from his current life, fit that description perfectly. He knew the fault was his if he'd chosen the parade of beautiful empty women with whom he'd kept company over the years since Gina had left him, a heartbroken and lonely soldier.

He laughed silently at himself as he brought up the rear of his group, now circling the lodge's exterior, grazing brush-like branches, crushing pine needles and cones underfoot, inhaling air that resembled city atmosphere as much as mint smelled like moth balls. He'd known for some time that he was ready to discard his immature and self-limiting attitude toward the opposite sex. He wasn't nineteen any longer, not even twenty-nine. Inevitably someone got hurt in every relationship that didn't end in marriage, but adults gained experience and memories, maybe to be prepared for that really great partner waiting down the street—or in the next office. *Now, finally, a fierce and determined woman I could spend my life with.*

A soft gust, as luscious, spicy and fresh as a Ponderosa, filled his lungs, and energy invigorated his every muscle. *Yep. I'm ready.* He flexed his shoulder muscles and arms, and clasped his fists over his head in a victory salute. Raye intrigued him, no doubt about that, like an itch he couldn't scratch. As he walked along behind her on the path circuiting the lodge, a surge of energy filled him, a curiosity and fascination he hadn't experienced for years.

Chapter Eight

Mornings at this altitude were cool, even in the middle of summer. There was no hoarfrost, but the sun created glitter and shine from the damp of near-frost on the ground. The Chosen Twenty-Five straggled to the central lawn in front of the lodge, clutching paper cups of coffee and hot chocolate in death-grips. All wore heavy jackets, and most had put on scarves as well. They stomped feet in hiking boots and checked the contents of the small backpacks they'd been given, complete with water bottles to dangle from straps.

Van Voorst appeared on the lodge's veranda, dressed in a pair of jeans so new that they still bore the lines of their original folds, and a leather bomber jacket, rubbing his hands together and blowing into them to warm his fingers. "Good morning, ladies and gentlemen," he crowed. "Ready for your first team-building challenge?" A few cheers were voiced and one whistle, then more people joined in as the group realized they should show some enthusiasm.

"Your leader for this day is our vice president of sales and marketing, Benjamin Buford." Van Voorst gestured toward the entry door where Ben now walked forward. "Let's hear it for Ben!"

Applause grew. Des liked the man, from what little he knew of him, and had discovered the attitude was universal.

"As you probably know, Ben attained the rank of lieutenant colonel in the Army, with experience in some of the toughest assignments overseas. I don't expect him to run you as hard as he used to run his men, but he'll challenge you. Ben, step up and say a few words."

As the man sketched out the day's activities, Des checked out his fellow employees. The men, by and large, dressed like him—jeans, hiking boots, baseball caps or bush hats. Some as hardy as Des wore cargo shorts, their numerous pockets bulging here and there with items and supplies that might help during the challenge. Des patted his thighs and rear where he'd stashed energy bars, sunblock and lip balm, a bandana for extra coverage or to mop off perspiration and a pocketknife...just in case.

Among the collected hikers, only six were women. There was Raye, of course, and Julia, along with Krystle Tanaka, whom Des had met previously when she'd dogged him down the halls at work. Three he'd only met briefly—chief counsel and Raye's boss Olivia, one from finance and the director of customer services. He was not impressed by the condition of the men or the women. Most appeared fit from hitting gyms and weight rooms, slow jogs around a park or Zumba classes, not hard-core training.

Ben continued. "Today's activity is called the Psych Hike. Assignments have been made and you're paired up with a person with whom you usually don't interact. You already know that a mile trek forms the core of the challenge. What you haven't been told is this is a hunt. You'll shoot…with cameras or phones. You'll get a list of items found in this terrain. The winning squad will be the first to complete the hike *and* also bring back photographic proof of locating the items. So this is a two-pronged challenge. Can anyone tell me why?"

Des immediately thought of an answer, but he waited for others to chime in. It was best to evaluate the competition before revealing his own ideas.

Roy Hudson, strategy officer, underweight but possessing a brain as sharp as a razor, raised a hand and said, "Because to compete in the real world, we need not only to be fast but also thorough and astute."

"Yes." Ben gave a nod of approval. With a stride forward to the edge of the porch, he revealed a new ploy. "It's time to let you in on an ulterior motive for this retreat. Yes, we're here to strengthen our relationships and build our management team. As an incentive, we'll have prizes for things like most improved, best squad, greatest enthusiasm. But to make things even more interesting, we'll be evaluating your achievements and factoring them in on a special award. A fifty-thousand-dollar bonus will go to the person who's been most successful at the retreat's challenges. And, who knows? Promotions may well be impacted by your performances. Mr. Van Voorst and I will make that determination."

Fifty thousand dollars. Quite a chunk of change, Des thought. *I sure could use that little bonus. Rather, Claudia could use it.*

A chorus of awe-struck whistles and applause greeted this pronouncement. Disbelief, yearning and hope competed for the dominant expression. "Incredible," said one man. "Fantastic," said another, "I'm going to try my damnedest." Another, Bill Pickett, the senior financial officer, overweight and approaching retirement, moaned, "Impossible for me to win."

"Hold it." Ben elevated his palm. "I'm not referring to winning or losing — or scoring points or being in the top three. We have all kinds of methods to appraise your progress. I don't know if our intention serves as a carrot or a stick, but factor the information into your approach.

"Let's gear up. I'll remind you... The trail may be rocky and tough, but today's task is only the first challenge. So don't give up if you perform at less than top efficiency. We're at ten thousand feet in altitude, a trial in itself. Make sure you have plenty of water, sun block, snacks and your brain. Now, Julia will distribute the scavenger lists."

Fifty thousand dollars, the exact amount needed to make four years of tuition at the college Andy hoped to attend. An exhilarating combination of excitement and fear twisted in Raye's chest as she wondered if she had any chance of winning. It probably depended a lot on whom she was partnered with. She compiled a mental list of co-workers, hoping to avoid this one, wondering about the skills of that one.

From the bottom stair where she perched, Julia stepped among them to distribute copies. Raye scanned the lengthy register as she asked, "What squad are you on?"

"Get serious," Julia murmured. "I'm here as the all-round assistant…a servant. I'm not going to be put on a squad."

Raye paused then said, "I'm getting an itchy feeling, the one that signals something's amiss. Why shouldn't you be part of the exercise? If the company's going to use our accomplishments as possible qualifiers for promotions, you deserve a chance."

Julia pulled a face of distaste and patted the top of her safari hat to secure it. "You know there's a caste system in this business. If someone's a woman and in an administrative position, she finds it nearly impossible to break out of the classification, even more so when she's Latina. Glass ceiling and all that."

"I hate to admit your analysis is correct, but I do," Raye said. "I had to fight my way up, even with Olivia supporting me. That's the truth."

"What's the truth?" Des somehow positioned himself between them on the gravel area where the co-workers gathered.

"Nothing," said Raye.

Des waved his sheet of paper toward her. "Looks like we've been assigned as a two-person squad."

"What? We don't get to choose?" Raye turned to ask Julia.

"No. The executive team used random assignments." Julia bent over the page she held and pointed to notes at the bottom. "You and Des are partners."

"Now how random was that?" Raye said. Julia assumed an expression of angelic innocence.

With a 'humpf', Raye snatched the paper out of Julia's hand and studied it. "Let's see—a purple columbine, some sort of animal droppings, a wild strawberry, three types of pine cones and a few more. It doesn't look like a tremendous challenge." She creased the paper into eighths and shoved the list into a pocket, hitched the sides of her shorts up a smidgeon, adjusted the shoulder straps of her day pack and tapped on the bill of the Colorado Rockies baseball cap she'd worn to protect her head from the sun.

She guessed it was okay she'd been saddled with Des. At least he was big and strong. With him along, she wouldn't have to worry about moving heavy loads or reaching up high. With his military experience, he wasn't a novice where survival skills were required. She had to admit to herself that he wasn't nearly as full of himself as some men. In fact, as she studied him from the corner of her eye, she decided he exuded confidence and power. She shook her shoulders and set off at a brisk walk on one of the trails that radiated from in front of the lodge, turning her concentration to the magic figures she'd absorbed. *Fifty thousand dollars.*

From behind her, she heard Des asking Julia, "Who are you paired with?"

"I'm not. Get going or you'll lose your partner."

His footsteps sped up until he appeared at Raye's side. The day, which had begun as cool and cloudy, changed with the rapidity of a summer storm. Every cloud dissipated, and the sun beating down from overhead jacked up the temperature to flat-out hot. The other squads, immediately spreading in all directions, left no trace of their existences. Des and Raye could have been on a desert island for all they saw of human impact.

Chapter Nine

Des slowed as he pulled off his lined windbreaker to tie it around his waist. Tough hiking boots and light-weight Merino socks ensured the comfort of his feet while several shirts — T and Polo varieties — enabled him to adjust his body temperature. He noted with approval that Raye was dressed in a similar fashion. *Although,* he admitted to himself, *she looks much better in her outfit than I do, what with her trim physique and the ever-present energy that animates even her silent moments, as if the energy were tamped down, held in check, harnessed for a growing surge.*

He trailed her as they walked on a stony path some four feet wide, sloping at a slight incline. *She's moving at top speed, although not much of a challenge immediately. What might interfere with our success? In this area, thunderstorms are common. I wonder if they'll hamper us?* His survey of the area included an intensive study of Raye's rear. She'd pulled her stick-straight ponytail through the opening at the flipside of the snapback cap, and it quivered from left to right half-way down her back, offering an irresistible temptation to tug it. He caught up with her and yielded to the urge. "Hey. Wait up. We're in this together, remember?"

She stopped to glower up at him, tossing off, "I hope you can keep up with me. I'm determined to do well on every single challenge." A belligerent bee, disturbed by their passage past a clump of Alpine parsley and its pale-yellow flowers, decided to dive bomb him. He pulled his safari hat off to bat the insect to the side, so her resolve changed to laughter. "It won't hurt you if you leave it alone."

"I know. That's why I'm shooing it away. I'd never squash a bee if I can avoid it. I value its role in the environment too much."

The interlude released a hint of the tension between them and they turned more companionably to continue up the trail. "Where there are bees, there's bound to be columbines eventually," she advised.

"I bow to your superior knowledge," he replied. "I'm a tenderfoot in these parts."

"You're from Kansas, right?"

"That's where I grew up. My parents, my sister and me."

"And no time anywhere else?"

"An occasional vacation in Mexico and Florida. After I enlisted, they moved out here, while I spent four years in the Middle East."

"Whoa. Somewhat different from Colorado."

"Somewhat."

She waited for him to add more, a squint of curiosity narrowing her eyes, but he avoided the opportunity. "Why do you need to do well on these challenges?" he asked instead.

"I'm seriously tempted by that fifty-thousand-dollar award. More than that, I'm lusting after it. I'm facing some huge financial commitments."

"I'm impressed by your tremendous focus. You're moving so fast that I can barely keep up. But that doesn't mean you'll win. Other people may be as motivated. What are your reasons? A new car? A vacation?"

"No, the money pretty much sums it up."

He waited for her to add more as he concentrated on tackling the narrowing path that was increasingly steep and rocky. *I'm almost panting*, he realized. *Hope we find one of the items on the list soon so we can take a breather.*

With a touch of reluctance, as if hesitant to reveal a personal matter, she added, "I'm a single mom. My son goes off to college next year, and school costs are out of sight."

Guess she's not just a pretty face. Des seized on the subject as a method of establishing a common interest with her. He groaned. "Don't I know it. My little sister finally graduated in May with her master's in social work. Eight long and expensive years."

Instead of responding, Raye crowed as she pointed. "Look! I figured we'd run across some columbines after we saw the bee." She pulled out her mobile and snapped a picture. "One down, seven to go."

Des squelched his disappointment at Raye's switch in subject. He unfolded his scavenger list to consult. "Three varieties of pinecones, Y-shaped branch, a piece of granite. Okay, my eyes will be peeled. Let's go."

To Des' delight, Raye resumed the conversation as she stepped out. "She must be significantly younger than you."

"She is. Twelve years. A surprise to my mom and dad, but a welcome one."

"How long does it take to get a master's? I know many kids take more time to finish school than they used to, but I'm hoping Andrew can speed through to hold down costs."

"It's a two-year program on top of the bachelor's normally, but Claudia has some extra challenges that interfered."

"I don't want to snoop if you prefer not to answer, but what?"

"She's diabetic. Insulin-dependent. As she went through adolescence, her body had to make major adjustments, as did her mind and expectations. Hey, I see several kinds of evergreens up there. Let's collect cones to compare."

Raye scurried ahead at top speed, while Des trailed, inhaling deeply to catch his breath. She bent over and scooped up double handfuls. "Yep. I'd say that one, that...not that...that." With precision she placed the cones on a rock with a flat surface. "Okay, snap away."

"I can't see much difference," admitted Des, as he pulled out his cell phone for photographs.

"That one's longer," she said, indicating the first. "It's from a spruce. The little one's a lodgepole and the ponderosa is plump and chunky."

"Okay." He gave a tweak to the trio for a better angle and complied with her directions. "Fascinating, how patterns or templates underlie plants and animals, even geography, and yet every little bit of nature is different, perfectly adapted to its needs. Next on the list? I'm also not expert at animal droppings. What about you?"

"Yeah, I have some experience, usually from accidentally treading on them. There are patterns there, too. Animals get rid of their waste, and their droppings are similar, as you can imagine. Smaller creatures' leavings can be easier to find than large, since there are more of them. They often look like dark pebbles. We have to poke around at the side of the trail, beneath the undergrowth." She proceeded to take her own suggestions and toed sticks and leaves, pushing them to the side. "*Hoy!*" she trilled.

"What?" said Des.

"*Hoy!*" she repeated. "It means 'today' in Spanish, but I think it sounds like an exclamation of joy, so I use it for that. I found some!"

"Funny. A similar sound is used in Yiddish, but it expresses dismay." Des bent over and spotted a small mound of dark brown pellets. "*Hoy!*" he mimicked as he raised his cell phone, still clutched in his palm, and clicked. "I think I located a lode."

She leaned in, too. "Yep. You got it."

"You seem to be an expert outdoorsman… woman…person. How'd you get so knowledgeable?"

They turned to tackle the trail again. "I've been mad for cowboys, horses and ranching since my kindergarten went to the National Western Stock Show. I loved the rodeo, the rope tricks, even the smell of the animals. My parents gave me a cowboy outfit and a lariat for Christmas when I was eight, after I pestered them for weeks," she said.

"Surely there was more. You act like a mountain man," said Des. He was starting to drag behind her.

"My dad's a hard-core camper, fisherman and hiker," Raye threw over her shoulder. "Not much of an eight-to-five guy, but talented in his own way. He dragged me along from the age of two. Blizzards or beating sun, made no difference. I learned how to put up a tent in two minutes flat, including pounding in stakes to ground the structure. I picked up a lot of woodlore as I went along."

"Lucky for me," panted Des. The trail, narrowing and getting even steeper, was definitely challenging him.

Nimble as a mountain goat, Raye leaped from one rocky outcrop to another on her upward journey. "You'd better believe it. You think any of these wusses with us know diddly about the mountains?"

"Maybe Ben. He was a twenty-year man in the service and was stationed in plenty of challenging locations," Des replied.

"Okay. I'll give you that," Raye threw over her shoulder as she continued her speedy progress. "But can you imagine Mason trying to identify an aspen tree? Or Krystle?"

"I'm still new, remember? Who's Mason?" wheezed Des. Definite pain and tightness across the chest slowed his steps.

"He's manager of network engineering," answered Raye. "If he spots an opportunity to make a racist comment about a Latino, he'll do it — or to wriggle out of work." She paused on the top of an immense boulder and turned toward him. She must have realized his condition at last because she studied him then asked, "Wait! How're you doing? What's the matter?"

Des whispered 'thank you' to himself as he caved in and collapsed on another large rock. "Now that you ask, do I look okay?" he wheezed. "Kansas City is about eight thousand feet lower than here. And you're setting quite a pace."

Raye jumped to the ground and approached him. "Oh my gosh. Are you sure that's all you're suffering from? What about altitude sickness? Do you have a headache? Are you dizzy? Thirsty? You're sweating like a pig." She swept the hair from his forehead with one hand and felt for a temperature.

"You're an expert on pigs, too?" He was thinking, *What a break. She must be a nonstop nurturer. All I have to do to get close to her is act needy.* Complying with his own advice, he allowed his body to slouch and opened his eyes wide in appeal, pushing his sleeves up his arms from the heat.

"No, I'm not. Sweating like a pig refers to producing pig iron, for your information. And what's *that?*" She pointed at the image on Des' bicep, hidden until now.

"What?" Des frowned down at his arm. "Oh, that's my tattoo. The Grim Reaper. Got it as soon as my first orders for overseas came through. You know how young men are, have to show hard."

"I hope not." She shuddered and snatched her hand back as if it burned. "I hope Andy doesn't feel compelled to permanently decorate his skin in that fashion. Anyway, I do have some experience with ignorant tenderfeet—tenderfoots? Whatever. Miscellaneous visitors from the lowlands, like you. But you're a tough guy, in the service, riding motorcycles, in great condition. I never expected you to be a victim of altitude sickness."

Plopping next to him, she offered him a swig of water from her bottle. "Drink up. No excuses. It won't hurt and it might help."

They sat together, relaxing, not speaking, as the sounds from the forest around them seemed to increase in volume—a bird twitter, a chorus of insect hums, the rustle of the breeze through aspen leaves, their own breaths. When the heat of the sun on their shoulders released the comforting scent of warm cotton, he became aware of other odors—pine, earth, a touch of dampness from decaying matter under the trees. Des carried the bottle to his lips and swallowed again, breaking the silence into which Raye now sighed with contentment.

"I love these times, these places. Being outside refreshes me, and I relax and forget my worries," she said.

"Agreed. The outdoors makes our troubles seem petty. But worries? I wouldn't have suspected much of anything bothered you. You're always calm and collected. I've never seen a woman so unreadable."

"Don't make assumptions. I know I come off as confident and unflappable at work, especially during meetings," she answered. "You can't believe everything you see. I've simply learned major control over my impulses to scream, run or duck and cover."

The breeze picked up, sending a fresh wave of the smells of growing things wrapping around them. Isolated as they were, away from people, machinery, the screech and moans of traffic and the pressures of city life, a comfortable isolation descended, and Des welcomed the instant intimacy it created. He supposed Raye was experiencing the same sense, because she dared to show curiosity.

"I suppose nothing makes you afraid?" she said.

"Why do you believe that?"

"You're a big, strong man, obviously super fit. I've seen you walk the halls, react in meetings. Nothing seems to bother you...except a few thousand extra feet of altitude." She giggled when he flinched.

Hmm. The second time she's mentioned my body, he thought. *That's a good sign, I think.* "I'd thank you not to mention my breathlessness to anyone. It's not good for my image. Very little makes me a worrywart, I'll admit. What good would it do me if I were bothered? Second-guessed myself? Brooded over this or that? It would slow me down."

"That's because you only have yourself to be concerned about. You don't have a wife or kids, do you? If you did, you'd understand."

His sister's face appeared in his mind, his mother and father who were aging — gracefully, but still aging, with a touch of arthritis here and a thyroid deficit there. "Don't *you* make assumptions. Everyone has someone or something to lose. I admit being faced with armed action clarifies existence in some ways. When you're under fire, you know you'll either survive or you won't. No mental hassles are necessary. And your greatest opportunity for survival is to get out there and do the best you can." He held his breath, hoping his candor raised a similar openness in her.

It did. "You know, you're nothing like what I thought you were."

The statement surprised him. "What did you imagine?"

"It's mostly what I didn't. I didn't think you'd be aware of the small joys of nature, be willing to admit you don't know the answers to everything or take direction from a mere woman."

For a moment he didn't know whether to be offended or flattered. He decided to express neither openly, instead shaking his head to laugh. "That's quite a verdict to admit to. But what do *you* fear?"

She leaned back and wrapped her hands together around her knees. "Mostly on behalf of my son. His father's not in his life. But if anything happened to me…" she trailed off.

"Parents? Siblings?"

"My mom and dad are divorced. I know they'd be there for Andrew in a catastrophe, but it wouldn't be easy for them because of money, other things." She paused, apparently considering how candid to be with him. She took a deep breath and opened like a morning glory in the sun. "I'm thankful that his dad's not involved. It makes life simpler. As for siblings, my only brother" — she inhaled again — "my only brother died in a motorcycle accident about ten years ago."

He hoped he hadn't distressed her. "Sorry."

She sat up and brushed some dirt off the rock next to her. "No, that's okay. I like thinking about him. It makes me feel like he's still nearby. Sometimes he seems to talk to me. Am I crazy?" She lifted those magnificent, expressive brown eyes directly to him.

"No. Not at all. Hence your hatred of the machines."

"Hence. When it happened, my mom and dad came to my high school, called me out of class and told me. It was a few days before finals. I truly couldn't take the tests. Most of my teachers were great, but one, when I sat there crying and saying I couldn't face the exam, said she'd flunk me. Then my homeroom teacher came in, took the papers out of my hand and directed me to leave."

"Then?"

"I was allowed to complete the tests several weeks later."

Silence fell again. Des didn't believe he had anything to say. It was similar to times in the service when the repellent visage of the Grim Reaper rose before him, and duty, not to mention his own mental stability, required him to tolerate a bereavement that ripped him apart in order to keep his troops sane and functioning. They'd lost buddies, support systems, collaborators, sometimes superiors or nonmilitary associates. Yes, he knew how little impact words had when confronted with sudden, violent death. He considered taking her hand or putting an arm around her shoulders, but before he could do so, she spoke.

"It's being outside in places like this that helps. When I look around and I see life surging around me, I glimpse patterns...like those crows on the tops of trees." She nodded toward a nearby stand of spruces displaying a collection of chatty, noisy birds like Christmas ornaments on their uppermost boughs. "I know that oftentimes when I hear their calls, they'll be perched up on the very top branches, come rain or shine. They'll call to one another, scold, tussle. No matter what year or what geographic location, that's how they behave."

"Nature draws me, too," he said. "I used to notice the lack of green growing things in the military. I missed lawns the most. I even wrote to my granny about the absence of grass, so she sent me a box of dirt and grass seed. Amazingly enough, I got it to grow. I sent her a photo of my bare toes wriggling in the green blades."

She giggled as she leaned back on her elbows and checked the empty sky around her. "There are patterns everywhere. Ever noticed that? The structure of an atom looks like the solar system, with its constantly moving ellipses around a central body. The way a pile of sand sloping downward on all sides resembles mountains with their cascade of rock. These things are constants. They give me reassurance that the patterns will continue, that *life* will continue, regardless of ups and downs."

"Have you changed the subject?" Des asked. He hoped not. She seemed to have dropped any defensiveness or distance. They were in their own safe little world.

"Away from my brother's death? Not really. It took some time for me to realize he was part of the patterns, too. There was no one and nothing to blame. The simple functioning of life was at work. There is comfort in that. Don't you agree?"

Far off, a roll of thunder sounded and Des looked toward the west. Clouds were building in billows, white and gold on top, dark gray underneath. *How did we get on this subject? And why do I feel self-conscious and uneasy with it? Because I don't discuss these types of things with women? Or because it brings up bad memories?*

"I've never thought about it. Too touchy-feely for me, I guess," he grunted.

Raye straightened up and shot him a challenging glance. "Come on. You were in the service in a military hot spot. You must have."

"You're getting way out of my league," he said. "I leave questions and answers like that to religion. Then I don't have to spend my time on them. Simplistic, I know, but I'm a simple guy."

Since he'd disguised this reality in a chuckle, Raye giggled, too. "Seriously. I get a sense of stability, continuity, eternity from my point of view," she said. "Oh, I know nothing is certain. Eventually, this planet, galaxy, even the universe may disappear. I won't be around, however. And I can't even grasp what these eons mean. So I go for the here and now, what I can grasp, and leave the answerless questions to a higher power."

Des couldn't come up with a response. She'd given him a shovelful to think about. Raye, though, shook herself and propelled the conversation to the task at hand. "Oh, rats. What are we doing sitting here babbling? We still need to find five items on our list so we can win this scavenger hunt." She jumped to her feet, patted her pockets and backpack down and took a swig of water. "Ready? Are you recovered?"

What do you mean, we're *babbling?* The thought twisted his lips in amusement. "Sure thing," he said. "The water and the break brought me back to speed. In fact I see the Y-shaped twig we're supposed to locate right over there." He nodded toward several branches on the ground.

Chapter Ten

Thirty minutes later, filthy, smudged, sore in every muscle and out of water and snacks, Raye and Des faced off under a twisted canopy of tree limbs and vines. Perspiration dripped from their bodies, and Raye wiped her scarf over her forehead and neck as she shouted, "You're flippin' crazy. That rock looks no more like President Clinton than it does the man in the moon."

"Please," Des pleaded. "We've got all the other items. The Y-shaped branch, the piece of litter... The last thing on the list is a rock that resembles a person, and we've been searching for fifteen minutes. We can turn my rock around and shove it into the dirt so the totally flat side doesn't show in the photo."

Arms akimbo, Raye shook her head so hard that the ponytail flipped like an angry snake. "Mine's an exact copy of Cher, down to the long, straight hair on the sides of her face."

Opposite her, Des posed in a similar position, but she couldn't help thinking he looked like a well-toned bodyguard to a major film star or a super-fit regular at the gym, and her rage evaporated. His stance quickly lost its visual punch when he took a step back and stretched his neck this way and that. "Okay," he breathed. "Let's agree to disagree. Compromise. Take shots of both rocks and decide when we get back. Our supplies are gone, and time is moving on. If you want a chance at winning, we've got to get back."

"You are so determined to have your own way," Raye accused, trying to stir up a sense of resentment, although she spared a moment to ask herself what was really disturbing her. "You won't give up or give in."

"Neither will you," he returned.

"Don't you dare act like we're similar," she said, even as she turned to go back to the lodge.

"Wouldn't dream of it." Des took his picture then adjusted his pack, jacket and hat, and followed her.

"Don't hang around when we're at the lodge and brag about how you found all the objects."

"Wouldn't daaarrre to."

She snapped her cap at the dust devils kicked up by her boots. "Don't think you can hang on my coattails and coast into winning."

"Heaven forbid," he breathed. Then, as a few fat raindrops hit his head and splattered on all sides, he added, "And heaven forbid we're caught in a thunderstorm."

"Eeek! It's raining." She set off at a gallop, leaving him yelling after her.

"I told you so." He groaned and trailed her.

"And don't ever, ever say 'I told you so' to me again." Even as the words streamed out of her mouth, she recalled why the phrase repelled her. Her mother had spouted the expression when Raye had gotten knocked up so many years ago, after failing to use birth control with Andy's father. But in this instance, a suspicion of a question wormed its way into her mind. Was she assuming, hoping or anticipating that she and Des would be together often enough for them to share an honest, comfortable conversation again?

Despite nearly tumbling down the mountain at break-neck speed, scattering pebbles, twigs and leaves in all directions, Raye and Des maintained a mostly mock argument about their finds, the competition, the weather and the impact of high altitude on the human physique. Low gray clouds continued to threaten rain but did little more than dribble water, which was sufficient to create rivulets of mud over which they were forced to leap, occasionally missing and spattering their shoes, shins and one another with chocolate spots.

The final one hundred yards before the lodge turned into a neck-or-nothing competition. They reached the porch simultaneously, breathlessly, while crowing, "I won," and, "No, I won," like feuding kids, interspersed with belly laughs. Julia, half-crouched at the edge of the overhang by the stairs, wrapped in a water-repellent windbreaker, greeted them. "You're the first squad in. Do you have everything on the list?"

"Do we ever," Des crowed as he pulled out his cell phone and switched it on. A picture of the purple columbine appeared. Just as he showed the screen, he glimpsed Raye's face over the equipment, and the lady was boiling mad.

"Of course you waltz in and make it seem like you did all the work," she said.

"No, no." He threw both hands up in the air. "We tracked the items together."

"Together?"

"Uh, no, truthfully, Raye knows much more about this terrain than I do," he admitted, turning toward Julia.

"As well I know," said Julia, grave as a school principal riding herd on tussling students, "having accompanied her on several camping trips. She can pitch a tent in sixty seconds, identify edible mushrooms, lure a hummingbird to a saucer of sugar water and tie a cowboy knot in a rope. She was the right one for you to pair with. But now, if you hope to be triumphant, let's go down the list one by one, and you can show me your confirming photos."

The three leaned on the porch railing to compare the numbered items with the images. They did well until the eighth and final picture—the rock that resembled a person. Then all hell broke loose.

"His rock looks like a squashed turd, with only the faintest resemblance to Clinton," Raye flung into the middle of the fray. "As a proud American, I refuse to let our squad submit an object that defames one of our presidents."

Julia exhaled a cross between a moan and a sigh. "I don't care what you enter, but hurry up. I can see three squads approaching the lodge and several more a bit farther down the trail. Plus, the skies are about to let loose." Sure enough, raindrops gathered strength and frequency, plopping thick as a sprinkler to release small puffs of dust when they hit the ground.

"Here's mine," Raye said and flicked her screen to photo images, now blank. Pop-eyed, she gave the phone a little shake. "Where is it? Where's the picture? I had it when we were up the mountain." A series of small hops did nothing to restore the photos, nor did the moans that poured from Raye's mouth. "Oh, no, no, no, no. I found an exact replica of Cher."

With the storm gathering intensity, the members of other squads jogged the final few feet to the porch and waved their cell phones in the air and stomped their feet to demand Julia's attention. She, in turn, stalled for time by turning her back on them. "You two are acting like children competing for a parent's attention. Straighten up. It appears to me you're out of time. What do you want to do?"

Des smirked. "I bow to the lady's judgment."

"We haven't much choice," said Raye. "I'd lose too much time trying to dig out a rock now. Go with Des' selection."

With a flourish of her marker, Julia checked off the final item on the list and motioned 'come here' with her free hand. "Step up on the porch to get out of the rain, everyone. We have a winning squad, ladies and gentlemen. But don't despair. Second and third places are still available, and we'll have a judging later on the best rock faces, so don't delete them."

For a moment Raye felt as if she were twelve again, trapped in some dismal classroom situation — say the annual art contest, during which, as a wanna-be artist, she'd faced the best students in the school. Her success at the time had depended utterly on competing against people like that stuck-up Angie

Berman, who took private painting lessons, and Rob Tower, a hottie even in sixth grade, where he'd ignored her in favor of filling page after page of paper with penciled images of race cars.

Roiling frustration with the loss of her rock photo set her feet in their hiking boots stomping across the wood planks of the porch. Or was it her reluctant dependence on Des' goodwill? She'd never run into a man so even-tempered, so slow to irritation. *What is he, some kind of a superhero?*

Des tracked at her side with words he probably thought were consoling. "Cheer up. At least we won. I've heard of sore losers, but never sore winners" and "We're a great team."

She swung to face him and poked his chest with a grimy index finger. "Listen here. You wouldn't even be in the running if not for me — and don't you forget it." *Thump, thump, thump.* She stopped, finger extended, when bewilderment overrode his features. *He looks like Andy at four when another kid snatched his favorite fire truck. What a rotten way for me to react, seeing as how he did pull half the weight of the scavenger hunt.* She stepped back and lowered her hand. "Sorry. I get carried away sometimes."

"Maybe you're just passionate," he said, his eyelids dropping to disguise his emotion, although a yielding at one corner of his firm mouth surely indicated humor.

"I've figured out what you are," she said. "A big goofball. I thought you were this tough guy ready to sacrifice everyone and everything around him to achieve success. No, you're a seething mixture of feelings overflowing an outsized kid who loves taking risks and irritating any susceptible target."

Tilting his head as if considering her judgment, he studied her. "Guess you'll have to spend more time with me to confirm your opinion. Are you ready to grab a cup of coffee? Tea? Perhaps even hot chocolate? The weather's made a major change."

She looked out from where they'd stopped on the porch. The rain could now be described as a deluge, as sheets of water poured from lowering clouds like a shower. She shivered. "The temp must have dropped at least twenty degrees." Enticed by his suggestion, she looked up at him then changed her mind. His scrutiny of her seemed to carry more than a casual invitation. It bordered on expectation.

What is with this guy? She backed away a few inches. All they'd done was poke around the mountains. Sure, they'd shared a few thoughts, but they'd also irritated one another. At least, he'd ticked *her* off. *Does he want something from me?* A little warning bell jingled in her mind, the one she'd developed courtesy of Michael and brought into sharper focus after each brush with a romantic disappointment. She raised her hands in front of her. "Thanks, but I need to clean up."

"Okay. I may catch you at dinner," he said.

She watched him enter the lodge's massive doors and stride toward the staircase. Julia appeared at her side.

"How did it go with you and Des? You sure were on his case about the photos."

"Kind of childish, I guess," Raye admitted, now feeling a bit foolish.

"Guess you got along well enough to work together," said her friend.

"Yes. Actually, he surprised me. He was pleasant enough, even when I snapped at him. I could almost say he's nonsexist, although he can be irritating as hell."

"Maybe that's sexual tension," said Julia.

"Ha! Don't you believe it."

"I think the two of you would be a great match." She continued by listing some of the most negative qualities any human could demonstrate. "You're both hard-headed, stubborn, determined, unwilling to compromise and focused on success. By the way, while you were tussling, I saw Ben observing you from the corner of my eye. It's a good thing you won this challenge. It should help your ratings for the promotions."

Raye snapped to attention. "Oh, no. We were told ratings depended upon way more than simply winning. Do you think he was evaluating our ability to get along? To collaborate? Did he look judgmental?"

"I don't know. I can't predict what goes through the minds of managers, assuming they have minds."

Raye couldn't stifle a burst of laughter. "I'd better watch my step from now on. Now to go get cleaned up before dinner. Ta-ta. Don't want the Chosen Twenty-Five to judge me a slob." She waved and bounded to the staircase, trailing the scent of damp rain and earth behind her.

Chapter Eleven

Quite an afternoon. What will the evening bring?
Des found himself torn between intrigue and
irritation with his female squad mate. She'd seemed
to resent him from his first misstep with her when
he'd asked her to get him a cup of coffee. And every
interaction with her since then hadn't been much
better, despite the draw toward her he sensed every
time they crossed paths — until they'd been paired
today.

The more he learned about her, how she responded
to pressure and challenge, her personal history, the
more he wanted to know. He didn't think she'd be an
easy, congenial acquaintance, one he'd simply share
a drink with occasionally, but the time and energy he
invested in getting closer to her would pay off, one
way or another. He didn't rule out romance either,
although something told him Raye wasn't the slam-
bam-thank-you-ma'am type.

Strange... Since he'd returned to Denver and his family, his single life was losing its appeal. His condo, sterile as a hospital room, sheltered no life except for the fern Claudia had passed along in the first week. Accustomed to batching it at his apartment in Kansas, light housekeeping, dishes and microwave meals came easily to him but held no appeal compared to the warmth and companionship his family showered on one another. When he left after a Sunday dinner, he caught himself wishing for a roommate, a cat or even a nosy neighbor — anything to break the solitude.

During a quick shower to rid himself of the lingering effects of the exhausting, frustrating and dirty romp of the scavenger hunt, he mulled over various relationships in the past. The most worthwhile ones had frequently been with challenging individuals, from the sixth-grade teacher who'd threatened to flunk him for lack of effort on a book report to the drill instructor in boot camp who'd seemed to have a personal grudge against him. More recently, a manager several rungs ahead of him on the corporate ladder wouldn't let him settle for a mediocre performance while a friend with a competitive streak a mile deep consistently beat him in rock climbs. A worthwhile friendship, to him, seemed comprised of equal parts intelligence, respect and camaraderie, as well as more than a dollop of competition or provocation. Funny, he'd never associated an eligible woman with those qualities...until now. Dinner might prove to be more interesting than he'd suspected.

* * * *

Drat it! Seats had been assigned at the meal, and Des had had to reveal six things about his childhood to his tablemates—who had not included Raye—during a team-building exercise. His admissions—he'd never learned to play marbles, he always hid lima beans in his napkin at dinner, he'd gotten lost on purpose in Target once so security would give him a candy bar, dark closets with open doors terrified him and a friend had dared him to run naked across the street.

Only one woman was permitted in each group, and somehow Krystle had maneuvered her way to his, where she spent the meal dropping embarrassing, cooing innuendoes into her conversation. When he mentioned he'd collected toy soldiers as a child, she referenced her ever-growing collection of lacy lingerie. He turned his attention toward awkward eavesdropping on the nearby collection of diners, including Raye.

The post-dinner gathering launched a crescendo of greetings and animated chatter when Des, a few minutes late following a quick text to his little sister, glimpsed Raye standing by the huge stone hearth. She was chatting with Julia and another woman, animation brightening her features as her burnished ponytail twitched with her gestures. He was considering an approach when a raucous comment reverberated through the area. He turned toward the sound.

"Yeah, after she's put a noose around some poor schmuck's neck to force him to support her for the rest of her life." Mason Mobley's guffaw shattered every conversation in polite progress around the lodge great room, and heads swiveled in his direction. He leaned forward to slap Tim Enoch, who was slouched in an adjacent easy chair facing the hearth, on the back in jovial fraternity.

Rigid, Raye pivoted to face Mason, moved closer to the duo and pushed her nose in the air. The tone of her voice ensured all nearby attention focused on her. "That's a ridiculous male myth, a fantasy men love to believe, that women will do anything to catch a man, tie him down and eliminate his liberty."

In inebriated and sloppy alliance, Tim now elbowed Mason. "Mase, ain't it the truth. A girl trapped my best buddy in high school by saying she was pregnant. All his hopes to go on the pro rodeo circuit, phfft, out of the window. Fifteen years and four kids later, he finally got free of her."

Des paused several yards away from the fireplace and next to Mason and Tim as they conducted their ardent discussion. *Don't barge in,* he told himself. *No knights in shining armor have been requested.* So far, Raye seemed to be holding her own. He waited for the drama to unfold.

Raye snapped a finger in the men's direction. "Hey, *hey!*" She lowered her voice to a tone only those in close proximity could hear, making a greater impact than a scream. "I suppose he made no contribution to the four kids appearing. They came from the stork or the cabbage patch."

Even Mason couldn't mistake the disgust in Raye's voice. "Who's asking you? This is a private conversation." He glowered like a jack-o-lantern.

"Can't be that private if I can hear from my distance. Anyway, you're at a work event, so I'd appreciate it if you'd keep your personal opinions personal."

Way to go! Des projected silent support in Raye's direction.

Mason turned an interesting shade of hot pink that clashed with his orange and blue Broncos T-shirt. "Listen, b— Err, baby." A quick twist of his lips converted his initial obscenity to a word acceptable in the current company. "Don't try to fast-talk me. The story's been the same since the beginning of time. Women are out to get a man, any man, and they'll resort to every trick in the book to steal his freedom."

Raye refused to back down. She crossed her arms and continued with a glare, "A flat-out lie. Men talk the talk but they don't walk the walk. Virtually every guy I've dated wanted me to be with him, only him, right away. He may not have mentioned marriage, but he sure as hell was hot on exclusivity — for me, not for himself."

Des couldn't pull his eyes from Raye. He didn't seem able to move his body, but he soaked in every detail about her — the straightness of her back, the flash of her eyes, the determination on her features. The long hair slicked back into a tempting touchable switch at the crown of her head swished back and forth in cadence with her words. Her tone, soft but resolute, overwhelmed Mason and Tim's stuttered grumbles.

Her strength and clarity of thought, marked by civility, resonated in his heart and mind. *This is the only woman in the universe for me,* Des thought at that moment. The idea exploded like a bomb in his brain. He wondered how long he'd known that without admitting it. While he tried to wrap his head around the concept, he decided to give her a break. He interrupted the discussion. "Freedom's another word for nothing left to lose. Isn't that a line from an old song?" he drawled as he swirled the liquor in his glass.

Ray' flicked her gaze in his direction before returning to Mason. She drew a deep breath, as if to adjust her temper. "Think about what you're saying and don't make a fool of yourself," she advised.

"Haw, haw, haw." Tim's hoarse attempt at laughter betrayed his embarrassment. "Mase is kidding, aren't you, man?"

"Hardy-har-har." Mason forced a faked agreement.

Diplomatic Raye twisted her lips. "Some jokes are funnier than others. Why don't you change your topic of conversation?"

A perfect solution, Des thought.

Mason, however, was past redemption of humor or reprimand. "Hell, no. You can take your opinion and stick it where the sun don't shine," he blurted as he struggled to his feet. The drink in his hand wobbled so far to the side that it was in danger of spilling. Mason tried to focus on the glass. A small stream dribbled down onto his fingers, and he lifted his glass up and back, likely realizing he clutched a handy weapon.

Even as his arm twitched to convert the movement into a throw, Raye spoke. "You're drunk."

The unexpected, if blunt, statement stalled Mason for a few moments while he mumbled to himself, stared at the glass then clutched his fingers once more.

"This is a business gathering. Don't do something you'll regret tomorrow morning." The smooth flow of words continued from Raye. "You need to go sleep it off."

Mason's eyes widened, blinked, half-closed, as he swayed on unsteady feet. His glass and arm remained at attention.

Enough. Even as he admired Raye's careful choice of language, knowing he would have simply spouted, 'you're a disgusting drunk,' Des quick-stepped to get between Raye and Mason. A wide sweep of his arced arm brought Mason closer so the three formed a semicircle. Des' voice turned as low and soft as Raye's. "I suggest you take Ms. Soto's advice and remove yourself from the vicinity. I'm sure your friend Tim is happy to accompany you so you don't injure yourself. Right?"

Tim, wobbly himself, had sufficient coordination to nod, stand and shuffle to the group. He grabbed Mason's upper arm in an ungentle grip and stumbled in the direction of the elevator. Mason staggered behind him, barely able to remain vertical.

Stolid as a statue, Raye watched their exit. "I didn't need your help," she murmured.

Des stood motionless beside her. "I'm sure you didn't. I'm pleased I was present to offer it."

"Although I'm quite capable of taking care of myself, thank you for your support. No one else did. What convinced you to step in?"

"You were magnificent. After I saw you in action, I had to provide myself an excuse for staying with you."

She gasped. "Desmond Emmett, whatever do you mean?"

"Those two need some lessons in etiquette," he went on without a pause.

Casting an oblique look at him, she agreed. "But getting angry or aggressive isn't the way. I've had some practice dealing with jerks," she said. "You never win if you let anger control you or if you flip out yourself."

"I hope you found my response suitable," said Des. "Now you can get a good night's sleep without a worry."

"Yes," she said and began to walk away. Then she paused, turned back and added, with a blush across her face, "Thank you again."

He stated nothing about his agreement with her perceptive summary of some relationships between men and women. A discussion about how, why or where men like Mason got their screwed-up ideas offered no benefits. Exclusivity with this woman was his only goal, not winning an argument. His lungs seemed filled with pure oxygen as he pledged to himself that her days as a single woman were limited.

* * * *

Aaarrrgghh. Where am I? Why did I have to wake up?

Des couldn't fight consciousness any longer, not with a blazing sun pouring in through the drapes he'd forgotten to close last night. *Oh, yes, that amazing night sky hypnotized me into forgetting that there's always a morning after.*

He remembered piling the stack of pillows soft as cotton batting into a heap, lying back on the oversized bed, pulling up the down comforter and surrendering to a fantasy of Raye beside him. Somehow, the fantasy had mingled with the incredible view of glittering stars and silhouetted mountain peaks. Somehow, the number of visible stars had quadrupled this high in the mountains and far from the disturbance of lights from civilization. Somehow, when he'd drifted off, the night had passed in dreams as exciting yet comfortable as a visit to Santa's workshop when he was a kid.

She can't be as perfect for me as I imagine. Lose the prepubescent attitude, he told himself in the full light of day. He jumped into the oversized tiled shower and soaped up from head to toe. One of the numerous skills obtained during his stint in the service was the ability to complete the whole package—hair, body, shave—in less than five minutes. He could even include a quick brushing of his teeth if necessary, which wasn't today. He preferred to include flossing and various picks and specialty items to keep his perfect smile perfect.

Ready to pull on the casual clothes suited to the retreat, he opened the drawers in the massive oak dresser just as his cell phone rang. A quick check told him Claudia was calling. "Hi, sweetie, what's up?" His sister's breathy high voice set off a litany of her job-searching woes then wrapped up with a near-complaint that she hadn't been able to reach him yesterday after his text.

"I told you I'd be hard to get," he answered. He propped the phone between his ear and shoulder so he could struggle into his shorts and socks as he spoke. "We're supposed to be unreachable most of the time, so we can concentrate on building our squad here."

A burst of pithy comments followed about her intense dissatisfaction over her inability to reach him on command. Des sighed to himself. This was one of the disadvantages to serving as a big brother. *I need to encourage her to be more independent, now that her diabetes and subsequent thyroid conditions are under control.* It occurred to him that she might need a suitable role model, a woman strong but sensitive, bright, classy, pleasant. *Well, maybe 'pleasant' is overrated,* he thought. *Better...courteous. Like Raye.*

He rubbed his rumpled curls with the towel as Claudia babbled about a concert she'd gone to with a new boyfriend. When his end of the conversation consisted of his abstracted "uh-huh" and "hmmm," she wound down to ask him if anything was wrong.

"Now that you mention it," he said, "I have two things. First, have you thought any more about the new treatment for diabetes I want you to enroll in?"

Silence.

"Claudia? You're not going to make me stop mentioning it by avoiding the question."

A small sigh slipped out. "Yes, I have thought." Des could sense the hope his sister was trying to suppress. "But since it's experimental, we'd have to pay a portion of the expense. We don't have the money and I absolutely refuse to let you go into debt for me. You've done enough, what with school and the extra equipment I need."

Des flashed on an image of Ben announcing the award. Fifty thousand would go far to underwriting the therapy. With all due respect, he didn't imagine many of his co-workers were equipped to be serious competition for him, especially if the challenges were physical. Most of them were decided desk jockeys, and although they were bright, their skills were office-centered. "Let's not worry right now about where the money will come from," he said. "Something may come along to help. But I have some news. I think."

Dead silence. Des filled in, "It's a woman I work with...at corporate headquarters."

"Have you found a new girlfriend? You always told me dating someone from your place of business was a risky, bad idea," Claudia responded.

"I'm not actually dating her. Not yet."

"So you're fantasizing about her?" She giggled.

This line of discussion with his younger sister made him uncomfortable, as if sand filled his clothes. "None of your business."

"You've broken up with Jennifer?"

"Who?"

"Jennifer. Your old girlfriend. The one who treated me like a brainless, fragile doll."

Des remembered several awkward holidays that he and Jennifer had spent with his family. When Jennifer had learned of Claudia's medical conditions, she'd responded with coos and pats on the arm. The last thing Claudia wanted was pity or pampering because of her health. As for his mother, she'd been impressed negatively, because not once had Jennifer volunteered to help with any household tasks. His father had admired her chest but nothing else.

"Yes, she's history. Actually, I broke up with her before I even moved to Denver."

"Good. What's the new one's name?"

"Raye. And I told you, she's not the new one. She's one of the Chosen Twenty-Five up here, too. We've been involved in some activities together, so I guess she's on my mind. We haven't even gone out. But keep this quiet from Mom and Dad." He checked his appearance in the mirror, smoothed his already-neat hair, rubbed his chin and bared his teeth in a final inspection. "Listen... I've got to run. We have an exercise shortly and I haven't eaten breakfast yet."

"Okay. But remember not to get serious until I have a chance to vote on this woman. This *Raye*."

"Sure. The day a sister can veto a romantic attachment for me is the day you can put me in a nursing home."

They both hung up chuckling.

Chapter Twelve

Too much food, as usual, Raye thought as she left the dining room. *No wonder Americans are overweight.* While she appreciated the made-to-order omelets, piles of fresh fruit and huge selection of pastries and breads, the excess appalled her. Her own family had always had to count pennies, and as a young mother, Raye's personal finances had ranked as poverty-stricken. When faced with surplus leftovers, she always wanted to hide the excess in her bag for later meals. Fortunately, and somewhat reluctantly, she'd been able to break herself of that habit. Replete but not stuffed, as she walked toward the central meeting room, she joined others streaming in and heard the buzz of voices. Spotting Julia huddled on the floor at the front, she moved to her friend.

"And now, ladies and gentlemen of the Chosen Twenty-Five," shouted Kabir, "we're going to create the Pursuit Telecom cheer! Woo, woo." He pumped his fist in the air.

A whisper passed through the assembly, gathering strength from person to person where they'd perched on couches, chairs and floor cushions. From her position near the front, hunkered down on the floor, Raye whispered behind her hand, "Is he serious? A cheer?"

"Now's your chance to become the cheerleader you never were," Julia murmured back. "You told me you had to drop out of the competition because you got knocked up. Well, Lady Luck's brought you a golden opportunity. If you help write it, maybe you can lead it at all-staff meetings, dressed in a tiny skirt and tight top, shaking sparkly pom-pons."

"Don't be ridiculous," Raye returned. "I'm hoping to be promoted at work, not humiliated."

"I'll bet Des would looove to see you decked out in a costume."

Raye blinked before surveying the people around her in a slow sweep. Some yards behind her on the edge of the audience, straight and still as a military guard, Des lingered between a long leather couch and several overstuffed easy chairs occupied by people high in the management chain of the company. He didn't seem to take note of her. She wondered what he thought of silly activities such as this one—a corporate cheer, for heaven's sake. *Absurd nonsense.* Another bellow returned her attention to the front.

Kabir, normally a tastefully dressed, sober and soft-spoken, incisive manager, had evidently taken leave of his senses. Not only was he wearing a discordant yellow T-shirt with a huge American eagle and flag over the front, surmounted by the phrase "*These Colors Don't Run*", but he'd also paired it with oversized cargo shorts in Irish emerald green. He dashed back and forth before the group, wielding markers in a variety of colors between his fingers. Behind him, an easel and flip chart provided access for notes.

"I've evaluated several well-known college fight songs that might serve as the melody. The Oklahoma Sooner's song, Notre Dame's Fighting Irish, the Michigan hail-to-the-victors. We can pick one refrain then write new lyrics. Any preference?"

"What are the tunes?" someone yelled.

With spontaneous zeal or as an outlet for excess tedium after round-the-clock enforced close company with co-workers, some voices la-de-da'ed the opening stanzas of one school song. Several more broke into another melody, then various others took up the final school's theme. Kabir struggled to establish a little restraint by holding up both hands and voicing dismay, but his speech failed to be heard. Over the period of minutes, however, individuals switched their selection to the Notre Dame refrain until they clearly outnumbered the other two.

Relieved, Kabir scrawled 'Notre Dame' on the flip chart in yellow and blue markers. A final burst of sound, a round of cheers and a rip-tide of enthusiasm carried Raye along like a piece of seaweed until she stood to swivel in all directions around those blocking her view. At the same time she located Des again, she heard a feminine squeal that permeated the air. Krystle pressed against his side, head flung back, giggles percolating between fading squeals of, "Onward to victory."

"Okay. Someone pitch me a suggestion for the first few lines," Kabir urged.

The audience settled down. "Pursuit Telecom, that's our name, we work hard to gain our fame," a voice shouted.

"No, no." Immediately some determined person disagreed and offered an alternative. "Pursuit Telecom, we're the best, searching north, south, east or west."

"Yuck. What about 'Telecom industry, who's passé? Pursuit leads in every way.'"

"Double yuck. We have to start with something positive, like 'cheer, cheer.' Cheer, cheer, Pursuit is the best."

Somehow a mock competition energized the crew and got them involved, whether the cheer concept inherently held appeal or not. On her feet, Raye yelled, debated ideas and cheered with the rest. In her occasional glance backward, she noticed Des seemed to be looking at her frequently. By the end of the one-hour session, the group had created an entire cheer, and people clapped and hooted as they belted out the tune. Raye started a cheerleader-type shuffle and kick, and Julia joined in, as well as a few others. A particularly creative type grabbed the morning paper and ripped it into strips to create pom-pons they could shake, while several grabbed cell phones to shoot video.

A sociable camaraderie seemed to be growing until Krystle waltzed front and center to lead the crowd. She waved her arms, interspersed kicks well over her head, added cartwheels, even flips. At this sight, Raye and Julia abandoned their efforts.

"She must have been a cheerleader in college," Julia murmured.

"Undoubtedly. Probably won national competitions," Raye retorted, although she was more interested in Des' repositioning toward the front of the group.

Kabir broke into the din of cheers and singing. "Great enthusiasm and participation. What a team! Now we're going to introduce you to a regular activity — Educated Exercise. These movements, which you can complete as vigorously or as carefully as you prefer, will keep us energized and alert. Studies show that physical activity actually enhances creativity. Brains operate more efficiently, and emotions are calmed. So here's our own Krystle Tanaka, Director of Human Resources, who happens to teach yoga, aerobics and tai chi in her spare time, to lead us in a few movements."

Krystle bounced to a position from which she dominated the entire audience. Raye and Julia exchanged looks, the ones they always labeled 'give-me-a-break', with lowered heads and slightly squinted eyes, as if exasperated to the utmost. "Of course she would teach all those," Raye murmured.

"You have to admit, she looks terrific."

She did. The happy possessor of the delicate build of many Asian women, she added the muscular development of an enthusiastic American athlete — slim thighs, toned arms, trim midriff. Clad in ultramarine blue shorts that surely contained a good deal of stretchable material, for they appeared painted on, she hopped up and down like a demented jack-in-the-box, smiled, pouted, whistled, clapped and generally occupied the entire strip of floor in the front.

Her ever-chirpy tone fit this situation perfectly. "Okay, gang, let's moooove it! One and two, and three and four. Get those joints flexing and those muscles warmed up." Jumping jacks segued into arm rotations, then to knee raises, waist twists, semi-squats and leg raises.

"Get to know your body. Be best friends with your physique. Not only will you feel better, you'll work better, play better. Even" — she drew in a breath and winked — "enjoy sex more."

Krystle's attention was completely focused on Des now. He, however, had somehow shuffled to maneuver himself out of the front row, backing his own well-developed derriere toward Raye and Julia. A collision was averted when they parted and stepped to each side of him. His head swiveled as he checked out his near-crash. Then came his grin. "I'm exhausted listening to her, aren't you?"

"She's playing to you," Julia said. "She'll be disappointed if you disappear." Raye tilted her head to concentrate on his response.

"I think the three of us are fit enough already," he said. He latched on to their arms and led them through the crowd toward the rear. "I saw donuts, pastries and coffee being brought in for a mid-morning break. We can be first in line if we try."

Stepping out like a majorette in order to keep up with Des, Raye managed to lean forward and talk to Julia over his solid chest. "Do you think she made major points with that fitness instructor act?"

"Probably." Julia leaned forward, too. "Because who's doing the evaluating? Men. And we have one example right here. Let's ask him."

"Oh, no. Don't you pull me into this discussion." Des dropped their arms and held up both palms in denial.

"This retreat was billed as a team-builder and morale-booster, with bonuses thrown in for certain winners. They mentioned squad prizes among others. Baloney. Everyone knows raises and promotions are going to hinge on our individual performances, in addition to the big-money award," Raye said. *And maybe even our jobs themselves, if layoffs occur.* "I'm determined to succeed in this competition."

"Hold on. No one's specifically tied raises and promotions to the retreat." Des ground to a halt. "Neither have criteria, conditions or rules been covered."

"You forget that I have a connection to insider information." Raye threw a sidelong glance toward Julia as they continued forward. "Someone privy to machinations at the top management level."

"Hmmm, you may be right. Behind-the-scenes intrigue, shifting alliances," said Des. "The patterns appear everywhere. These are standard operating procedures in major corporations, the armed services or any type of large organization, for that matter. In any case, you'll have many rivals. Me for one. I'm not used to losing. Nothing energizes me as much as a challenge and topnotch competition."

"Is that a back-handed compliment?" said Raye.

"I think I know Raye's motivations to win." Julia stopped and pulled Raye to a halt. "Des, what inspires you? Is clawing up the corporate ladder the reward? Power over people and the system?"

"Yeah. At heart I'm a mini-dictator, eager to exercise authority over the masses." A sarcastic twist marked Des' lips as he urged them on again toward the buffet table. "I might dial down my efforts if you stuff me with enough pastries, though, or if I'm convinced Raye's reasons are good enough."

"I'll believe that when I see it," said Raye. "You both know my main one—a kid in college. He's got temptations and pressures—gangs in the neighborhood, girls chasing him. Definitely his lack of a decent father contributes."

"What about your dad?" Des asked. "Didn't he fill in?"

"The best he could. But I couldn't call his employment history a template for success. And there were other...problems." *Which I refuse to talk about,* she thought as she snapped her mouth so tight that she figured not even Des would continue the subject.

She was right. After casting one curious glance at her, Des directed the women with a palm on each of their backs toward a spread of delicacies. Pausing to *ooh* and *aah* over lavish cream frosting dripped over miniature cinnamon rolls, chocolate-dipped strawberries, almond croissants, piles of nut meats and juices interspersed with champagne and vodka for make-your-own drinks, they soon loaded their plates.

Julia continued, "No, really. What drives you, Des?"

"Oh, I've got some family reasons, too, that I can't go into right now, as well as a strong competitive streak," he said.

"I'm betting on lots of sabotage, especially from certain people. Krystle's single and has no kids," said Raye. "She's consumed by her career. I've heard she deliberately rated an assistant low on evaluations just to keep the woman tied to her desk."

"Raye!" Julia shrieked. "I told you that in confidence."

"Des won't run around babbling. He needs his eyes opened about her. I'm sure Krystle's out gunning for every advantage she can grab. I wouldn't mind a fair fight, but there was no need for her to cavort around the way she did. Kicks over her head...really!"

"I thought she was kinda cute," said Des.

Raye snorted. "You would!"

Chapter Thirteen

A wave of other employees were swelling their way, intent on the food. "Uh-oh," Raye warned. "We'll be lucky to get crumbs if we don't hurry."

"Finish loading up, ladies," said Des. "Then we'll retreat to the patio."

Des set the pace, loading his plate to the utmost. Julia copied him, even as she raised her eyebrows at Raye so she'd do the same.

The trio exited with haste, ducking behind louvered French doors, pulling them closed as they headed for striped lawn chairs. Julia didn't wait to sit down before she plucked a raspberry-laden tart from her plate.

Raye, however, set her small china plate on the teak occasional table next to her and ignored the mini croissant. "So you're a fan of Krystle's?"

"Nope. Didn't say that." He spread a generous dollop of veggie cream cheese on his poppy-seed bagel and took a huge chomp.

"You said she was kind of cute."

"I don't know many fifty-year-old women who can move like she does."

"She's not fifty, maybe forty-five."

Des chewed then swallowed. "I dunno. She has that hard kind of edge that usually indicates some surgical improvements to the features of aging females."

At Des' analysis, Julia, who'd taken a mouthful of coffee, choked and spewed liquid.

"And her body?" he continued. "It's sculpted. Oh, I admit she must work out strenuously, but work's been done there, too. Plus, she's way too skinny." He took another man-sized bite.

"I'm astounded at your summary of her looks. I thought you were captivated, the way the two of you lingered at the back, nearly wrapped around each other," said Raye, all her attention evidently on the plate of food next to her. She hovered her fingers, as if to make a choice.

"Noticed, did you?" Des waggled his eyebrows at her.

Raye looked up and gave him a narrowed glance. "It was impossible to miss the show when you moved to the front of the group. Anyway, her looks aren't important to the subject at hand unless they affect the likelihood of promotions and raises."

"How much competition could she be?"

Julia walked past Raye to reach for her friend's untouched food. "She's cut-throat. She'll sacrifice anything or anyone to get ahead." She removed a small bunch of grapes and popped two in her mouth.

"She's as phony and artificial as a three-dollar bill," he dismissed. "No likelihood she'll win. One of you has a much better chance," said Des.

"Why ever would you imagine that?" Raye said.

"I've seen both of you in action, and you're the most pulled-together, hard-working, creative people at the firm—first at work, last to leave, always ready to offer assistance, finish assignments in advance of deadlines, develop solutions to problems. Always pleasant. Well"—Des looked from the corner of his eye at Raye—"nearly always courteous."

Raye raised her dark eyebrows at Julia as high as they'd go. Julia snickered and popped another grape into her mouth. "You can count me out of the contest," she muttered around the fruit.

"That's very kind of you to say, but I'm betting that in the final evaluation, the qualities you mentioned will count for *nada*," said Raye in reply to Des. "Even more to the point of how to succeed, Krystle's an egotist, a quality important to ensuring you get noticed by management."

"Egoist or egotist?" said Julia.

"Actually, in her case, both. An egoist puts himself ahead of everyone else. An egotist thinks he's superior."

"How so?" Des opted for a neutral question.

"Because every time she's in a conversation, she dominates it. It's all about 'me.' Haven't you noticed? No matter what the subject, she has a handful of observations and even more advice, usually illustrated with some vignette from her own life to illustrate her exemplary qualities. She rarely pauses and never, but never, asks you a question about your own opinions."

"And that's your assessment." A slight frown marred Des' face. He brushed crumbs from his hands, stood and strolled to the edge of the patio to face the encroaching forest.

"My analysis, based on observation and interaction over several years." A twinge of guilt shimmered through Raye. *Am I being unfair? Judgmental?* 'No' to the first because she'd reported the truth and 'yes' to the second because she'd applied her own values to Krystle's behavior. "I don't want to tell tales. You can make up your own mind." She paused to take her first bite of croissant. "Truth be told, though, I've noticed hard work and talent aren't necessarily the qualities that get rewarded in life. Take Julia…"

"No, no. Don't go into that," said Julia. The speed with which she spoke indicated her unwillingness to delve into the subject.

"I know she doesn't like to dwell on it, but because she's an admin, Julia's ignored for many opportunities. For one thing, she's not on a squad at the retreat, so she doesn't qualify for bonuses or whatever other perks are in store."

Julia jumped forward, her face flushing bright pink. "I haven't complained, have I? Leave it."

"No, I'd like to hear about this," said Des, over his shoulder. "Go on."

Raye looked back and forth at her companions then proceeded. "She's treated like a bond servant—go here, pick up all the reports, find that misplaced file, assemble the statistics, pay these bills, dust the office, make the airline reservations. But when kudos are handed out or opportunities for development or advancement occur, she's overlooked."

Des turned back to her. Raye didn't out of her chair. Julia sank into an adjacent one, shoulders slumped and head bowed. "Isn't that what admins are supposed to do?" he asked Julia.

Raye answered instead. "Yes. But surely an outstanding admin should have the chance to move ahead. Talk about a glass ceiling. Women in lower levels of management suffer from bumping their skulls repeatedly on that. Witness the lumps on mine. But admins have the problem quadrupled. Add that Julia's Latina and even more barriers appear."

"I really wish you wouldn't talk about it," said Julia as she raised her head.

"On top of all that, Julia's family depends on her. They're way behind on car payments, and they've got to make good soon or they'll lose their transportation. She helps with the rent as well as her mom's health issues, and her younger brother and sister need financial support with their educations."

Unable to stop as the resentment on Julia's behalf increased, Raye gripped her croissant so tightly that she squished it into a wad of dough. "You've seen her translate fluently. Van Voorst depends on her to plan and implement all his brilliant ideas. She deserves a promotion and she certainly could use one. She's first-generation and an American success story. Pursuit Telecom should be spotlighting her as the face of employee accomplishments, not hiding her behind the boss' door."

"I never realized." The words trickled in an undertone from Des' lips.

"Men usually don't," Raye said as she fingered the remainder of her croissant into her mouth.

Des added, "I should talk to the big boss about this. As a member of the management team in Kansas City, I helped create the firm's national employment policies several years ago. We pride ourselves on not discriminating, we follow up immediately on every suspected case of sexual misconduct, but we fail to utilize our employees' skills to their fullest. That's bad business."

Raye and Julia stared at him open-mouthed. "What?"

"I'm floored," Raye said. "I never expected you to take me seriously, let alone pursue action!"

"No, no." That was Julia. "Please don't. I appreciate your intent, but this isn't the time or place to raise the issue."

"Are you afraid something bad would happen?" asked Raye.

Julia's fingers trembled as she reached for her coffee cup. "Yes. I could lose this job." She took a long sip. "Raye, I don't have to predict consequences for you."

"No. You don't."

"Then explain them to me," Des said. So deep in the dark that he was nearly cross-eyed, Des searched for an explanation. *If Julia lost her job, she'd sacrifice medical benefits, her parents might shun her, she'd be forced to declare bankruptcy or rob banks, she couldn't afford the dentist and her teeth would fall out...* The possibilities were endless but baffling. He began to feel that bewilderment accompanied contact with these two as a natural condition.

"How naïve are you?" said Raye. "If an immigrant from Mexico is canned from a decent position and has to hit the pavement to search for another, her chances of finding a comparable job inside of six months are nearly zero."

"That's bull," Des said.

"I'm afraid it's not," said Julia, so softly that he struggled to make out her words. "I know from experience. About five years ago, the company I used to work for closed up shop and laid everyone off. It took me fourteen months to find this position. And I had the perfect experience as well as great references. I could tell as soon as I walked in for an interview what the response was going to be. It was never so overt or honest that you could discuss it or counter it. Just a careful 'we'll be in touch.' That's the cue you'll get a form email rejection...if you hear back at all."

"A major reason why I don't job-hop," said Raye.

A light seemed to flood Des' mind. He'd read about subtle discrimination tainting corporations and institutions, even discussed the impacts of intolerance on morale and performance, whether in the military or on the civilian side. He'd never felt a personal connection to that kind of discrimination before. Soul-searing anger welled up in his throat. He interrupted the conversation continuing between the two women.

"I understand," Raye was saying. "Van Voorst knows how valuable you are. I won't do anything to disturb your position."

"Knowing you've lived through similar situations and support me helps," said Julia.

"I disagree," Des said. "I won't do anything on my own, but at some point each of us has to step up for what we believe in, be an influence for change. However, you're the ones directly affected by the situation, not me. So for now, let's do our best in this competition." He made a silent vow to be alert for the opportunity to help Raye, Julia and everyone at Pursuit Telecom succeed or fail on their own merits.

Chapter Fourteen

Okay. We can do this. Everyone in Colorado likes Mexican food, and Julia and I are expert cooks, at least for anything with chili peppers in it.

Still, Raye wondered what demon had encouraged her to raise her hand as volunteer chef for the third night. Oh, yes...Olivia. After the whole crew had gathered for this morning's final instructions for participation in a 'design the perfect staff room' contest, the recruitment had been announced. Olivia had poked Raye in the ribs and whispered, "Raise your hand. Good brownie points."

Even with Julia's immediate, loyal back-up, as soon as the words had flown from Raye's mouth — *'I'll fix burritos'* — she'd wished she'd wired her jaw shut. As part of the go-for-broke competitive atmosphere of the retreat, Kabir had casually announced that those staff who hosted a dinner would earn the gratitude of Mr. Van Voorst. *Translate that to 'earn brownie points',* Raye figured. She and Julia couldn't lose. Her home-made salsa recipe—courtesy of her father and a favorite of her brother's—always won raves. Its secret ingredient? Cinnamon. Crank out a mess of spicy, tasty burritos lashed with plenty of cilantro and cheese, pour icy margaritas down everyone's throat and they'd have no rivals.

The two dinners so far had been the first night's casual burgers, brats and fresh salmon and top-grade meat and nice trimmings of asparagus, sweet potato fries, biscuits with butter oozing and the like. Everything had been quality and tasty, but was hardly outstanding in creativity.

What can go wrong? Plenty, she realized as she puttered in the professional-grade kitchen, surrounded by granite counters and stainless-steel appliances. She gripped a utility knife, sharp as a sliver of glass, over a deep sink full of piles of fresh produce, ordered courtesy of the lodge's manager from the local farmers' market at her request.

One person could be vegan, another lactose intolerant, several someones gluten-free… That was precisely why she'd suggested burritos. Corn tortillas instead of flour, choice of beans or meat, cheese and sour cream on the side and all options were covered. The lodge manager had assured her he'd found every item on her shopping list, even fresh cilantro.

But…the stuffing could burn on a new-to-her stove. Diners' digestive systems sometimes balked at the potential intestinal upset of piquant foods. Her co-workers could sneer at the relative modesty of the menu.

Julia appeared at her elbow. Gently tugging the knife from her hold, she set it on the counter and plucked a generous bunch of fragrant cilantro, bright green as the aspen trees outside, from the colander. "Here, start stripping this. I'll get the beans going."

Raye favored burritos for meals like this one because they were quick, easy and expandable. She might prepare for ten, but she could serve double in a pinch. Tonight's guest list ran about twenty-eight, but who knew what their appetites would be like after the day they'd experienced? By cracking open an extra can or two of beans, grating a spare hunk of cheese and chopping another onion, the stuffings could be stretched indefinitely.

Ever health-conscious, she trimmed calorie counts and upped nutrition by using fresh products, warming tortillas in the oven rather than frying them and sneaking in shredded veggies like celery and carrots. "Don't complain until you try it," she'd advised Julia, who'd quickly become a convert to the cause. So this evening, once Raye had plunged into the routine that was tightly controlled by the clock, she'd forgotten to be nervous and simply moved into the rhythm of food preparation. She and Julia had mini-competitions—who could prep an onion the quickest, how many plates could be balanced to carry safely to the buffet line, amount of time for Julia to crush tomatoes for salsa versus Raye chopping avocadoes.

Giggles gushed between their lips as they sampled and tweaked their work. "*Hoy!*" Raye crowed as she submerged herself in the process. It didn't hurt that an audience gathered—including, she noticed, her squad partner. Des sat on a high stool on the opposite side of the pass-through counter where she was setting up the buffet. He was cushioned between several others, with more onlookers standing behind.

An occasional hand darted out to sneak a snippet of cheese or a tiny bit of tomato, as if the witnesses couldn't restrain themselves. Her confidence and sense of acceptance by these people, in this place, increased moment by moment, and she realized with some surprise that she was enjoying her sense of acceptance.

Charged with the creation of a tasty vegan filling, Julia was reaching the apex of her achievement. She gave a final few stirs to the beans—a mixture of several varieties, along with corn and summer squash, decorated as much as flavored with green onions, cilantro and red and green peppers, spooned the concoction into an earthenware serving bowl with Southwestern hues, and carried her offering to the head of the buffet. Moans of hunger and appreciation rose in a tide, which transformed into a low chant of "Julia, Julia, Julia."

Julia glanced over her shoulder at Raye, still at the stove. The way she widened her eyes and pursed her mouth let Raye know that her friend was thrilled at the spontaneous friendly action.

"Ah, the wonderful aroma of beans. I should have known I'd find the two beaners from the office. Just joking, just joking…" Mason's grating voice chuckled with false humor, drifting over the others, and his face, twisted with a sarcastic sneer, peered out.

Raye froze, the spatula for the frying hamburger in her hand. *What an obnoxious ass*, she thought. *Surely he can't think he'll get away with a comment like that here and now.* She snuck a look at Julia. Motionless, the younger woman remained by the buffet line, as if fearful that a twitch could bring attention down on her.

"I hope there's another choice. My stomach gets upset easily." What a fool! Mason simply wouldn't give up.

Julia seemed to shrink inward, like an origami folding in on itself. Raye examined the others, who also remained motionless. Raye couldn't tell if shock, disgust or agreement tinged the atmosphere. From the group, she picked out Des' face. His eyes glittered and moved from person to person in his line of vision. She didn't know if she feared or hoped he would leap into what could become a fray, but she refused to wait for his response.

"You're welcome to come in here and cook up another meal for the crew, Mason." With perfect control, Raye set down her utensils, reached for a hot pad and toted the meat filling to the buffet line. "I didn't see you leaping up to volunteer earlier."

Mason held up both palms. "Oh, not me. I *never* cook."

"I'm not sure how many people would want to test an experiment from you then. They know by their noses and eyes how delicious our meal's going to be."

"Ha, ha, ha." Mason's guffaw grated on her ears. "They can be sure you have lots of experience with the tastes of janitors and mowing men and house cleaners." When a murmur of disapproval answered this statement, he held up both hands. "Hey. What's the matter? Can't you all take a joke?"

Still moving with the utmost grace and talking in the tones of diplomacy, Raye fetched a stack of plates from one end of the counter and moved them next to the food. She knew from long experience that comments bordering on racist were best handled immediately, politely and informally. To involve a corporate big shot, fling quotes from official policy or argue defensively would gain her no supporters and certainly would not change Mason's behavior. She twitched her long ponytail at the very end as she gathered her thoughts. "I'm half German-American, too," she said, so sweetly that butter wouldn't melt in her mouth. "Therefore I'm also genetically prepared to deal summarily with pig," referencing the national meat of Germany while dealing a subtle insult.

This remark flew over Mason's head, seemed to rebound against the refrigerator and smacked up against Des. He blinked then stifled a chortle. However, apparently taken aback by her ability to stick up for herself, Mason mumbled an unintelligible comment, scooped up a handful of grated cheese with his bare fingers and exited, head ducked. Low-pitched nattering from observers, interposed with soft whoops of laughter, convinced Raye of their sympathy.

She moved to Julia's side. "Never mind what that jerk says. But you really need to learn how to react with some forcefulness. Be calm yet assertive. People like him... They take silence for fear, courtesy for cowardice. Like mad dogs, they attack and attack to drive you away." She noticed tremors quivering up and down Julia's arms. Now it was Raye who tugged the utensil and bowl out of Julia's fingers and ran her hands over her friend's forearms. "I know. I know how scary a situation like that can be. But you have nothing to lose and everything to gain when you train yourself to respond to the nonsense. Right?"

"Yes." Julia turned her palms upward and captured Raye's hands. "Thank you. I know you're right. I'm so used to not making waves. That's how I survived the tough school I went to, where every group and gang challenged the others. It's how I keep peace in my family. But I need to stick up for myself."

"Yes. And against stupid, small-minded stereotypes of any kind." Raye traded the mutual arm-grip for a swift hug. "Never forget… *Todos somos luchadoras*. Now, get busy putting out the rest of the condiments." Twirling Julia by the shoulders, she gave her friend the sort of pat on the rear common among sport teammates to hurry her on her way to the pantry.

"Most impressive." Des' low rumble interrupted Raye's contemplation. She swung back toward him, anticipating she'd catch him in a sardonic mood. *No.* Everyone else had left, some to grab a glass of wine, others for a final primping before dinner, but he leaned forward, chin propped on fist, focused solely on her, as if entranced. He'd worn the same intense gaze today in his deep eyes as when they'd brainstormed together to design the perfect, if imaginary, staff room, complete with amenities like a juice bar. It was strange how his obvious interest in her made her feel like the center of his every sensation. He seemed unable to tear his attention from her.

She took in a tiny gasp of air. It was surprising that a person's concentration could animate his entire being and make him as attractive as a present she'd want to open at Christmas. For a moment she forgot the dinner she was preparing for her co-workers, who soon would evaluate her venture.

Olivia, who must have come downstairs for dinner, appeared in the periphery of her vision and broke into her trance. "Oh, Raye, what a spread! We're going to have some stuffed stomachs around here."

Raye's boss hadn't been present when the verbal tussle with Mason had occurred. Raye twinkled at her. "You advised me to volunteer."

"And you never take half-measures, as well I know," said Olivia. "I can't wait to taste the final products."

With a ta-ta wave of her fingers, Olivia departed, leaving Des and Raye staring at one another over the food-laden counter. The zesty, meaty aroma of sautéed hamburger mingled with tomato so fresh that she could smell the sweet, earthy pungency, cushioned by undertones of corn from tortillas, along with sharp cilantro, and her mouth watered. She licked her lips, and Des copied the motion. *Just what are we licking?* she wondered.

"Looks like another success for you," he said.

"This isn't part of the actual competition," she said.

"No, but you can count it as extra credit. I'm not complaining, mind you. Not only have you concocted a delicious meal, but also you met the enemy and he is yours. Congratulations on a definite classy victory over an oaf."

She started to cover the dishes with plastic wrap until the official start of dinner. "I had to respond to him. It was a real challenge to keep my cool while reacting to him."

"Yeah, I could tell. I thought your head was going to burst, you were so tightly wound."

"I hope Mason didn't know." She tugged a piece of plastic wrap over the last bowl.

"I'm sure he didn't. He's singularly unaware of anything outside himself."

"I would have walked away if Julia hadn't been around. But she's a novice. She lets this kind of nonsense get under her skin. I wanted to show Julia how a jerk can have the ground cut out from under his feet without the use of foul language or screaming like a fishwife. And what is a fishwife, in any case?"

He threw back his head and laughed. "You may be aptly described by *fishwife*. She was a woman who worked as hard as a man and didn't take guff from anyone — and sometimes known for her beauty."

She looked at him from under her thick dark lashes. *Is he trying to flirt with me? Put moves on me?* She waited but he added nothing, so she asked with a trace of suspicion, "Are you paying me a compliment?"

"Yes," he said. "Yes, I am."

Chapter Fifteen

Karaoke. What can be worse than a bunch of people who should be on their best behavior making fools of themselves?

Des was not a fan, but the musical entertainment was scheduled for this evening's activity. He had to attend. Certain compromises always seemed to come with the territory of being part of a group, whether it was his high school football team, military unit or corporate office. If he wanted to be accepted, if he hoped for encouragement and assistance, he had to get involved with the company.

But he didn't have to sing.

In fact, he still was focused on the earlier discussion with his sister. Not the experimental medical procedure he hoped would help her, but her response to the idea of Raye in his life. On automatic, he left his room, paced down the pine-paneled hallway and massive log-and-plank staircase, then on to the central lounge in which most indoor activities were being held. In immediate view loomed a large screen, several microphones and other machines heralding the evening's fun. Ben, Julia and Kabir clustered around the makeshift staging area, fiddling with the equipment. In an armchair at the end of the first semi-circular row of chairs perched Raye, earliest of the audience.

Hmmm, some advantages now occur to me. He grabbed a nearby chair and pulled it closer to her as he weighed the various topics to bring up. *'How 'bout them Broncos?'* wouldn't cut it, he already knew from the ride up. "Your meal was a raving success," he said, quickly adding a question so she'd be forced to continue the conversation. "Was the vegetarian choice more popular than the beef?"

"No, about equal. Although lots of people took beef and beans. And there were no more nasty comments about beaners or indigestion," she said. "We are in Colorado, where there are more Mexican restaurants than any other specialty. Mason's going to have to learn to watch his tongue."

"Especially if he hopes to receive advancement. No matter what he thinks personally, he should know he can't get away with questionable comments," Des added.

"And what do *you* think?"

"What do I think about what?" Truly puzzled, he tilted his head and looked at her. "Oh, I totally support corporate policies on anti-discrimination and harassment." When she made no response, he wondered if he'd passed or failed some sort of test.

In the lengthening silence, he broke in with his own concern. "So, about this karaoke... Think we'll be judged on performances?"

"Nah. Julia told me it's for entertainment. No one will be forced to sing." She gave a little bounce in her overstuffed chair and tucked her feet under herself, making her ponytail flick on her shoulder. She slid her eyelids closed as she hugged herself. "I love karaoke, especially if I can sing *Proud Mary*."

Background music started playing and light flickered from the screen at the front as song titles and lyrics cycled through for a last-minute check. "I assume you'll perform?" Des said over the echoing sounds. "Seems out of character. A public humiliation could be in store."

"Oh, no," she said. "It's vital for me to participate in these activities to show my ability to be part of the team. Anyway, I love karaoke. I'm a frustrated rock star. Wouldn't miss it for the world. How about you?"

"I'm an audience member, not an entertainer."

"Even with a nip or two in you?"

"Especially not then." His adamant refusal allowed no wiggle room, he hoped. Some close scrapes in his teens and even when first in the service had convinced him that if he wanted to keep his dignity, not to mention his money and his reputation, he should avoid drinking to excess and public appearances resembling mob scenes.

"Okay. Your loss." She got to her feet, smoothed down her brilliant tangerine cami layered over a striped tank, tossed her matching beaded earrings and pulled the scrunchie securing her hair to the very top of her head. Using movements that resembled a witch casting a spell, to Des' way of thinking, she wrapped, tucked and pulled strands through the mass until she boasted a loose bun with curls falling this way and that.

"Looks like you're preparing for your appearance," said Des. Raye's primping set off a tremor inside him, which he tamped down.

"Yes, indeed. Can't sing or move with all that hair flying about. I need freedom. Freedom! *Hoy!*" She yelled as she flung both arms in the air then leaped, hopped, kicked to the cleared area with the equipment at the front of the room, where Julia welcomed her with a cheer and a fist pump over her head.

She's as limber and fit as Krystle. Des let his mind wander briefly to consider what that might mean in an intimate setting.

As the other members of the Chosen Twenty-Five poured in and filled the chairs, laughing and chatting in apparent anticipation of the entertainment, Des leaned back to recall his own search for freedom. Ah, yes, he remembered that yearning to chase the phantom of independence, for he knew now total liberty was an illusion. He'd always had to battle an urge to run, to escape whatever cage currently confined him. When he was much younger, he'd frequently surrendered to that impulse, rebelling against his parents' stupid rules, sneaking out of the house, slouching late into school, running wild with his buddies through the dark streets that seemed to promise excitement.

Those episodes hadn't turned out well, he recalled. They were part of the reason he'd abandoned any post-high school education immediately after graduation, accepting every cruddy job simply to have pocket change. Then, when he realized he was on a never-ending treadmill to nowhere, his father had been forced to file for bankruptcy because of his sister's medical bills. Des had figured he could sign up in the service and send checks home to help. The enlistment bonus had sealed the deal. He'd fled to the military, which he'd imagined would be a life-altering challenge. It had been, but not in the way he'd anticipated.

I wonder what Raye's pursuit of freedom has been like.

In the open area serving as a stage, Raye was set to go. She radiated energy and enthusiasm, executing a dance-like shuffle to the side, then up and back, rotating her shoulders, clenching and unclenching her fingers, like a boxer preparing for a bout. Stepping in front of her and positioning himself with a microphone, Kabir assumed the role of emcee to usher in the fun. Raye hardly waited for him to finish before she grabbed the mic and belted out the song lyrics on the screen.

Nearly three hours of revelry followed, liberally oiled by glasses of wine and bottles of beer, creating that amorphous, almost tangible, atmosphere of good will and camaraderie that results when people are restricted to an intimate setting and forced to relate. The interaction tonight was minimal for those, like Des, who didn't want to perform. All they had to do was maintain a cheerful mien and applaud at the conclusion of each entertainer's selection. Des, of course, made sure to put lots of energy into clapping for Raye, along with cheering and woofing.

Every hopeful soloist in the troop had the chance to sing, but Raye was implored to perform over and over. She threw heart and soul into her delivery, soon pulling the scrunchie from her hair to allow the curls to go their wanton way around her shoulders and down her back. Des wanted to jump up next to her and sing back-up, warbling like a canary. Fortunately he controlled himself, for with his lack of skill, he'd most likely drive the audience out of the room. And he'd lose whatever semblance of dignity he possessed. Still, he knew if she crooked a finger at him, he'd be by her side in an instant.

He wasn't embarrassed by his growing feelings for Raye. It was long past time to put that bad break-up years ago behind him, the 'Dear John' letter from Gina in high school, a girl as wild and feisty as he'd been. She'd promised to wait but had dumped him less than a month after he'd enlisted. Broke his heart, it had, but not his spirit. In fact, the grief had toughened him, enabled him to thrive in appalling conditions of boredom, heat, danger and suspicion, covering the gamut from physical to emotional trials. However, he'd never again approached the emotional bond he'd once shared with Gina, although he'd had plenty of physical liaisons and dozens of women who'd seemed eager to extend a mere fleeting connection into something more permanent, like the late, unlamented Jennifer back in Kansas.

Being with Raye the past few days had enlightened him. Over the years, without consciousness, he'd been waiting for a woman to emanate a sense of welcome and home for him, to elicit in him a mixture of desire and longing and relief and safety. The time was now, the woman was here, yet approaching this touchy, distrusting, independent woman would be the challenge of his life.

* * * *

"What are you doing here?"

Raye heard a low undertone that broke the night's silence. Everyone had retired after the karaoke event. Raye had thought she'd be alone.

She froze at the bottom of the massive log staircase from the second story that led to the lounge area, then scanned the leather sofas and chairs and the Native American blankets that decorated the walls. A few table lamps remained burning, and the flames in the stone-encrusted fireplace were making their final desperate flickers. To the left of the room, a rectangle of light shone from the side leading to the kitchen, and she finally spotted a silhouette backlit from the doorway. She rewrapped the tangled locks sitting haphazardly on the nape of her neck into tighter control with the scrunchie.

"Des. I could ask the same question of you," she whispered back.

"Okay. Let's both admit our failing. You're here to scout out leftovers from dinner, right?" Des moved back out of the doorway and motioned for her to follow, which she did on tiptoe. He traveled to the island in the middle of the kitchen, a granite top perched on row upon row of drawers and shelves. Strewn across the flat surface was a gourmet feast of remains from dinner — tortillas, beans, avocado, corn, hamburger, tomatoes, salsa, even half a four-layer chocolate cake from dessert. Des must have retrieved them, because she and Julia had left the kitchen spotless.

Raye gasped. "I'm starving. After hours of singing and applauding, my blood sugar's low. But do you think it's okay if we have a snack?"

"Yes." With a smirk, he added, "Remember... We're being evaluated on taking initiative. So I took it. I talked to the concierge after dinner. He said the chef never checks, and all the help plunders the remains when a group like ours visits. What are they going to do with all of this? Just throw it out? So I unloaded the fridge. Dig in. Here's a plate and some silverware."

Silence reigned again as Raye and Des scooped, piled, sliced and stirred. Then there were only the clink of utensils, the sounds of chewing and swallowing and, finally, satisfied sighs. The refrigerator's hum as the motor switched on provided background rhythms, and Raye felt she was in a Disneyland-type setting amid the sparkles and shines of appliances, lights and glistening white cupboards.

Des smothered a burp. "Guess it's clean-up time."

"And you probably think that should be my job, right?"

"Yes."

"Because I'm a woman or because I'm Latina?" She held her breath as she waited to see if he would charge toward the red flag she'd deliberately waved. Would he realize she was pulling his leg? Testing his good humor? He was damned either way he answered the question.

"Because I'm lazy," he inserted smoothly.

A cascade of giggles poured from her at his reply. He'd outmaneuvered her. "You should have seen your face. like a mask had dropped over it. I wanted to see how you'd react." Raye stuck her finger into the frosting on her piece of cake and licked the chocolate like a lollipop, considering her next statement. *Sharing food reminds me of Communion in church,* she thought. *A private time apart.* Of course, a few drinks plus drowsiness increased her inclination to let down her guard. *What the heck?*

She began, "I'm not overly sensitive. I don't search for ethnic innuendos in every corner or under every table. I think that sort of thing is ridiculous. I am what I am, and I'm proud of all my ancestry. Not overly proud, but aware of my heritage and the history and achievements and culture that go along with it."

The two of them cleared their mess away, stacking their few dishes in the sink, storing any sizeable leftovers in the refrigerator. "Why can't we simply treat people as individuals?" The question popped from her as if of its own volition. "We spend so much time getting ready to be offended or tiptoeing around political correctness that we lose sight of one another's humanity."

She slammed the refrigerator door closed, but she giggled. "That reminds me of a time here in Denver when the police were writing parking tickets and used the word Mexican. They caught hell from all sides of the political spectrum for the term. Turned out the violators had parked in the space reserved for the Mexican consulate."

As she laughed, Des joined in. In a contagious reaction, he set her off more, until they collapsed on the counter. Then he grabbed a damp rag to swab the surfaces and continued. "Don't try to con me. I've seen the way you boil if someone tosses out a stereotype about Hispanics, like implying you're slow-moving or lazy. That 'beaner' comment by Mason, for example. I thought the top of your head was going to detonate."

"That's different." She paused, salt and pepper shakers in hand, poised to place them in a cupboard.

A shadow darkened her ebony eyes. "That's blatantly racist. Deliberately trying to be offensive."

Maybe the conversation is getting too serious for him, she thought, when he changed the subject abruptly.

"That's some nightwear you're wearing. Comfortable, homey. A sweat suit, right?" A smear of dried salsa came under an especially thorough attack with the wet rag.

Raye looked down at her body, swathed in a light brown pullover and pants. "It's warm and clean," she protested. "My son outgrew it and I didn't want to let it go to waste. Not every woman wants to waltz around in a skimpy lace negligee, especially in the middle of a lodge during a work function."

"I'm not taking issue with your choice. You look cozy, as if a massive drop in temperature wouldn't make the slightest difference to you. And you resemble a teddy bear. A huggable one." He was rinsing the rag in a stream of hot water at the sink.

She blushed. "I don't know if you're admiring me or not."

Des turned to face her. "Since when do you want approval from me?" A few paces brought him to the dregs of the night's liquid refreshments, including a collection of half-empty wine bottles, and he grabbed one.

Raye had to ask herself the same question. Somehow, over the past few days, Des had become less antagonistic, less arrogant. He'd shown a caring, human side of himself in the discussion about the bias Julia faced, demonstrated a healthy—if sarcastic— sense of humor as he teased Raye on the scavenger hunt, exhibited deep affection toward his sister every time he mentioned her and had even added a twinge or two of neediness, like his comment driving up about women only valuing the material things a man brought them.

Or was she the person changing?

She gave a low, challenging laugh. "You've certainly built up a vivid scenario in your mind — teddy bears, coziness, comfort — not at all what I'm really like. I'm actually tough as nails. I've had to be." She stopped.

"You can't halt there," he said. "What's your story?" He topped off her flute of wine before he swiveled around to the counter again to capture a bottle of beer and uncap it. He clearly wanted to keep talking, because next he scooted two sturdy plastic kitchen chairs from the kitchen to the other side of the counter, positioned them facing the spacious dining room side by side, and motioned an invitation for her to sit.

She gave a self-conscious groan as she took the chair next to him. "A very old one. Ancient. Part teenage rebellion, part screwed-upness. My brother had been killed and my father must have had some sort of breakdown. I didn't know which way to turn. That's when I met Michael. First he became a distraction, then a refuge."

She sipped the wine and gave a wry grin. "My parents disapproved, but I thought he was wonderful, despite his brushes with the law and a drug habit. Surely feelings as strong as mine would be eternal, right? My love would save him, so I took off from home. Then I got pregnant. A shotgun marriage followed, thanks to my dad."

"Then?" He swallowed a slug of beer.

"Actually, very little. Once we'd gotten married, he hung around for a few weeks then disappeared except for sporadic contacts. I know I was fortunate. I didn't think so at first, but when I compare my situation to other women who have to tolerate violence or their guy stealing all their money, pawning their valuables or dictating their lives, I've been blessed."

Chapter Sixteen

The confession seemed to confirm the dilemma facing Des as he considered how to get closer with Raye. She was a strong woman, perhaps so independent that she'd never open up to a man like him. She'd already made it clear that she despised — in fact feared — motorcycles and distrusted men who rode them. They'd bumped heads on several issues that seemed to be grounded in unspoken hierarchy, male-female stereotypes or plain crankiness, such as disagreements over items to collect for the scavenger hunt or her opinion of men, as she'd succinctly stated during the drive up. The last thing he wanted was a pissing contest with her. Maybe if he related some of his personal history, she'd start noticing similarities between their outlooks rather than differences. There were plenty.

He blinked when her next question offered him the perfect break. "What about you? Do you have a sad story to tell?

"Well, I suppose I do," he said, then delayed by taking another swallow of beer before he continued. "I had a serious girlfriend years ago—Gina, in high school. She was built like a brick house, up for any mischief I and my buds thought up. She ran around a lot, wild and crazy, but was absolutely loyal to me once we started going together—or so I thought." He inserted the tip of a fingernail under the label pasted on the beer bottle to tear off thin strips.

"She didn't have much supervision and even less in the way of rules. And she didn't get along with her family, so we spent all our time together—a good deal of it getting into trouble. A car wreck was one example. I managed to total the vehicle, give myself a concussion and break her arm."

"Oh, no," Raye breathed.

He looked straight at her. "It wasn't all that terrible," he said with amusement. "She got sympathy up the whazoo. Guys carried her backpack and teachers hand-led her through assignments. As for me, my reputation as mad, bad and dangerous to know grew." He rubbed his chin with its five o'clock shadow, in the time-honored gesture of men who appear to be checking on their testosterone, and resumed his label-peeling. "Then followed some months of going berserker, if there is such a word. In fact, the description of your ex isn't off the mark when it came to my behavior."

"But you were, what, eighteen? Not thirty-two like Michael was. There was some excuse for you."

"Thirty-two?" Des sat up straight. "Wasn't that a little old for you?" In the faint light of the lounge area, highlighted by the overheads shining through the rectangle opening for the kitchen where Julia and

Raye had prepared the food, her figure was indistinct. He wished he could read her expression better, so he scooted his chair so close to hers that he could have touched her.

"Exactly what my parents said. But what teenage girl in love ever listens to adults? And, FYI, most teen mothers are impregnated by men over the age of twenty."

"Wow! Where'd you learn that statistic?"

"Playing catch-up in a post-natal parenting class — which I attended by myself, of course." She swigged a mouthful of wine around, as if to remove the bad taste on her tongue.

"Must have been tough."

"Now that I look back, those times were more challenging, even exciting, than they were catastrophic. I was determined to show my parents that my baby was a blessing, and I was equally determined to make a success of my life independently...despite my lack of money, training or resources. Beans, rice and ramen became the gourmet highlights of my menus, and I'm delighted to say that I outfitted myself and Andy for years from thrift stores. Poor but proud."

"Ah, yes, the illusion of freedom." Des leaned back and laced his fingers over the beer resting on his chest. *There must be more to her story*, he sensed. In this late-night, story-swapping atmosphere, he should be able to learn more about her, given that he was a sympathetic listener. "The times when you think you are or should be in control of your life, making every decision. Somehow you believe chance and circumstance play no role."

"Seems like you're familiar with the motivation."

He scrunched his features, as if sampling a lemon. "Yep." *Should I reveal my family's sordid history?* He studied her features, a mixture of embarrassment over the situation when she was young, along with pride that she'd met life's tests. Yes, they had much more in common than she might imagine. He spoke abruptly.

"The main reason I enlisted wasn't to escape my wild reputation. It was bankruptcy. My sister's medical bills got so horrendous and creditors pressed so hard that my parents had to go through the process. It was a nightmare — the forms, the extra bills — because, of course, legal bankruptcy costs money — the time, the humiliation. My mom reacted as if the plague had hit us. My grandparents, as immigrants, had been poor, and she'd wanted to escape the stigma of poverty in the worst way. She'd thought she'd achieved that goal when she married my dad."

"Didn't you have insurance?"

"Yeah, but like many folks, it only covered part of the costs. And our household income was too high to qualify for Medicaid."

"But bankruptcy?" She shuddered.

"Now I'll throw a statistic at you. You probably don't know that fully a third of all bankruptcies result from medical bills."

"No. No, I didn't."

"Anyway, the thought that I could send my checks home for my parents tempted me. Then when I learned I could get an enlistment bonus, I sealed the deal." He sat up straight again. "You must have some nightmares about finances, given your youthful indiscretions. What are they?"

She groaned and covered her eyes with a palm. "Those collection agencies. The mailings and calls never stop. I'm so familiar with their techniques. Thank God for caller ID. Bloodthirsty monsters." Raye pounded the arm of the chair with a fist.

"How so?"

She rose and strolled to a dining room window near Des' chair. Like most of the panes in the lodge, it faced the forest-clad mountains — dark at this hour, but still containing unknown possibilities. Without looking back at him, she continued. "I don't know bankruptcy but I know desperation. My parents lost our house…through foreclosure. I remember the flood of notices, the threatening messages from the mortgage company, my feelings of helplessness. My parents fell apart.

"This was right after my brother died, and my father must have had some sort of breakdown. He stopped going to work, and my mom's job paid peanuts. She nagged constantly, and he simply stared into space. That's when I met Michael. I escaped the tensions at home. I retreated, isolated myself from my family and left my parents to clean up the mess. My mom found a cruddy studio apartment, my dad moved in with his mother, my parents divorced and I got pregnant. End of story, except for the bad taste in my mouth and an endless terror of the wolf at the door, of being homeless again." She turned back to him, one palm outstretched as if in supplication, the other clutching the wine glass, eyebrows raised in hope. "I've got plans to ensure that never happens. I buy a lottery ticket every month. When I win, I'll never need to worry."

Des gave a half-smile, unsure if she was serious. "I'm familiar with the feeling of desperation," he said. "Your life's going nowhere. All around look like dead ends. As for me, I figured the service offered unlimited opportunities. Little did I think Gina, the love of my life, wouldn't agree. I figured she'd join me after basic and the world would be our plaything. The Dear John letter arrived before I even finished training."

"Yikes! Fast." She returned to his side.

"I don't know why women use enlistment as a reason to dump a guy," he said as he extended both legs and crossed them at the ankles. "Most of 'em are just shallow, I guess. Won't stick with you through the hard times."

"Now just a minute. I could make a case that men walk out on women as soon as they give in and have sex. Guys are looking for a one-night stand or a relationship with no stress." She chugged the rest of her wine, and Des reached toward the floor where he'd placed the bottle, to refill her glass, but she pulled the flute away.

He set the bottle back down as he disguised the hurt that had lingered for nearly twenty years with a flippant, mocking tone. "Not in my experience. Women generally are as faithful as fish. Dangle a desirable piece of bait and off they wriggle to catch it. The best lures are sparkly, like jewels or money, or tasty, like expensive clothes and vacations."

"I can't say much for the women you've tried to tempt." Raye was focused on tipping her empty glass one way then another, as if trying to capture the last drops of liquid. Des saw, however, that a certain tightness to her lips and squint to her eyes seemed to indicate intense dissatisfaction with his comments.

"Rather, I can't say much for the manner in which you've tempted them. If you look for superfluous, shallow relationships, that's what you'll get." Raye thumped down the flute on the floor next to her chair.

Des cast his thoughts back over the series of babes he'd been with since Gina. 'Bimbos' was the kindest description for them. Gina's features then came to mind, twisting his throat as if she were choking him. Preferring not to reveal the pain he still suffered when he thought of her, he coughed to clear his throat. "I tried. I tried damned hard with Gina. I was ready to surrender my lifestyle to marry her and make a home and family. As for the others, they weren't worth any sacrifices."

He knew those comments would infuriate Raye, fervent feminist that she was, but at this late hour and level of exhaustion, he had grown unguarded. Her hot temper caught fire from his, and she jumped to her feet, ready to take him on.

"Oh, grow up," she warned him as she leaned forward. "It's been years since that incident." She pointed her index finger in the direction of a nonexistent sheet of paper in her left hand and shook the digit. "You're the same as Andy's father, everyone's picking on you. So you got a Dear John letter in the service? Gina was straight with you. She didn't do something like knock you up, desert you and leaving you penniless. Then you'd have a reason to complain. You're a typical sexist male. Nothing's ever your fault."

Still in his chair, Des' spine was so straight, his shoulders so tense, that he could have snapped in half. He wanted to calm her, but he knew this quarrel couldn't be resolved by simply backing down. Like a noxious weed, its widespread roots grew from Raye's history with her ex-husband, her brother's death, her parents' divorce, even her heritage as an ethnic minority. If they didn't learn to handle these types of situations, there was no future for them. He issued a deliberate, if over-stated challenge. "I'll be ecstatic to grow up when you stop being a man-hater. Bad-mouthing every male in sight."

"You're a woman-hater. An automatic reaction to any barrier in front of you? Blame the nearest female. Ignore logic, ignore anyone else's emotions. Big babies, all of you." Raye stepped immediately in front of Des, her fists planted on her hips, chin thrust out.

Although he wanted to tone the conversation down, two contradictory impulses wormed their way into his consciousness. The first? To tell her how cute she looked when angry. The second? His unruly wit. He nearly tried a joking, '*Do you want a swift punch in the jaw?*' Fortunately, he swallowed his snide comment. But they both were so heated at this point, so emotional, that he felt he had to pull some response out of his pocket, one that would disarm her. "Misandrist." He hissed the word out, knowing she wouldn't have the least idea of its meaning.

She drew herself up to her whole five feet four inches. "How dare you call me a, a...?" she sputtered. "*What* did you call me?"

"A misandrist. A female misogynist. A woman who hates men." His head cocked to the side in silent inquiry.

"How dare you call me that?" Her features, twisted into a scowl, began to quiver, her mouth trembling until she no longer could suppress another disabling round of giggles, which, once he realized her anger had evaporated, he joined. "You are ridiculous."

Somehow his arms wound up around her as she swayed forward and wrapped hers around him, both of them murmuring, 'misandrist' and 'misogynist', 'man-hater' and 'woman-hater'. Her breath brushed his throat and she tilted her head upward until their lips were a fraction apart. He could smell the trace of the meal's seasoning from her mouth, the faint fragrance of her perfume, even the warmth throbbing from her skin. He drew in air.

A melody pealed from her pocket, and they both froze. Her eyes widened, then narrowed. "My cell," she said. "The only one who would call here now is a family member. I'd better check."

She unwrapped her arms from his waist, stepped back with a tremor and dug her phone from a pocket. "My son," she said to Des before she pressed a button. "Yes? An accident?"

Chapter Seventeen

She moved a pace or two farther away and tilted her head to bring the cell nearer to her ear, covering her free ear with a palm, as if that might help her hear. Des made a movement to close the distance between them, but she waved him back.

"Are you all right?" Panic clipped her words to staccato. The connection was poor, and Raye had to concentrate to catch Andy's speech. In the background, she picked up on passing traffic and the stammering static from a police radio. "Who are you with?"

"Cameron. I feel okay. I think. They're planning to take me to the ER to get checked," Andy said.

"What happened? Where are you? How's Cameron?"

"On I-25 south by Northglenn. Cameron and I were headed home from a coupla hours of rehearsal. Some jerk was following too close behind us, and when we got to the road block by some construction, he rear-ended us. You know that section where it seems every nut case on the road puts his brain on slow-mo."

Raye nodded. "Oh, yes. You can never get through that section without some accident or near miss. Back to you. Broken bones? Cuts? Concussions?" Andy's status being her sole apprehension, she continued to look in any direction except Des'.

"I don't notice blood, and no one's clutching a limb like we're hurt. Both cars are major wrecks. You should see the traffic. It's backed up for miles!"

The excitement in Andy's voice reassured Raye that he hadn't sustained any major damage, but knowing he might be in shock, oblivious to injury and that trauma could show up hours, even days later, she aired a Mom mini-lecture. "You let them take you to the ER. Call Grandpops as soon as you can. He can drive to the hospital and let me know how you're doing while the doctors are poking and sampling. He'll take you home, if they release you. Does he know where you are, by the way?"

The wail of an emergency siren swelled in the background.

"Yep. Don't get all over-protective on me, Mom. I'll be fine. Cameron will be fine. It's only the car that's not."

"Ours or Cameron's?"

"Ours. It's pretty much totaled. Listen… I gotta go. The ambulance is here." His voice became weaker as he must have turned his head to talk to his friend or the police.

Her heart sank to her toes, even while she reminded herself that the single most important fact was her son's safety. Predictable phrases flowed from her mouth. "As long as you're okay. We can survive without a car for a while. We'll face this crisis together."

Still, her thoughts sped faster, each one leapfrogging the previous. *How on earth am I going to find the money for repairs? The deductible alone could take every penny I possess. Even if the other driver's at fault…*

"Were you at fault?" she croaked, ready to bite back a stinging rejoinder if this were the case.

"Naw. The other driver was ticketed."

"Does he have insurance?"

"I dunno, Mom. Cripes, this just happened. I'm taking off. Bye."

As the conversation abruptly ended, Raye thought, but didn't add, that she wished the auto involved had been Andy's friend's. His family was much better off than Raye, and for them, a damaged vehicle could be easily handled. Raye, however, would be faced with paying for a loaner out of her own pocket, cutting back on necessities like clothes or Andy's school expenses to cover her deductible and similar inconveniences, even if the other driver's insurance eventually reimbursed her. The thin wire she walked as she tried to balance income and expenditures once again skyrocketed her stress level, excluding any of her curiosity about the new rapport with Des. Her stomach lurched, ready to expel dinner, and she nearly fell back into the chair, now trembling from the ordeal.

Several feet away from her, Des tilted his head with a question. "What's up? That was your son, right? Was he in an accident? How serious?"

"I don't know. He's off to the ER. I hate being this far away from him." She bit her thumbnail, substituting mistreatment of her innocent digit for maternal action, then realized she was shaking. "I wish I could get back home tonight, but we're not supposed to leave the premises."

"I'm sure this situation would be considered an emergency. You should go. You won't be able to concentrate on anything as trivial as the challenges here at the retreat."

Gratitude flooded her. Des was correct. She belonged with Andy right now, not thinking about amassing brownie points during some inane activity such as developing a marketing slogan or redesigning a nonexistent staff room. *But...* She slapped her forehead with a palm. "I don't have a car here. There's no way I can get back tonight."

"I'll drive you," said Des.

"Then we'll both be at a disadvantage for the prize. That's not fair to you," she offered.

"Hmmm," said Des. He held his arms out, palms up, as if weighing something. "The distant possibility of winning some money"—he dropped his right arm—"versus helping a friend reach an injured relative." He dropped his left arm down and his right shot up. "I wonder which is more important in the balance?" Now he alternated raising and lowering his hands in an assessing motion.

His obviously bogus expression of bewilderment generated a laugh deep within her. "I can't reject your offer," she said, as tears threatened to well up. "That's so wonderful of you." Tears spilled when she couldn't suppress the deluge of troubles she faced. "I don't know what I'm going to do about our car."

He dropped his arms. "Listen... I'll take a look at it. I'm experienced with engines. Had to be overseas. Those motorcycles, delicate creatures that they are, taught me quite a bit. What say we postpone this conversation and get you home? I'll meet you right here in forty-five minutes. Is that enough time to gather whatever you might need? I'll let Julia know what's happened." Des already was turning toward the stairs to the lodge rooms and grasped her elbow to lead her in the same direction.

She went willingly through the darkened lobby, dim mounds of furniture reminding her of the problems looming on her horizon, choking back a lump the size of a pinecone. *He called me a friend,* she thought. That point seemed more important than any other previous exchange between the two of them.

Chapter Eighteen

The crisis never happened. The next morning found Raye explaining the incident to Julia as the group gathered for the day's challenge.

"Andy called me back before we set off. Our good luck held. The doctor in the ER cleared him of major trauma, so he hung out at Cameron's for the rest of the night. My dad can handle contacting the insurance company and getting the car towed, that sort of thing. I tell you, I thought my heart would stop when my son first phoned. It's the incident that every parent dreads, refuses to even consider. I was so glad Des —" She broke off.

Julia anticipated what she'd been going to say. "You were so glad Des was with you, right?"

Raye nodded.

"I told you he's a good guy. He's perfect for you. You're like peanut butter and jelly or butter and popcorn. Together you make sense."

"You may be on to something," Raye said slowly.

She'd had plenty to consider during their assignment — create a social media campaign for a new corporate website. As people broke into their squads and squirreled away in corners of the lodge, the wrap-around porch and the nearby grounds, toting legal pads and pens or electronic tablets, depending on their level of comfort with technology, she realized the sight of Des offered her immediate reassurance. A link existed between them, a closeness she hadn't sensed before last night. A grin spread over her face, and she could feel herself light up when he approached. His face replicated hers. She nearly held out her hand to touch his, but she restrained herself.

* * * *

The day had gone well, thought Raye as she lingered after dinner, coffee mug in one hand, brownie in the other. The plan she and Des had created for their hypothetical campaign had received the most votes from their co-workers in the straw poll, so she was more confident her squad was doing well. The meal, cooked by two men in sales, consisted of pizza laden with five toppings. *Too much is never enough when it came to pizza toppings*, she thought. She then trekked to the evening's entertainment designed to let everyone escape completely, a shoot-'em-up action film. But where was Des? She'd missed him in the dining room, and he didn't appear to be in the audience now. Sitting on the floor, she craned this way and that to try to spot him.

At last he appeared at the rear of the group. She waved over her head to him, and he hesitated but finally walked over and hunkered down beside her, crossing his legs under him. She thought his eyes showed strain in the shadows around them, the way his lids drooped, and his normal alert stance had wilted. "What's wrong?" she asked, wondering if she should be worried.

He shook his head and pointed toward the screen to direct her attention there. Although she complied, no way could the rock-'em, sock-'em action, the explosions and flares compete with the tension she felt emanating from him. The screen sent flickers of bright rays across the room, highlighting his profile and torso. In the shadows, his nose, jaw and chin were almost too drawn, too strong. Something was bothering him. She noticed a beer in his fist, from which he sipped regularly. Strange, because he hadn't drunk much previously, and from his comments, she thought he was a careful alcohol consumer, by and large.

Others in the audience must have found the movie as tedious and commonplace as she had, because by the time the credits rolled, only a few of her co-workers remained. A small stampede for the stairs ensued, leaving Raye and Des side-by-side on the rug. She scrambled to her feet, saying, "Guess it's time to hit the hay. Another busy day tomorrow," and silently cursing herself and him for the awkwardness between them.

He grasped her ankle with strong fingers and halted her mid-stride. "Stay," he said, although he kept his head bent.

Now she was thoroughly confused. She sank back to the floor. "I'll stay, but only if you tell me what's going on with you. It's like you're behind a huge wall and I can't reach you."

"Last night you got bad news. Today was my turn. My parents called to tell me my kid sister had gone into a diabetic coma from hypoglycemia. It's when your low blood sugar falls extremely low and you lose consciousness, which she did."

"Oh, no." Raye didn't know how to respond. "Is she all right? Do you have to leave? Is there anything I can help you with?"

He shook his head and pushed his hair off his forehead as if wiping away rain. "Thanks for asking. My mom found her before any major damage occurred. My dad got the EMTs over. They ferried her to the ER, and all is well now. It's just that"—he pounded the rug with a fist—"she can't continue this way. She shouldn't have to. Neither should my parents. They're getting old. What might happen in the future? I don't mind if she lives with me, but she says over and over that she doesn't want to hamper my life because of her medical issues."

"She sounds like a lovely young person, but what can you do other than what you're already doing?"

His mouth quirked up at the corner. "Be patient. This brings me to the award here at the retreat. The specialists tell us of a promising experimental treatment—one that insurance won't cover, of course. That's why I'm so keen on winning, which places me in direct opposition to you."

Raye's mouth fell open, her mind whirling. *That's my award*, she thought, fully realizing she had no control over who won but counting on fate or luck or skill to succeed. "You better believe it, cowboy. I need it to get a new car and send my son to college. Do you realize how hard it is to get a Latino boy through school? The temptations for him to get a job, or join a gang or hang out with bad company?"

He drained his beer before answering. "Actually, yes. Most boys, unless they come from upper-middle-class families, are torn between some ill-defined macho image and getting a blue-collar job just to put money in their pockets. That was my situation."

He doesn't sound angry or upset with me...or life. Still, what did his home life have to do with the award? She sympathized with his desire to help his sister, but her son was just as good a cause. Yet she definitely didn't want to view Des as an opponent, not when she felt so connected to him.

His eyes, fixed on her, seemed to be weighing her reaction. Quick as a flash of lightning, he blinked and gave a chuckle. "Look at us, so serious when we should be enjoying this break from our work routine." He headed toward a coffee table where someone had abandoned several unopened cans of beer, bent to collect them and dangled their plastic six-can holder from his fingers before he returned to her side. "Let's relax for a while."

She rubbed her palm on the colorful Southwestern-style rug. "True. The retreat's been fun. A challenge, but fun. I have to admit that I had some trepidation before I arrived. I'm not used to being in luxurious lodges where people waltz around in five-hundred-dollar boots."

Des threw back his head and chuckled in that all-encompassing manner he had, as if his entire body were indulging in the humor. He made Raye join in simply because she was in his vicinity. "You come off as completely confident. I'd never have expected that response. Why do you feel out of place?"

"My family's very working class. My dad's parents immigrated from Mexico and my dad has worked in a supermarket all his life. My mom — I think I told you that they're divorced — handles admissions for a local HMO. I'm not like most of the others at Pursuit — no fancy university, no expensive wardrobe and certainly no flashy motorcycle or car." She looked under her eyelids to gauge his response to her subtle dig at what she thought was his background.

Des said, "Just a minute. We have more in common than you might think. On one side my ancestors came from Ireland after the potato famine and the dismal conditions it created. They were quite familiar with the signs stating *No Irish Need Apply*. On the other side, my grandfather's people were poor immigrants from Norway who farmed. He was forced to drop out of school in the eighth grade and became a machinist in the local power plant after the sudden death of his father."

"Incredible. The luck of the draw for both of us, right?"

"Right," said Des. "Especially the luck that brought us together."

There was no doubt. He was putting moves on her, and she didn't mind at all, Raye admitted to herself. She wondered if he was planning some hanky-panky, then she wondered if she'd hanky his panky, given the opportunity, although she couldn't image anything happening in this setting. There were too many co-workers and bosses in the lodge. As for the great outdoors, she couldn't envision any environs in which intimacy might occur, given all the rocks and thorns, prickly needles and mud, insects and small animals. *Such discomfort!*

"So both of us have battled our way through barriers," said Des. He crushed the aluminum can in one hand and reached for another beer. His second, Raye noted to herself. He popped it open and drank. "My parents are like yours, hard-working and focused on meeting day-to-day challenges. When I started getting in trouble, Dad was the one who suggested or pressured me into the service. *'To straighten me out,'* he said. I let him believe that was the reason I left."

"That approach worked for you," she said. "Older and wiser heads prevailed, but my parents' advice didn't for me, not even the confession from my mom that she was knocked up with my brother when they married. Although I can't blame my parents for the six years I spent trying on different jobs and lifestyles like dresses, I was the one who thought massage, teaching yoga and selling candles at home parties would make me a fortune. Guess I still was hung up on Michael's stupid, ridiculous fantasies. If there ever was a person who trusted in the American dream, it was Michael. He really believed someone could become a millionaire with no effort—overnight, instantaneous power, success and fame. Of course his visions got a little confused with drug-induced delusions."

Alarm for her wrinkled his forehead, and she shooed away his reaction by waving her hands, unlocking some final barrier, an automatic protective reflex inside herself. She became almost slap-happy as giggles took possession of her. "My *abuelita*, my father's mother—she's the one who taught me to cook—was so matter-of-fact about my pregnancy. *'Mija,'* she said as soon as I gave her the news, *'life without sex is safe but dull.'* She also told me to accept my parents' help when I had enough of struggling on my own, which I did."

Des said, "She sounds like my granny, the Irish one—down-to-earth, practical, funny. She's the one that named me when my parents couldn't agree." Raye noted that he drained his beer and popped another one. "She was my best audience for stories about the service. I'd write or call her with descriptions about the innumerable rules and regulations, some of them crazy, the orders barked by my granite-jawed superiors, the dangerous physical challenges. I learned to survive, adapt, even thrive." He closed his eyes, as if lost in memories. "She especially enjoyed hearing about adventures like me getting lost at night in the desert, the softball competitions played under less-than-ideal conditions. I never told her about the bad times. She's been gone now for seven years."

He broke off with a whoosh, like a gush of icy water plunging over a cliff, and covered his eyes with one hand. Raye saw it was trembling, and she wondered at the sudden change in his mood. He'd been exuberant, at times hilarious as he'd related examples of what were, she was sure, milder episodes of his deployment.

In a voice so low she could hardly hear it, he said, "Sorry. There were good times, occasionally. But when I think of those poor bastards..." He stopped again.

Raye didn't know how to respond. Des came off as so typically macho-strong that she never would have anticipated this emotional reaction. He seemed to be in real pain. *Or is alcohol to blame? Isn't that his third drink in his hand? Is he consuming too much? An alcoholic?* Haunting memories of her ex-husband out of control, yielding to the domination of alcohol and drugs, flooded her, upsetting her emotional equilibrium. "Pretty rough, was it?" she managed to say.

It was as if she hadn't made a sound. He drew in a shuddering breath and lowered his hand, stared at the field-stone mantel and build-out that framed the fireplace where the blaze burned vigorously. Showers of sparks flared when a log reached the breaking point, and the cascading fragments warned of the fire's latent power. Reflections of yellow, blue, orange flames traced his face.

Trance-like, he spoke again. "Most of my company were good, so damn decent. A few were real bastards, enjoying the terror in native kids' eyes, yelling strings of obscenities at cloaked women, who, thank God, couldn't understand them. At least I hope they couldn't. But in the end, it didn't matter. Good, bad, indifferent—when a bullet gets you, a grenade explodes or a bomb blasts a crater, you're all just as dead. Meat, that's what they were, meat to the machine of war, civilians as well as troops."

Raye realized she'd been holding her breath during the entire recitation. As he stopped, she released it soundlessly. He closed his eyes again, as slow as the quiver of moth's wings, and tears begin to slide down his cheeks. "Those poor sons-of-bitches. Life was cheap there, as cheap as it is here when an oil slick kills millions of fish or a mass murderer mows down shoppers in a mall."

Reaching across to him on the rug, she squeezed his fingers, and he jumped as if he'd forgotten her presence. He flexed his arm, nearly reaching to hide the wetness on his cheeks, but for a moment she clung to his fingers so he couldn't escape. Instead, he tilted the can to finish the beer then set it aside. "That was my third, more than enough for me. Blame the alcohol for my maudlin frame of mind and for talking too much."

Relieved that he'd recognized when to stop, she hoped she was giving him an unspoken message, support and compassion — as much as she, unfamiliar with the trials of war, could do. His fingers lay flaccid in her grip and his eyes searched hers. Whatever answer he was expecting must not have appeared, because he sighed deeply, squeezed her fingers back then withdrew his hand.

"So I learned to value instant gratification, especially of the senses." He grabbed her by the shoulders. "Like this." Lowering his mouth, he tasted hers with a kiss neither gentle nor rough, as though he were concentrating on receiving every sensation her lips could deliver. She found herself responding like a drowning person reaching for a buoy. She hadn't realized how hungry she'd become for the touch of an adult male. No, she corrected herself, for this particular man. She leaned in toward him. He reciprocated, but with restraint she could sense.

That brought her to her senses — or her one common sense. If anyone appeared downstairs, they'd see her and Des necking like a couple of teenagers. *Not a good idea.* Palms flat against his chest, she scooted her bottom away then tugged her T-shirt into place. *Now what?* A barrier had been breached…and by both of them. She had no idea what went next or if she even wanted it.

"Better close up shop," Des said as he stretched his arms over his head then shrugged his shoulders before rising. "We've got to get up early for that ridiculous—I mean that 'challenging'—exercise in team-building at six. You and I both have major incentives to do well at this retreat." He offered his hand to help her rise.

He'd shut himself away, she realized. She gave a mental shake. If he didn't want to discuss what had happened between them, she certainly wouldn't. She clambered to her feet without his assistance and felt in her pocket for her room key. "Appears to me that we're going to bump heads…hard. Our loyalties are to different objectives and our hopes centered on opposite outcomes. So what do we do?"

Des frowned as he reached over his head to pitch the can with a basketball toss into a nearby recycling container. "One of us could deliberately allow the other to take most of the credit for what we do and set one of us up as the most likely winner. But it ain't gonna be me, lady. I need the award too much."

"I'm not asking you to do me any favors," said Raye. "I don't need you to give me extra advantages to win."

"And I'm not offering to. I'm simply pointing out I have a kid sister with major problems who comes first in my life."

"Ditto back. My son's my top priority and deserves every consideration." She restrained the irritation starting to taint her words. Des wasn't attacking her, and she would certainly avoid the least sign of annoyance she felt toward what she viewed as his patronizing attitude. She swung around, her long ponytail swishing like a whip, shoved her fists into her pockets and tramped toward the stairs, carefully controlling a bottom lip that seemed to be quivering on its own.

Des reached out and touched her arm with his fingertips. She stopped immediately, although she kept her face turned away. "Hey," he said softly. "Sorry for getting under your skin. I don't know what came over me. I know asking for special consideration is the last thing you'd do. You're more likely to break your back jumping over every hurdle. Guess I'm upset 'cause I'm powerless when faced with Claudia's problems."

Blinking furiously, she rotated back to him. "I get you. I'm frustrated over Andy's situation. I'd appreciate it, though, if you'd remember I'm not your enemy."

She scurried to the stairs. *Enemy, enemy,* echoed in her thoughts. She wondered how much of his instant defensiveness came from his time in the military, how deep he'd tried to bury his emotions and reactions, if his experiences indelibly colored his every thought. As she mounted the stairs to the wing with the bedrooms, she wondered how he'd endured, how any human could survive the conditions he'd served in, functioned in the turmoil he'd undergone and remain semi-normal. War was inhumane, she thought—a banal conclusion, but war itself was trite, if terrible. When she got to her bedroom, she locked the door as fast as her fingers would move, leaned her back against the frame and cried alone in the dark—whether for Des, herself or what might have been between them, she didn't know.

Chapter Nineteen

Still saddled with Des as her squad mate and with no way to avoid an awkward intimacy, if the previous days' tests were any indication, Raye wrapped a long scarf around her hair and tightened the knot on the bright yellow windbreaker she tied by the arms around her waist. Flashes of images darted through her mind. Each featured a snapshot of Des in one of their companionable activities — laughing at her attempts to scale the low wall they'd been required to climb over, jaw clenched when he'd dragged her bodily out of the moat of mud surrounding the company flag on a pole, forehead wrinkled in thought as they'd drafted a social marketing plan for the firm. *Maybe the partnership isn't so bad after all.*

She walked through the lodge lounge, swinging her own well-worn knapsack by the straps, and connected with Julia as they'd agreed the night before.

"Doing okay?" Julia asked. She, too, had dressed for the day's rough and tough agenda. No shorts for this occasion. Sturdy denims and thick socks, plaid jacket, even gloves, and Julia's pack appeared to be stuffed to its limit.

"Yes." Raye knew her soft answer would be nearly unintelligible, but she failed to summon the strength for false enthusiasm. They turned together to stroll to the porch.

"I spotted you with Des as I snuck out in the middle of the movie. Did you two stay together until the finale?"

"Yes, although we weren't paying much attention to the plot." She hesitated, wondering how much she should reveal to Julia or if that would betray Des' confidences. Even as she decided she could be diplomatic and not blab too much, the pressure built inside her to share some of her insights with a friend.

"He got pretty bent out of shape. Talked about the service and some bad things that happened. Told me about his kid sister's medical condition. It's why he wants to win the award."

Julia halted and her load of supplies shifted in her arms. "That's no good. You've got to win to cover your car and Andy's college expenses."

"Yes, but his needs are as huge as mine." Raye frowned in uncertainty and distress. "Oh, Julia, he really is a great guy. After he'd had a couple of beers, he knew he was drinking too much and stopped on his own. Do you know how amazing that is for someone like me to see? Did I tell you he volunteered to look at my car and see if he could repair it? And he's a great brother. If I could, I'd give him the fifty thousand. Yet I feel I'm balancing on an avalanche, trying to control the uncontrollable. I'm afraid I'm coming to care for him too much.'

"I'll say. You're moving way too fast, way too soon. I'm starting to regret setting this relationship in motion. You've got to put on the brakes. It sounds like you're hurt right now, but I think you did the right thing. Getting the award for your son has got to be your highest priority. If Des can't see that, he's not the man for you."

Slipping sunglasses over her eyes, despite the day's overcast sky, Raye strode with a heavy tread. "Enough, enough. I'm so confused. Please, Julia. Leave it for now."

"Okay. *Somos luchadoras.*" Julia's touch halted Raye and the younger woman hugged her briefly.

"Yes. We're fighters."

They continued to the designated trailhead. Raye tried and failed to control herself from searching for Des, but he was nowhere in sight.

The Chosen Twenty-Five plus Julia milled around like random billiard balls. Today's challenge loomed larger than any previous task. A path meandered through the federal forest surrounding the lodge. It was partly paved and partly rock and dirt, and Pursuit Telecom Ltd. had promised to have its top executives walk miles of it to check conditions and make necessary repairs.

As Raye and Julia strolled, they overheard snippets of conversation centered on squad and individual scores to date, heated discussions about the day's possible activities and never-ending complaints over the weather.

"Hope it doesn't rain," said one man.

"What's the likelihood of that?" said his companion. "It's been pouring buckets almost every day since we arrived."

"I've got a poncho, just in case." The first man tugged at an eye-searing orange swath at his waist.

"Rain's the least of my concerns," murmured Raye. They paused at the back of the clearing. Ben and Van Voorst materialized toward the front after a few minutes. Today they were both dressed in hiking clothes with assorted pieces of equipment — water bottles, compasses, whistles — slung around their necks and across their chests. Ben stepped to the front.

"Yes, ladies and gentlemen, our CEO and I are accompanying you today, you'll be pleased to learn. This is the major and final challenge we're issuing. As you know, community involvement and social improvement agendas constitute important components of Pursuit's corporate mission.

"We'll be monitoring the trail through this area, refurbishing it in a manner consistent with the natural, native environment, while ensuring safety for humans. Over to my right" — he nodded toward a pile of tools near him — "are shovels, rakes, clippers, hammers and other implements to carry out renovations. To my left" — he inclined in the opposite direction — "are materials that may be needed — gravel, some dirt, boards, wire. A few wheelbarrows, dollies and foldable carts will help you haul things in and out. Julia will be going with you and checking periodically to see if you need supplies, water, snacks or other assistance."

"Your goal is to make the trail as accessible as possible to regular hikers," said Van Voorst. "Most people enjoy a challenge but not so much of one that they might injure themselves. To that end, Julia has printed guidelines for trail maintenance and construction based on advice from national and local organizations responsible for similar activities."

As the leaders answered a question here and there from the group, Des appeared at the side of the crowd and made his way toward the women. Julia hauled a stack of printed instructions from her knapsack, but before she could distribute them to the crowd, Raye turned to Julia to beg. "Come with me, at least when we start off. I don't think I can be alone with him right now." The tension in her neck and shoulders was swiftly progressing to a headache that throbbed with each pulse.

A friend like Julia served as a safe place, a refuge. "Okay," she said. "I'll wait a few minutes to distribute the flyers." Raye abandoned any pride, even grabbed Julia's hand to clutch, hiding the grip between them. She noted that Des' countenance remained grave even when he spoke.

"Good morning."

Somehow a tiny niggle of satisfaction wormed up from Raye's heart. At least she'd judged him correctly. He was struggling with their disagreement and chaffing under their coolness as much as she was. She took pity on him. "Good morning. Ready for the final challenge?"

"Absolutely. And may the best man win." He stuck out a broad, hard hand. Raye dropped Julia's to grasp it and shook, although she yearned to hold it longer than seemly. "What's first on the docket?" he asked as he nodded toward Ben and Van Voorst.

"We're about to find out." Raye pivoted to face the leaders again, wriggling her shoulders as she sensed Des' solid form at her back. While she listened further to the leaders and their description of the difficulties soon to come, she admitted to herself that she was grateful her squad included a man with the physical strength to meet the challenges.

Ben and Van Voorst were speaking in that semi-joking repartee men use to disguise a tendency to bully. "A great deal of fun," Van Voorst was saying.

"As long as you thrive on hard work," quipped Ben.

"Under brutal conditions."

"Making every muscle and joint ache."

"And with sweat spouting from every pore," Van Voorst finished with a flourish.

A splatter of rain sprinkled the gathering, making some recoil. Ben wrapped nature into his remarks, smooth as the strum of a chord on a guitar. "Can't guarantee you'll sweat up a storm. Noting the weather, it might be a different type of dampness."

Those collected looked up and saw one small dark cloud poised and threatening overhead. Otherwise the pewter sky simply covered any ray of sunshine.

"Just a drop or two. Appears to be no problem now, so let's hit the trails." Ben modeled the action he wanted by striding to the equipment stack and shouldering a shovel.

While Julia circulated with the flyers and most of the Chosen Twenty-Five surged toward the supplies, Raye remained immobile, surveying the sky in every direction.

"Up and at 'em," Des said, with a puzzled glance at Raye.

"I don't like the look of the conditions," said Raye. "Looks threatening, as if something major's building up."

"You're a weather forecaster now?" Julia joked. "I checked right before we got together. The call is for ten percent chance of scattered showers. You're not going to wriggle out of today's activities because of the weather. You'll still be required to be part of your squad."

"I know, I know. But there are things bigger than this competition, bigger even than our jobs. Safety, for instance."

"We can always hike back," said Des, "if it starts pouring or something." He swung a brand-new backpack onto his shoulders and adjusted the straps.

"True." Raye mentally balanced the likelihood of a storm against the very tangible promise of a treasure to be won. *What's a little dampness compared to my son's future? No debate.* "Okay, let's go."

After selecting extra equipment, the Chosen Twenty-Five plus one set off in a clump but soon strung out as the first challenge presented itself, a few yards that contained not only two smaller routes that branched from the trail but also a channel or gully that had obviously carried run-off from rains over the years. Now merely muddy, its three-foot width presented no major challenge, but the hikers had to scramble down a bit then up its channel. Squads of two and three pounced on and staked out successive sections of the path in two-hundred-yard increments.

As the trio swung down the trail, they realized they'd sabotaged themselves by waiting to bring up the rear. Although the path plunged and ascended, it generally climbed, placing late-comers Raye, Des and

Julia at the end, smack at the start of a steep rocky incline where the canyon carrying the burbling stream below them narrowed even more. By unspoken consent, they paused at that point to take stock.

While the chittering and whistles of birds flowed around them and voices from their co-workers farther along the route rang out, they momentarily wordless. Then dismay flooded Julia's voice. "Now what? We got stuck with the roughest section. The only way to make this trail accessible is to level the mountain."

"Ben said to make the route accessible to an average hiker, not to everyone. We can assume people needing oxygen or with major infirmities aren't among the group," said Raye. Hands on her hips, she turned from one side to the other. "The debris from the spring storms must be playing havoc with not only the path but also the stream downhill." She poked an index finger in the direction of the refuse as she spotted items. "Leaves, twigs, branches, even huge limbs. Pebbles. Piles of mud where it dried. Exposed tree roots that could cause falls. And, worst of all, human garbage."

"The difficulty and angle of the path shouldn't make a spit-load of difference," said Des, "as long as we keep working slow but steady. In fact, we'll probably impress the honchos with our determination to overcome all odds. How about if we climb a way farther and look down? That could give us an idea for our strategy. For example, maybe we can push some things down the hill to where they'll be easier to deal with."

Again Raye offered silent thanks for the presence of a strong, competent man. She turned to reassure her friend. "Julia, officially you're exempt from menial labor anyway. You're the go-between for all the squads. You don't have to help us."

"Sure…" Julia's response was loaded with disbelief. "I'm going to sit here and watch the two of you sweat and strain while I count petals on a blossom."

"You wouldn't do that," said Raye in apparent seriousness. "It's illegal to pick wildflowers in this region."

Gurgles built into uncontrollable giggles that swamped all three. "I'm glad I wound up with you two," Des said, "with your quirky senses of humor. I had eight years in the armed services, part of it in Kuwait, plus ten long years climbing the corporate ladder to teach me that most people don't appreciate an off-the-wall perspective."

"You mean I don't have to fear walking into a doorway blocked with plastic wrap?" teased Raye.

"Nope," Des said, "and no candid photos of staff with the governor's or president's head photoshopped in. My big practical jokes now are all reserved for my sister on April Fool's Day."

The laugh loosened them up, and they set off up the ascent, which was easier to scale than it had first appeared. As they climbed, branches of evergreens brushed their bodies and combed their hair, winds whispered in their ears and pebbles under their hiking boots shifted, at times rolling from a careless kick. On their left was a sheer wall up comprised mainly of blocks of rock. On their right was another steep cliff down, this one of earth sprinkled with boulders and decorated with grass and vegetation.

Clumps of hay-colored spikes grew between sagebrush and, between these, a frenzy of greenery and flowers so bright and lemony-yellow that they illuminated their surroundings.

"I love this." Raye breathed out. "If I could, I'd live right smack in the middle here."

"In a tree?" Des asked.

"In a muddy cave?" Julia topped his selection.

"What about predators? Bears and skunks and such?" Des initiated the issue, tongue in cheek, as the gender traditionally inclined more toward hunting.

"What about worms and snakes and mosquitoes? And beetles?" Teasing back with a stereotyped response toward creepy life forms, Julia made her point.

"I don't care. I'd risk it all," said Raye. She pulled the paisley scarf from her neck to wave in the air. "Run naked through the forest, leap fallen logs, eat berries. Whoo, whoo, whoo."

Chapter Twenty

That was a vision to bring Des to a screeching halt — Raye leaping naked through the brush, probably festooned with violet, white and yellow wildflowers, dark gleaming locks flowing over her shoulders, inhaling mountain air and exhaling the joy of living. He allowed himself to enjoy his fantasy without mentioning a word of it. Instead he refocused his eyesight and resumed walking. "I think you'd bruise the bottoms of your feet substantially, along with getting scratched by the branches."

"You have the soul of a shopkeeper," said Raye, "or a scientist. Where's your romantic streak?"

"I lost it in the Middle East." He regretted the words as soon as he'd voiced them, because they doused her enthusiasm as sure as a bucket of water killed a fire. Scrambling to recover their previous camaraderie, he tossed out a weak joke. "How about you, Julia? Ready to give up the trappings of civilization? Are you a mountain maiden like your friend?"

"Absolutely not." Julia shuddered as she walked, knocking a water bottle against a pine branch that intersected the route. That sent a shower of dried needles, a few pinecones and one oversized spider on her arm. She screeched and brushed her clothing off. "A picnic now and then is pleasant, a stroll in a park with sidewalks and trimmed grass, even a day at a beach, all fine occasionally. But no roughing it for me. My family struggled to get away from the land. My grandparents were poor farmers, at the mercy of weather and big business that bought the produce they raised. They didn't even have indoor toilets. No, give me modern life and all its trappings."

"Julia!" Raye paused. "You never told me that. I thought you were eager to go on a camping trip with me."

"Why do you think I always find excuses? Humanity has spent thousands of years crawling out of the muck before we got plumbing and heat. I'd never scoff at progress."

Des choked back a chortle. Raye might appear to be the protective mentor in their duo, but Julia was proving she was no blind follower. The exercise facing the three of them should bring him additional entertaining insights into the women's personalities. Still he had to focus on the task in front of them — restoring their section of the trail to decent condition. As they reached a level area — small though it was — he stepped to the side of the path. "All right, ladies. It appears to me we should maneuver that fallen lodgepole pine smack off the side of the mountain. That's the easiest way to deal with it."

The trio began to unload backpacks, jackets and extraneous items. "Oh, dear," Raye said in mock distress. "Your new knapsack has some major streaks of dirt on it, not to mention the miscellaneous needles and leaves clinging to it." She brushed at the equipment vigorously enough to nearly knock Des off his feet.

"Hey! Watch it, lady. I'll take care of my things. You focus on our challenge."

"I'm game," said Raye as she strode toward the barrier while tugging on well-used work gloves.

Julia refused to be left out. She took her place next to Raye. That left over half the trunk for Des to maneuver, but he welcomed the challenge. *Can't let them show me up,* he thought. *I'm sure I have at least the strength of two city-dwelling women.*

Bending forward slightly to place their palms on the rough texture of the tree, all of them pushed. Nothing happened. Exchanging glances, the three inhaled, exhaled on a groan and shoved harder. Still zip.

Des straightened. "A little more effort," he said. "If you will notice, I'm breathing heavily. I don't want to put you down, but neither of you appears to be breaking a sweat. Now, on the count of three."

Together they recited, "One, two, *three.*" *Grunt, growl, moan, shriek.* The log gave a small shudder, encouraging them to still greater effort as they set up a kind of rocking that eventually overcame inertia and a furrow in the earth in which the tree lay partly buried. With a creak and the rustle of dried boughs, the log rolled over a few times, gathered speed and slid down the steep slope directly toward the stream. It came to rest a few feet from the water.

Instantaneous exhilaration... Their whoops of satisfaction echoed down the canyon, raising a response from the workers farther away.

"What's up?"

"This isn't supposed to be a picnic."

Even, "If your section's so easy, come help us."

Des, Raye and Julia choked a semblance of control over their voices while pumping fists in victory and hanging on to one another. *Simply a reaction to our collective achievement,* Des told himself. *Raye doesn't mean anything more than that, although I wish she did.*

"Lady Luck's with us for sure. What next? I'm raring to go." Raye approached a scattering of rocks that had cascaded from the cliff face on one side, boot extended for a kick.

Wiping perspiration from her face, Julia shook her head. "I should make a quick run to see what the other squads are doing — if they need bottles of water, have run into problems or whatever." She checked her wristwatch. "Shouldn't take me long, then I'll be back."

"Surrrre." Des drew out his response in pseudo-skepticism. "Now that the grunt work's coming up."

Julia snapped his shoulder with the end of her scarf. "Right. See you soon." Lowering her sunglasses over her eyes, she marched back down the trail with only an occasional stumble over pebbles that covered the path.

Des observed her descent while trying to suppress the only thought in his head. *Raye and I are out here alone.* He gave a shrug, then a suggestion to Raye. "Those rocks don't appear significant to me. A little smoothing out and we're good to go. However, the vines and small twigs surrounding the tree trunks right next to the path could trip hikers. How about we attack those next?" He whipped the guidelines to trail maintenance from his rear pocket and read,

"Completely remove saplings, briars, vines and other smaller flora. Dig them out. Don't just cut them off."

"Yes, sir." Raye gave a mock salute. "Good thing I chose a small hoe as one of my tools. Multi-purpose."

Des scrambled to a collection of equipment he'd hauled up and pawed through it, finally holding dilapidated blue sheeting high in the air. "And I have a tarp to collect the refuse."

They tackled chopping, snipping, cutting and heaving, setting up a dissonance against the natural sigh of the wind through the trees and the hum of insects. Yet somehow their presence wasn't at odds with their setting. *Maybe this kind of physical exertion is as natural as our surroundings,* Des mused. He gave a final huge *twack* to one particularly obstinate low branch and tugged it to the tarp before pausing to examine the sky and landscape. "A nearly perfect day," he said.

"What do you mean? Look at that thunderhead building up in the west." Raye dumped her armload to stop next to him. "We've got to be cautious. That could very well mean a downpour upstream."

"Naw," Des said. "Take a chance. No pain, no gain."

As she continued to point out various atmospheric formations and scattered bursts of light to illustrate her off-the-cuff lecture about weather phenomena in the mountains, Des tuned out her words.

Here I am alone in a forest with a woman instructing me on meteorology. She's dressed in grubby clothes, her hands are filthy and we're both sweaty as hell. We bump heads and argue, plus she's a co-worker who deserves every aspect of workplace courtesy. And all I want to do is grab her and kiss her. I must be nuts. That or...

The rest of the thought escaped him as a blast of wind blew through the ravine, fluttering leaves and swirling bits of twigs and dirt into dust devils. Des lowered his sunglasses immediately, while Raye blinked rapidly then rubbed her eyes. He pulled out a clean pocket handkerchief, snapped it and leaned toward her. "Here…let me," he said as he clasped her chin and dabbed around her eyes. "You wouldn't want to damage your sight this far from medical help."

All the while, thrumming through his head, *I wonder if I stare into her eyes hard enough, she'll catch the drift of my thoughts.* Which were? He didn't give a damn about their falling-out the night before. Yes, the thought of failing to win the prize money to fund his sister's medical treatment created a distressing tightening across his chest, but the achievement of his goal would create insurmountable distance between him and Raye, force them to become mere polite co-workers. Then he wouldn't be able to breathe at all.

Under his fingers, Raye's eyelashes fluttered, watered, cleared and she cupped her hands around his, clinging as if she had lost the strength in her legs.

The sharp crack then tremendous rumble of rolling thunder startled them apart. *What in the name of all that's rational am I doing?* Raye had no answer, yet she'd prided herself on her honesty ever since she'd discovered her high-as-a-kite ex was still using and abusing years ago. She'd learned then that the only way to pry herself loose from a bad situation was to face reality, as she'd done with him—no false hopes, no excuses, no minimizing damaging consequences.

Although being close to Des wasn't a bad situation, it was simply much too tempting.

The urge to lean into him overwhelmed her. Bubbles seemed to be percolating up her throat, a pleasant sensation, but inappropriate in the middle of a business function, not to mention throwing her off stride in the competition for a monetary award she very badly needed. On top of everything else, a storm was threatening.

I've lost my sanity.

When she spotted a bolt of lightning over his shoulder, she seized on the storm as an excuse to break away from the intimate climate Des had created, lowering her hands. "Hey! Over in the west... See that mass of dark ugly billows I pointed out before? There's a definite rain shaft descending, very large, probably dumping lots of water."

"Yeah?" His hands, still cupped where she'd pulled away, finally fell. "Well, I wish you'd pay more attention down here."

She peered upward with greater concentration. "I need you to focus. These are the perfect conditions for a flash flood. I think we should warn the others. We all need to return to the lodge if there's time — or head for high ground."

Des searched downward past the craggy face of the mountain over which the trail roamed. "Are you kidding? I can barely spot that pathetic excuse for a creek alongside." He crouched to get a better perspective. "I doubt if it's more than three inches deep." He studied the sky. "Nothing threatening overhead. I admit the west's foreboding, but those thunderheads are miles away. Are you spineless?"

"I prefer to call myself 'prudent'. And I'm telling you this area has had flash floods several times over the years, immense ones. These mountains don't need rainfall immediately nearby to suffer. In fact, if there's a downpour miles upstream, that can create an even greater probability. Look…" Her index finger extended, she slowly swung from one side to the other, pointing as she went. "Narrow canyon, very little width for the path, steep yet short slope down to the water's channel… All this means that if a flood comes, it'll be fast and furious and have nowhere to go but through here."

Des unwound from his position and stretched to his full height while fumbling in a pocket. "Tell you what, I'll access my smartphone to find out about the weather."

Too polite to make a snide comment, she rocked back and forth on her boots, hands in her pockets. Des poked and stabbed at his phone, stared into the small display, turned it off, turned it back on, even shook the instrument gently. "No connection," he muttered. "I suppose you knew that."

"Yeess." He looked so sheepish that she couldn't bear to crow over his error. "Of course, that means we can't call the others to alert them. We're going to have to reverse down the mountain."

"What about the tools and supplies?" he asked.

"Let's stash them as high up the side of the mountain as we can reach without taking too much time. Then we'll make tracks."

"No way a flood can get up this high," he said, "but okay." He obeyed her directions and wedged a shovel, small saw, clippers and bags of gravel, all wrapped in bright blue tarps, nicely between a stand of sapling aspens barricaded by a boulder in front of them. Then he grabbed their backpacks and stuffed in a few extraneous items—hand ax, rope, hammer.

"Why are you adding weight to our packs? They're heavy enough," she said. "We need to be as mobile as possible."

He scoffed at her. "These? Heavy? I'm used to fifty pounds minimum, going up to a hundred. I knew you were a weakling."

What a nasty thing to say. Her blood pressure climbed and she prepared to snap back. Then she realized from the way his mouth tucked in at the corners that he was pulling her leg again, simply to see her reaction. "Your wretched sense of humor on display?"

"I admit it. I told you that under normal conditions, I can control it. I usually limit my victims to my younger sister."

"It sounded like a challenge to me," she said. She grabbed her pack from his hand and threw it over her shoulder. "You've been out of the military for years, while I've been hiking and mountain climbing nearly every weekend this spring. We'll see who's got more endurance."

"It's a deal."

She nodded agreement. He waved her ahead of him and allowed her to take the lead down the slope. She had her mobile in hand as she jogged and a finger twitching constantly.

"What's up?" he yelled.

She tossed over her shoulder, "Signals come and go up here. There's a chance I can connect to some sort of weather report."

"Any prediction on how long until we reach everyone?"

"Going back is easier than trudging up," she said, "but you need to be careful because a misstep can mean a broken bone. I'd say it took twenty minutes to where we started, right?"

"Agreed." He was slipping and sliding on loose dirt and gravel as he followed.

"And the squads are spread out some. So I'd guess we should spy the first group in a few minutes. Our job's made easier because everyone concentrated on this main trail. The teams should be perched like beads on a string, although, as we walked up, I spotted some side ravines that might have tempted them. I wish we could connect with Julia though."

"Why's that?"

"Because she's so plugged into everyone's work style that she'd probably lead us right to the others plus advise us on how to persuade them to get to safety." Raye leaped from side to side on the trail to avoid the shakier, rockier ground in the middle, holding both hands in the air for balance.

"You're still convinced a flash flood's possible?"

Skidding on her heels, she halted so abruptly that he nearly collided with her. "Listen!" Pointing upward with an index finger, head tilted, she concentrated. "Those rolls of thunder in the distance? That can mean more rainfall back there."

Des took a swallow of water and wiped his lips with the back of his hand. "Okay. You're the expert." He set off before Raye could respond, quickly outpacing her.

"Hey. Wait up," she said.

"Nope." He shook his head, a major accomplishment at the rate he was moving. "You're making me look like a wuss, and a big strong guy like me can't tolerate that."

"Oh, now I see," she said as she galloped to catch up. "I was right. You *are* sexist." She hoped his increasing momentum didn't foretell an accident. Then a thought came to her. *Slow down so you can enjoy the scenery.* Des looked good from this angle, his long legs scrambling and succeeding to achieve a rhythm that showcased his fitness.

Voices broke through the background of forest rustles and murmurs. Clangs of metal rang around them. Des and Raye slowed to shout greetings. "Hey, everyone, urgent information," said Des. He galloped the last few yards, skidding, grabbing for branches to help him slow down. "Raye's convinced something's brewing with the weather, and we'd better prepare ourselves."

"You would say that." Mason Mobley turned from where he hacked at a branch, laid the saw on the ground and rubbed his shoulders and neck. "Wanting us to stop our work so your section will look better. But any excuse to take a break."

The second man, his frequent cohort Tim Enoch, also halted his transport of a small log, pulled out a damp bandanna and wiped his forehead. As Raye joined the small group, she noticed Tim's red flush and shirt wet with perspiration, a match for Mason's.

"No, it's true." With calm determination, she relayed information to the novice woodsmen. "This area is susceptible to flash floods, and with the rains we've had since we've arrived, plus the clouds building up in the west, anything could happen."

"I'll check," said Mason, waving an expensive smartphone over his head.

"I'm doubtful you'll get through, but go ahead," said Des, with a wink toward Raye.

Both men on the squad ignored him and fiddled with their phones. When they couldn't connect, they were immobile with surprise. Tim found his voice. "If you can't get a signal, how do you know we're in danger? A few drops of rain don't mean a flash flood's coming. And so what if it storms? The creek's a good ten feet below us."

"Just our luck to run into these two bozos first," Des murmured to Raye.

She choked down a giggle but reverted to a stern, schoolteacher demeanor to answer Tim. "You obviously lack experience out in the wild. But we don't have time to waste. The squads farther on should be alerted, and we all must head back to the lodge while the weather holds."

"And if it doesn't?" Mason's sharp tone showed his skepticism.

Raye waved her hand, indicating the steep slope up the mountain. "That's our best bet."

"You've got to be kidding. No way I'm scrambling over all those boulders and trees," said Tim. "I'll get all scraped up and filthy."

"Fine. I don't have time to try to convince you. It's your decision. You two stay right here. Des and I will go warn the others." With a turn so swift that her ponytail swung out in a circle, Raye was off down the trail, muttering all the way. Des hot-stepped behind her.

"Idiots, idiots, idiots," she mumbled. "Would serve them right to be swept away."

"Be reasonable," said Des. "We don't know for sure a flash flood's coming. Nothing may happen to them."

After several moments, Raye agreed with slow reluctance. "You're right. Still, I can hope, can't I?" She flashed a teasing, tooth-baring leer.

Chapter Twenty-One

Every time I think I know how this woman will react, she surprises me. She can't be as perfect for me as I imagine. Des balanced for a few moments on several rocks on the trail. *Yes, she could be perfect. What a refreshing circumstance. Not only does she never bore me, she also shows intelligence, sensitivity and humor.*

More than ever, he was determined not to let her escape. The huge question mark about her, however, lay in her attitude toward a new relationship. The few things she'd mentioned about her ex-husband had brimmed with frustration, if not anger, and she never hesitated to be candid about her opinions. Did he dare reveal her appeal to him? *No, not yet. Especially not under these uncertain conditions.* He turned his attention to their very real dilemma.

"How should we approach the other squads?" he said. "If Tim and Mason refused to believe you, persuading the rest of the group may be equally difficult."

Even as he spoke, the heavens opened and intense rain commenced, dripping down every plant, splashing from impermeable surfaces, before long soaking the trail into a slippery, muddy trough that erased their footprints behind them. "Won't be a problem too much longer," said Raye with an impish grin. "We're gathering evidence even as we walk. Better put your rain gear on, not that it will help much." She barely broke stride to follow her own advice.

They quickly came upon the second squad, then the third. The members of these confirmed Julia had passed by. They were more amenable to taking Raye's advice than Mason and Tim had been, after they'd all checked their phones and confirmed no connections, hence no information, existed. In fact Krystle and Kabir bordered on hysteria, calling for rescue by helicopter or favoring high-speed races over rough terrain back to the lodge.

I wish I could administer slaps across their faces, Des thought, as Raye reacted instantly by grabbing Krystle's and Kabir's arms and bestowing abrupt, strong shakes. "Control yourselves. Nothing jeopardizes us as much as allowing panic to run free. We're not in immediate danger. Now, take a few deep breaths. Hold on to each other if you want." The two calmed down, clasped hands and circled to the end of the line of crew.

"What a fraud," Des breathed as he resumed the hike.

"Who?" said Raye.

"Krystle."

"I thought you considered her cute?"

"Her cuteness is overpowered by her phoniness. Didn't you see her out-squealing Kabir? Every time he raised his voice or moaned, she doubled the volume."

Raye chuckled as she and Des led, the others trailing behind, chattering about the storm and complaining of the cold, until one by one, they fell silent. While the rain's patter could be described as 'soothing', the same wasn't true of the rumbles of thunder now increasing in volume and frequency.

Although he trusted Raye's experience with mountain storms and flash floods, since it had to be greater than his own, Des couldn't suppress a qualm or two. "What can we expect in terms of timing? Will the downpour increase? Will there be any signs from the flow of water in the creek? It seems as if getting back's taking longer than climbing up."

"I haven't the foggiest," said Raye. "I've never actually been near a flash flood." She soldiered on through mud, which was now ankle-deep.

"What?" Alert to the possible repercussions of an abrupt halt on their followers, Des slogged after her.

"I did a research paper for physical geography about Colorado's weather systems. Fascinating." She sank further into mud and her boots made sucking sounds when she raised her feet. "Read transcripts and viewed videos on a number of inundations. I've been interested ever since. You can't tear me away from local weather reports during storm season."

"Then why on earth are we subjecting ourselves to this hike, which might turn out to be an exercise in futility?" he whispered.

"You're the ex-military hot-shot," Raye said. "Surely you're familiar with preventative measures. If you thought an enemy might attack, you'd line up your defenses, right?"

"Right."

"No different now, except the weather's the adversary, not humans. Everything I've read, heard or been taught instructs us to do exactly what we're doing—try to return to a shelter, keep an eye on weather and flood conditions and head uphill immediately if things worsen."

She was right. No options existed except for everyone to stick together and take one step at a time. *Funny, though,* thought Des. On the way out to the maintenance locations, the trail had seemed as close to a gentle stroll as possible for a pebble- and brush-strewn footpath, probably because he and his companions had been intent on the competition as well as spirited conversation. Now Des could have sworn the grade of the route had doubled as it fluctuated up and down the mountain, testing his every step. *Some of the squad members must be struggling with the surprising exertion. Hope there's no fall-out from that.*

"Okay, okay." A streamlet of ice-cold water ran from Des' baseball cap straight down his spine and he shivered. He wondered if this was a portent of forthcoming disaster and couldn't suppress the lightning-like thought that, although he'd survived extreme weather conditions before in Kuwait's intense heat and brutal dust storms and was accustomed to snow and rain in Kansas City, a flash flood was beyond his purview.

The added burden of ensuring the safety of a gaggle of city slickers failed to daunt him, however. He'd learned in the past that a challenge invigorated him, put him on full alert. Energy surged from his toes and fingers, up through his arms and legs, to his core. For a split second, he wished he could set off running, leaping like a stag along the trail.

Strangely enough, the parallels between the military and a national corporation lay in the sense of responsibility they cultivated in personnel, along with the ordeals they presented that challenged people to succeed in spite of themselves. It was a mental return to the foundations of human development, when a man pitted himself against a saber-toothed tiger.

For the first time, though, his partner in the endeavor wasn't someone of similar background, experience and skills — wasn't even a man. He looked at Raye's erect posture, her strong stride, her firm shoulders, arms and legs, and he felt the same confidence that he'd developed in his soccer teammates, his regiment, his work unit. He decided that today's trek, weather and all, was a pleasant interlude, although he wouldn't have been able to explain that conclusion, even if he were paid to do so.

Raye continued. "To give you some reassurance, I'm keeping my eyes peeled for more indications of a flash flood. Rising water levels. increasing stream sounds and water current, unusual debris in the stream, that sort of thing.'

"And have you spotted any?"

"Unfortunately, I have. The water level is increasing somewhat."

"And we've been out — what…ten minutes since the rain started?"

"Yes."

"Shouldn't we head for higher ground?" Des wasn't embarrassed to admit his ignorance of a flash-flood pattern.

"I'm hoping we can get to all the squads before we have to climb or run. I'd rather not lose track of anyone. I wonder where Julia wound up?"

Des nodded. As they approached the next small group scattered among saplings, intent on their repairs, he hallooed them. "You may have noticed the weather's worsening. Time to change our plans."

The fourth squad, bolstered by the presence of Van Voorst and Ben, required no persuasion. The members agreed to retreat at once and added they'd been troubled themselves about the idea of floods. When Des reported Mason and Tim's skepticism as the reason for their absence, the two top men exchanged glances.

Raye broke into the confab, even as she herded the additional people into the pack. "Has Julia been by?" Receiving denials, she said, "I'm concerned about her. With no phone connections and no one spotting her since she passed the third squad about ten minutes ago, I hope she hasn't run into problems."

The tramp continued, adding members of the various squads as the main group passed. The line now resembled a queue of disgruntled school children obliged to come in early from recess, and Des caught an undertone of grumbling about the weather, the forced march, fatigue, hunger and every other discomfort possible in the situation, despite the prospect of a flash flood. In the absence of greater danger — like actually being swept away — Des hoped the group would remain focused more on safety measures rather than complaints. This was no squad of elite commandoes, not even a corps of foot soldiers. Sometimes civilians couldn't recognize directives, panicked for no reason or simply refused to comply with what they were told. He cached the thought in the back of his mind. Although thinking of possibilities helped him prepare for an emergency, he refused to expend valuable time on the scenario when he had higher priorities.

At a sizeable shelf on the path, Raye called a halt. "If you all are as exhausted as I am from battling the weather as well as anxiety, we should take a break for a minute. Eat a bite. Take a drink of water." She bracketed her mouth with her hands and called Julia several times.

Her co-workers sagged in relief and they regained their voices, with several of them asking about distances. "How far have we come?" said one, while another was more troubled by the distance yet to travel, adding, "This is taking forever."

"That's because conditions have deteriorated, and we're counting every minute until we get back...if we can. Remember, each squad was positioned a little over five hundred feet down the path, so with eleven squads, that's about a mile and a quarter, not over a mile and a half, from start to finish. We have, what" — she appraised the entire group — "nine squads together now? One squad didn't want to set back, and we're still missing Julia and whoever she wound up with. But I'd say we're fairly close to our starting point. Walking's harder in the mountains and takes longer than flat land. My estimate is about ten minutes."

One intrepid explorer clambered up the hillside, trying to spot the lodge or out-buildings, loosing an extra shower of water on his companions. They groaned and booed. Raye motioned Des to her side. "I don't like the looks of some of our people," she said and nodded in the CEO's direction. He half-leaned, half-sat on the edge of the clearing, and his face displayed a definite grayish tinge.

"I wouldn't worry," said Des. "He's a tough old guy, despite his desk job." Without confirming Raye's apprehension, Des silently agreed. Something was off-kilter with Van Voorst, but the last thing Raye needed was another major alarm. "I'll walk next to him, just in case," he said.

"Would you?" Raye's features brightened with gratitude. "Thanks so much."

"But before we set off again, I want you to nibble on some trail mix." He opened a small plastic bag with an assortment of nuts, seeds and candy and held it out to her. Even as she took a handful to chew on, he sensed a minuscule release of tension from her body.

A tilt of her water bottle to her mouth, a shrug of her knapsack and she said, "Okay. I'm ready to go. How about you?"

He nodded, then turned to make his way back to Van Voorst's side, where he disguised his assistance by offering a handshake quickly converted to an upward tug. "On our way, Mr. Van Voorst. Not much farther until we've rounded up all of them," he said with false joviality.

"This has turned out to be quite an excursion," said the CEO, controlling a wobble as he resumed walking.

At his other side, Ben Buford also stepped close, an arm extended in the air behind and slightly below Van Voorst's back. "Yes, it has, sir. But we're safe and nearly there." Des glanced over at Ben, who raised his eyebrows at Des. Now that he knew reinforcements were at hand, Des concentrated on quick-stepping and voicing soundless thoughts of encouragement in all directions.

Riding herd on the straggling line, Des began passing people. He heard, from the front of the group,

Raye taking up the refrain of the children's song *Rain, Rain, Go Away*, substituting 'Pursuit Telecom wants to play' for the usual 'little children want to play'. It proved a distraction, because the chant caught on, and people launched rounds, replete with shouts and cheers.

Des shook his head in stunned amusement. She surely must be one of the few who would have come up with this idea to elevate spirits and unify the group. Soon others offered suggestions for additional melodies, some familiar like *It's Raining, It's Pouring*, *Raindrops Keep Falling on My Head* and *Singing in the Rain*, and some not so well known, like *I Love a Rainy Night*. When people didn't know the words, they hummed, yodeled and la-la-la'd. Their voices reverberated among the trees in counterpoint to the low rumbles of thunder.

The group approached the initial point at which all eleven squads had set off that morning. Des hustled to catch up with Raye in the front, where she'd reach the large gully perpendicular to the trail. It had only been a little wet when they'd first set out — easy to clamber down, cross, then climb up. It now contained a rush of muddy water, threatening to spill over the banks. Raye stopped to extend her arms across the path, halting the hike for everyone behind her.

Next to her, Des stopped, and his bulk more than hers provided the barrier. "Hey, guys, we need to reconnoiter," he announced to the group at large. "What now?" he asked Raye.

Her rain hat being insufficient to meet the demands of this storm, Raye's hair plastered her forehead and neck. She blinked away water while keeping her face immobile and her voice subdued. "I think our best bet is to traverse the ditch as quickly as possible then take il going toward the lodge. I'm not sure where the other ones go." She pointed at the second, smaller path slightly behind them that appeared to move generally at a right angle to them, as well as a third even fainter that branched who-knew-where.

"You really think that's necessary?"

"I don't know, but we can't continue to stay here. This part's lower than the slope preceding this location or the trails leading onward, and if we go back, we're farther from the lodge." Raye made an up and down motion that mimicked the dips and rises in the trail, which generally led down in the direction they were moving but contained alternating ascents on the way.

"I think we're at the point we'd better brief someone with more authority," Des said. "So far we've been moving on automatic. I'd like to consult with Ben, if you don't mind. He's second to Van Voorst, whom I don't want to involve right now. Ben has experience leading groups in all sorts of weather and levels of danger. I bet he'd have some ideas."

"Anything that might help," breathed Raye. "I don't know how much damage we can survive from this weather."

Des wished she'd complain she was cold so he could wrap his arms around her to help. That was a warm, comforting thought. He turned and backtracked through most of the stationary crowd, meeting the puzzled glances and questions about weather and path with as much appearance of calm competence as possible, accompanied by a handshake here, a slap on the shoulder there, trying to reassure people with his comments. "Nearly there... Feeling okay? Quite a challenge... We're a great team."

He approached Ben and Van Voorst with what he knew was a shit-eating grin and called with a wave of his hand. "Hey. Slight delay. Mr. Van Voorst. Mind if I borrow Ben for a few minutes? He has more experience than I do with physically challenging conditions."

The boss man, perched again on a large boulder, eyes at half-mast and torso drooping, looked about as ready to survive a major thunderstorm as he did to run a marathon. Even as he rubbed his neck and jaw, his breath came in short gasps, but he managed to pant, "Sure thing. I'm not feeling chipper, so the sooner we can get out of here, the better."

Behind Van Voorst, Ben's tweaked eyebrows signaled a silent alert to Des, while he spoke to Olivia, standing beside him. "Olivia, can you give Mr. Van Voorst a hand? He may need some water." Ben pulled his rain poncho from his body and repositioned it over the CEO's shoulders and torso, wrapping the waterproof nylon material around him. "This may help warm you up a bit." Then he headed straight for Des, stepping over someone sitting on a tree stump to stretch his legs.

"Is he as bad as he looks?" Des murmured when he led Ben back toward the gully.

"I'm afraid so," said Ben. "It's not only fatigue, maybe a heart attack or congestive heart failure. We've got to get the hell out of here."

"A small challenge," Des said over his shoulder, his strides so long and fast he was slipping in the mud now coating the entire path. "Remember the gully we went over this morning? It looked insignificant at the time. You could scoot down and across, no problem.

It's now a large trench filled to the brim and overflowing with run-off. Raye and I want to consult with you about possible choices."

"What choices? We should simply leave this area immediately."

"You'll see when we arrive."

The two hustled through the collection of Pursuit Telecom executives, who, after half an hour of pouring rain on their heads and ankle-deep mud on their feet, resembled refugees escaping from an armed conflict rather than business leaders. *The seriousness of our situation is sinking in*, Des noted. No smiles, the jokes and songs had stopped, incipient frowns... Even the few queries held an undertone of desperation.

Ben halted next to Raye and studied the swirling brown torrent at their feet that was inching higher and higher. "I see what you mean," he said to Des. "This is not looking good." He directed his gaze to survey the sky, which roiled with angry clouds. "And you say these are good conditions for a flash flood?" he said to Des.

"Raye's our resident flash-flood expert, sir," said Des. "At least as close as we have."

"I'm certainly not going to guarantee a deluge, sir," Raye said, "but you'll notice a rise in the level of the water, indicating more rain upstream. And debris is increasing, too." She turned, and Des and Ben looked over her shoulder at the stream. No longer a burbling, sunlit show of sparkles and ripples, the water's bruise-like colors swept past them frantically, carrying along an occasional plastic bag or litter.

Ben turned back. "I've never dealt with mountain flash floods. What are our options?"

Chapter Twenty-Two

A wave of uncertainty swamped Raye. Her formal rank on the corporate ladder didn't include the responsibility of leading a group like this. She'd been so focused on the possibility of a flash flood that she'd overlooked her lack of authority, not to mention the danger to her co-workers if she made poor decisions.

She hesitated, not wanting to impinge on her superior's position and expertise. "What do you suggest, sir?"

"We don't appear to be in immediate danger, so my S.O.P. is to ask members of my team for their recommendations."

Still she stalled, preferring to give Des an opportunity to strut his stuff, which he did. "The logical two are either push on or retreat. But I'm sure there are corollaries to both of those we should consider. Raye?"

Ben spoke instead. "A third would be to head up the hill immediately."

"I wouldn't suggest that, sir." Raye felt she had to speak. She shook rain from her head and wiped her eyes. "At least not at this minute." She pointed up the steep cliff bordering the path on their right. "You can see the run-off is increasing. If we proceed, we'll isolate ourselves on the mountain with no chance to get back without outside assistance. Whereas if we ford the gully crossing our path, we still have the option of climbing up if we need to, on a less-steep incline on the other side. Plus, I believe rescuers could reach us more easily."

"Well...." Ben looked left and right at the slopes.

"Raye has experience in these mountains — at least more than you or I do. I say we follow her advice," said Des.

Ben adjusted his backpack. "Agreed...and the sooner the better."

"One more point, sir," said Raye. "We're short at least five employees. What should we do about them? Des and I saw Mason and Tim, who refused to accompany us, but I haven't been in touch with Julia since I started. She was going to try to contact every squad to see if they needed help."

"So who else is missing?" asked Des.

Ben ran a palm down his wet and exhausted face. "Through a process of elimination, that would be Bill Pickett and Roy Hudson. They were teamed."

Raye groaned. They were probably the two least suited for a survival test, since Bill was overweight and well past fifty while Roy's asthma challenged him regularly, even in the office. "So what do we do?"

Des broke in. "We've got to take care of the folks who are here now. Then we'll strategize about the missing."

"I agree," said Ben. "Raye, you lead off. Des, you've got long legs. Can you station yourself with one foot on each side of the gully and extend a helping hand? As a precaution. We wouldn't want anyone to slide along the gully then down the bank into the stream below and get swept away. I'll do the same opposite you. Ready?"

Raye held up a hand. "One more thing. Mr. Van Voorst still appears to be in less than top form. Can he go as soon as possible? And I'm wondering if anyone's carrying aspirin that we can have him take as an added safeguard."

The three turned back to look at their top boss. He remained perched on a large boulder, breathing slowly, as if he might shatter into pieces if he twitched. "Agreed," said Ben

"And I've heard aspirin is more effective if chewed, rather than swallowed whole," said Des.

"I'll bet my boss has some," said Raye. "Olivia's got several kids and always seems to have emergency supplies with her."

"I'll check with her," Des said.

She watched his progress to the back of the line as a ripple of concern passed over her. She recalled how Mr. Van Voorst had taken time years ago to give her a few words of welcome when she'd first started working at Pursuit as a lowly temp. He'd done even more when Olivia had been staffing her department by dropping a word in her ear suggesting that Raye be hired permanently. As for Olivia herself, she'd always taught and encouraged her, given her a strong foundation in management, even dried a few tears now and then over the years. A squeeze in the area of her chest told Raye she was unconsciously suppressing anxiety for her work colleagues. *Action,* she told herself sternly. Only positive action would help the group.

"We'll start the process of moving people along," Raye said to Ben. As Des fast-stepped back to Mr. Van Voorst, Raye raised her voice, along with her arms. "Hey, everyone. Ben, Des and I recommend bridging this gully and continuing to move back toward the lodge."

"Is it safe?" came a voice from the crowd and a murmur built.

Raye sensed discomfort growing in the group, doubtless over what should be done. Somehow she knew she had to project calm and disarm any insipient panic. "Relax, everyone. The change in location should prove safer than here," she answered. "You probably remember that this morning the gully had very little water in it. That's dramatically different now. We figure we'll be a bit closer to the lodge, and if flood conditions continue to escalate, at least we'll be in a better position to be rescued."

"So you're saying a flood is imminent?" came another question.

"We can't predict with certainty. However, the stream contains more water and you've probably noticed a fair amount of debris—branches, mud, leaves, even saplings. That usually indicates activity farther upstream."

"Hey! I see a kid's travel crib floating down," said someone else. "Must be a camper's from the national forest site."

Voices rose and a tangle of conversation tinged with hysteria took substance. "How much time do we have?" a query broke through.

Raye threw a look of appeal at Ben. She doubted she projected the inherent authority needed to get people to respond without debate. He stepped in. "Now's not the time to natter and hypothesize," he said. "We can do that after we're all across the gully. I'll stand next to the gully to provide a hand to those who need it and Raye will cross first. One or two at a time. Don't push, but don't delay either."

The babble continued, but people started lining up and moving after Raye.

Ben spread his legs bridge-fashion, one on each side of the gully, and extended his hand to Raye. She leaped across, thinking silent thanks that she'd kept up her fitness and exercise routine over the years. She succeeded with barely a splash of her boots in the water. Almost automatically, Ben extended his palm to the next person in the queue and continued the process to subsequent hikers.

"Hey, wait up!" Two voices broke through the cluster of splashes and gasps, the ricochet of thunder and roar of water rushing in the stream below. "We're coming. Don't leave us."

From her position on the gully's far side, Raye saw the figures running — or at least moving as rapidly as they could, given the mud's slimy surface under their slips and slides. In a few moments, she recognized Mason's and Tim's waterlogged figures, nearly indistinguishable from the dripping, gray-green plants around them. Forcing their way through part of the group at the back, they paused by Des, Olivia and Mr. Van Voorst then followed as the trio pushed through to the front of the crowd. Everyone seemed to sense that Mr. Van Voorst was in a bad way, as no one attempted to question him or claim priority, and many exchanged worried glances.

Des guided Mr. Van Voorst and Olivia across the gully, giving Raye a tight-lipped smile and a thumbs-up signal as he passed. Once on stable ground, he instructed them to keep walking, slow but steady, and to leave room on their left for others to pass them where the trail was wide enough. Olivia braced her arm under the boss' armpit. Tim's and Mason's passage coincided with Des' break, and they babbled nonstop about their decision to catch up with their co-workers, laced with criticisms of Raye and Des for not conveying the seriousness of the danger they faced. Off they slogged, still mumbling, and Des and Raye exchanged silent shrugs of shoulders.

"I think you should head down the trail next, Raye," said Des. "You'll pass Olivia and the big guy in a few paces. The other two won't listen to anyone else's suggestions, so you can ignore them, but the people still coming up can benefit from a confident leader...meaning you."

"Okay," she said, then touched his shoulder lightly. "Be careful and as quick as you can."

He nodded.

She adjusted her hat and wrapped the scarf more firmly around her neck. "I'm still worried about Julia. And there's one more squad with two people that we haven't come across."

"They may have already proceeded up the trail. Maybe they were more concerned about the weather than we were and started back," said Des.

"I hope so." While Des returned to the gully to assist Ben, she set off with a firm tread, wishing she felt as strong and confident inside as she tried to project on the outside.

As the trail meandered steadily downward, interspersed with the inevitable up-slopes as yard succeeded yard, Raye concentrated on watching the stream below, now as rapid and roaring as an angry cheetah and close to overflowing. The rain had, in fact, nearly stopped, although every few seconds a branch released a small shower against her damp cheeks, as if a child had pumped a squirt bottle at her. While her jacket had protected her from the worst of the soaking, that wasn't the case for her jeans, which were damp from ankles to thighs. She scanned the slopes around her, hoping to spot Julia's plaid jacket, but no bright red flashes of the clothing's pattern caught her eye.

When she turned to check the progress of the group, she noted with relief that everyone had crossed the channel. At the end of the line, Des waved to her. How lucky they'd been that he was part of the group. And part of her life, at least for now. Strong, steady, intelligent, good-humored, as dependable as the sun's cycle, he certainly differed wildly from her first, snap-judgment opinion of him.

The retreat back toward the lodge, transitory as she hoped it would be, absorbed her entire attention. She could barely recall her condo, felt no nagging unease over work at the office, failed to worry about her son's status. Not a word from radio, television, newspapers or the internet news returned to dog her. The rest of the world had disappeared, so wars, recessions and plagues had vanished. 'Restful' described the ambiance, strange to say.

Yet every physical impression intensified and sharpened, as if she'd never fully experienced sensation before. Her brother had loved hiking in the mountains. She almost seemed to see him beside her, striding along. Although clouds and forest dimmed the light, each leaf, twig and pebble appeared as clear as if it were under a microscope. In her mouth, the taste of nuts and honey and raisins lingered. The feel of a slight breeze, the damp on Raye's face and hair and the firmness of her tread were distinct. The noises made by the hikers' boots moving over the ground and the call of a solitary bird cutting through their chatter all sounded like a microphone had amplified them.

As for odors, the evergreens towering high overhead provided a variegated canopy through which the drizzle skittered. The fresh, invigorating smell of the rain filled Raye's nostrils and throat, made her lungs expand and set off a tingle on her arms and neck that made the hairs on her body rise as a whispered alarm seemed to fill her ears in her brother's voice.

Say what?

"Drop to the ground," she yelled at the top of her lungs as she followed her own instructions, even scuttling crab-like from under the cluster of trees where she was currently walking to move up and back several feet to a bare patch of ground.

An eye-blinding detonation of light flashed from the sky to the trees where Raye had walked previously. A cannonade of thunder shook the ground. A metallic, chlorine odor permeated the air. The hikers' screeches and cries rose immediately, proving they knew at once they'd been the target of a lightning strike. As Raye peered back over her shoulder, she saw most of the group had followed her shouted instructions. Several of them rushed to Raye to help her brush off her clothes.

"I think Lady Luck's flashing a signal to hit the road," she joked. When she noted puzzled glances, she clarified. "I mean, the hill… It's time to abandon this trail and head up the hill to that rock ledge above us. The stream below is approaching the level of the trail rapidly, and the lightning signals greater amounts of water coming toward us. To avoid more strikes, we also need to get to an area bare of trees."

"You're nuts," said Mason. Mud covered him to the knees, and with no rain poncho or coat, his damp clothing testified to many brushes with wet vegetation. "I'm freezing and filthy. I'm going straight back to the lodge. Not a thing indicates we won't make it. Yes, there's more water in the stream, but the trail's not covered. And even if that's a possibility, we can wade through. Your scare tactics are preventing us from reaching safety. Who's with me?" Arms outstretched, he pivoted around and appealed to the others.

Raye could see Des and Ben toward the back of the crowd, craning their necks to locate the source of the delay and the forceful voices. Mr. Van Voorst and Olivia stood slightly in front of them. Thankful that Mr. Van Voorst's color and posture seemed much improved, she concentrated on responding to the dissenter. While she wanted to start screaming, 'Stop arguing! Get up that mountain!' she knew the least overt friction might send her co-workers stampeding off in different directions.

"I can't force you to take my advice," she said, grinding her teeth with the greatest calm. "Keep in mind, though, that this area has experienced floods several times in the last fifteen years."

From their position some yards away, Ben and Des offered support. "I'm not wasting time debating," said Ben. "The size of the objects being swept away now is large. Look... There goes a septic tank."

Along with most of the crowd, Raye looked at the stream and spotted a large, bright blue plastic cistern bobbing menacingly along the riverbed, hitting banks and trees, rebounding under the water, which now bore no resemblance to the placid trickle from earlier in the day. Close behind the tank floated part of a child's swing set, its empty chains wrapping and unwrapping from its legs. Fencing and lawn furniture drifted as if on a pleasure cruise.

"Where are these things coming from?" asked the woman from the finance department. "I thought we were in a forest."

"We're in a watershed with lots of drainage winding around and through the mountains," said Raye. "I'm sure some of the streambeds have overflowed. Upstream and around to the east there're several lodges, as well as cabins and camping grounds."

"We can use some help here." Raye recognized Des' voice and realized his request was helping direct people into action and up the hill—an intentional result, she was sure. He motioned to several men to assist Mr. Van Voorst and Olivia up the slope while he extended a hand to a stocky man challenged by the steepness of the incline. More people surged around Mason. He was left motionless, hands still stretched out on both sides. After several moments when he found he'd been virtually ignored, he shrugged his shoulders and plowed after his companions.

"One, two, three…" Raye added under her breath as she ascended. Counting herself and Des as well as Ben and Van Voorst, twenty-five people were laboring up the slope. That left three still missing, including Julia. Raye had no choice but to continue with the group rather than search for her friend. A few feet off the trail, going perpendicular to it, she had to help others clamber over random branches and logs heaped in piles like pick-up-sticks abandoned by a giant child.

Then the going became truly difficult. Thin branches slapped the passersby on faces and shoulders, leaving scratches in their wake. Forced to cling to tree limbs and wedge themselves between trees, people grabbed trunks to balance themselves on the upward journey. Those who'd forgotten gloves soon had an overload of dirt, bark and even more grime covering their hands. Olivia and Mr. Van Voorst moved at a snail's pace, bracing their backs against trees as they went. When they came to a complete halt, Des, with Ben positioned beside him, called from a large outcropping of rock above the main group.

"Hey, I think we're high enough. The top of the slope is just above. And this stone shelf has an overhang to protect us if a downpour threatens us. It's almost a cave and there are no tall trees to attract lightning. I hope."

From the back of the hikers, Raye scurried as fast as she was able without knocking people over. When she reached Des, she pivoted to look behind and below. "*Hoy*! We made it!" she said to the group in general as she pumped both fists over her head. Faint cheers and many gasps and pants answered her. She spun to Des. "I agree with you about the location," she said, as she spotted the roaring stream a good forty feet below. "We're lucky we could get this high and that you found a decent shelter."

Around them, their co-workers were making themselves as comfortable as possible, given the cramped quarters and the hard ground under their shoes. The only rock at a comfortable sitting level went to Mr. Van Voorst who, despite obvious discomfort shown in his rigid yet stooped posture and the paleness of his skin, soldiered on in his best strong-jawed fashion. Van Voorst exchanged a word or two with his employees and accepted a handful of dried fruit from Olivia with a murmur of thanks.

Some people dropped to the ground to rest cross-legged, while others shook out jackets and scarves. The strenuous climb had produced lots of perspiration under their heavy clothing. Sharing snacks, water, lotion and bottles of hand sanitizer, people seemed euphoric, proud to have met the challenge to climb straight up the mountain. A few paused near Des, Ben and Raye to study the surrounding panorama featuring the continuing show from the blustering, bullying storm.

"Oh my God, a car," one breathed.

Sure enough, a battered and rusty Olds twisted and bumped down the raging flow, too large now to label as a 'stream', ricocheting off a cluster of large logs snagged at the side then coming to a rest. Behind that car a few more vehicles cavorted from side to side as they smashed into one another. The water churned as if it were coming to a boil and surged around blockage in the passage. Faintly, growing in strength by the second, came a roar that quickly revealed itself to be a wall of water.

Raye took a massive breath then whooshed out. "Here it comes…the wave front. It's a good thing we climbed when we did."

"Looks like our resident expert was right about the flood," said Ben. "What happens now?"

"I've heard there can be several wave fronts, spread out over hours, if the storm continues upstream. Each one usually is higher. So although the rain's slowed down here, there's no guarantee we're out of the woods, so to speak."

"So to speak," Des said at the same time. They didn't attempt to suppress the mirth bubbling up at their common response. *His off-beat humor replicates mine,* she thought.

As the small group on the rim looked down, others on the outcropping joined them one by one and comments and exclamations increased. A wall of water at least ten feet high surged below them, now dark brown and spotted with rocks, twigs and other debris, making it appear like coffee with grounds intact. They could make out miscellaneous yard and household objects from cabins upstream—shovels, laundry baskets, more fencing, bicycles, fireplace logs. These barreled along like a high-speed billiards game.

"I can't imagine getting caught down there," said Des.

"I'm praying Julia and the others didn't," Raye said. "They'd never survive."

They both became quiet. She shook off her dejection to paste on a hopeful smile. The appearance of Mason at their elbows, with his ever-present shadow Tim, halted any brooding on unsolvable problems.

"What now?" said Mason. "We can't perch here forever."

"Yeah," echoed Tim. "I'm getting cold and hungry."

Then call a taxi. The sarcastic response popped into Raye's mind spontaneously.

"You can always call a taxi," said Des.

Raye suppressed a beam. It was amazing how much she and Des thought alike.

Chapter Twenty-Three

Mason's face reddened and his jaw clenched. Before he could spit out a challenge, Des sighed. "Sorry, man." He slung an arm around the other man's shoulder. "I'm stumped. I'm sure you can see we don't have much control over the situation. We could really use your and Tim's leadership. How about circulating to tell folks to go easy on their food and water? Then see if you can compile a running list of supplies. We may have to combine our assets and dole them out bit by bit—ditto on extra clothing. Most of us dressed warmly, but a few may be feeling the chill now." Not by the twitch of an eyelid did he single out Tim, clothed in a grungy gray sweatshirt, shivering and with bare hands tucked under his armpits.

"The rain here's let up a bit, but that's no guarantee more won't move in. In fact, the clouds just over the ridge appear to be more ominous," Raye said.

"It's what?" Des checked his wristwatch. "Three in the afternoon? We have a good five hours before night. We've got to prepare."

"Keep track with a pencil and paper." Raye extended the items, pulled from her pack. "We need to conserve our electronics."

Ben threw his authority behind the suggestion. "I'll come with you to encourage complete honesty."

Together Raye and Des observed Mason and Tim march up to a cluster of people, list at the ready, their mouths moving and heads nodding as they relayed directions. As the alpha male in the set of two, Mason led in emphatic gestures — arm waving, fist pounding, frowning for emphasis. Tim's more restrained motions mimicked his pal's. Ben's occasional nods and gestures bolstered the presentation.

"They are unbelievable," Raye murmured.

"Actually, not that unusual," said Des.

"Where have you run across their clones?"

"From high school on. The military, business, even, much as I hate to admit this, occasional family members." He kept his eyes on the pair. They seemed to be providing directions, productive activities, everything he could have hoped for. "They are a standard personality type — not necessarily brainless, although that's possible. Often people uncertain about their status in the hierarchy or apprehensive about rejection bluster about their position and opinions."

"They're doing no harm and may even help," said Raye.

"Agreed. Then there are the whiners and complainers." Des nodded toward Krystle and Kabir. "They act so sensitive, like they suffer more than the

218

run-of-the-mill person." The duo's dissatisfaction was obvious in their frowns and drooping shoulders. Des turned back toward Raye. Without thought, he wiped a raindrop that was running from her hair toward her forehead. When she instinctively startled, he explained. "Sorry. Didn't want the water to get in your eyes."

Is that a hint of shy response in her glance? Des could only hope. Maybe an unintentional gesture of help was strengthening their connection.

"Thanks. I mean…that's all right. Uh, no problem." A few soft, hesitant huffs before she continued. "I'm sure someone at the lodge will be trying to contact the authorities about our absence. It's not as if we're stranded out here forever — or even days, most likely. But it's possible we're facing a day or two of isolation. It kinda puts the thought of layoffs into perspective, doesn't it?"

His expression turned grim. "We're isolated, but under what conditions?" He shook his head. "No, I've got to be more optimistic. This group has shown outstanding abilities to stick together in the face of huge challenges, even the least likely." He nodded toward Mason and Tim.

"You may have dreamed up the tasks for the amazing duo to keep them busy and out of our hair, but you performed a service for the Chosen Twenty-Five as well. We need to institute rationing based on our pooled supplies, so Mason and Tim's work is the first step, unless you can conjure a rescue group for us," Raye said.

"Happy to. I'll pull one out of my…sleeve," he said. "Really, you should be thanking my military training. That's where I learned most of my management skills. Straightforward and honest. Nothing mysterious about it. Kind of an 'everything I needed to know I learned in kindergarten' approach."

"I'm sure you're downplaying the effort you put out."

"What I'd say in my favor is I don't need to be hit over the head to learn a lesson," said Des, wishing he could add, *Or to make sure you and I are on the same wavelength.*

"Look! Look over there!" Olivia, Raye's boss, yelled with no warning. She'd joined several bored individuals who'd been occupying their time by pitching pebbles into the torrent below. Her attention was focused downstream.

Raye turned a smidge to her right and followed Olivia's pointing finger downward. "What? I don't see a thing except more flood."

"No. A bit lower. On the opposite side downstream, under that stand of tall aspens. Some people. I think it's the rest of our group."

Sure enough, three figures perched downstream, blurred by distance, mist and branches. One of them, clearly female, wore a bright red plaid jacket. Raye scurried to the farthest lip of the rock overhang and leaned from the waist.

"It is! It's Julia. And the others, of course. Julia! Julia!" Waving her arms over her head, she tried her best to whistle. When that failed, she increased her volume and hooted. "Over here."

Des joined her and, placing his fingers in his mouth, gave a shrill loud warble that drew the attention of the trio across the way.

"They look worse off than we are," Raye said.

Indeed they did. They must have been caught at one point in a greater downpour, as their clothing sagged, probably from water. Julia copied Raye's gestures, first doing a double take, then bending forward, finally crying and waving her arms. Des could make out her communication over the water's roar if he concentrated. "How are you?" said Julia. "Is everyone else over there?"

"Yes. We're fine. How about you?" shouted Raye.

"Wet and hungry. Otherwise, okay. Do you have a cell connection?"

Raye shook her head violently from side to side.

"Neither do we," said Julia. "What now?"

"Consider this a mini-vacation."

Eyes glued to the folks on the other side, Des muttered a negative. "'Fraid not. Trouble may be brewing." He nodded in the direction of the trio.

"What?" Raye asked.

He drew her to one side to avoid alarming Olivia and the others. "The flash flood's undercutting the riverbank right where they're caught." he said softly. With a small jerk of his head, he alerted Raye to a rapid, strong current forced to the opposite side where the water was gobbling bites of earth and carrying the muddy mess away.

I will not faint. I will not scream. I will not panic. A trio of forbidden reactions rotated through Raye's mind, loosening a hysterical giggle from her throat that she couldn't control. At first Des looked askance at her, but when the giggle burbled louder and didn't stop, he grabbed her shoulders and shook hard.

"It'll be all right. We'll think of something."

"What?" she said. "Can we fly? Jump several hundred feet? Materialize ropes out of thin air?" As she finished the litany, tremors began to shake her from head to foot.

He grabbed her and held on tight. As she regained a modicum of control, he rubbed her back. "There's always something to be done. It may not be obvious, but we'll figure it out. Ready, fire, aim... That's my motto."

She stifled a chuckle. *I don't know if I'll ever be able to give this man up,* she thought. *Someone who can make me laugh in the middle of a crisis and keeps his head on top of that.* "Okay, big guy. Tell me what."

He stepped away from her and rubbed his head with the knuckles of one hand. "First, they're across the river, right?"

Raye nodded.

"But they must have started on this side like the rest of us, right?"

She nodded again.

"Therefore, they must have found some way to get there. If we discover the route, we may be able to help them."

"And at least we won't be sitting around on our hands," Raye finished.

"Right. The first thing we have to do is warn them back as far as possible from the edge."

"Agreed," she said.

As one, they wheeled to address Julia and her cohorts only to receive another shock. "The flood's eating away at the bank so quickly that only a few feet remain before they'll be dumped in the water," said Des. "She's most likely to take a warning seriously from you. Yell to her."

Raye complied. Forming a megaphone shape with one hand on each side of her mouth, she drew a full breath. "Julia. Julia. Listen to me. Emergency! Move back! Move back!"

Julia's faint tones came back. "You better believe this is an emergency. Almost no water and sharing sticks of gum." Panic accentuated her laughter, strong enough to carry across the way. "Plus the trail back to the lodge on this side has been washed away."

My attitude now may mean the three live or plunge in the flood and probably die, Raye thought. Burying the notion under determination, she somehow infused a holler with composed insistence. "Cut the crap. Step back from the edge. At once. All of you."

"Are you kidding? The entire mountainside is mud."

"That's the problem. You're perched on a heap of mud, but the flood is eating away your foundation. You're about to fall in."

"Fall in? Have you lost your mind? We're not going in there," yelled Julia.

"No!" Although her throat was getting sore from yelling, Raye sucked in another lungful and tried again. A second voice joined hers—Des. "Get back and up. Up, up, up!"

The two of them, with accompanying flapping arm motions, got through. Julia whirled around to consult with her companions and the trio moved away from the edge and even managed to scramble up the steep hillside a few feet. Raye exhaled in relief. Eddies of water swirled around the opposite side of the banks, and she could see that the distance between the torrents and the top of the bank was shrinking. Breakers of liquid hit the earth and flipped back in the opposite direction like huge surfing waves to rejoin the main surge, which struggled to break free of the bed and spread out, only to gush ever forward in greater force.

A chunk of the bank some three feet wide broke off and fell. The entire body of water was so dark that debris being carried along couldn't be seen unless it broke the surface. rush

Julia's scream underscored the chaos as she realized the chunk had been inches from her previous position. "That's as far as we can go. Now what?" came the question from the three across the way, who joined voices to ensure they could be heard.

If the situation hadn't been so dangerous, Raye would have giggled at their positions as she thought, *That's one way to create attrition in the work force.* Clinging to roots exposed in the hill from the rains and a small branch here and there, backs outward, the stranded looked like tree frogs or lizards that scampered up walls. Their faces, pale and glowing, emerged moon-like from the background.

Raye and Des conferred again. "I agree with them. What now?" said Raye.

"I think we should see if we can get over there as soon as possible. We can't do anything from here. Maybe we can use the rope you thought we should abandon," Des said, admirably allowing only the slightest superiority to surface.

"Okay." She threw up both palms in surrender. "You were right. We can borrow more line if people brought theirs along, and we can take food and water if we have enough to spare."

"Let's ask them how they crossed."

A slight sway in the direction of the three increased the force of Des and Raye's voices as they chanted in unison. "How did you get to that side?"

The reply. "Go downstream. A small path branches from the main. It looks like a shortcut to the lodge, over a log bridge. It's now submerged in the flood, as is the downstream path."

"Must be farther on than we've explored before." Raye lowered her voice to address Des.

Ben materialized at their side. "I see you've discovered our missing employees."

"Yes," said Des. "Not in a good situation, however." He quickly filled Ben in on details and what he and Raye planned. "We think we should make an effort to reach them and, if possible, bring them to the main group. Are you okay on your own to supervise developments here?"

"Do you think there's a question about being able to return?" The absolute immobility of Ben's features indicated the seriousness of his inquiry.

"There may be," Des said. "We can always stay over there if necessary."

Considering the two men, Raye felt more tacit communication was being exchanged than voiced. Through the control of their bodies — muscles flexed, eyes alert — they appeared ready for any eventuality. She knew the question of her participation was inevitable. "I'm eager to go with Des," she said before Ben could articulate the issue. "Julia's a good friend of mine, and I feel a responsibility to my co-workers with her. Plus, I'm more familiar with this terrain than anyone else in our group."

"Raye and I have worked well as a team during this retreat," Des said. "Our skills complement each other's."

Ben opened his mouth, but before he could speak, Des added, "I'm sure you're ready to lead the charge, sir. But you're needed here. With Mr. Van Voorst's condition uncertain, only you have the authority and the skills to assure calm, along with cooperation."

"Believe me, the days of me in the front line, exhorting the troops to superhuman effort, are long gone," said Ben. "I'm content with bossing others around. You two go for it."

Chapter Twenty-Four

Des lacked the time to wonder why he and Raye worked so smoothly together. He simply knew they did and spared a moment of thanks for the fact. Within minutes, they'd hit on several people to lend rope, food and water, strapped and stuffed the items on their persons and set off back the way they'd originally traveled. Although this meant plunging downhill to get to the trail, little impeded their quick passage. He discounted mud, since the entire area was coated, and because he and Raye were the only travelers, they were limited solely by the speed of their own feet.

In a strange way, the situation enchanted him. He and Raye were alone in a world he'd never before experienced, a cloudy and gray atmosphere that somehow held mystery and beauty. The waters next to them surged and sparkled, a slight breeze blowing the indescribable scent of damp earth and growing plants. A hint of that first garden, Eden, pervaded the terrain, and Des nurtured the hope and excitement infusing him from this thought. *If only Raye and I could be alone, treading fresh territory, exploring a corner of a new world as we discovered one another.*

"Look," said Raye, as she stopped. She indicated a shaft of sunlight pouring through the clouds in the distant west. "I bet the thunderstorm's coming to an end."

"Good news," he said, although a tiny part of his brain wished nothing would ever change, that they would forever be strolling down this mountain path surrounded by simple, unique, blessed nature. "At least there won't be significant amounts of water being dumped into the stream."

"Yes, but it will continue to be flooded for a while as it clears farther upstream."

They were approaching the flooded gully, which now appeared like a flat surface some ten feet across. At the gully's junction with the stream below, a tangle of fallen logs and branches had lodged like a beaver's dam, redirecting the more rapid water's flow into the stream away from the gully. Raye stuck the tip of a boot in. "It's spread from the primary ditch but only appears to be an inch or two deep here. I think we can safely shuffle forward to test for depth then help each other over the deep part."

"Okay. I'm ready if you are."

Adjusting clusters of intertwined straps, bottles, scarves and gloves, Des led, extending one hand for balance and grasping his supplies with the other, while Raye followed. For several feet, water barely covered their shoes, but at the gully itself, a greater depth and slippery slopes offered a real challenge. Still, Des' height and strength, solid as a linebacker's, ensured Raye would suffer no harm.

In a few yards they spotted the two alternative trails. One of them started climbing right after a bend in its route and surely went farther up the mountain. The second intersected with their current path and was almost imperceptible, weeds and vines flourishing next to and across it. So faint were its traces that it could have been a mere wildlife route. "That must be the one that leads to the opposite side," said Raye. "I hardly noticed it before."

Des knelt, balancing on the balls of his feet and his heels to avoid the mud. "Fresh boot prints," he said. "Several different styles of soles, so I agree with you." He stood. "Now we're into unexplored terrain." Again he led, a bull-like thrust to his shoulders and chest.

As if timidly entering the Garden of Paradise, the two checked left and right where the landscape became even wilder. Small blossoms, delicate as spider webs, decorated stems of flora so abundant they protected much of the ground from footprints. Large, smooth leaves still glistened from the recent rainfall, while needles of evergreens borne aloft on supple twigs protected the wilderness from human violation. Still, the signs of recent passage by people could be noted in an occasional bent limb and skid mark in mud.

"Can't be too far," Raye noted. "They weren't much beyond where the main group took refuge."

Almost as she spoke, she and Des halted. The path didn't peter out. The flood's ravages had chopped off the land, along with the trail. On both sides of the swollen stream, a few broken log stakes bearing strands of wire, snapped as if wire cutters had been at work, bore witness to the previous existence of a small, primitive bridge. In between, a gush of water showed the original channel, but somehow, the stream's violent temper had surged beyond and out of the bed to create a second tributary, leaving a kind of isolated island or peninsula in between two strong-flowing branches.

"That explains why they couldn't cross back to our side," said Des.

"Should we try to get over there? And how can we accomplish that?" Raye said.

Des drew several deep breaths. He quieted the clenching in his guts, an automatic reaction left over from his time in the service. The hypothetical situations he'd received in basic training had materialized into reality when he'd shipped out. Even though he'd avoided actual combat, the state of the world today dictated eternal vigilance for violence. At the time he'd been a risk-taker, a daredevil. Experience had taught him different. *I wish I could walk away from this. I thought I was done with extreme rescues when I left the service, no more gambling my life for someone's questionable behavior. But I can't with Raye looking to me to perform miracles for her friend.*

"I know from practice that it's best not to go off half-cocked in a potentially dangerous situation," he said. "Best to assess the strengths and weaknesses. Sometimes an alternative action holds more promise than simply charging forward. So what do you think is our challenge here?"

Raye considered. "Getting Julia and the others out of their isolated spot and over to where the rest of us are."

"That's certainly one possibility. But if the probability of failure is too high? And what would make the odds overwhelming?" Des was glad Raye devoted some attention to his questions. It showed a certain maturity and intelligence.

"I guess the risks would be too high if one of us, you or me, endangered ourselves—or if the same were true of the three across the stream. Unless, of course, a more pressing threat existed," said Raye.

"And in that case, they'd be better off hunkering down and simply biding their time, right?" Des added.

"Right. But we should at least let them know we're trying to get to them, doing everything we can. Having a positive attitude can help you survive anything."

"I agree. Is there a third choice?" Des could have been lecturing a class.

"Maybe moving them to another spot entirely, if we can find an appropriate one."

"Again, I agree. So that means we should—"

"Scout the territory," Raye filled in. By now the rain had almost completely stopped, although drops of water continued to fall periodically from where they'd been caught on leaves, branches and trunks.

Des could see yards ahead, behind and around. No inch of the environment escaped his study. He noticed Raye copying him, her eyes so focused they nearly crossed. Des choked back a chuckle of delight at her attention, even as he imitated her action.

"The strip of land appears to continue downstream, probably as far as Julia's group," he said.

"Then why haven't they returned this way? From what we saw, they're stuck pressed against the hill."

"Aaah... The question we must answer." He paused for further evaluation of the vicinity. The stream still overflowed its bed and up the banks, its contents closer to sludge than water. "It appears to me that we might be able to get across the branch of water closest to us. It's not deep, maybe six to nine inches. *If* we can figure out a way to do so safely." His eyes narrowed. "Boy, that water looks as if it has the force of an ocean riptide. No way we can wade across. Let's conduct a simple test." He scoured the immediate ground for an object, hefted several stones from hand to hand, then selected a short but weighty limb nearby. Dragging it to the bank, he heaved it into the water's flow where it bobbed once, hit bottom, spun twice then rocketed down the stream with the speed of a race car.

"Yep," he said. "Fat chance we're attempting that without some sort of safety system, even if we can see the bottom."

"The ropes," Raye said. "We can use those to get across." She pointed to the two broken log stakes or posts on the opposite bank still present after the bridge had been washed away. "Not just one. Two, distanced a couple of feet apart, from this side to the other?"

"That would do it. *If* the ropes could be secured across the way. But we have no assistance over there."

"Listen, buster," she said. "You're in the Wild West now, remember? I learned to throw a lariat at my father's knee."

"You're pulling my leg."

"Nope."

He tossed back his head and hooted so hard he nearly fell over. "You never cease to amaze me. Throw a lasso."

"Technically the line's a lariat. Lasso is a verb. Hand over the ropes."

He pulled four from his knapsack and passed them over. Raye held each one individually, slid them between her fingers, balanced them, pulled and tugged, twirled them around her head in a small circle.

"These two should do," she said, holding them up. "They're a little short. They should be forty feet, but once I get them across then secure them on this side, we should be good to go."

"What's your plan?"

"I'll lasso those, then you and I can tie the ends of the lines on this side to the trees behind us, a foot or two apart, like rope banisters. We can hang onto them as we walk across."

"I'll agree to that, but only along with tying ourselves to the cables as a safety backup. If one of us loses our footing, at least the connection should prevent us going downstream."

"Okay." Stepping as close to the stream's flow as she could without falling in, Raye tied a slipknot on one end of a rope, inserted the other end to make a small loop, ran a hand down the line to check for irregularities then coiled most of the rope in her left hand. Some loose rope remained between the coil and the noose. She launched it around her head from right to left, gradually increasing the size of the circle. As she worked, words flowed from her continuously in a nervous gush. "You have to remember that it's been years since I tried this. I used to practice hour after hour with my dad. His family had a *ranchito* in Mexico. I may take quite a while to lasso the posts. You've got to be patient."

Her swinging hand moved from back to front, she advanced a small step and shifted her palm forward and down to shoulder level, as if aiming at a post across the stream. With a snap, the lariat flew through the air and landed around the upstanding log.

"*Hoy!*" She tugged as hard as she could, then gestured to Des to join her in the same effort. They both pulled until they were confident the noose was secure. Next they hauled the remainder of the rope away from the stream to wrap several times around the trunk of a large pine. Des lashed the cable with a solid knot, stepped back and brushed his palms against each other.

"I see you know how to knot," she said.

"Yep. Another skill courtesy of the military."

"It may be we'll owe our success to the armed services," she joked as she picked the second rope up from the ground.

"Or your childhood infatuation with cowboying,' he said.

Again going through the previous series of motions, she allowed her wrist to move easily and act as an axle as she swung the noose. Nonetheless, this time, even though the lariat easily flew to the other side, it went far beyond the second post, falling to the ground beyond with a slither.

"Ooh, too bad," he said. "Another try." No success. The next attempt dropped short, several flew to the right or left, one landed on the log but rebounded off. *We've gotten too cocky. I should have known it wouldn't be this easy.*

Raye teetered on the edge of tears as she re-coiled the rope around her arm and hyperventilated. "I'm giving up. This idea is futile."

He went to her and pulled her close. "Take it easy. Try to relax a little. You're coming very close to roping it, but we've been working on a solution for quite a while. Maybe rotate your shoulders, walk around a short distance, breathe deeply." As he talked, he rubbed her shoulders and back. Her gasps slowed then resumed a peaceful rhythm.

Chapter Twenty-Five

He has a magic touch, Raye thought as she relaxed in Des' arms. *I feel so safe here.* With a jolt, she realized she hadn't experienced this sense of security for years, not since she'd been a child. Becoming a mother herself had put her on twenty-four-seven alert. Each new situation had held potential horrors and terrors for her son. Did Andy have all his shots to avoid deadly diseases? Did he need braces? Was he being bullied on the playground? Any chance his father's addictions and immaturity might pass down to him? Regular bouts of insomnia had nagged her sleep. During these times, she'd sneak in — first by his crib, then his cot, finally his futon — listening to him breathe, counting the soft whistles in and out that qualified as his snoring, praying he'd be safe and she'd pass the tests of a being good mom.

She tightened her arms around Des and inhaled the wool and waxed-cotton scents of his shirt and jacket, delivered through his body's heat. Her nose tickled and she hoped it wouldn't run. *How embarrassing!* A small sniff took care of that potential problem and gave her a chance to recover her equilibrium. Here she was, stuck out in the wilds in the middle of a storm and flood, no contact with the outside world, the potential for danger looming all around her. Somehow, panic, fear, insecurity, were all evaporating, moment by moment. *Des brings solidity and confidence to the situation.*

She pulled away to look up at him. "Okay. Ready to try again." Grabbing the rope, she tested, reknotted, coiled, swung in a rhythm that felt solid and productive. As she swiveled to launch the throw and an intermittent mist from rain interfered with her vision, a figure seemed to materialize across the way next to the post. *Is it Carlos? Is he urging me to throw?* She shook her head, blinked her eyes.

The rope seemed to become an extension of her arm and take direction from her vision. The log post across the stream turned out to be no distance at all. With the certainty of a child's belief in Santa, she knew she'd succeed this time. *Whffft!* The lariat flew through her fingers. Her sight fled with it almost like a telescope, magnifying the log to ten times its size. The noose settled inevitably around the post. She pulled it tight. "*Hoy!*" she yelled.

"Yah-hoo," Des bellowed, cowboy-fashion. He grabbed her with both arms and lifted her from the ground. Feet dangling, she still held fast to the rope as she leaned backward and let loose her own crow of delight.

As he lowered her to the earth, she prepared the cable to lash to the pines behind them. "Aw, shucks, 't'weren't nothing," she said with comic humility.

In short order, the two of them had both ropes readied for their passage and an extra length secured around each of their waists as well as tied in a slip knot around the temporary rope railing. Des removed his orange-and-tan field jacket and fastened it around his middle to leave his arms free, then inched out into the stream first, hands gripping the handlines firmly as the water and sediment climbed inch by inch to his calves. On his way, he managed to sidestep or leap over a large crooked branch and the battered remains of a doghouse. Fortunately most larger items had been swept downstream along the current of the more sizeable torrent farther away.

Raye watched until he was halfway, across then she felt her way. Completely assured by Des' success, she achieved the other side with no mishaps. As she waded through the knee-high, icy rapids, the waffle soles of her hiking boots held firm to the rocky stream bed. She could almost hear her brother urging her on, telling her she'd be safe. Yes, the water's power could well have knocked her over, tossed her down the current like an abandoned doll, but she knew it wouldn't, not while she clung to the ropes and had Des' brown and orange plaid jacket in her view.

Leaping the last few feet of the stream and jubilant with their achievement, they paused to toast one another with water bottles before Raye urged Des on. "We should find Julia. There's not a lot of daylight left. I shudder to think of them being isolated out here in the dark."

The peninsula on which they walked resembled their basic trail. Water-soaked vegetation, tree trunks and branches showed damp streaks where rain had soaked in. Underfoot lay shiny, slippery mud, and the silence of the mountains now seemed ominous and threatening, broken only by the river's roar and a crescendo of clanging as large items bounced along the current and rebounded off one another and rocks along the bank. Simply to keep her mind occupied and free from fear, Raye began chanting the rain song.

Faintly drifting to her through the air, she caught a few bars of the melody and some words. "*Lluvia, lluvia, vete* —" She gasped and froze where she stood. "Stop. Stop! I hear something."

Des halted, turning his head from side to side to capture any hint of a sound. "So do I," he said. "Very weak."

"It's Julia," she said. "She's singing the same song, but in Spanish. She's letting us know where she is and that she's all right." A giggle at Julia's irrepressible humor burst from her. "Come on. This way." She plunged forward but a bit to the left as the peninsula widened. All the while she sang at the top of her lungs, much as a trumpet blast might herald their friendly presence to Julia.

"Careful," said Des. He lengthened his stride and pace to keep up with her eager steps. "We don't know the condition of this strip of land. It's obvious the original streambed allowed the flood to diverge around a slightly higher bar. But if we get another surge, if there's more rainfall upstream or if the side canyons let loose, we might find ourselves in rapids up to our necks."

Raye made an impatient jerk with her hand. "Even more reason to hurry. The condition of Julia and her group is uncertain. They could be dangling from a branch over a whirlpool at this point. There's no time to wait."

"That's why we should be alert and ready for anything."

"*Now* you advise discretion? What happened to the grandstander?" she said, although she realized Des had to be speaking from experience. He'd faced many more dangerous situations than she had by about one hundred-to-one. In fact, she couldn't recall ever dealing with a greater hazard. Still, it didn't stop her impatience. She felt they were moving in slow motion, a nightmarish, sluggish quality to her every sense.

In a matter of a minute, she was glad he'd put the brakes on her. The ground before them turned into swirls of mud over gravel and sand, showing where the flood had surged then retreated once. A short distance away, several feet of water still prohibited easy passage from their land bridge over to a hillside where they could glimpse Julia and her two companions clinging to roots and branches, isolated from their would-be rescuers.

"What do we know about Julia's sidekicks?" Des asked. "I still can't recognize everyone in the central office by sight."

"We may have a challenge. The husky one, CFO Bill Pickett, obviously would rather munch on chips than walk around a block. Roy Hudson, our strategy officer, has a severe asthma condition. Not much help there." She raised her voice to call. "Julia. Julia. Are you okay?"

"Sure thing. I'm just waiting for a bus," Julia said.

Raye lowered her head, fighting tears, biting her lip. *How like Julia to joke about her situation. She's a fighter!* "*Todos somos luchadoras!* Keep fighting." Raye made her response equally happy-go-lucky. "'Fraid there's only us. Me and Des. We'll do our best to get you outta there."

"'K. I don't have much choice. Just hangin' here."

Raye dropped back a step or two and turned to Des. "What now?" She couldn't imagine her emotional condition had he not been with her. Yes, she had experience in mountain camping and hiking. But flash floods and rescues were way beyond what she'd ever imagined she'd confront, although every few years she soaked up television and Internet news reports on these incidents. If she allowed herself to consider the challenge now before her — to help save her best friend in the world as well as two others from possible injury, even death — she was sure she'd turn tail and run screaming in the opposite direction. But here was calm, confident Des, who didn't appear worried in the least.

He was unfastening the rope tied to his belt and indicated she should do the same with the length she still carried from their first fording of the flood. "I think we can duplicate our previous crossing, but we'll have to use only one rope as a grip."

"Should we go back and collect the other two?"

"No, we haven't the time." He nodded toward the rivulet moving between them and Julia's group. "We were too optimistic. The flood's not winding down. There must have been a surge up-river. It's increasing again."

Sure enough, the water level was rising. More to the point, the small bulge of land on which Julia and the others were isolated now served as a point where debris was pounding, recoiling, then catching to create a dam. Water built up, swelled higher in its rush to escape the barricade. Again Raye felt she was moving with the deliberation of a snail, every action hampered, despite her desire to respond quickly.

With narrowed eyes, Des studied the setting in which their colleagues were trapped, took a few steps forward, backward, left, right, crouched on his heels, rose then turned to Raye. "I think our best chance of success, and smallest possibility of injury or death to any of us, is for us to toss them one rope and have them secure it to something sturdy over there — rock, roots, limbs. We stay on this side to help anchor this end. You'll notice we have nothing on which to fasten our end that's strong enough to bear a lot of weight, so we'll have to provide the bulk of the muscle."

Raye shook her head. "I don't like it. I don't want to leave them on their own to slog or swing their way over here. We don't know the water's depth or speed. Bill's overweight and Roy would never admit it, but he's handicapped by his asthma. Julia's a total city girl. Come up with another method."

"Short of braiding vines or constructing a ladder, which we lack time and tools to do quickly, there isn't an alternative."

"How about if we strap the rope to the broken pine back there." Raye swung around and pointed in the opposite direction.

"Number one, if I'm the only one to add my muscle to supplement the trunk, I doubt it's strong enough to hold a struggling, swinging, fearful adult. Plus this rope's on the short side. There's not enough length to tie it on both ends over that distance."

A stubbornness straightened her backbone and a mulish feeling came over her. "There must be something. They have no experience with this weather or physical exertion. They need help."

Des' words slowed and gained precision and clarity. "Yes. And that's what we'll give them. We are not miracle workers—and they're not helpless."

Yikes! Raye'd never seen Des controlling his temper before. She imagined he'd looked like this when in a tough command position in the military—clenched jaw, grim-eyed, stony-faced, controlling every word that passed his lips. He was scary…and implacable…and somehow utterly reliable, steadfast as a rock.

On the other hand, she couldn't foresee the future. She wanted to screech, hurry, hurry. She folded. "Okay. So we toss the rope and tell them to try to ford the rapids."

"Yes, but we have them take safeguards. First, only one of them at a time on the rope. And that individual ties the second rope around their body as securely as possible, so there's a back-up if they get swept away. Nothing's a guarantee, but that may help."

"Okay. Let's get started."

Together, they turned toward Julia, who immediately unleashed an outburst—*fully justified*, Raye thought. "It's about time. Get us the hell out of here."

"Calm down." Des motioned downward with both palms. "Hysterics help nothing."

"That's what you think," Raye murmured. She couldn't tell if he'd heard her.

"Here's what we want you to do," he said. "This is a cooperative effort. One rope goes over to the other side to you, where it gets lashed around something as immoveable as possible, like that large pine." He pointed toward the tree. "Then Raye and I anchor this side, and one by one we trundle, shuffle or hop you over here."

"What do you mean 'we,' white man?" shouted Julia.

Raye cracked up, and when Des recoiled, laughed even more. "She's pulling your leg. I'm glad she's got the spirit to sass you." She spoke more loudly. "Julia, get your troops ready for an assault. Des and I have to stay on this side to hold the line on this end because nothing's strong enough to fill that function over here. But you'll have a second rope to secure to yourself and the first rope, to…to—"

"To keep us from being washed down with the flood. I get the idea. Let me tell the others." Julia wriggled around to address her companions.

Even as she spoke, the skies opened and rain came down in sheets, instantly soaking everyone and everything. Des shrugged into his field jacket while Raye held her hands over her head in a useless motion. It was nearly impossible for Raye to make out the figures of her co-workers, who appeared ghostly and insubstantial, like figures on an out-of-focus television screen. She shivered, as much from fear as from the chill. "Julia, Julia! Get over here now! This downpour means more upstream flooding coming toward us."

Chapter Twenty-Six

Des didn't need to say a word to indicate his agreement but simply tied one end of the rope to a stone the size of a softball and heaved it across the stream. The same action ensured that the second rope also reached the other side. He circled the rope to a stand of aspens, large enough to anchor the rope's end but too small to bear all the stress. Then he and Raye circled handholds on the line for them to grasp. The message came through to Julia and the others as clear as a foghorn, because they hurriedly tested a pine tree to see if it would support a person's weight and fastened it. Then Julia began to tie the second rope around Bill Pickett's chest below his armpits.

"No," Raye yelled. "Julia, you should go first."

"Nope." Julia didn't even pause. "This is my group. We're here because I wanted to go this way. I'm responsible for them." With a final jerk, she ensured the knot on Bill would hold then looped the rope around the hand line in another loop, leaving some give yet guaranteeing that if he lost footing or was swept away, the cable would connect him to the line.

Before Raye could open her mouth again to protest, Des hushed her. "Let it go. We'll waste more time debating in what order they should come over than if they decide it themselves." He faced the line and Bill's husky form on the other side, grabbed a handhold and circled the entire rope around his arm for good measure. "Okay, big guy, you ready?"

Des was right. They could delay no longer. The storm hadn't let up. Although she'd been a little damp before, now she was soaking wet. It was a strange feeling—one moment nearly dry, the next sopping. Water cascaded down from sky, trees and earth in sheets. She could see the deluge washing a torrent of mud into the waters flooding past, thick and dark like wet mortar sluggishly heaving over a brick wall. If someone risked stepping into that morass, would they be stuck, glued or shoved downstream like the rest of the debris?

She looked up to prepare herself for Bill's crossing. She'd never seen fear so obvious on a human form before. Although the rain pouring over his head and features obscured his facial expression, his shoulders curved inward toward his chest and belly, as if to protect them, tremors cycling over his entire body. That could be due to the cold. *Late afternoon in a downpour is not conducive to retaining body heat*, she thought. She was freezing herself, although fortunately gloves offered her hands and fingers some protection. She'd need them working properly if they had any hope of getting three people across the divide. To go one better than Des, she turned around to wrap the rope around her waist and dug her heels in. "Come on, Bill. Think of all those folks waiting back up the mountain with power bars, drinkable water and even trail mix. *Todos somos luchadoras!*"

Julia translated for her crew. "We're all fighters!"

The older man gave a wave over his head and grasped the guideline in both fists. "Full speed ahead," he called. Taking small shuffling steps like a baby learning to walk, he inched into the water. There was no way to tell how deep the rapids were in this course of the flow. Raye held her breath hoping, praying for a solid streambed not far below the surface.

"Hooray!" she shouted before the flow hit Bill's full weight, putting intense pressure on the rope. As she braced herself and pulled in reverse, she realized how lucky they'd been. It appeared this section of the canal was higher than the normal streambed, so water flowed only inches, rather than feet, deep. Of course the rapidity of the current's speed was nearly insurmountable, so Bill was fortunate to have the guideline to hold on to.

When he reached the other side and struggled through the sludge, Des and Raye couldn't relax until Bill untied the second rope. There were hugs and back slaps all around before Des urged them again into action, assigning Bill as additional support on the line. Lofting the second rope back across the gap courtesy of another stone, Des resumed his position as the primary anchor. The second person to cross, chief strategy officer Roy Hudson, was thinner and, aside from his asthma, in decent shape. He shouted, "We are all fighters!" and made the trip with no incidents.

Relief grew in Raye's chest. She'd hardly let herself hope, but they were going to succeed—drenched, exhausted, hungry and freezing, but alive. Now there were four on the correct side and only Julia lingered on the hazardous bank. Raye resumed a firm grip on the rope as she watched Julia fasten the safety rope around her chest. Then she happened to glance upstream. She screamed. "Oh, my God. Julia! Julia!"

Des turned in the same direction. A solid wall of water was headed straight for them. Only yards away, it filled the entire width of the bottom part of the canyon. The side on which the quartet halted had a gentle slope upward, but the side with Julia surely would be inundated. With almost no time to shout a warning, Des made an attempt. "Hold on, Julia. Don't let go. The rest of us, up the hill!"

Everyone managed to cling to self-control enough to back up the incline while retaining a grip on the rope. Despite the three additional people reinforcing the anchor, Des' arms were jerked nearly from their sockets as the full strength of the water wall hit Julia, breaking her grip on the guide rope and sweeping her into the flood.

There was no time for anyone to scream or swear, cry or think what to do. All Des could do was just hang on, every muscle quivering with effort. Not a noise came from Julia either. She'd been submerged too quickly. No, her head bobbed up momentarily. Back down. A booted foot kicked out. A few seconds later, an object hit a collection of tree roots protruding from the bank. Julia's body? Apparently so.

Slowly, slowly, as the safety cable whipped through water and air, twisting this way and that, it tautened, extended to its full length. *Must still be attached to Julia,* Des thought. *A good sign, although she might be severely battered.* He managed to gasp a few positive words to the rest of his gang. Raye's ashen face turned back toward him momentarily. She didn't appear able to respond to him.

Yes, there was Julia's head. Her scarf was missing — ripped from her head by the water's force, he assumed. But she'd managed to wrap her hands around the tight safety rope and was bobbling up and down at the end like a fishing lure. *Yes, yes,* Des urged her silently. *Cut across the current so we can help you control your position.* A gulp of air, liberally doused with the ever-present rain, enabled him to voice instructions.

"Julia, toward the bank."

As if released from an enchantment, the other three joined in. From the end of the rope, Des coached the team. "Hang on. Move up and toward the left so we tow her in the direction of the bank." They complied. Vision continued to be limited by the downpour, but the heaviness on the line convinced Des that Julia was still attached. Plus, the group's movement back up the slope and over toward stable ground showed they were making progress. He didn't want to think they might be towing dead weight.

Damn! Down went Bill, knee-deep in mud, then planting a facer. The others instinctively stiffened to counterbalance his loss. He struggled up and resumed, covered in grime from chest to toes. Des threw his body backward and felt a distinct 'give,' a brief loosening. Maybe a series of short lunges would help, like reeling in a large game fish. He put his idea into action and was rewarded with a blurred but distinct outline of a form in the rapids. Then a hand appeared and grasped the rope.

"She's moving," Des yelled. "She's alive and trying to get to us."

Sure enough, a second hand and arm shot through the raging waters and grabbed the rope. Then Julia's head, her mouth gasping for breath, foam and dirt swirling around her, pushing her away from the bank and her friends. Again time moved in slow motion as a shoulder appeared. Everyone on the opposite end of the rope was getting into the rhythm Des had set — lunge, dig in heels, lunge, lean toward the side, lunge, let gravity add to the pull.

Inch by inch, Julia moved toward the safety of this side of the flood. Occasionally her head went under again, intermittently her chest surfaced, but she was approaching the sloping bank. Des saw her waggle in the water. She must be feeling some sort of more stable ground under her feet and was trying to gain traction. Yes, her shoulders definitely were out of the water, now her waist. *Blast it*, now she slid back a bit. *There*, she'd recovered and attempted a thigh-stretching stride forward.

Des sensed Raye wanted to let loose and run to the bank to haul Julia to solid ground. "Don't even think about it," he yelled in her ear. "She's got to have firm footing. Then you can help."

Another grimace over her shoulder, but Julia held strong. Only when she staggered from the knee-high flow at the edge of the flood, pitching forward on her face full-length, did Raye drop the rope, rush to haul her up to a sitting position and deliver a bear hug. Heedless of the filth completely covering her friend's front, Raye rubbed her palms up and down Julia's body and head.

"Oh, my God, Julia, are you all right? I don't feel anything out of place. Do you hurt anywhere?" She pushed Julia's hair off her forehead and cheeks, examining her face, then lifting her hands and checking front and back. "You're all scratched up and some bruises are forming." Raye noted Julia's boots, socks, scarf and backpack were missing, stripped from her by the flood's angry force. Only the rope around her chest had saved her from being topless.

One by one the men had released the rope and were grappling to disentangle themselves and their knapsacks from it and one another. Des strode toward Raye and Julia while looping the rope from his palm to his elbow in circles for storage. Next to the pair, he stopped and leaned in, placing a hand on Raye's shoulder. "Don't bother. She's in mild shock." He squatted and turned his attention to Julia, taking her hand in his.

Voice low, he rubbed her fingers. "You're safe now. Relax. The water can't get you here, and we're with you. Take some deep breaths." Tremors began to shudder over Julia. "If you feel shaky, bend your head between your legs." He guided her into the position. Turning to the others, he said, "She's lost some of her clothing and her shoes. It's important to keep her warm. Does anyone have extra clothes, a blanket, scarves we can lend her?" He swiveled on his heels to collect items as people held them out.

Raye scrambled to pull her long muffler from her neck, even though it was sopping wet. "It's wool," she said. "It will help preserve her body heat even though it's soaked."

Bill and Roy both located spare pairs of hiking socks in their knapsacks, and Des pulled the cap from his head.

Julia shook her head and blinked at them all. "I'm okay...now. Thanks to all of you." She tugged on the donated items. The quaver of her voice belied her statement but Des chose to believe her. Since the torrent around them continued unabated, the alternative—that she was incapable of proceeding—was unthinkable.

Raye's earlier words came to mind, and he recalled her warning about a succession of walls wreaking devastation as ravines and chasms first collected water then overflowed, sending new surges downstream. "Given the wall of water that hit us, the rise in water level, and the continuing storm, I think we need to get back to the main group. They're located on a rocky plateau maybe twenty feet above this elevation, which should protect us from any additional rushes that may develop."

"Soldier on, soldier." Bill made a weak joke as he adjusted his clothing and pack. He looked like a child's plump float toy, drenched and abandoned in a bathtub, his baseball cap useless, drooping, leaking rivulets of water. Next to him Roy wrapped his sweater-clad arms around himself for warmth and hoisted his shoulders to help protect his neck.

"Let me give you a drink first," said Des. He fumbled at his backpack for a water bottle, uncapped it and tilted it for Julia. "Does anyone have chocolate or other sweets? She needs lots of calories fast for the hike ahead."

Raye fumbled in the back pocket of her knapsack without removing it by crooking her elbow. She held a clenched fist high. "M&Ms," she said, transferring most of her hoard to Julia but retaining a few for herself. Julia looked as grateful as a starving puppy for the handout.

As she sucked on the treat, Des dropped his pack to the ground and whipped his orange-and-tan field jacket off, taking her arms one by one to thrust into the coat's sleeves, wrapping its oversized body around her. Then he undid his windbreaker from around his waist and donned it.

"How are the Chosen Twenty-Five minus two?" Julia said, in a faint voice.

"They're fine," said Raye, with a grin, "except for missing your bunch." She murmured to Des, "If she's cracking jokes, she's recovering."

"Okay, team, up and at 'em," Des snapped in his best officer's tone. There was no hesitation from anyone. As one, they set off after him, helping each other over rough spots, lending a hand to sock-clad Julia, who had the biggest challenge.

A surge of astonishment clogged Des' throat as he caught a glimpse of his rag-tag troop. Not one of them had complained, no one asked for special treatment, all moved as quickly and efficiently as the individual's body allowed. He couldn't have asked for more effort from them. They may not have had the excellent physical condition of soldiers or athletes, but their determination and courage could not be matched.

He bent his head into the slanting, frigid rain. Mud sucked each step into the mire, making movement forward like maneuvering through thick chocolate frosting, minus the happiness that usually accompanied a cake at a party. No, he amended. He was happy, and he bet the others were, too, simply for their own survival. *So far.* They still had a distance to go. Wind lashed the branches of aspens and bushes until they bowed and touched the ground. Some of the fury's power originated in the waters crashing downstream only feet from them. Gushers of liquid shot up from the torrent and banks. It was useless to try to escape the inundation gushing from the sky, cascading off the vegetation and making it impossible even to wipe water off his face.

Beside and below them, but not far enough away to reassure Des, thundered the rumbling, angry flood waters, so even strident conversation was impossible. A sort of trail remained visible, although every so often the waters ate through the bank, which crumbled off into the flow like an over-baked cake.

Barely evident as an orb, the sun would soon set and visibility would decrease even more. Des patted the pockets on the front of his jeans to locate the flashlight he knew he'd shoved into one of them. Yes, it was there in case they didn't escape this mess before dark, but if they were lucky, they'd reunite with their colleagues in the not-too-distant future, provided the path was passable and the gully no fuller than before—and if everyone in their little group continued to function.

"Des, Des." A bellow came from the end of the line of hikers. Raye was calling. "Stop! We've got to stop!"

Chapter Twenty-Seven

He called a halt and everyone slumped in relief. Raye and Julia limped forward. Julia leaned heavily on Raye's left arm that circled her waist.

"This isn't working," said Raye as she reached Des. "The socks are unraveling and getting holes in them. We're going to have to carry her or do something for shoes."

Bill and Roy came in close and all five leaned in, like horses sheltering in a pasture. While some were debating what to do, Bill shrugged off his backpack and opened it. "Okay. This may sound screwy, but I have a large plastic water bottle. How about if we cut it in half and trim it down to fit the bottom of Julia's feet? That would give her some protection."

"How does she keep them on?" Roy said.

"If any of us have especially long shoestrings, we can cut some off. We don't need to lace our boots all the way up," said Bill.

"Great idea!" Des bent down to unlace his shoestrings. His boots extended a good four inches above his ankle, so the laces had to be seventy-two inches.

In short order, using Des' Swiss Army knife, Bob sawed away at his water bottle to cut it in half, trimmed off the useless top, and poked holes on both sides of each section so laces could be tied across. Others donated pieces of material — handkerchiefs, gloves, spare small clothing — to pad Julia's feet from the hard soles.

"It's not great, but it should do," said Des.

Bob's proud grin spread across his face, and Julia sighed with satisfaction. The new accessory infused not only additional energy but also humor into their group. Julia pranced back and forth a few feet, wriggling her bright blue handmade sandals at the crew, who applauded and cheered.

"Okay," said Raye. "I suggest Julia lead the way, since she's the best-dressed. And remember, *todos somos luchadoras!* We are all fighters!"

This got the group moving again. Des dropped to the rear to confer with Raye. "Inspired and inspiring," he said to her, lowering his voice below the roar of the flood that continued unabated next to them. "But brace yourself. Even worse is ahead of us."

"What do you mean? We got them off the dangerous peninsula. We're on this side. Now all we have to do is get back to the main group."

He stared straight ahead, as if hesitant to reveal bad news. "Let me rephrase. We have an exciting challenge. The water in the stream has risen by ten to twelve feet. The path back to our party, which we're on now, is descending. Remember the gully we had to ford on the way here? It's bound to be inundated for yards on either side. There's no way we'll be able to get across there."

Raye gave a soft groan. "I've been thinking one step ahead. I never thought of the rest of the trail. What should I prepare for?"

"The best scenario would be to scale the mountain and cut directly across the rise. If I recall, I don't think it's impossibly steep. The worst? To find the way impassable and be forced to shelter close to here."

"What? No cover, no way to keep warm, no food? Impossible. At least with the main group, we'd have more body heat as well as pooled resources and the protection of the overhang."

"We may not have a choice."

Raye wished a fairy would appear and whisk her away, preferably to a spa where a good warm soak and massage awaited—or that this was all a bad dream and she'd wake in her bedroom at home, surrounded by photos of her friends and family. At the least, she could collapse on the ground and weep. Since none of these were about to happen, she kept plodding, each boot feeling heavier by the step. When, at the head of the line, Julia resumed singing, *Lluvia, lluvia*, Raye felt about as much like jumping into the flood as she did singing, and only her determination not to discourage the others compelled her to join in.

The scene as they approached the gully gave her little hope. They didn't need to stumble to the top of the channel to make a decision. In fact, they couldn't even approach it. As the trail they were on started to plunge toward the gully, a backwash had completely filled the whole elevation. No way could they safely traverse it to continue their trip. The five stopped as one.

"I'll be a monkey's uncle," said Raye, so stunned she couldn't have moved if a tree fell toward her.

"I hope not," said Des. She smacked his arm, even while thinking, *What a guy. Nothing can bring him down.*

"I'm not eager to spend the night out here," said Roy. "One of the triggers for my asthma is cold weather. We're very exposed in this position."

The rest of them agreed with Roy, when Des spoke up. "Fortunately the mountainside's incline is gentle. True, there's no trail, but I think we can go directly across the ridge and approach the route the others took to higher ground."

"Isn't the way really rough?" said Julia.

"Yes. But it's that or bunk down on this inhospitable, rocky, muddy, narrow trail."

"Plus, if the water's already up this far, what can we do if we're hit with another wall?" said Raye.

"*Nada*," said Julia as she rocked on her unusual hiking sandals. "I'm the worst equipped, and I say to go for it."

Once again pausing to share water, candy and trail mix as needed, they began to climb up and over. Raye launched another musical round of *Rain, Rain, Go Away*.

Des' prediction was correct. The small group spotted the rocky ledge outcropping from the mountain after only ten minutes. They were about halfway between the primary trail the squads had walked in the morning and the refuge where most of their co-workers now gathered. Several, including

Ben, were surveying the flood waters and the downslope.

"Whoo-hooo!" Raye sang out, and she swung her arms high in the air. The others joined in, hollering and cheering, to be met with the same jubilant noises from their co-workers above. Now eight or ten heads peered over the edge of the outcropping, smiles wreathing their faces, hands waving.

Des schlepped through the muddy undergrowth until the crew reached the passageway their co-workers had originally used to climb the ascent. He stepped to the side to allow the others to precede him. As the quintet labored upward through sheets of rain that continued to pour down, they mounted the outcrop. Plenty of assistance was offered, with an intertwining of fingers here and a grasp of elbow or arm there.

While the women in the group grabbed one another and hugged, Ben approached Des. "What's the condition of your troop?" he asked, automatically using the military term he must have been accustomed to.

"Not bad, sir," said Des, responding to both Ben's position as a senior vice president for Pursuit as well as his former Army position. "Julia's the worst of the bunch. But aside from losing some of her things, being nearly drowned, then walking a distance in plastic soles, she's in amazing condition. They're all real survivors. How about your company?"

"Pretty well, pretty well." Ben swiveled on his heel to inspect the people from Pursuit. Approval slowly relaxed his features. "Other than the chief, very few complaints. Sure, lots of apprehension, debates and theories about what happened and what's coming but some seem to gain energy from the challenges they're facing."

"And Mr. Van Voorst?"

"Doesn't seem to be in immediate danger."

"Any sign of rescue? From what I can tell, we're going to have a real ordeal returning some of our people to the lodge. I was hoping the authorities would call up helicopters. It's unlikely, of course, until the deluge stops and they can evaluate the situation."

Crossing his arms, Ben chewed his lip lightly. "You're right. We're going to have to bed down here for the night. Even if the downpour ends, I'm sure any rescue effort will wait for full daylight before sending out a team."

"So the next step is to inventory food, water and coverings?"

Ben nodded as Raye materialized at Des's elbow. "Still no mobile connections," she said. "What now, oh fearless leaders?"

That got a chuckle from both men. "We're just agreeing we need to check with Tim and Mason about the inventory of supplies," said Des. "And if there's anything that can be used for covering. We're fortunate there's some protection, what with the overhang of the hillside as well as brush."

"And that the outcropping we're on is mainly rock," added Ben.

Des, Raye and Ben appraised the group in front of them. All the marooned looked restless. Some milled around the small space on the ledge, some chatted with one another. The entire bunch appeared exhausted and wet. "I think if we give them some tasks, they'll perk up," Raye said.

"Agreed." Des called Mason and Tim over from where they'd stopped in a shallow, water-filled indentation on the rock ledge. They couldn't have appeared more miserable than if they'd gotten their severance notices, but they brightened up considerably at his appeal. "I know you made a list of supplies several hours ago, but the three of us"—he glanced at Ben and Raye—"think it's now time for rationing. Do you agree?" Mason's and Tim's chests swelled visibly at the honor of being consulted, and they nodded vigorously. "Am I correct that individuals still have their own supplies?"

Again the other two men nodded.

Ben took charge. In the way that informal groups seem to acknowledge a leader when he steps forward, the Pursuit employees snapped to attention as Ben raised a hand and spoke. "Folks, you don't need me to tell you we're in a precarious position. Our mobiles won't connect and we've seen no attempt at rescue. Still, we've got to believe the danger is minimal. We're all together now, we're in a somewhat sheltered location and none of us is seriously injured or ill. And"—he paused for dramatic effect—"I've seen no signs of vampires, zombies or wild beasts, so we're safe for now."

The crowd laughed, *with a little too much gusto for such a lame joke*, thought Des. Not that he was complaining, even to himself. Humor always made people feel more optimistic.

"On the plus side," said Ben, "if you have a co-worker you've always wanted to be closer to, now's your chance. We're quarantined here, at least for the night. We're already wet and chilled. We may get cold. So be prepared to snuggle together and share coats, scarves, sweaters, gloves, whatever. Remember, what happens on this mountain stays on this mountain." A second burst of chuckles.

Des rocked on his heels, hands stuffed in pockets, and inspected the twenty-seven humans totally reliant on themselves and good luck. "As for food and water, I'm asking each of you to dig in your packs and pockets and remove every single one of these items. Mason and Tim will circulate to collect these and store them in one cache. We'll have someone monitor and distribute these supplies fairly. Of course, anyone who's not in tiptop shape" — most eyes swiveled toward Mr. Van Voorst — "or has other special circumstances will have top priority."

"Like what?" someone shouted.

"Like diabetes or pregnancy. Anyone here pregnant? And willing to admit it?" Another round of giggles.

"We should choose the monitors," came a suggestion from a man Des recognized as definitely not a fan of Mason's or Tim's. "I suggest Julia and Raye."

Maintaining the teasing spirit of the proceedings, Raye said, "Suuurrre. Let the women do the housework."

As a ripple of motion moved through the crowd, Des could tell the proposed monitors were popular. He agreed mentally. People trusted the two women, and he knew they'd be absolutely fair as well as sensitive to special needs.

"Okay. All in favor?" said Ben.

The crowd roared, but as the din lessened, people looked at one another, then away at the sky, the forest, the flood below. They rubbed their arms, buttoned their coats up to the chin, shuffled their feet. Des knew uncertainty strongly flavored with fear was building and his colleagues needed something positive to do and focus on.

"You and Julia move to that little hillock," he murmured to Raye. "We've got to get these folks acting, not reacting."

Chapter Twenty-Eight

"I agree," Raye said. "I'll empty my knapsack so we have a place to protect any snacks we gather." She strolled over to Julia, who was perched on a rock at the edge of the ledge, and consulted with her.

As Des and Ben watched the two women, the older man commented. "If we'd wanted a personalized method to evaluate our employees for traits like leadership, initiative and determination, we couldn't have ordered a better trial than this catastrophe. My eyes have certainly been opened in regard to some of our staff." His glance flicked toward Mason and Tim. "Others have shown unexpected talent in leadership and planning. You, of course, are performing exactly how I would have predicted."

"And is that good or bad for me?"

Ben chuckled. "Fishing for a compliment? You have nothing to worry about in regard to the ultimate purpose of this retreat."

"I thought it was to compete for a prize."

"Yes-s-s." Ben laced the answer with insinuation. "You might be surprised to learn there's more to the exercise."

Des questioned whether Ben should be revealing anything to him. He gave a mental shrug. Over the years he'd known superiors who strengthened the loyalty and built the skills of subordinates by confiding in them. He admitted to himself that he felt flattered Ben trusted him. "And what is that?"

"I don't need to ask you to keep this confidential. Permanently. Van Voorst and I believed we could get a good reading on top level managers to guide us as Pursuit tightens its corporate belt. There'll be some layoffs as well as some promotions as we restructure."

His throat tightened as Des thought about Raye. As a single mother, she couldn't afford to lose her job. As bad for him personally, he'd only begun connecting with her, and if they didn't work together, growing closer could prove impossible. Then there was Julia, who was becoming a friend. Although younger, she was equally vulnerable in the importance of her employment. "You can't mean, uh... You haven't reached decisions...um. Do you know already what direction you're leaning?"

"Do you have a concern?" Ben asked.

"Raye? And Julia?" The words popped out before he could think, but then he paused. *Never hurts to think twice before speaking,* Des told himself. Then he recalled his mother's advice, *'In for a dime, in for a dollar.'* In other words, if he started something, he should see it through. He cleared his throat. "Sir, I feel a responsibility to speak up. I know you personally wouldn't ever be affected by someone's sex when decisions are being made. After all, you're—"

"Black?"

"Yes."

"Des, it's okay for you to mention that. I've known it for years."

Des chuckled. He should have known what Ben's response would be. Still, he recalled Julia and Raye's words when they'd been on the patio, chomping on bagels. "But—"

"But?"

Des took a deep breath. "I've heard some talk about instances in which Pursuit could be more aggressive about promoting qualified women."

"Oh, really?"

"Yes. I trust you're not offended."

"No. Not at all. I simply think we should discuss this further at a later time. Preferably when we're off this damned mountain and back in a warm place with food."

Des studied Ben. Nothing in his demeanor or responses hinted at negativity. Des decided to relax and let things take their course. Certainly nothing could be accomplished here and now. "Right. Well, guess I'll go help with the supplies." Making a small gesture with his right hand that came close to a salute, he grabbed his backpack and made his way to Raye and Julia.

"Need extra storage?" he called as he held the bag high.

"Sure thing," Raye said as she reached for it. "But what's happened to it?" Small clumps of mud clung to the material, and the entire bottom was covered with grasses, leaves and twigs. "Looks like you tried for a camouflage effect. It was pristine this morning and now it's filthy. Did it receive a baptism by fire?"

"No, by flood," said Des with a grin.

Moving slowly to stretch out the chores — after all, what could they do with fifteen and a half granola bars, seven partial boxes of raisins and craisins, some candy bars, M&Ms and a miscellaneous assortment of partial bags of trail mix? — the trio organized and packed supplies.

"At least the rain's tapering off again," said Julia.

"Which brings up the other essential we're short on," Des said. "Drinking water. We should try to collect some as it falls. That will be less polluted than catching run-off from plants or ground."

"I wonder what's happening upstream and downstream from us?" said Julia. "Is this location better or worse off?"

"No way to tell until help shows up," Des said. "All we can do is stay together and keep our spirits high."

"I had an idea for an activity everyone can participate in." Raye spoke with forced enthusiasm "I think we should start a pool about when we're going to get rescued. Except…"

"Except what?" said Des.

"I don't know how to set up a pool." She slumped in mock exhaustion.

"A perfect activity for that group of layabouts on the other side of our little refuge. They look as if they've run out of busy work." Des considered about twelve of their fellows who were tossing twigs into the swollen waters beneath the ledge. He grabbed his now-grubby backpack, dug in a waterproof pocket and pulled out pencil and small notepad. Before pacing toward them, he silently marveled at the relatively high morale demonstrated so far among his colleagues, but he wasn't about to allow them time to brood over what they couldn't change, such as falling temperatures, low supplies of drinking water and lack of privacy for personal functions. That little challenge had been solved much earlier by declaring a corner as private and shoving some small branches in the ground and hillside as a visual barrier, but it still was barely adequate.

"Hey there, dude," said Tim, as he approached. "Glad to see you back. We're about to search for some dry wood to start a fire. Warm us up and be a signal at the same time."

"And you have matches?" Des was unsure whether this idea was a good one. He doubted dry wood could be had within five miles, but the hunt would occupy some of those currently twiddling their thumbs, and, if successful, would do much to improve everyone's comfort.

"No. I have a cigarette lighter. I still smoke occasionally," said Tim with a hint of embarrassment.

"What luck. Good for you." Des slapped him on the back. "Another suggestion. How about running a pool for the hour of rescue?"

"Don't you mean day of rescue?" joked Mason. A general moan greeted this statement.

"I certainly hope we're not here for days," said Des.

Chapter Twenty-Nine

With absolutely zilch left to organize of the few supplies on hand, Raye and Julia did what comes naturally to two women friends bored and on their own. They gossiped.

"Are you dried out yet?" asked Raye.

"Pretty much. That last trek to here got my blood circulating," said Julia. "Right now I'm more tired than anything. I'd love to stretch out."

Raye looked overhead and around. Although not visible through a dark cloud cover, the sun was descending, and its rays fought the showers still scattering the area. While most of the ledge was rocky, patches of muddy earth seemed to glow with suppressed reflected light. "We could relax on the ground. After all, we're about as filthy as we can get."

They promptly sat down, trying to use the mountainside that ascended behind them for some protection. Up and down the ledge others followed their lead, except for the small group across the way around Des. Raye noticed he was the vortex of that collection. All eyes were on him, and camaraderie accompanied by friendly masculine punches on the arm orbited the circle. She marveled at his high spirits, even if they were feigned to bolster other people's optimism. He looked as comfortable as if he were in his own living room. A kind of charisma drew others to him, relaxed them and encouraged friendly banter.

Julia bent her legs and circled them with her arms, then spoke softly. "So, what's up with you and the big guy?"

"Nothing." Raye flushed. "Nothing at all. We're still together on our squad."

"So I noticed. You seem to work well together."

"Do we have a choice here, now?"

"There are lots of people who aren't cooperating and doing their best. Take Krystle. Her constant, upbeat cheeping has vanished. All she's done is complain, whine and moan. She seems incapable of figuring out how to function in this crisis."

"Yes," said Raye. "And those two boy wonders, Mason and Tim. I didn't know them well before this retreat, and I'd never voluntarily work with them again."

"Unlike the big guy."

"Unlike the big guy," Raye admitted.

"What do you think of him now? I know you were suspicious of him before. You had doubts about whether you could trust him, if he were genuine."

Raye copied Julia's position and drew her knees up. With nightfall, the chill factor had escalated and her teeth chattered. "I have to admit he seems absolutely solid. When we trekked to locate you, I could rely on him. Not only physically, although he's in great shape and has the strength of an ox, but his judgments were also careful and considered, and he weighs his options before he decides. He's not bossy, not convinced he's always right."

"Hmmm. I told you I thought you and he would make a good pair."

"Listen. We're not talking about a romantic relationship here." As Raye spoke, her heart gave a leap. She sternly suppressed it.

"Really? Last night you seemed headed that way until I left for bed. Then this morning—was it only this morning? Unbelievable. I met you, and you acted as pissed as hell. I figured it was a lovers' tiff. But you and Des have been together ever since, and now you're acting not lovey-dovey, but in sync."

"I guess we are. That doesn't mean we're together. We both have our own lives to consider. My top priority has got to be Andy." Andy's face came to mind, his boy-teetering-on-the-edge-of-manhood appearance, a shadow of beard, the light in his face when he talked about his dream of becoming a psychologist or mentioned his rock band's new playlist. She never wanted disappointment to cloud his life, although she was realistic enough to know she couldn't shield him from failure and mistakes. Just as baby Andy had to fall and skin his knees to learn how to walk, adolescent Andy had to discover his strengths and weaknesses through experience.

Here she sat, cradling that little kernel of enlightenment close to her. She missed him terribly. Did he have an inkling of the situation she was in? Or were he and his grandfather sitting around to watch an action movie, play a video game or chow down on popcorn? For the past few evenings she'd squeezed in a quick telephone call, even though contacts with the outside world had been discouraged. What would he think when she failed to ring? *Probably nothing.*

It was impossible to comprehend the changes in her life in less than twenty-four hours. What was the saying? *Man proposes, God disposes. Better yet, man plans, God laughs.* No, everything didn't revolve around Andy. She knew that. But ultimately, protecting his welfare directed her life. No way could she let the temptation of a relationship with Des threaten that. Standard good business practices actively discouraged relationships between co-workers. She needed her job, depended on it absolutely. It wasn't as if she were beating off corporate headhunters. Anyway, the competition and strategizing for the big prize at the retreat automatically made her and Des rivals, not romantic partners.

She'd been fortunate today, she knew. A few scratches and bruises and a thorough soaking were the sum total of her adversity. She hoped she hadn't used up all her good luck during the retreat. She prayed enough remained for her to win the award.

A quiet interjection shook Raye out of her thoughts. Des materialized at her feet. "I've done all I can do right now with the rowdies." He nodded at the group he'd been talking to. "They're not ready to relax. I think anxiety's keeping their blood pressure up. They finished the pool and gave up the idea of a fire when they realized all the wood in our vicinity was wet. Now they're lobbing pebbles at a target. Better than at one another. But I think those of us who realize we're exhausted should try to rest."

"Agreed," said Raye and Julia simultaneously.

"Why don't you sit down between us," said Julia, her voice ringing with innocence. "You can keep both of us cozy." She winked the eye away from Des at Raye. Before Raye could object, he agreed.

"How can I reject an offer like that? Two beautiful women?" Des took his place in the middle and slung an arm around each of them

Definitely warmer, Raye thought, *though I'll never get to sleep.* As drowsiness made her head nod and her muscles relax, and as she was trying to decide if a glimmer of moonlight was evident, she fell asleep.

* * * *

The uncomfortable poke of a sharp object in her ribs woke her up some time later. She shifted on ground as hard as a rock when she realized the surface she was resting on was, indeed, rock. Burying her head under a warm cover, she came to partial awareness. Her legs were frozen and her knees ached and cramped. Then she remembered she had no blankets, duvets or quilts. What was over her, keeping her torso warm? She lifted her arm and felt the weight of someone else's arm go up, too. Julia's, she knew by instinct. *Where is Des?*

Up she sat, shifting the cover which she now saw was Des' heavy jacket. Her movement disturbed Julia, too, who rubbed her eyes with knuckled fists, mumbling, "What's happening?"

"Looks like the middle of the night," said Raye. "And Des is nowhere in sight. He left us protected with his jacket, but where is he?" She peered through the shadows at other figures huddled together in small clusters across the ledge. Though the clouds had disappeared, a full moon illuminated the upper reaches and stars shone brilliantly, dazzlingly — typical for these mountains. She still couldn't spot him. She stood, shaking herself loose from his coat. A light, she needed a light. Then she remembered the flashlight in her knapsack, so she rummaged in its depths until she located it.

The beam, bright as a star, circled and bobbed, its aureolae throbbing with greater intensity, like a bullseye. Three forms lay on one another in a heap on one side of the mountain shelf, a cluster of most of the stranded huddled around two upright yet snoozing figures, which Raye surmised were Mr. Van Voorst and Olivia. Everyone had taken refuge with at least one additional person to benefit from shared body heat. Even as she looked, one individual reared up then sat. Ben's eyes shone from his dark features, and when he noticed she was awake, he got to his feet, wrapped his jacket tighter around himself, pulled his maroon beret down securely over his ears and picked his way to her. She shone her flashlight at his feet to help him.

"Do you know where Des went?" she whispered. "I fell asleep, and when I woke up, he was gone."

"He told me he was going to check out the terrain nearby," said Ben. "We can't be sure rescuers will be able to find us easily any time soon. We may need to march out on our own."

"Isn't that dangerous?" Raye couldn't control the quiver in her voice. "Wild animals, unsure footing, more bad weather? He could fall or be swept into the flood waters."

Ben shot her a sharp look. "Worried?" She nodded. "I wouldn't. He's a big boy with lots of experience in potentially dangerous situations. He went to reconnoiter. In addition to the full moon, I lent him my high intensity LED, and he said his own was fully charged. He's the type who can't sit still for any length of time and needs to be solving problems. He'd want you to sleep, not knock around the woods worried about him."

"I can't sleep." *Not with Des gone*, she added to herself.

"Then at least relax. You'll probably need every ounce of energy tomorrow."

"You're right." She wasn't doing anyone any good fretting like this. "I'll get some rest. You, too." She squeezed his arm briefly and returned to her place by Julia, watching Ben retreat to his original spot. Julia stirred at her side and sat up.

"What's up?"

Raye pulled her legs toward her chest and wrapped her arms around her knees for warmth. A quivering moan arose from her diaphragm. "Ben says Des went to scout out the area and see what we can do on our own tomorrow, in case there's no sign of rescue."

"I'm sure there will be. Of course the lodge would have notified the authorities when we didn't return."

"We don't know if they have power or some form of communication—if they're even above water. Can you remember what the layout of the land was around there?"

Julia squinted as if to reconstruct mentally what the grounds close to the lodge looked like. "The area around the lodge entrance is flat, but I know we hiked down quite a bit when we headed toward the trail. Then the path itself ascended some."

"The stream's a distance from the building, so even with the flood, I don't think the water would have gotten clear over to the facility. Anyway, I'm more worried about Des right now. What in the hell does he mean wandering all over these mountains in the middle of the night, unfamiliar with the terrain, no back-up, no one knowing where he is?" Raye said.

"You sound worried."

"I am. Aren't you?"

"Not as much as you." Julia pressed both palms over her mouth to hide her giggles, eventually rolling over on her side because of the strength of her mirth. "Oh, Raye. You've been slapped upside the head and punched in the gut. You're in lu-u-uv."

"I am not. I barely know the man." Surely emotions were something she could control through sheer effort. No way this man she'd known for such a short time was threatening her peace of mind.

"Then you're in lust. Have a crush. Whatever."

"Keep your voice down." Raye checked the environs for any twitching eavesdroppers or tossing limbs indicating wakefulness. "I don't need any random gossip in this group about my personal life."

"I notice you're not denying it."

A wind, which had been breathing softly for some time, now picked up strength. Raye heard the whisper of evergreen limbs brushing against one another and bending in the breeze. The brushstrokes of clouds still remaining overhead were swept away. There was no diminishing of the water's din below the mountain side, but during the hours the castaways had been asleep, most of the shrieks and clangs and bangs of large items in the flood had stopped. *All of the large debris must be miles downstream by now.* Surely the gradual return of the weather to normalcy must be a good sign, and her psychological state would soon do the same.

Who am I kidding? Every second she spent with Des made her value him more. Their beliefs, their actions, moved smoothly in sync. The thought of him injured in these dark mountains or disappearing off the face of the earth created pain as if she'd wounded herself. thought

"I have no need to contradict you," Raye said. "What I have to do is decide what in the hell I'm going to do next."

Stretching out to recline gingerly onto the rocky surface, she closed her eyes with no hope for sleep.

"All I know is the sparks fly between you two every time you brush up against one another," said Julia. "*Muy caliente*. Hot, hot. So you jump his bones," she whispered in Raye's ear.

"I can't," Raye whispered back. "I'm a mother. Mothers don't do things like that."

"Of course they do. How do you think they get to be mothers?"

"Maybe before their first baby — or after their kids are grown. Certainly not when they have kids at home and one of them is a teenager who might, just might, be toying with the idea of having sex himself. How would I keep a straight face delivering advice and lectures to him?"

Julia turned to her back and exhaled. "I'm not suggesting you stay out overnight all the time or run naked through your condo with Des chasing you. It wouldn't hurt for you to give him a little encouragement, though."

"I've got to focus on my career and my son," said Raye. "No matter how tempting a strong, stable, intelligent, funny guy may be, you know how poor I was when Andy was born. I didn't want to admit I'd made a mistake with Michael or that I couldn't take care of myself."

"Yeah, that's when you were a waitress then a retail salesclerk, then a masseuse with your own business."

"Yeah. And I went broke and nearly starved. That's why I'd never do anything to endanger my position at Pursuit Telecom with its nice benefits package. You know we're discouraged from dating co-workers. I'm sorry, but the uncertainty of getting to know Des better can't compete with medical and dental coverage, annual leave, short-term disability insurance and retirement."

"They won't keep you warm at night."

"I've obsessed over money plenty of times," Raye said, "and everything it does or doesn't buy—rent, house payments, hot water heaters blowing up, car leases, snow tires, clothes, guitar lessons, replacement home appliances, Christmas presents, little tiny vacations to cheap motels... The list's endless. How am I supposed to save for emergencies? For Andy's college? My brilliant plan to invest in lottery tickets has accomplished zip. I've got to win this competition."

"You have no control over that now. We're at the mercy of fate. Forget about it." Julia started breathing in deeply and exhaling through her mouth, an annoying sequence after about ten repetitions.

"What are you doing?" Raye said when the cycle seemed never-ending.

"I'm trying to unwind. It's a meditation technique. You concentrate on inhaling and exhaling to wipe your mind clear of worries. Let the universe speak to you and through you."

"Does it work? Will it wipe out the effects of being threatened by a flash flood? Even nearly drowning like you were?"

"Try it."

For several minutes the two women breathed in and out in unison. When Julia's breathing slowed and the normal sequence of sleep overtook her, Raye decided she wasn't a good candidate for meditation. Regardless of her efforts, she couldn't free her mind of a frantic round of what-ifs. What if through sheer chance she tripped off the mountain — or a sidewalk — and broke her ankle, permanently disabling herself? What if the downturn in the economy continued and she was laid off? How would she support herself and Andy? What if she was walking down the street and a driver lost control of his car and ran over her? What if a tornado followed this flash flood and she never got rescued?

Chapter Thirty

She rolled onto her side. She knew these incidents were highly unlikely, but, after all, so was a huge flash flood, trapping her and her co-workers. She tugged Des' jacket more firmly around her body. It held his scent, faint as a nearly forgotten dream. Inevitably, with the power of a strong magnet, her thoughts embraced him. She hoped, prayed, he was okay. If he were freezing cold, that would serve him right for deserting her, but she didn't want him catching pneumonia or falling off a cliff.

The cold made her nose drip and she sniffed. That didn't help. In fact, the effect multiplied, and her eyes filled and overflowed. Dabbing at her cheeks with the sleeve of Des' jacket, she scolded herself. How could she be weepy and depressed after everything she and her co-workers had endured? They'd escaped with their lives and virtually no injuries. Now it was simply a matter of enduring tedious boredom and discomfort until rescue appeared.

Except for the small matter of Des. Nothing could happen to him. He had to be okay. She realized her entire body had tensed, every muscle contracted, so she made a valiant attempt to relax, limb by limb. What was wrong with her? She knew he was a strong, intelligent man, possessing many more survival skills than she did. But somehow his safety had become top priority in her mind.

Flopping to her other side, she peered at the mountain's inky silhouette next to her, submerged in an infinite navy-blue pool with floating stars. Strange how the weather had changed from fine to terrible and back to fine in the space of less than a day. Strange how people who'd arrived in these mountains without knowing one another beyond a polite 'good morning' and 'good evening' had learned they could depend on each other for help in an emergency. Strange how a man she'd felt no ties to, no sympathy with, now seemed as familiar as her own right arm. And if he disappeared? It would be as if she'd lost that arm.

Patterns. Patterns everywhere, in nature, in human behavior. She buried her face in the crook of one arm, not to sleep but to enter that half-dream state which supplants both slumber and consciousness in times of stress and conditions of extreme pressure. She knew people were nearby, and they, too, were struggling to keep themselves calm, hopeful. All any of them could accomplish was to while away the hours until dawn in dim shadows, populated by their cohorts or by ghosts. Like her, they surely lacked the energy and courage to discover which.

* * * *

In the early morning light, Des stared down at the sleeping women snuggled against one another. Raye's arm enfolded Julia, whose leg was thrown over the other woman's thigh. Des' jacket managed to stretch from one side across to the other. They couldn't be comfortable, he thought, yet they must, to be so unresponsive to the birds' songs, loud and mellifluous with individual melodies. The earliest rays of the sun slanted across the plateau, still barely able to alleviate the night's gloom, while vertical shadows of trees seemed to stretch as long as the mountains they pierced.

There was no reason to wake the women. With the dearth of food and water, absence of news or contacts, hours were best spent in a state of suspended animation. Lacking that, to be unconscious if possible. He parked his tush on a collection of pine needles at the base of a tree, leaned back against the trunk and closed his eyes to take his own advice. It was a challenge when his thoughts circled like a whirlpool around his discovery during his midnight hike. If and when they survived their ordeal, he had to guarantee Raye was his for life. The hours of absence from her had taught him that life without her would be a constant battle for mere survival that was not worth waging. As for the contradiction between his priorities of Claudia and Raye, he'd figure something out. Everything didn't have to be solved at once.

Several hours later, he regained awareness bit by bit, with no shock, no anxiety, as if slipping away from the soft caress of a summer breeze. He fluttered his eyelashes and realized Raye was sitting at his side, studying him as he'd slept.

She looked wonderful. He didn't say a word, simply gazed his fill. The storm and the night out in the open hadn't been kind to her hair, which was snarled and knotted under the scarf she still sported. Yet the effect was as natural, as fresh, as vibrant as the living vines and branches tangled in the landscape. Whatever makeup she may have had on the previous day had been washed away, but she needed no artifice. Was the mountain air responsible? Her natural good looks? His joy at seeing her and remembering the dangers they'd survived? He didn't know and didn't analyze.

"You're gorgeous." The words slipped from him without conscious decision.

"Probably because I'm alive and unharmed and got some sleep," she said with a twist of her lips, "thanks to the offering you left me. How was your adventure?"

"A failure." He groaned and threw his head back with an "ouch" as he thudded with the tree trunk. He closed his eyes. "I found nothing. Despite plenty of illumination from the moon and flashlights, no other marooned hikers, no secret and easy path out and certainly no rescuers." Now he was dealing with the effects of yesterday's constant damp, the lack of food and decent sleep, the strain of struggles to move in new, challenging and strenuous ways. "I don't suppose you have a cup of hot, strong black coffee on you?"

"No, but we do have a bit of water. Remember? Last night we set all the water bottles up along the edge of the plateau and collected some. While you were catching your Zs, I checked."

"That'll work. Then we need to start planning what to do with this crew." He struggled to his feet with a growl, stretched in several directions, rotated his shoulders and smoothed down his hair. "Who's awake?"

"Almost everyone."

"Then let's go talk to Ben. He's the person in charge for now. I assume Mr. Van Voorst's condition hasn't improved significantly."

"No. He's holding his own, but he's better off with as little stress as possible." She scrambled up and adjusted her clothes as best she could but avoided his eyes.

Something's wrong, he thought. He wondered what. As she swung around to head in Ben's direction, Des stopped her with a hand on her arm. "You're upset. I don't want my partner to get into a tizzy. What is it?"

She looked up and straight into his pupils. He'd never seen a gaze so guileless. He could have fallen into those eyes, bottomless, laced with the unknown. Before he could get carried away with the romance of it all, she sputtered. "Don't you ever, ever do anything like that again. Disappear without a word to me."

"No, ma'am," he said.

"When I woke up and saw you were missing, I thought I'd die."

"Yes, ma'am."

"Do you realize what could have happened to you out there? The dangers?"

"I hear you," he said. "Now let's drop the subject."

She drew in a breath as if to continue but simply expelled air. He slung an arm around her shoulder and squeezed her close as they strolled toward the cluster around Ben. All the while he wondered but gave thanks that somehow, he seemed to have made a place for himself in her heart. *Have I been too curt?* he asked himself as he noticed all animation abandon her features. *I should let her know something of what I'm feeling, even if we're early days.* He halted to put both arms on her shoulders, then said, "I know one thing that I hope you realize, too. You're much more to me than a temporary partner at a corporate retreat. It seems almost like we were destined to be together."

She gulped and liveliness lit her up from within. "The same for me. About you, I mean."

He waited, but she added nothing. *I can tell she's still incredulous, still not willing to take a huge risk. No problem. I'll wait.* He released her shoulders but kept one arm around her.

As they crossed the rocky plateau, they saw the destruction wreaked by the storm far below and around. The waters had receded significantly, leaving devastation in their wake. This was no small incident, nothing to be minimized or glossed over. In places on the lower slopes and by the stream, the ground had been scoured clean of any living thing, along with all pebbles, stones, limbs and paraphernalia. There was mud on the banks, while the water continued to escape the normal confines of the stream. That material looked like a giant child had pushed clay or Play-Doh into huge swirls. Here and there the water had dropped debris, much of it piled behind large items like a toppled tree trunk, even a vehicle, to collect like a junkyard

Up a bit from the flow, rain had driven new crevices and gullies into the mountainside, cut cliffs that dropped straight down, made the slopes steeper and robbed the mountain of some of its ground, using avalanches of dirt. Here and continuing higher, the force of wind and rain had ripped leaves and small twigs from trees and bushes, leaving them scattered afar. By the time the couple reached Ben, they lacked the ability to make any comments, as language provided a puny method to express the emotions they held in.

"We need to decide on a strategy," he said. "Des, did you discover anything that might help us get back to the lodge?"

Des dropped his arm from around Raye. "Nothing. The full moon gave me plenty of light, and the flashlights lit up the shadows. There wasn't a person, not a human sound, not a vehicle in sight, no sign of anything that could facilitate a rescue. The only plus — no hostile forces, only hostile nature. I imagine downstream tells a different story, where more people can be expected to be stranded — if they were lucky." He left unstated the fate of the unlucky. "I think our best bet is to send several strong climbers up and along the ridge. There's no real trail there, but a natural drainage network should make the going a little easier. Then they could make their way — "

A buzz interrupted him. Then a jingle. "What the h — Shut those things up," Des barked, until his own pocket vibrated and he realized what was happening. A chorus of several mobile phones in the vicinity rang simultaneously. He turned toward Raye as she pawed at the case that hadn't left her side for more than twenty-four hours. At the same time, they connected with their callers, wonder tingeing their greetings.

"Hello?"

His sister's soft voice squealed at Des. "Is it really you, Des? I've been so worried. I haven't been able to get you since day before yesterday."

Des recalled the quick call he'd made that evening to Claudia. "We've had a flash flood up here. We went out for a hike and got trapped by the waters. We're all safe, though."

"Why didn't you call?"

"No one had reception. In fact, when we hang up, can you contact the authorities and tell them a group of about twenty-five are stranded on the west side of the stream? Uh, river. Uh, flood. I'd say we're maybe a mile and a half northwest of our lodge."

"Oh. My. God." Claudia's response captured her shock. "I heard about flooding in the mountains but I had no idea it was near you. Are you really okay?"

"Yeah. Except that we have almost no food and very little water. Listen, I can't talk much more. I don't know how long my power will last."

As he chatted, Des caught snippets of several other conversations being conducted in the group. Their twenty-four-plus hours of silence had created alarm among friends and families. Those not contacted directly tried their own connections to the world. Raye was one of those on the phone. He sidled closer to eavesdrop.

She held on to self-control, barely, the same way she gripped the mobile with both shaking hands. "Andy, what are you saying? You had a premonition about a flood?"

On the other end of the connection, words flowed from Andy as fast as the waters had rushed. "Yeah, Mom. I'd come back from practice and was taking a shower. All of a sudden, I had the strangest feeling that the water wasn't going down the drain. It was mounting higher and higher in the stall, and I swear I heard your voice calling to me to be prepared, that we were going under. I dried off and tried to get you right away, but there was no service. Then I turned on the news and learned about the massive flood. I kept dialing off and on all night, but all I could get was voice message, until now."

"That's amazing, exactly what happened."

"Are you all right?"

"Yeah, except for being filthy as a pig and starving. But we haven't heard or seen anything about how to get out of here."

"I wish I could airlift you a bagel or a breakfast burrito. The news is non-stop about this emergency. They said hundreds of people are stranded, and some cars got swept away."

"That's probably downstream from us. Here the branch is relatively small—or it used to be. Some things drifted by but didn't lodge near us. Other than ourselves, we haven't seen refugees. What do they say about rescue efforts?"

"Not much. There are constant references to helicopters and National Guard. They say many phone calls are getting dropped or simply don't go through. That no one should make nonemergency calls now."

"Listen, can you do me a favor? I just thought of folks at the office."

"Of course, Mom."

"They need to know what's happened. Can you call and tell them everyone's safe? I'm thinking the authorities can track our location by our cell phone signals now, but we don't expect a rescue for hours, even days. We've been uneasy about Mr. Van Voorst, but he seems okay right now. And have them get in touch with emergency contacts in the personnel files."

"Sure. Take care. Love you."

"I love you," she replied.

"Everything okay?" Des asked her as she pocketed the cell.

"Yeah. Fine. But what about us?"

"Now I'm afraid we're in for a boring stretch. Or I should say, we're lucky to face boredom rather than more danger," he said. "Ben will send a few volunteers out to try to connect with the world at large."

"I'm guessing one of those will be you," she said. "I won't even try to persuade you not to go."

He chortled. "You're learning more about me in a short amount of time than usually occurs in a new relationship. Guess that's what happens in a disaster."

"Yes. A definite bonus. The truth, the whole truth and nothing but the truth. No one can lie or fake their way out of a flood. But what's this about a relationship? Aren't you jumping the gun? We haven't had any sort of formal connection or even talked seriously about one."

He turned to her and again grasped her shoulders, to trap her glance with his. "I think what we've survived qualifies us to take a giant step forward. We can remember all this when we tussle over things like which restaurant to go to and the names of our kids. We're grounded in mutual trust and faced momentous dangers, so we'll survive anything in the future."

"Giant step?" she gasped. "More like a leap of miles."

He pulled her close. "You feel what I'm feeling. Don't deny it. We're not starry-eyed teenagers with some absurd fantasy of love, a soft-focus film complete with hearts and flowers."

It felt so good to her that she didn't want to move, but before she could answer, a thump-thump-thump sounded and blasts pushed the air around, tossing leaves and twigs in whirlwinds. Raye angled her head and saw a helicopter approaching over the crest of the mountain. "Looks as if we'll have to delay any major decisions. The cavalry has arrived!"

Chapter Thirty-One

Sure enough, Raye saw the Colorado National Guard's dark olive helicopter pulsing slowly through the air, passing over the mountain's summit, conducting a zig-zag pattern over the trees, obviously checking for signs of life. The Pursuit Chosen Twenty-Five plus three — Julia, Mr. Van Voorst and Ben — sent up an immediate 'hooray', accompanied by whoops, cheers, arm pumping, waving and screams and her hoot of *'hoy, hoy!'* Several swung handkerchiefs and scarves around. No way would they be missed.

The aircraft spotted them and fluttered toward the outcropping past the group, to hover over the flooded area. Raye could see the pilot and other personnel inside the tinted windows, binoculars and headsets in use. From the copter came a vibrating voice, amplified to a tinny echo. "Hello, below. How are you?

"Fine. Super. Okay," proliferated along with thumbs-up and A-okay finger signs. Des released Raye and jerked a tiny twitch of his head in an unspoken question to her. "Go, go," she said, waving her hands in a shoo-shoo motion. "You and Ben have been our leaders since the beginning." She watched him bound over to Ben and launch an intense discussion before she located Julia to help her move the crowd toward the shelter of the mountainside.

Ben broke free and stepped to the edge of the ledge. Lacking a microphone, he relied on gestures for most communication, supplemented by shouting between palms up on either side of his mouth. At his side, Des duplicated the pantomime and screams. The craft hovered about ten feet above the ledge and a yard away from the perimeter. Its rotary blades continued to circle, creating a strong breeze over everyone.

"How many folks with you?"

Ben flashed fingers to total twenty-eight.

"Condition?"

Holding up one hand, Ben touched thumb and forefinger to make a circle, indicating 'okay'.

"Any medical needs?"

Ben lifted a single finger high, while Des thumped his chest in the area of his heart and grimaced.

"Supplies?"

Des made drinking motions and mouthed 'water' as Ben motioned eating.

"Confirmed. Food and water," came the response. A brief silence as the crew of the helicopter consulted, then the voice resumed. "We'll take the medical along with up to five additional. Anyone down there with experience getting civilians aboard?"

Ben and Des checked with one another. Ben answered by raising two fingers.

From her point of view, Raye could see a shuffle and wave run through the group. Those surrounding her knew rescue was at hand and were eager to escape. The precursor to disagreements and fights over priority. Since triage was essential to maintain order, she cut through the crowd to touch Des on the arm. "Can I help?" she offered. "I'll bring over the highest priority passengers."

"Yes. Thanks."

No consultation was needed to make the initial selections — Mr. Van Voorst, Olivia as his aide, along with Roy and Bill, both of whom had major challenges in physical effort. Raye and Julia quickly located them and lead them to the front. But then, who? Two small disturbances broke out in the crowd, like rocks around which the flood waters had surged. Krystle began to moan and weep, despite the efforts of those around her to comfort and quiet her. Then, with their customary savoir faire and the egoism of the selfish, the disrespect they'd showed when drunk several evenings ago and disregard of the group's safety during the current misfortune, Tim and Mason started to force their way toward Ben, whacking into people and demanding passage.

"We're better off without them," Raye murmured to Des. "They'll disrupt our retreat from the mountain. You know what havoc they created when we were trying to pull everyone together as the flood first threatened."

"Agreed," he said. "Especially Krystle. She's worthless."

A sudden movement at the cliff edge showed the copter now hovered mere inches away from the periphery with little wavering. A strong rotor wash flung vegetation and twigs around as well as tangling long locks of women's hair and lightweight scarves. Some protected their faces with their hands or arms. The door to the craft slid open like a huge mouth, revealing a yawning blackness, framed by several uniformed troops. One man, equipment slung over his shoulders and across his chest, propelled himself through the opening. He carried an armful of water bottles, as well as a supply of protein bars.

"Can you squeeze in six in addition to our medical during the evacuation?" Des asked. He, Raye and Julia relieved the soldier of his supplies and handed them out to the crowd.

"Sure," said the man.

Des waved Mr. Van Voorst and Olivia toward the helicopter. With the soldier's help, they clambered inside, making way for Krystle, Tim and Mason, whose eagerness placed them ahead of Bill and Roy. Raye caught Roy's eye and she shook her head in disbelief, matching his contemptuous smirk with her own. He gave her a small flip of his hand in farewell and disappeared.

As the helicopter's panel door slowly slid closed, a crew member tossed more water and bars to the waiting crowd, while another communicated again through his mic. "We'll let the command know your location and condition. It shouldn't be too long before you're cleared out."

"How're conditions downstream?" Ben shouted to the men in the door.

"Not good," came the reply from one who stalled the closing with his hand "You're lucky. You missed the worst."

"That was quite a feat," Raye said to Des as they turned back to their remaining co-workers. She held her hair down in the continuing wash of the rotors. Then she felt rather than saw the craft increase speed, dip slightly and take off. A sigh seemed to flow through the group, as if they'd all released breaths.

"I'll say. Must be highly experienced pilots to evacuate so smoothly from a relatively inaccessible area."

Julia approached the two while most of the remaining employees straggled toward the trailhead, gathering water bottles, scarves, hats, all the paraphernalia they'd lugged on the hike from the first step. "What now?" she asked.

"Ben will probably pull us together to trek back. Since we're on the nearer side to the lodge and everyone left's in decent shape, there's no reason to delay," said Des. "Boy, it's getting hot now." He patted his pockets as if checking on his remaining supplies, stripped off his jacket and pushed up his sleeves, revealing his tattoo.

"Boy, I never expected such an adventure when we left for the retreat days ago," said Julia. "They wanted to test their top employees, and they got a doozy."

"And now?" asked Raye. "Is the award still a possibility? Or is mere survival enough of a thrill?"

"I'm sure they'll give it. I made time to talk to Mr. Van Voorst to get directions for my return to the office, and he's adamant. It was part of his and Ben's schemes to ratchet up employee morale and role models." She stopped, her eyes darted left and right, her mouth pursed and she leaned in a trifle. "Guess who's at the top of the list of candidates?" she whispered. She bit on her lower lip. "I shouldn't. I shouldn't tell you."

"Aah, come on," said Raye, jiggling up and down in a pseudo-teenage entreaty. "We won't let anyone else in on the secret."

"No. I can't," said Julia through the fingertips she now had plastered over her lips.

Raye turned to Des. "You ask her. If both of us beg, she won't be able to refuse."

Amusement twisted the corners of his mouth. "I hardly think I need to."

"Why?"

"It's fairly obvious the strongest candidate is me." When Julia joined Raye in delivering mock blows to his biceps, his grin widened as he crossed his arms. "Don't be a sore loser, Raye," he joked, slowly sinking to his knees as if they were battering him down.

Their laughter turned to gasps for air, then mere giggles, while they clung to one another. Julia straightened first. "He's right, you know," she whispered. "Des is definitely among the most likely. So are you, Raye."

Raye was surprised by the news. Despite the couple's rank bang-smack in the top few squads in every challenge, the mere idea of terminations choked her, making her gasp for breath. "What about the plans for downsizing? Are they still on?"

"Oh, yes," said Julia. "Come hell or high water."

Another round of chuckles burst forth. "Who knows what will happen in the future?" said Des. "Concentrate on the here and now."

The renewed thought of fifty thousand dollars left her motionless for a moment as she thought of the possibilities for using the money. "Thanks for telling us," she whispered back. "I hope it comes true. Of course I hope I'm the winner more than that Des is."

For some unknown reason, that statement set off their giggles once again. As they collected themselves, Raye noticed the three were last on the far side of the stone shelf. "We'd better get ready to go."

"Oops," Julia spouted. "I've got to catch up with Mr. Buford. Mr. Van Voorst may have left me some instructions." Off she trotted.

Raye surveyed the remaining employees, who made vague movements as if to tidy themselves and gather their few belongings. "What now?" said Raye.

"Grab a protein bar and some water and settle in," said Des. He pulled a treat from his pocket and broke off a square of chocolate to pop into her mouth.

"We've got almost nothing to pack, no change of clothes or makeup to put on, so I guess we can relax," joked Raye around her mouthful, even as his words about giant steps, names of their kids and quarrels over restaurants lingered in her mind. A shiver ran up her spine. A serious, in-depth discussion should surely be coming up. They ought to trade information about their families and obligations, hopes and fears. His sister could be a challenge, as would Andy's plans.

"But first," said Des. He surrounded her with both arms, enfolding her. She hadn't realized the mountain chill had saturated her skin until he stepped close. He brushed her forehead with his lips, her cheeks, finally her mouth, and she held her breath to experience every sensation. *A discussion can wait,* she decided.

* * * *

The trek back to the lodge seemed to require the same easy effort as slipping down a slide. The cluster of log and fieldstone buildings appeared almost the same as before. Aside from the vigor with which rain and wind had obviously whipped through the rustic setting, stripping loose leaves and abandoning small pools of water here and there, no other damage appeared. Raye inspected the landscape from her miniature balcony and drew a deep breath of mountain essence. So much had happened in less than two days, especially in the closeness she now felt toward Des.

She assumed him to be as busy as she was — showering, donning clean clothes, calling family and friends who all must have heard the news of the flash flood. As for her own relatives, her mother's motto always had been *'Never trouble trouble until trouble troubles you,'* so her mother hadn't been worried, assuming instead she would have been notified had real disaster struck. Her dad had received news from Andy, of course, but he'd called Raye soon after the Pursuit group had returned to assure himself of her status. She again gave silent thanks to him for the survival training he'd provided courtesy of her childhood camping experiences.

The mood inundating Raye — a curious combination of glumness now that a frenzied apprehension overlaying the entire experience had receded, along with relief at their rescue — thwarted many questions.

It's strange, she thought. She wasn't worried about cleaning her knapsack, the cost to replace ruined clothes, the appeal of a nap to catch up on sleep or the fingernails she'd broken while tugging on Julia's rope. She'd learned a lot from the ordeal. The primary concern in life was the well-being of loved ones. And, sure enough, she placed Des firmly in that group.

For a moment she stared dreamily at a sunny, placid view with not a hint of the violence that had overtaken their group the day prior. The scene reminded her of life itself, how she could be moving along smoothly then a sudden storm upset emotions, stirred up longings, threatened peace of mind…in either a bad way or a good way. She wasn't sure what Des' presence would turn out to be, but she realized she was eager to confer with him. At the thought, euphoria filled her with a bubbly sensation and the sun seemed to shine brighter.

She'd learned a lot from the retreat, most of her instruction having been unplanned. She never would have predicted the disasters they'd faced. Yet among all these lessons, the pinnacle, the prize, was finding Des, discovering the real man, his intelligence, reliability, strength. She squelched aspirations for a future with him, but she couldn't suppress the dream.

As a red-tailed hawk spread its majestic wings across the cobalt sky, flashing its rusty tail feathers overhead, a disturbing thought stabbed her consciousness. *The competition! Who led?* She exhaled. It held little interest for her now. Sure, the money would come in handy, but she knew — win or lose — that she'd survive, Andy would go to college and she'd make do with or without a car.

No, her most important task was to determine if she and Des possessed a future. How should she approach this issue? Blurt it out to him? Start talking casually about the policy at work covering co-workers dating? To avoid a resolution was out of the question. Life was too short not to pursue possibilities. No longer would she hide or deny hope. She turned back to the room to dress and prepare for a debate with him.

Chapter Thirty-Two

Des stared into the bathroom mirror as he shaved, but he didn't see his own image. Raye's features constantly filled his mind, becoming more essential with each passing second. If he'd thought, a week ago, that he'd be consumed by the most compelling, frustrating, charming, entrancing woman he'd ever known, he would have scoffed at himself. After triumphing over numerous close calls with her, he didn't puzzle about his obsession. It was a relief to give in to it.

A surge of joy swelled in his belly. He couldn't wait to connect with her again, talk about their near-misses with death, edge toward the mutual commitment he knew was coming after they played the little back-and-forth games every couple went through. He looked forward to the minor uncertainties about if they were a good match, if they both loved spaghetti, drew up careful budgets then tossed them to the winds to splurge on a gourmet meal or avoided reality television like the plague. Discovering their differing opinions would be even more fun. He guessed she'd oppose his tendency to leave dishes in the sink for days and would be lukewarm about attending football games. That was fine. That was fun.

He set his razor aside to lean on the sink, both arms extended, studying his reflection. Surely he deserved some companionship, some love after so many years without. He'd denied himself a great deal. Not that his life was tough, far from it. He was one lucky son of a bitch. He'd evaded the limitations of his working-class family, escaped the worst possibilities of armed conflict, somehow accidentally wriggled out of several romantic entanglements that would have been fatal for him and fallen into a career path with financial advantages as well as a sense of fulfillment. But he'd delayed that deep, heartfelt satisfaction of a true partnership with an equal. He longed with passion for a little peace, the kind studded with exciting interludes of discovery and intimacy.

His phone buzzed and he walked to the bedside table to check the caller's identity. His mom. He groaned and wanted to ignore the contact for now, but remembering Claudia's recent emergency, he answered.

It was not good news. "Des, the doctors are saying Claudia's developing signs of kidney failure." His mother's inability to start with a greeting showed how upset she was. She continued with open-ended babble, somehow quoting nurses, doctors, neighbors, Claudia, Internet sites and church friends in a tottering tower of dire predictions.

"Mom. Mom," Des said. "I hear you. Sounds like you're very upset. How's Claudia reacting? And Dad, what does he say?"

"Claudia's taking refuge in her meditation. She's convinced that will solve all her problems." His mother whooshed out a puff of air to underscore her disagreement. "Your father's putting all his hopes on this experimental treatment. But you know we don't have the money for that."

From his toes, a chill moved up Des' entire body. Most of his disposable income already went to help with Claudia's medical expenses, assistance for college, occasional caretakers when she hit a rough spot. Gaining the award here at the retreat was fast moving from desirable to being an absolute necessity. He was going to have to do everything in his power, play every trick in the book if necessary, to win. That included hiding his overpowering attraction to Raye. No way did he have a faint hope for a normal life with her for an undetermined length of time until Claudia's dilemma was resolved. He'd be forced to hide the dream for any kind of relationship with Raye deep within himself, to stifle his feelings.

But how could he accomplish that? She'd be expecting a response from him, some sort of contact after all they'd been through. He couldn't cut himself off completely from any dealings with her. He worked with her. They saw one another daily. He grimaced as he thought of his own pain, to be near her and never reveal his feelings. Somehow he'd have to convince her that his feelings had changed or that his feelings were fickle—or that he'd been temporarily influenced by the crisis they'd survived.

A knock broke into his thoughts. He strode to the door and swung it open to see Krystle beaming, all her teeth displayed like a beauty pageant contestant. A few hours' respite from the rigors of storm and flood had been enough to restore her store-bought sheen. Her glossy waves caressed cheeks tinted with blush, and her lustrous lips looked as plump as berries, while dangling turquoise and silver earring medallions brushed her shoulders. Moving down, a fringed leather vest topped a pair of carefully distressed jeans, frayed strategically across thighs and calves and tucked into high black cowboy boots. If ever a woman was dressed for the hunt after a man, Krystle won hands down.

Anticipation clutched Des' belly. "Hello, lady. I see our recent troubles only made the sight of you more appealing," he said while thinking rapidly that the perfect alibi for ignoring Raye had appeared. Krystle had been after him since he'd first entered Pursuit's doors. Just as important, Raye knew of Krystle's infatuation and should figure, if she were quick enough on the up-take, that Des was acting like a typical male in taking advantage of whatever Krystle offered. It was a perfect method to discourage Raye's friendship. He stepped forward while tucking Krystle's hand under his arm. "Shall we go down for our late farewell lunch?"

* * * *

In front of a paneled wall displaying Western artwork, Raye paused, hands clasped behind her, to study a painting of buffalo being chased by Native Americans armed with spears. Blood dripped from the points, flowed from the sides of the stricken animals, dotted and smeared the horses controlled between the thighs of the hunters. Next she strolled to a bow and quiver of arrows on display, then marveled at other Western paraphernalia — six-shooter, holsters, rifle, tomahawk. Every memento reminded her of the inborn aggression in humans, as well as their drive to survive. Perhaps the crew from Pursuit had more in common with early residents of the West than she'd thought.

The clatter of footsteps on the stairs to her left alerted her to someone's entry, and she swiveled on her heels in time to spot Des descending, his head bent close to a woman's. Raye felt pleasure blossom on her face, an automatic reaction she couldn't have controlled even had she wanted to. She'd stepped forward toward him before she realized the woman was Krystle and Des seemed in no hurry to end the conversation or involve Raye in it. *Sometimes I'm thin-skinned*, Raye admitted to herself, so she plastered on a welcoming expression and greeted both newcomers. Still, between her shoulder blades came the itch that always warned of something provoking her.

"Ready for the final lunch?" She checked her watch. "Almost two. I'm starving for a decent meal. It certainly will be a refreshing change from water and trail mix." A small maneuver brought her to Des' other side. The three of them continued toward the dining area, but Raye couldn't avoid noticing that Des walked closer to Krystle than to her. They went through the buffet then took seats at one of the round dining tables. Somehow, Des wound up at the end of the line, with Krystle in the middle.

What followed was the most excruciating experience Raye had ever experienced. The sub sandwich with spicy Italian meats seemed to turn to dust in her mouth as she suffered through Krystle's babble, who, like a compass pointing north, ensured every topic led back to her and Des, a pervasive buoyancy coloring each "Wasn't that great!" and "I can hardly wait!" Raye attempted but failed to make general conversation about the weather, the retreat and the trip home. When the meal finally drew to a conclusion, Raye thought only a false accusation of shoplifting or someone shouting swear words at her in public could be worse. Nothing else seemed likely to approach the humiliation.

By the time Raye had sat through thirty minutes of this tactic, she hardly felt the flatware as she tried to sample the dessert. She might have been a stuffed rag doll for all the attention her conversation received. Rather than stifling her distress, she drew upon long-ago lessons learned from Michael, through the misunderstandings and ill will he insisted on raising between them. She'd found blazing anger burned away unproductive emotions and served as an excellent foundation for constructive action.

She bided her time until Krystle and Des finished stuffing their faces and made noises as if to leave. Then she reached out and deliberately placed the fingertips of one hand on his forearm. "I'd like to speak to you alone for a few minutes." He hemmed and hawed, making insignificant excuses to escape, but she refused to let him go.

Krystle could hardly stay when Raye had nearly told her to leave. Once the clicking of her boot heels vanished, Raye studied Des, thinking, *I still see those lovely eyes, that strong jaw. But what's hiding underneath?* "Have I been deceiving myself about you?" The question forced itself between her lips.

"I don't understand you," he said.

"I thought we'd been through so much together that surely we'd be frank with one another. What's going on?"

He was silent.

"If you're interested in Krystle, it's no skin off my nose." Her cheeks were burning, but she raised her chin high.

"I can't be with you. Not right now," he said.

Something made him edgy. Some guilt or secret forced his eyes to flicker everywhere around the room but at her. "Are you trying to tell me that after all we've survived, you didn't believe what you said? Our team was so much more than a one-time partnership? We seem almost destined to be together?"

"You know in times of crisis people say things they may not mean." He stood to place his empty coffee mug on the table then shoved his hands into his pockets and shrugged his shoulders. "I guess I jumped the gun. We don't know each other very well. It's best to take things slow."

She got up to face him and clenched her jaw. With careful enunciation, she said, "You are a rat." She pronounced every word as if she were spitting poison. "I don't know if you're afraid to admit we have—had—something good between us or if you were playing some sort of game with me. Either way, you're worthless—like Mike, like nearly every man I've known. I've had a lucky escape."

She whirled and stomped up the stairs with the energy of a toddler throwing a tantrum, hiding her emotions under a frozen mask. As she entered her lodge room for the final time to collect her luggage and splash some cool water over her face and hands, she realized she faced a dilemma. She was scheduled to ride home with the same crew she'd come up with. The idea of giving Des a cold shoulder or, even worse, making small talk, terrified her. Surely Kabir would welcome a seat in the front where he could babble away in man-talk with Des. She went to her room phone to call him. While Kabir's extension rang through, an insight flashed through Raye's thoughts. *I know what's behind all this. The award.* She didn't know if she was disappointed that he would sacrifice her for money or if she should be proud that loyalty to his sister was his priority. She hung up before Kabir could answer.

Now Des figured he understood how Benedict Arnold must have felt during the Revolutionary War, when he abandoned the cause of American liberty to return to Britain's side. *Like shit.* As if he were making the biggest mistake in the world. Raye's words revolved in his mind. *Rat, rat, rat, rat.* Her expression of complete betrayal. Her instincts were excellent. She'd intuited his infatuation with her, their mutual rapport and, yes, damn it, his desire. Then to drop her flat, completely contrary to her every perception... He closed his eyes as the image of the pain she felt grew on her features, the slow change to anger flooding her.

He had no choice. Claudia. His little sister. She deserved every chance he could help her obtain. He remembered the bully-tormentor-tyrant types who'd picked on her in school. They weren't limited to males. Females also exhibited that terrible behavior, although they tended to be more mental than physical in their nastiness. High school seemed to be a malevolent breeding ground for cliques of girls who ran around, delighting in the terror they created in their victims. Every time he recalled how Claudia would swallow her fear, give him a trembling smile, shoulder her backpack and climb on the school bus, day after day, knowing what lay in store, pride swelled his chest. Things had improved for her in college, he knew, even as her health slowly eroded. He had to ensure she had an opportunity for a normal life.

If he had to choose between Raye and Claudia, there could be no contest. He'd just met Raye and Claudia occupied part of his very being.

Chapter Thirty-Three

There was no contest, Raye thought, back in her room. She folded her clothing and tucked it into her tote. If she had to choose between Andy and Des, Andy was higher priority every time. She had to do her damnest to win the award, even if it meant losing Des.

Yet couldn't they be honest with one another? This uncomfortable itch between her shoulder blades came whenever someone's attitude didn't ring true, like Mason's racist comments or Des' fawning over Krystle. She thought back to every encounter she'd had with him, and, funny, wasn't it, that she could remember them all and he'd always been candid, honest. Even the times they'd disagreed, he'd been straight and true as a bullet. When he'd pulled her leg, he'd quickly let her know he'd been teasing her.

She held up the pieces she'd worn over the past two days. They were filthy, snagged, damp. They'd need a good soaking. She stuffed them into a plastic bag and continued pondering Des' strange attitude.

Why was he so uneasy and wouldn't meet my eyes after lunch? She slapped her forehead with a palm as she realized the reason. He was too honest to be evasive. If he wouldn't come clean on his own, she figured she should confront him, for his own good. *Yeah, sure,* she thought, *not because you're still holding out hope for a relationship with him.*

To give her courage time to build up, she finished packing up her green tea skin care lotions, mascara and the few eye shadows and liners she'd toted to the retreat. *If he's in his room or I bump into him before we leave, I'll say something. Otherwise, I'll wait until we're back at work.* She made sure every item was lined up in an orderly fashion then inserted them into her makeup bag, where they promptly jumbled together.

He hadn't checked out. Her soft knock on his door brought an immediate response. Not a welcoming one, however. His mouth was pulled down a little at the corners and his eyebrows pinched inward as he tried to hide dismay, while a vertical furrow in the middle of his forehead made him appear so uncomfortable that she longed to smooth it away with her fingertips.

She decided not to ask permission to enter but simply to take control of the situation, awkward as they both may be. "I need to talk to you. We should talk."

She walked in and spared a few seconds to look around. Most of his gear was neatly packed and stowed in a military-type duffle bag. On the dresser rested a few toiletry items, a brush and an iPad with a wallpaper photo of a family, including a delicate, appealing young woman. Her ice-blue eyes matched Des', but her loose curls were a dark auburn.

Raye strolled to the dresser and gestured toward the screen. "Your sister?"

He briefly stretched out a hand as if to stop her, then relaxed it by his side. "Yes."

Stop delaying the conversation, she told herself as she returned the picture to its place. "I think we should clear up some misunderstandings."

He neglected the courtesy of asking her to be seated, so she propped her rear on the arm of an easy chair as a half-measure. "First, I'm sorry for calling you a rat." She held up her palms at his automatic refusal of her apology. "I was hurt. You were rejecting not only me, but us. I knew... I *know* we have a connection. I also realize helping your sister is your major goal, like helping Andy is mine. There's no shame in that, but if we both plan to keep working for Pursuit — and I'm certainly not in a hurry to search for a different job — we'll need to remain cordial. Any closer dealings may be out of the question now."

She tried to control the blush flooding her cheeks, as she remembered his hands on her waist, the solidity of his grasp helping her scramble up slopes and rocks, the strength of his torso when they'd tugged the rope to rescue Julia, telling herself to concentrate on more important issues. "I believe honesty will enable us at least to remain friends."

"You're right," he said. "I've noticed since we first met that you say what you mean. No shilly-shallying around for you." He stepped to the window and pushed the drapery to one side.

He was posed against the wonderful, rugged scene of mountains, pines, rock slides and billowing, embracing clouds she'd noticed from her own room and wanted to be part of that picture. She stepped to his side, placing her fingertips on his arm, telling herself he was worth taking a chance for and hoping he agreed she was worth the same. "So what do you say? Let's allow all this work rigmarole to play out as it will. We can relax and enjoy a friendship."

He turned to her, and for a moment, she thought he was going to quash her every hope, walk out of the room, tell her she was nuts. His eyes narrowed and focused only on her. "You're right," he said. "You're braver than I. All I wanted to do was hide from you. The act of a coward."

"Never that," she said. "You're such a contrast to my ex-husband. He'd never admit any shortcomings. I don't think he had the least awareness about the impact his actions had on other people., was never willing to discuss or compromise."

"I know you had a tough time with him."

"Believe it." She focused on the distant view, not ready to watch Des' expression while she admitted the truth. "You want to see a coward? That's what Andy's father was, the biggest con man in the world. He'd tell you any lie that crossed his mind to convince you he was successful. He told me he was a close pal of the President's chief of staff, and I believed him. He knew all the names, described all the parties and political wheeling and dealing. Beat all the right liberal drums, and because I'm Latina, he knew exactly what patter would appeal to me. He dabbled in popular drugs and was especially charming when he'd had a drink or three. He poured on the sympathy I thought I needed. My dad was old-fashioned and tried to discourage things like makeup and certainly no serious boyfriends. I was such a naïve fool."

Wow! Where did all that come from? she wondered. "I thought I was completely over him. I apologize."

"No apologies necessary. I think when we're young, we're in love with love, in love with some fantasy in our heads. So what happened? You told me you were pregnant. But that doesn't necessarily equal marriage."

"Believe me, my dad can be ver-r-ry persuasive, especially when he spouts nonsense about statutory rape. He admits his decision might be different nowadays." She sighed. "Now I'm embarrassed, crying on your shoulder over a story that ended long ago."

"Listen, you can cry on either one or both shoulders at any time. You're a brave, strong woman and I'm proud to call you my friend." He reached for her, wrapping both arms around her shoulders and squeezing.

She gave a smothered half-gasp into his chest. "You should know inside I'm a shaking, obsessed worrier, riddled with fears. You can't imagine how terrified I was in the first staff meeting you attended. I challenged you to address the security system of the legal department. I knew what I was talking about, but I thought you'd pooh-pooh me because I was a woman."

Des stopped her. "Never. I think that's when I started to feel something for you. You were fierce and determined. Then, on the first tour around the lodge, I thought I could spend my life with a woman like you, ready to take on all challenges."

Leaning back into his arms, she traced his Grim Reaper tattoo on one forearm with her fingertip. "Are you saying you think we might have a future together?"

"Yes. Some day. I hope. If we can overcome all the apparent barriers."

"Why does life have to be this hard?" She moaned. "Why can't we make a decision and bam, that's it, instead of feeling first one way then another, then thinking it will never work, then thinking it's got to work? Why can't we just know our minds and do it?"

Des chuckled. "It's never that easy, not that clean or well defined. We're humans and our emotions are messy. I'm thankful I bumped into you at this time, this place, and that we're headed toward mutual surrender with a peace agreement."

Her heart bounded upward, and she thought that with him next to her, they could meet any difficulty.

"Time to head home," Des said as he released her. "This has been quite a corporate retreat, more like a pitched battle against the elements."

"I hope you think we've both triumphed in the struggle with nature."

"Absolutely."

* * * *

Des' family greeted his return home from the mountains with joyful fervor. His mother made him promise he'd come by the family home before heading to his own condo. As soon as he pulled into the driveway, his mom, dad and Claudia rushed out, tossing confetti made of clipped newspaper and bestowing hugs and kisses. Both Claudia and his mom wiped tears from their eyes.

"Hey, ladies, no biggie. Here I am, safe and sound, with another adventure under my belt. The trip didn't come close to my tour-of-duty experiences," he said as he attempted to put his arms around all three of them.

His mom looked up at him. "We didn't know where or how you were. There was only a void out there in the mountains. Even the radio and TV stations had no information."

Claudia untangled herself and danced in a back-and-forth step. "Yeah. They're saying it was the worst flood since the Big Thompson in 1976. Even with all the Department of Transportation road signs, warnings and reverse nine-one-one calls, several dozen people were swept away."

He gave his sister a special strong one-armed squeeze. "Well, that didn't include me or anyone with me."

"Like Raye?" Claudia twinkled at him.

"Now you behave yourself," he joked. "My personal life doesn't enter into this."

"Who's Raye?" his mother asked.

"I want to meet her. You haven't seemed this serious about a woman since...since forever. I need to know whether to be jealous or not." Claudia squeezed him back.

"Who's Raye?" his mother repeated.

"A woman at work," Des said to his mother. "She was my squad mate at the retreat, had a lot to do with our survival."

"Sounds pretty special to me," Claudia said with a wink to her mother.

Des looked down at her glossy curls and the tinge of pink in her cheeks. She appeared healthy enough except for the thinness of her arms, the delicacy of her build. This treasured little sister of his, who had come into his family so unexpectedly, years after his parents had stopped trying for another child, was irreplaceable. Nothing could happen to her. And it wouldn't, if he had anything to say about it.

"She and I decided that now isn't the time for us to get serious. We're both too involved with work," he said. He directed their steps toward the house.

"I'm sorry," she said as she blinked up at him. "You deserve a chance at a soul-shaking love. Could Raye be that?"

"While not the business of a younger sister, I'll admit she very well might. But don't you worry your head about it. Let's take care of you first."

Claudia was worth any sacrifice. The retreat award seemed to take shape in his mind. He could envision either a huge check being handed to him or a stack of cash so tall it nearly toppled, and anticipation forced him to stumble before he recovered. "Tell me about the experimental program you're applying for."

"The research people have been working toward an artificial pancreas for decades, and they've been given the go-ahead for a test on humans," said Claudia. "There's a possibility of a grant for participants, too." She chattered away merrily, as always conveying minute details tucked in her brain about her condition and related studies.

Des relished every enthusiasm, each burble. "Sounds great. Perfect timing, too. The award from the retreat venture will come in handy."

"You're that sure you'll get it?" she asked.

I won't let a doubt enter my mind. Negativity creates its own penalty. "I'd say I'm very confident. Raye and I are definitely the top team, and my role in the whole rescue effort was more visible."

"And you're okay with that? What does Raye think?"

"Oh, we talked. We agreed we were moving too fast, and may the best man — person — win. That would be me. I need the money more."

He refused to consider that he might be sacrificing a special harmony with Raye for his sister. Would Raye be willing to wait months, years, while he resolved his personal troubles? Was he throwing too many roadblocks in their path toward being together? Still, he couldn't help wondering about Raye's every action, the emotions going through her head. Were she and Andy commiserating about the boy's accident? Was she desperately praying to win the award as she struggled to balance household expenses, hoping to change deficits into income by adding figures again and again, each time praying for a different result?

When Claudia broke into his pensiveness, with "What's up?", he realized she'd sensed his preoccupation. "Nothing," he said. Telling Claudia about his personal struggle with emotions would solve nothing. "Let's go in and eat Mom's meal. I missed a few in the mountains."

His mother had gone the distance and prepared his favorite — corned beef and cabbage — but somehow it didn't taste the way it usually did. Oh, yes, dill, onions, mustard seed, garlic, they all flavored the dish, but it lacked its normal pungency. His movements were clumsy, and the fork handle slipped between his fingers. Pieces of gristle forced him to chew and chew, like a squirrel with a nut. Around him conversation flowed, laughter flashed, but he couldn't have repeated any topics or jokes if his life had depended on it.

Claudia, who sat next to him, jabbed him in the ribs with her elbow. So much for his ladylike, gentle little sister. "Mom asked you a question," she murmured from the side of her mouth.

"What, Mom? Oh, yes, we got thoroughly soaked for most of a day. None of us came down with pneumonia, although the big boss had some heart troubles." *As did I*, thought Des, finally admitting to himself how much the disagreement with Raye had disturbed him and his relief they'd patched things up, at least a bit. "Yes, some people were evacuated by helicopter, but most of us were quite able to hike out. I haven't seen much of the news coverage. Maybe we can catch some tonight on the all-news channels."

His suggestion, met with enthusiastic agreement, meant they all moved to the family room. Claudia lowered the lamps on the small tables and flicked the television on, sending colored lights dancing across faces and bodies as they took seats on the overstuffed couch and armchairs. The Emmett family's relief at regaining their son and brother fueled their banter back at the newscasters. The atmosphere reminded Des of his return from his tour of duty years ago. Their unspoken fears now replaced by gratitude at Des' safe return, his mother and father pointing at the screen when an old news flash contained an alert that had made their hearts stop. Statistics about missing persons. Moving images of cars and trucks drifting down a raging torrent. Still shots of debris piled up against a bridge, threatening to overwhelm it.

"We could pry no news from the authorities," his mother said. "In fact, it was impossible to get through to them. When Claudia finally connected with you by phone, I'd nearly given up hope. It was too much, on top of Claudia's situation."

His sister broke in. "Mom, I told you the researchers are hoping to locate grants for all the patients."

"Yes, yes — but that's not for certain."

"It is for certain that one foundation is underwriting some patients. All I have to do is write a letter, and you know how great my writing is."

Sitting on the rug next to Claudia, Des shifted and surreptitiously checked his smartphone for the time — or for a text from Raye. They hadn't discussed staying in touch, but he hoped. Stretching his arms over his head, he yawned and said, "Well, folks, it's been a release to get back after a long, hard experience. I'm bushed. Think I'll take off."

"Hold on," said Claudia as she pushed her chair back. "I'll walk you out to your car."

Outside, not a sign of clouds marred the evening sky, while a breeze helped the city cool down from the early summer heat. When Claudia remained silent, Des got the sense that his sister was struggling to find a way to tell him something personal. She strode slowly, arms across her chest, eyes on the sidewalk dimly lit by the porch light. Something in his chest clutched, and he wished he could fulfill Claudia's every wish.

When they reached his car, they paused. "So, kiddo, what's happening?" he asked.

She looked up, her unblinking azure glance matching his. He realized anew his sister was no child. "You've talked so much about this award at work. You're sure you'll win, and you'll give the money to me. I'm concerned, though."

"What about?"

She turned and braced her arms on his car. "Partly about this new woman. You sound different every time you mention her—as if... As if she's deeply important to you. I don't want you to lose an opportunity with her by concentrating on me too much. She may not be available forever."

"She is important to me. But right now, not as crucial as your health."

"That's the other thing." A deep sigh preceded her words. "I'm twenty-six and an adult now, and I should be stepping up to solve my own problems. Which the medical procedure is not, a problem I mean. I have that covered. You should concentrate on your own issues. Like, what's stopping you from going after a woman who might be the perfect partner for you?"

"You've got to have the money to move forward with the medical procedures."

With her effervescent response to life, Claudia rose on her tiptoes, fluttered her hands and danced in a circle. "Des, have a little faith that things will work out." She swooped to a stop as she grabbed him around the waist. "What would you tell me if I'd met the perfect partner for me? You'd say what you always do. If I'm hesitating, you urge 'Go for it! Don't let this chance escape you.' Right?"

"Ha! I've told you that?"

A tiny smile etched Claudia's lips.

Words slipped from Des that sounded as if his own courage had evaporated or he'd suddenly turned into Claudia's grandfather. "That's great, but dreams and wishes don't bring happily-ever-afters in romance or in health. They certainly don't pay bills." He didn't want to crush her enthusiasm, but he couldn't permit her to be hurt by wild hopes.

Confusion tugged at Claudia's features. "I don't get it. I thought you always told me to take reasonable risks. I'd learn a lot, gain experience and eventually be successful."

Chapter Thirty-Four

"True," he said. "*Reasonable* is the operative term here." He continued to deliver a lecture-like series of clichés, all the time thinking, *Why do I feel like a pompous ass?*

Eyes on his face, Claudia appeared to be thinking so hard that her forehead wrinkled. He paused. She choked out a cough, covered by her palm. He pontificated. She appeared to suck up a sniffle. He instructed, using terms like 'learn the easy way, through thinking' and 'never risk more than you can lose'. She hacked. He babbled.

Then she collapsed in giggles.

"What? What?" Des said.

Nearly breathless, she propped an elbow on the car and gasped. "I can't believe the words coming out of your mouth. You, who enlisted in the service at eighteen and saw each dangerous assignment as a lark. Who moved across the country to take a job, no friends, no family nearby. Who rides a monster motorcycle, goes rock climbing, never turns down a dare. *You* are advising caution."

If she'd yelled or cried or bitched, Des would have ignored her point of view. Instead, he became convinced that this response proved one thing, even as it made him think about his own reactions. "You're an adult," he said, surprised at the realization.

"No kidding!" Choking down her laughter and wiping the tears from her eyes, Claudia straightened up. "Yes, I'm a woman. It's about time you faced reality. I'm fully capable of making my own decisions."

"Come here." Des stepped forward to meet his sister, and they shared a body-shaking hug, leaning so far they nearly fell over. "You're right. I need to butt out and let you take responsibility for your own life."

As Claudia started back to the house, pausing once to give him a last wave, he detected several responses rising in himself—pride, certainly, for the mature, thoughtful, bright young woman he'd had a small part in raising, but also increased determination to ensure she'd be selected as a final candidate for the experimental procedure whether she obtained a grant or not. *I need to guarantee she doesn't realize I'm still doing my damnedest to win the prize money,* he thought. He'd protect that new womanhood to the limits of his ability.

Sliding into the driver's seat, he started the engine. As he prepared to turn on the headlights and pull out of the driveway, he noticed the full moon over his shoulder and paused to consider how different the landscape around him was now compared to the flash flood in the mountains. Then he'd sensed danger to himself, a woman he cared for and several dozen co-workers. Yet even though the situation had been menacing, the midnight sky had lifted him out of himself, enabled him to transcend fear.

Tonight's heavens spread in the same manner, despite the difference below. On the ground in a suburban enclave, he was encircled by lawns and yipping dogs, sturdy, cozy residences that resembled one another in the same manner, as did the nearby tulips and irises and daisies. Somehow the similarity of the two night skies comforted him, reminded him that certain things were eternal and those that weren't still created wonder with their variety.

He'd always looked toward the heavens when he was in the military or out rock climbing. Thinking about the distance between himself and the stars made him and his worries, his pleasures, his achievements miniscule. *Not a bad thing at times.*

A new thought flooded him with such force that his hands dropped from the steering wheel. *Claudia's right. I can relax. Give her the freedom and respect to make her own decisions. Do my best and concentrate on what's truly important. My sister, certainly. but also Raye. With her by my side, I bet anything is possible.* His lungs swelled with surprised delight and a sense of peace seemed to flow through his veins. It was astonishing how the realization energized him. He steered toward his condo with a swell of anticipation in his chest as he figured out the best possible way to repair his connection with Raye.

As soon as he got back to his condo, he made his plan and began his attack.

Whr do u live? I want 2 ck ur car.

Not necessary.

Does it wrk?

No

Then necessary. Pls

And when she didn't agree, he vowed to continue his assault until he was successful.

* * * *

I give up, Raye thought. Des had been texting over and over, asking to look at the trashed automobile immobilized in her garage like a discarded pile of recyclables. Every time he connected, an ache to see him swamped her. She fought it, knowing they both wanted clear boundaries between them for now.

The garage wasn't much more than an enclosed carport, but some prior owner had tacked vinyl siding over the wooden framing that formed walls. She slumped down on a collection of cardboard boxes with old toys, clothes and household goods stored for a garage sale—her favorite pair of jeans that had finally worn through the rear, a Mother's Day mug from Andy, chipped in an accident. It seemed her car, a loyal servant, was about to join the assortment in her personal solid waste stream. She scrutinized the chaos around her. Lowering her head into her hands, now propped on her knees, she pushed her hair back as the cumulative mass of the discards weighed on her shoulders.

Maybe she shouldn't maintain the barriers between herself and Des. They consumed so much effort and energy. Like an armed conflict, she had to remain on guard constantly. *Am I ready to surrender to my urge to let down my guard? It would be such a relief. I wouldn't have to do more than be cordial, let him come over and poke around the car, offer him a cup of coffee. What's the harm?*

She knew what she was afraid of. Getting comfortable could lead to wanting to be closer, hoping she could open up to him, depend on him, everything she'd lacked over the past eighteen years as she fended off any relationship with a man who carried emotional weight.

"Mo-o-om." Andy's warble echoed from the kitchen doorway, and his physical presence soon followed. The look of bafflement on his face startled her.

"What's wrong?" she asked.

"I've got something to tell you." He swung around to perch next to her on the boxes. "But first, you. Why are you sitting here alone in the middle of this chaos?" He gestured at the garage's contents—several bicycles and a toddler trike, the bicycle that was his current favorite, a pile of balls, bats, tennis rackets, skates, trash and recycling cans and a rickety card table piled with hand tools and hardware.

"I'm wondering if I should get depressed," she said.

He interlaced his fingers and inclined his head toward the dented auto in the middle. "What are we going to do about our car? Is that what's bothering you?"

"A major cause of depression. When you had it towed here, it wouldn't work?"

"Not at all. Can we get by without one? I can bike or catch a ride with a friend for nearly everything."

"Before I jump into looking at financing, used cars and carjacking I'd like to get someone to poke around to see if it can be repaired."

"Who? Would Grandpop be able to?"

Raye burst into laughter. "That's about as likely as you."

"Then what? Who?"

"Good questions." Did she dare? "There's a guy at work who was my partner during the retreat. He got some experience as a mechanic in the service. He offered to help when he heard of your accident."

"Cool. Seems perfect. What's holding you up?"

"You're absolutely right. I'll contact him tonight. Now, what were you going to tell me?" In the few seconds before he answered, she smoothed a lock of his hair back from his forehead.

"About college. I think I've found a way to help underwrite it, rather me and my buds have. We'd share the profit." Andy chewed his bottom lip, a sign since childhood that he was nervous and uncertain.

Raye considered the cost of a college education — thousands and thousands of dollars even if a student started at a community college — but she knew better than to verbalize anything negative. There was no better way to kill enthusiasm than to dwell on what could go wrong or the teeny-tiny probability of success. So she kept her tone neutral as she asked, "What's the plan?"

"You know how I've been practicing with the group all this year?"

"You mean the three boys from your class who meet you in the garage, sing, pound on drums, and play instruments as loud as a sound system in a stadium?"

"Yes, the same one. Kids, particularly girls, have started hanging around during our practices to hear us."

"The group our neighbors complain about in warm weather when you play with the garage door open?"

"Yes. Also the group that had a standing-room-only audience at the school show."

"The quartet of soon-to-be-graduates who are all heading in different directions?"

"Yes. Meaning quadruple the contacts at our colleges. Mom, we've listed our band on a crowd-funding site. You've heard us. You know how great we are. People can't classify us. We're part rock, part folk, part blues, part jazz and a touch of hip-hop. We appeal to everyone, even old people your age."

"Thanks a lot," Raye said, even while thinking, *I probably seem old to him, perhaps as ancient as I sometimes feel, but chances are they'll attract no one if they don't specialize in a specific type of music.* "Are you sure the website is legit? What about the creeps out there who prey on inexperienced dreamers? What if you don't collect enough money to produce the music?"

Andy ignored her warnings. "We figure that with all our networks and connections, we'll be able to reach thousands. There're four of us in the core group, plus our manager and a couple of others who handle the recording side and promotion. We're all going to different colleges, will all work this summer for different businesses and there are our connections through sports, families, hobbies, churches and other interests."

Raye couldn't choke back her immediate reaction to advise him. "You know there are jillions of worthwhile causes out there. You'll face a lot of competition. Don't get your hopes up too high."

Excitement continued to gush from him, like a fountain of hope. "I know, but because our appeal will be tied to the concept of supporting a brand-new band, our friends will be fighting to get in immediately."

Raye accepted the inevitable. *I'm always too cautious. I need to let loose and take a risk.* "What the heck? Go for it. Nothing to lose, right?" She froze. "I'm assuming there's no up-front money required."

"Correct. The site takes a percentage of sales — recordings, merchandise, events. We pretty much have the fourteen songs we want to showcase. We're talking to a friend who's a designer about a cover and art for the site. There are a few other details to take care of and we're off!"

"Sounds fantastic." Not for the world would Raye give voice to her doubts again. "And if you make something, you can help underwrite your education. You won't change your plans for college, will you?"

"Naw." Andy stood and stretched both arms high over his head. "I've wanted to be a psychologist ever since I learned what the term meant. I might even combine music with it for art therapy. Who knows?"

"That's great, Andy. Reach for the stars. Both of them." She reached for him and hugged him in the way he avoided if other people were near, but he accepted her arms all the way around him, as well as a kiss on the cheek.

Two huge risks in one day — Des and Andy's music career. I must be changing. Well, in for a penny…

OK. U can lk @ car. When?

When gd 4 u?

Sat a.m.?

K. Donning bells now.

Chapter Thirty-Five

Des brought everything but bells when he appeared Saturday morning, a week after the return from the retreat. The red metal toolbox with two drawers, nearly two feet wide, contained so much gear that Raye couldn't have named half the paraphernalia. Strapped around his waist, Des wore a heavy leather belt that stored wrenches, gauges, wires and who-knew-what in pouches and dangling from loops.

"You certainly look the part," she said as she met him in the garage, two cups of coffee in hand for immediate consumption. She repressed the memories raised by the leather tool belt of the one male strip show she'd attended years ago. "Aren't you a bit over-prepared?"

A sheepish air came over him. "When you gave me the go-ahead, I grabbed every tool and piece of equipment I could put my hands on at my dad's. I wanted to impress you."

She struggled to control her laughter. "Believe me, you have."

He seized the mug she offered. "Perfect," he said as he sipped. "This will get the old brain in gear." A few steps and he circled the vehicle to examine the body. "I can tell it was rear-ended. That's where the bulk of the damage is."

"Is that good or bad?" Raye dogged his footsteps, bending when he did to look under the auto. As he straightened, she found herself face to face with him, about an inch apart. A relaxation came across him, a release, and he looked almost tender. She lowered her eyes, but looked back up immediately. "Is that good or bad?" she repeated.

"Is what good or bad?" said Des.

"If the damage's in the rear." *What are we talking about?* Raye wondered, losing track of the discussion.

Des shook his head and walked toward the car's front end, where he opened the driver's door to pop open the hood. "Depends on whether the body or the frame was affected.

"I'll give the engine a quick once-over." He pulled a wrench and screwdriver from his belt and ducked under the hood, from where clangs and squeaks soon alternated with mutters that sounded like profanity.

Raye giggled into her palm. She was familiar with this approach to handyman-ship. Her father seemed to have a litany of suspicious phrases he mumbled under his breath to facilitate his maintenance chores. "Speak up," she called. "I can't understand you."

Des' features reappeared. "Let's try the engine," he said.

Digging into her front pocket, Raye jingled the key from her fingers then slid into the passenger's seat.

Des skootched in the driver's spot, took the key and inserted it.

A chug-chug-chug sounded and a few lights flashed on the dashboard. Otherwise, nothing. Not a shudder, not a hum. Des flicked the key off and on several times to no avail. When Raye reached across to try it herself, he held her back. "We don't want to wear the battery down."

"What could be wrong?" she asked.

"I'm not sure." A wrinkle materialized between his eyebrows. "Something with the fuel line or the tank? I'll look underneath."

Des disappeared under the car on his back, heels thrumming to push him. Raye wished she had one of those wheeled creepers used by mechanics, but all she could offer him was a stack of old newspapers. Again she heard bangs and squeaks rotating with mumbling and an occasional flicker from a flashlight.

Finally he emerged, wiping a grease-stained sleeve over an equally smeared face. "Appears to me you have a lousy fuel line. That could have happened in the impact. Without removing it, I can't tell if it's loose, damaged or what."

"So what does that mean? It sounds expensive."

"Not extremely so." Tugging a rag from a back pocket, he swiped his tools with long deliberate strokes. "If you let me install it and don't put up any ridiculous nonsense about 'I couldn't impose' or 'I insist on paying you'." The look he shot her dared her to attempt the feat.

Raye's shoulders and torso relaxed, as if releasing a huge pressure. *He really is quite a guy. Why was I so suspicious of him initially?* "Wouldn't dream of it," she said. "Unless I win the lottery."

"That still your plan for a personal slush fund?"

"Nothing else has occurred to me. I might need a stash if I get laid off."

"Surely you're not still worried about that?"

"Always and always."

"Mo-o-om." Andy's voice warbled through the garage.

She held up her index finger. "I do have one requirement." She watched as Des fought back a snippy reply, pursing his mouth as if he he'd sucked on a sour pickle. "You let Andy watch you, maybe even get him to putter around with you."

"I think that's a great idea," he said. "I'm sure your kid has to take after his mom — bright, personable and hard-working. I'd welcome his help."

Raye didn't even try to hide the beam of pleasure that flooded her features. "Thank you so much, on behalf of Andy and myself." She reached for some tools Des had left on the hood of the car, to help him pack up. "By the way, how's your sister? I seem to recall you'd had a crisis when we were wrapping up the retreat."

Des joined her in the chore, ensuring each piece of equipment went in its proper place. "Yeah, a couple of developments. First, she gave me what-for because I'm too bossy and protective. Says she's grown up now and doesn't need for me to win the award in order to pay for medical procedures. I should make decisions based on my own happiness." He squeezed the bright orange, plastic-covered handles of a pair of pliers to check their grip. Then he set them in the toolbox. "She also informed me she has a plan."

"A plan? What kind of plan can a twenty-six-year-old have? Is it like Andy's plan to fund college?"

"This is news. Sounds like we have a couple of geniuses on our hands. What's Andy's idea?"

"I'm almost embarrassed to tell you. You've heard of crowd-funding, I trust?"

"Of course. But you have to have a product or service to offer before you can ask people to support you—or at least some off-the-wall idea. Is he going to hustle investments in himself? What's he plan to study? Something lucrative?"

"No, at least not immediately. No fortune guaranteed." She gulped. "I didn't tell you Andy's a musician."

"In addition to being a student and a soccer player and a bicyclist and whatever?"

She simply nodded.

"Let me guess. His plan's to make a recording that will bring in a fortune?"

She nodded again.

Des' face slowly turned an alarming shade of red as whoops of laughter burst from his mouth. Spasms shook his body until he seemed compelled to put all equipment down and bend over, clutching his midriff. "That's about as ditzy as Claudia's idea. She claims there's a foundation that will support grants for her procedure, and all she has to do is write a knock-down, drag-out essay and application."

"Presto!" Raye snapped her fingers. "Our challenges are met." Her laughter joined with his.

"We are lucky, lucky people to have such talented, motivated relatives around us." As his chuckles died away, Des propped his leg on the car and crossed his arms. "I'd say we've been given a sign to leave Andy and Claudia well enough alone. They'll solve their difficulties."

"I wouldn't go that far," she said. "But I agree we've been too hung up on trying to do everything for them. They deserve the chance to try their wings."

"I concur. Now what?"

"Why don't you come in and have a beer? You deserve one." As Andy's call again echoed, she added, "I'll introduce you to Andy."

Chapter Thirty-Six

Sleep will be a challenge, Raye thought on Sunday night as she leaned toward the mirror in her home bathroom to squirt lotion on a cotton ball and swirl the makeup remover over her face. Des had welcomed Andy's involvement. Even better, when Des had promised to be Andy's first investor, the teen's enthusiastic comments each evening revealed the older man swiftly was becoming a luminary to him. Raye cheerfully tolerated a never-ending stream of terms about auto mechanics and insights into the mysteries of repairs, as though her son were briefing her about a foreign culture. The car finally was fixed, although dented and scratched, and was safe and drivable. All the results were what she had hoped for — a functioning automobile as well as a good male role model, a rarity for the boy.

She stopped her hand's movement as she considered. The problem? She and Des still disagreed about the award. Julia's confirmation that Raye and he were the front runners created a tension that grew by the day. Both knew the money to be necessary for them to reach their goals, yet both also longed for success for the other. *Maybe we could share the wealth*, Raye dreamed. Then, with a sigh, she told herself to stop spending money she didn't have.

Somehow, though, her action soothed her, dissolving tension. The mint fragrance brought back memories of candy canes from her childhood — Christmas mornings with her brother, mother and father, who had been as excited and joyful as she was.

Of course, those reminiscences had occurred before her brother's death — speeding, spinning, falling, crashing over an embankment on the highway — followed by her parents' divorce. The tragedy had amplified tensions between Mom and Dad, who differed radically in their approaches to life. Mom…ambitious, demanding, upwardly mobile. Dad…relaxed, live-in-the-moment, unmotivated. For them, grief had become a wedge that had shattered love.

Raye liked to think she combined the best of both parents. Did her current indecision over a future with Des contradict that? She reined in her wandering attention. Though his visit two days ago to look over her car showed proof positive of his good intentions, and even better, displayed his charismatic personality… *I don't want to go there*, she told herself, *and I don't have to. I can think about candy canes and Christmas without continuing on to sad memories. And I don't have to decide what my future might be with Des. I can just sleep.*

A tug on the covers and she climbed into bed, punched up the pillows, lay back and closed her eyes.

Moments later, she threw two plump, colorfully striped cushions to the floor and pulled the nearly flat feather pillow of her childhood forward. On her stomach, sleep usually came easily.

Not this time. She flopped over onto her back and linked her fingers behind her head. She simply couldn't get Des out of her mind. Even though a week had passed since the Pursuit group's return from the lodge and the aftermath of the flood, and routines at work had reasserted themselves, his face, his fingers, the feel of his shoulders and arms when she'd embraced him seemed embedded in her brain. The images and sensations had flipped through her — the flood, storm, evacuation, their conversations after the rescue.

Now that she'd seen him in an ordinary situation — at her home and working with Andy — optimism surged in her that their closeness was growing. She suppressed it. She wouldn't allow herself to hope. They were too far apart in their goals, too different in their lifestyles, too competitive over the award.

There was nothing she wanted more than a real relationship, even marriage. Why, then, couldn't they agree on the basics? She refused to believe the issue of who should win the prize from the retreat could keep them apart. Des deserved victory. Everyone's survival had depended on him. He'd demonstrated every quality top management wanted — intelligence, courage, initiative. The bonus should be his. Yet for the life of her, she couldn't choke back a desire so strong it swelled her throat for the money that would ensure Andy's education.

The advantage of her childhood pillow was its flatness. So little stuffing remained that she could fold it in half, even thirds, to use it in any location that seemed to require its comfort. Scrunching it into its tiniest form, she buried her nose in it. Perhaps the relative smotheriness of this position blocked enough oxygen to allow her to slide right into sleep.

She was back in the forest, on the mountainside during the flash flood. This time, however, she was alone. Where was Des, she wondered, as isolation from human contact nearly paralyzed her. She had to climb up this trail, slick with mud, pine tree limbs slapping her face and poking her with needles, catching in her ponytail. Although she continued the energy-sapping scramble, nothing stopped her constant scrutiny of her surroundings to find some sign of people. She'd never felt so lonely.

A final bound up and over a pile of rocks brought her to mountain's summit, as the sun broke through heavy, striated clouds, sending a swathe of rays ricocheting down to a clearing, a long-grassed meadow embracing a bench of rough-hewn logs. Perched on the bench was her brother Carlos. She gasped, held her breath, close to the point of fainting. She said, "Carlos. What are you doing here? Aren't you dead?"

"Hola!" Carlos patted the place next to him, inviting her to sit. "Depends on how you define 'dead'. I don't waste time on it. I'm here and I'm happy to see you. I've missed you."

"I've missed you," Raye said before she burst into tears and hugged her brother. He seemed absolutely solid. She even smelled the pungent after-shave he always wore. Her sobs slowly ceased, and she straightened in his arms.

He smoothed her droopy bangs out of her eyes. "For a while there, mija, I thought you'd be joining me, gagging along after me like you always did. I'm glad I was wrong."

"You mean the flood? But why didn't I join you?"

"A whole life's out there waiting for you," he said. "It's not your time yet. I don't know what's in store, but it will help you grow into the woman you're supposed to be."

"I don't understand. Why did you have to go? Can't you return?"

"No, I can't." He sighed and pushed her back so he could look in her eyes. "But always know that I'm with you. I care about you. I see you and Andy, and me gusta. *It pleases me. Nothing better than knowing you're* ¡viviendo la vida! *And Mom and Dad, too, of course."*

"They got divorced."

"I know. It was painful for everyone. But no one knows what goes on in a marriage other than the two people involved in it. I'm not going to judge them."

"Dad told me recently, 'Don't let my mistakes limit you. After your brother was killed, your mother and I couldn't get along. We should have supported each other. Instead we moved apart, isolated ourselves in our grief.'"

"They're doing the best they can. As should you."

"What does that mean?"

Carlos repositioned himself to lean forward until his elbows were propped on his knees, his fingers loosely laced between, so he was looking out over the valley below the summit. The view reminded her of the landscape where the mountain trail had meandered — verdant, lush with pines and vines and aspens and brush, snow-clad mountains in the distance. "I never tire of seeing this. So full of life's energy and sensations. Magnificent!" He turned toward her again.

"Monita, all I can say is you have a great adventure before you. You'll know love and loss, success and failure. Live every second. You already know what's important in life and it's not money, not getting ahead at work, not chasing things, stuff like clothes and cars and fancy houses."

"Then what is important?"

"You tell me. What are the first things you think of when you count your blessings?"

"Andy. My parents. Friends like Julia. And" – she paused – "and Des." To cover a touch of embarrassment, she freed her locks from the ponytail and shook her head to let the wind cool her.

"You got it in one try. Now, why don't you lay your head on my shoulder and rest? You've had some busy and thrilling times. You can let yourself relax."

Raye did as Carlos suggested, a happiness filling every cell. Her brother, back. Her brother, unchanged. She closed her eyes and drifted to sleep.

The next morning, her pillow was soaked with tears, but she awoke with a smile on her lips. The way was clear now. She knew what she had to do. She didn't care if she won the award. Reaching for the phone, she dialed Des.

The line was busy – and busy again five minutes later, still busy ten minutes after that. Thumbs flying, she texted him then scurried to the closet to dress for work.

Chapter Thirty-Seven

Fifteen minutes early for her first work appointment of the morning, Raye used the time to flick on her computer, check messages on the office telephone and sort the mail, all on automatic and almost simultaneously. A week ago last Friday Ben had scheduled today's meeting, prefacing his email communication with what had become his standard spiel for serving as a proxy. "Due to the indisposition of our CEO, I am implementing on his behalf plans, created previously, which have his full endorsement."

In this case, his message contained no additional details, other than the names of the recipients — Raye and Des. She recalled Julia revealing that the retreat would be used to determine layoffs as well as promotions. With her native pessimism, she feared she was in line for firing. On the other hand, Des was Pursuit's golden boy. No way he'd be shafted. She had to think the engagement had something to do with the award from the retreat.

Nothing had been officially announced before the Pursuit team had left the lodge. It would hardly have been appropriate, Raye believed. The scene had been heavy with emotions bordering on hysteria as co-workers hugged, called best wishes, pledged unending affection and support following their trial. Individuals she'd never seen in any condition other than perfectly groomed and smiling slightly, confidently, in the office, had cried openly, tear-streaked faces stamped with happy relief. Everyone's thoughts had centered on survival from the storm and flood. They'd all been reminded of the fragility of life, the lack of control humans really have over circumstances.

Raye would have had to be deaf and blind, though, to overlook Mr. Van Voorst's enthusiastic support of her and Des at the lodge right before he was transported directly by ambulance to a hospital for a thorough exam. Clasping their hands, he'd thanked them over and over for all they'd done during the trial. Then he'd called Ben to his side to dwell in embarrassing detail on their actions. "Your decision to bring the crew up to the ledge saved all our asses. And organizing us so we all got some shelter and food then getting us the hell off that mountain? Amazing! Sorry I was out of it during some of the operation. Goes to show, though, we had the right people on the team. Agreed, Ben?"

Ben had immediately supported Mr. Van Voorst's comments.

During the week following her return to the office, Raye hadn't been able to walk down the hall without someone snagging her by the arm to thank her or dredge up an incident or emotion they'd had during the flood. The award was mentioned over and over and linked to her and Des as the two who most deserved it. Because of the public praise, coupled with Ben's message last Friday, she could think of no reason other than the retreat and the award for Ben to want to talk to them — unless it was advance notice of dismissals.

But why together? She thought only one could win. It seemed far more likely to her that an announcement would either be private for the one winner, or — knowing how top management adored a public to-do — at an all-staff gathering.

Whoever was selected — almost certainly Des, with her only a teeny-tiny possibility — that person would be convinced the other would suffer intense disappointment. They were closely connected now. They'd been through too much together. When the winner was broadcast, she pictured the two of them bowing, scraping, touting the reasons why the other should have been declared triumphant, the studied politeness, the delicate reassurances that the other had been essential to the rescue. Although, come to think of it, neither of them had done anything extraordinary, given their backgrounds and experiences.

That had formed the basis for Raye's new brainstorm she'd had that morning, as she'd headed to the bathroom for her health and beauty routine. Tooth-brushing had always set free new thoughts, innovative insights. She'd begun with flossing while she'd revisited her dream. She liked to consider her brother's spirit as an influence. Thoughtfulness and generosity had always marked his interactions with his friends and family, from the way he'd let her tag around after him from the time she was a toddler, how he'd try to referee Mom and Dad's arguments and his volunteer time with a preteen boys' basketball team.

She'd reached for the toothpaste and toothbrush and scrubbed rhythmically, tilting her head this way and that. Drifting wisps of sensations lingering after the dream had ignited her imagination. Raye could do nothing better to honor her brother's spirit than to encourage notice of the most deserving person at the retreat.

Julia should win! As organizer of the event, she'd provided the foundation for the entire retreat, as well as responding calmly, intelligently to every crisis. She'd saved three people, including herself. She'd suffered Mason and Tim's racist remarks with dignity and learned to rise above them.

If need were factored in, Julia's ranked up there right alongside Des' and Raye's. She couldn't afford to get married or even move in with Eric unless she found money to clear up her family's delinquent loan. Other opportunities hinged on this single action — her hopes to encourage her younger siblings to continue their educations, her own desire to advance to a more responsible position at work.

Raye had turned on the water full blast to rinse her toothbrush. Plus, Julia embodied the very concept of teamwork, she'd mused — no muttering under her breath at requests for extra attention to a document, never a negative remark about a boss' orders, always an extra step to help a co-worker. Raye had walked to the closet to gather clothes for the day, her plan firmly set.

Now she wondered if Des would support her in a proposal to give the prize to Julia. She couldn't be sure. By her desk in the office, Raye paused mid-step to pull her cell phone out and text him again before the meeting. When Olivia waltzed in, Raye shoved the cell into her pocket to prepare herself for the challenge.

Her boss had shown no adverse reactions to the mountain ordeal afterward. Today a taupe suit resembling smooth armor, as if ready to do battle with enemies without and within the corporation, caressed Olivia's fit torso. The clothing wouldn't have the nerve to wrinkle. It was quite different from Olivia's appearance following the group's misery on the mountain. Then she'd been as grimy, tattered and wet as everyone else.

Her boss typically launched a barrage of orders and questions at her every time she entered the room. Today was the exception. "I'm so happy for you," she said. Normally demonstrative as a mushroom, Olivia leaned forward to squeeze Raye's arm with her perfectly polished fingertips, leaving a faint trail of Chanel No. 5 in her wake.

"Thanks," Raye said. "But for what? We're all happy we survived, right?"

"An adventure to pass along to friends and family," Olivia said, swapping a warm smile with Raye, as if sharing a pleasant memory.

Then Olivia stepped away to reach for her mail in the sorter on Raye's desk. Immediately occupied with her communications, she added, "You'll find out your cause for happiness shortly," and Olivia tapped off to her office in her four-inch heels.

Nearly nine. Time to get to Ben's office for the meeting with Des. Raye hoped she could intercept Des beforehand to mention her idea about Julia. If she had a few moments, she was sure she could convince him to support her. After pressing the button in the elevator to take her to the top floor, she marshaled arguments she thought might persuade Des. "Julia's been overlooked too long." No, that sounded whiny, didn't stress her outstanding qualities. "Julia supervised every step of the retreat." Nope, too clerical and administrative in its message. "Julia risked life and limb to save two men." Yes, that was the ticket. The doors slid open, allowing Raye to step out of the elevator, confident as a general who'd never lost a battle.

Ben's office, immediately next to Mr. Van Voorst's, had no sentinel to guard access. In these times of tightened budgets and centralized technology, vice presidents shared one assistant then drew additional support from temps and various departments as needed. So Ben's door was open, and Raye could hear Des chatting before she walked in. *Too late to catch him.* She paused, sucked in her stomach muscles, smoothed her dark hair in its low chignon, assumed a pleasant but not cheek-stretching expression and strolled in.

"Have a seat. Have a seat." Seated at his desk and affable as ever, Ben gestured to the cushiony chair across from him and next to the one Des occupied. It was difficult for Raye to remember the vice president exhausted, filthy and, yes, face creased with worry about the flash flood and alarm for his employees.

"Now that things have calmed down for us, I'm ready to implement the changes Mr. Van Voorst wanted to launch after the retreat."

"How is he?" Des asked.

"The surgery was successful and his doctors expect a full recovery. After many weeks of convalescence, of course. He and I talked before the procedure and very briefly yesterday. He reiterated the approach we already had agreed upon." As if deliberately to build tension and nervousness in his listeners, Ben stopped, laced his fingers across his chest and apparently studied the view of benign, plump clouds drifting across the horizon, visible through his wide window. "Quite a different spectacle from a week ago, eh?"

"Yes, sir," said Des.

Whack! Ben had unlaced his fingers to slap the desktop with both palms. "Back to the business at hand. First, the award." He beamed. "The two of you blew us away. Going into this event, we were unsure how things would develop. There were a number of contenders. Then, thanks to Mother Nature and the hardships she handed us, we quickly realized that two candidates had come to the top."

Chapter Thirty-Eight

Raye drew a deep breath even as she opened her mouth to speak, but simultaneously Des butted in. "Ben, if I may make a suggestion before you proceed? I haven't had an opportunity to talk to Raye about this, but I believe an individual accompanied the group at the retreat who served as the backbone for all of us. Often overlooked because she's always present, she went above and beyond during the flood. She should get the award."

Des was leaning forward a bit, intent only on Ben, almost as if he were avoiding looking at Raye. *Julia.* He was referring to Julia. *That rat!* He'd gotten the jump on her. The momentary flare of rivalry was quickly submerged in delight. If she needed proof the two of them belonged together and agreed on the important things in life, there was no need to look further. *Is it a sign? Or common sense? Absolute reason and logic? Self-deception? His generous nature?*

Never mind. At that moment Raye vowed to have the man. To hell with doubts, questions, minor arguments or shilly-shallying, whatever that was. They had to be together.

Ben was watching her, not Des. She shoved her momentous decision into a mental cubbyhole and scurried to add her opinion. "I agree completely. Julia's been ignored for years because she's so good that no one ever has to give her instructions or check her results. I was about to make the same suggestion but Des beat me to it."

Smooth as a spring breeze, Ben continued the litany. "And she assumes responsibility, solves challenges. She's the ultimate team-builder. Yes, I know. Mr. Van Voorst knows. In fact, he's experiencing some major twinges of guilt for being selfish in the past. She's such a mainstay for him that he doesn't want to lose her. We have plans for Julia."

Sounds ominous, thought Raye. No, he wouldn't have mentioned the fact if he hadn't meant his comment in a good way.

He stretched his arms over his head, legs extended under the desk, leaning back in his chair as if rebelling against the physical restrictions an office placed on him. Through the window a hazy path of sun's rays illuminated the room, and he bounced to his feet, winced at a twinge in his body, then peered through the glass. "I'm still feeling the effects of our adventure," he said as he rubbed his shoulder before continuing. "I need to confess something to you. The competition and award were something of a sham."

Raye and Des exchanged raised eyebrows in curious glances. "How so?" asked Des.

"Van Voorst and I came up with the scheme to help us make decisions about reorganization." Ben clasped his hands behind his back and rocked on his heels. "We felt throwing all of you into an unfamiliar situation that required you to develop new relationships and respond to challenges would enable us to make judgments about who to lay off and who to promote."

"That's… That's unfair." Horrified at having the rumors confirmed, Raye thought of the members of the work squads who had, in good faith, sweated their hearts out on the sometimes foolish, always pointless exercises at the retreat. Most did the best they could at work and had families to support at home. A few exceptions came to mind whom she avoided considering. "Putting us in physical danger to facilitate your decision-making. Setting us up to make fools of ourselves."

Oopsie. She probably shouldn't have been so blunt. It was usually not a good idea in the setting of a major corporation and with an executive vice president.

"Hold on," said Des. "The danger came from the storm and flood, things no one could have predicted or controlled."

Raye's heart melted. Des must be trying to rectify her hasty words.

"I find the concept of the retreat intriguing," Des said. "Look at the qualities people exhibited, traits we never could have predicted here in the office. Many displayed kindness and generosity, far more than I would have predicted. Few complained or groused. Still"—he paused to consider and addressed Ben—"that makes your decisions more difficult."

"Not really," Ben said. He resumed his seat, giving a small grunt of release. Raye could sympathize. She still felt occasional aches from physical stress of the retreat. "While we were over the moon about the teamwork and consideration displayed by most everyone, we still were able to gain insight into uncommon qualities like leadership and initiative. As I've hinted previously, our findings will be reflected in the upcoming round of promotions and layoffs."

Ah, just as Julia predicted. Raye forced herself to interrupt. A typical management technique during bad economic times was to reorganize then shrink numbers by firing low and mid-management staff. *Why do top managers seldom get the ax?* she wondered. "Can't you handle layoffs through attrition and transfers? I hate to think anyone suffers because of the forces of nature."

Both Ben and Des flashed her inquiring looks. *What? Didn't they consider the human cost of the proposal?* She didn't care if Ben thought her a bleeding heart, but she hoped Des' reaction would be sympathetic.

"Certainly we'll try. That reaction is exactly what I'd expect from you. But back to the award. Naturally, we'll make good on that. We've decided to split it between both of you."

"I really wish you wouldn't," said Raye, even as Des spoke, too.

"Please, don't."

"We were in the right place at the right time," Raye said.

"We did nothing more than anyone else," Des said simultaneously. It was as difficult to separate their voices as their thoughts.

"You're serious." Ben exhaled as he leaned back in his chair. "This isn't false humility, I hope."

"Not at all," said Des. "Let me give you some reasons to go with Julia. First, if you distinguish us, resentment inevitably occurs with an award like this. Almost every person feels he's accomplished wonders that simply haven't been noticed, so envy and gossip begin to flow."

"Yes," said Raye. "But everyone knows, or at least everyone with any perception knows, what Julia achieves, so they'll support that decision. And, really, if there's anything our terrible experience taught us, it's that the most important things in life are not money or position." Her eyes drifted closed as the vulnerability she'd felt in the wild swamped her again. She reopened them to see Des and Ben motionless, apparently stifling similar reactions.

"You still can use your findings for promotions," Des pointed out.

Ben cocked an eyebrow in his direction. "I take it you both won't object to a promotion with an appropriate raise in salary and bonuses, because—"

"Oh, no," interrupted Raye. "Please do. I'd be most grateful, as would my teenage son and the college he plans to attend."

"Ditto," said Des, adding hastily, "not my teenage son, but my younger sister, who hopes to get some advanced medical treatment."

"This is most unusual, to let employees have a voice in bonuses and awards." Ben frowned and pulled on his bottom lip with thumb and finger. Raye held her breath.

"Certainly nothing I wouldn't predict from you two. Expect the unexpected, I've learned after a week in your close company." He looked at both of them then nodded. "All right. It will be as you suggest. I guess that's that then." Ben extended his hand to shake. "As I was about to say, because it appears to me you two are headed toward a closer understanding between you. Am I correct?" He added his soul-sunning, stunning grin.

"It's too early to tell," Raye said, "but perhaps."

"Not too early for me," said Des. "That's what I'm hoping."

They both stood while Ben continued with a warning. "But remember Pursuit's guidelines about co-workers dating. You're safe right now as long as you're discreet. The only complete prohibition is for people in the same department or one supervising the other."

Raye released a sigh as she and Des exited. "That turned out well," she said. A giggle accompanied her next words. "I couldn't believe we both came up with the same idea about Julia."

"Great minds think alike." Des winked at her. "Or fools seldom differ."

"I'm also glad we didn't start arguing about who would make the bigger sacrifice. We both realized those kids have the right to make decisions about their lives, not blindly follow our orders." At that moment, she couldn't think of another place she'd rather be, walking down the hall next to a guy so much in sync with her. Their minds seemed to function in the same way and their feelings duplicated each other. Family was important to him, as it was to her. Doing his best at work was another given for him, just like her. Besides, his face had become the standard by which she judged men's looks now, and his body the same. She wasn't ashamed to admit it.

"Now that we appear to have found the treasure at the end of the rainbow, what's the impact for Andy?" said Des. "He's a great kid. Spent most of his time with me talking about his recording venture."

As they strolled, she responded. "I'm thrilled to know about the Pursuit promotion because I'm not as confident as he is about the crowd-funding scheme. I have to admit that it's been up online only a few days and pledges are coming in, though, mostly from friends and friends of friends via social media. But I'd hate to count only on that source of funding for college expenses."

"Don't tell me you're actually ready to abandon your lottery tickets investment scheme?" Des pulled a face so droll that he was nearly cross-eyed.

"Unbelievable, yes?" She chuckled. "Guess I'm putting away childish things. I added up all the money I'd spent and it was way more than I ever won. Andy's dreams already brought in a fair amount. Let's say I'm cautiously optimistic. What's Claudia's status?"

He paused and turned toward her. "That's a good description of how I feel about her—cautiously optimistic. She's sent in her letter, along with the required form and statements of support from her medical team. So it's promising. If we have to, we'll take out a loan."

"Or you could do a crowd-sourcing project, too," Raye joked. "Looks like we're almost ready to be surplused. Made redundant, isn't that the term? A more acceptable description than useless."

Then a flippant thought occurred to her. "Know what?" Leaning to Des' ear, she whispered, "If anyone's let go, I hope it's Krystle, Mason or Tim."

Des threw his head back and chortled. She loved the way he laughed, experienced every nuance of the joy, displaying his teeth and crinkling his eyes. "Me, too," he whispered back.

"I love you," she gasped around her own giggles. Another oops. She covered her mouth with one hand and held her breath.

"Finally admitting it, eh?" He stole a look around the hall. Seeing no interlopers, he grabbed her for a series of soft kisses over her face and neck. "The feeling is definitely mutual."

Although she didn't draw away, she still protested. "The big bosses won't like co-workers getting together like this."

"Hey, they'll adjust. We've got reputations now as leaders and innovators." Des spun her around to start toward the elevators. "Don't forget—"

"*Todos somos luchadoras!*" They said...together.

Want to see more like this?
Here's a taster for you to enjoy!

Love's Command: Running Scared
Billi Jean

Excerpt

There has to be some kind of mistake.

The MapQuest directions sat on the truck seat next to Lacey, outlining that this was the right exit. She hadn't accidentally decided to take a wrong turn. Besides, there weren't any decisions in her life right now, only directions. She smiled at the thought. Yeah, her attempts at making colossal, life-changing decisions had landed her here, in the middle of nowhere, with no one and nothing around her.

Well, not exactly nothing. There were mountains everywhere. Huge, monstrous mountains, like the kind you could see on the travel channel seconds before some giant paw-waving, open-mouthed, roaring grizzly ate the cameraman.

Oh, yeah, this had to be some kind of mistake. Lacey needed the beach. And people. At this point, she'd settle for a pizza from her favourite beach shack. To hell with anyone else. She needed out of this truck, she realised, surprising herself with a broken mini-sob.

There wasn't a car in sight when she pulled her truck off the turn lane and stopped a few hundred yards onto the cracked asphalt of the old highway.

Two fumbles at jerking the door handle open, and she jumped down, the map in her hand. Blue sky, a cold November breeze, clean air and mountains filled her senses immediately. One deep breath, two, and half the tension simmering along her skin disappeared. Not the unease, though. The breeze felt different from home. Smelt different. Was different.

This has to be a mistake.

She rubbed her hand through her hair at the thought. Yeah, sure, this had to be a mistake, right? Wrong. Throughout this mess, she'd kept thinking that any time now she'd wake up, that this couldn't be happening, that there had to be some kind of freaking mistake. Life couldn't turn from normal to horrible in the blink of an eye. A decision to go outside a club trying to avoid a creepy guy couldn't destroy everything she'd worked so hard to build.

But, yeah, one look at the rugged, wilderness reminded her that, yeah, one thoughtless decision had ripped her life to shreds.

If she could reverse time, she'd—what? If she'd known that by leaving the bar she'd witness a mob hit, would she have taken her chances with the creepy guy? Probably not.

So here she was, standing on the side of a road on what looked like some crazy Wild West movie set.

Reality sucked. Delusions worked so much better — at least for about ten seconds. Lacey hadn't witnessed a murder. She hadn't been beaten to within an inch of losing her life. She hadn't spent months in a hospital trying to breathe on her own. She hadn't been forced to testify against some of the nastiest criminals in the world. She hadn't been left out to dry like this, forced to move, alone, to a place so remote and far from normal she might as well have been on another planet.

She was used to people, sunshine that smelled like the ocean...heck, music and noise, for God's sake. She was used to delis filled with adorable little old Italian men, smiling at her and asking about her day. She was used to Jewish bakeries with bagels that she'd get up at seven for on a Sunday morning. She was used to coffee shops brewing wicked espresso by the cup. She was used to nice people. Beaches. Safety.

The landscape facing her she was not used to. Big open grasslands, lined with the brilliant colours of fall foliage. Yellow and burnt cinnamon, deep green pines next to the white bark of some other kind of tree—beech or aspen, she didn't know—all created a wildly beautiful picture.

The view gave her the creeps. Maybe she was afraid of wide-open spaces. Agoraphobia was a possibility.

Humour bubbled up and she rubbed her face with both hands. The map crumpled a little, reminding her of the brutal reality of her new life. She was running scared. Nothing was going to change that. Not standing here, not staring off at the mountains, nothing.

So many regrets washed over her. Tears stung her eyes—she felt like they were clogging her throat. Lacey fought them and ignored the deep hollow pit in her stomach.

She needed a plan. Action washed all the turmoil aside—always had. She'd always filled her life with action. Being forced to sit in a truck for days on end had driven her slightly insane, no doubt.

The real estate office in Troy couldn't be too far. She'd find that, then her home, and see her new address for the next... Ah, God, who knew how long she'd be here?

Forever?

And didn't that thought put a huge dollop of pity into her pity-party sundae? Two blinks and the tears held off, so she focused on the mountains. The peaks looked white, possibly ten feet deep in snow by now. She could hike up to that snow; feel the cold on her face, maybe trail run along the ridges and ravines? They would be a challenge. Something to do. Later, maybe, after she'd settled in.

A truck slowed behind her, bringing the heartbeat she'd settled down to normal skyrocketing. What felt like ice water flooded her veins, while goosebumps beaded along her arms and a huge whoosh of adrenaline raced through her veins. The FBI agents had been clear: do not act anything but normal. What that meant, really, after all she'd endured, was a bit unclear. She didn't feel normal in her own skin, let alone here in this wilderness. Besides, she doubted she would look normal to a small western town filled with redneck cowboys. She was a beach babe, had always been one, and didn't think the changes of hair and scenery were going to make a difference.

Truck doors closed and she turned to face two guys — two cowboys, she corrected herself, taking in their jeans, rough looking tan jackets, scuffed boots and dusty black cowboy hats. Both walked over, and she panicked. What was she supposed to say?

They don't look Russian. The thought ran a frantic circle in her mind, followed by, what does a Russian hitman actually look like? God, did he have to be Russian? Or even a he? A humorous hysteria built up, but she took a deep breath and clenched her hand around the map. She steeled herself not to take a step backward as both men walked right up, almost breaking her bubble of personal space.

"Miss, can we help ya out?"

Home of Erotic Romance

Sign up for our newsletter and find out about all our romance book releases, eBook sales and promotions, sneak peeks and FREE romance books!

About the Author

Bonnie McCune has been writing since age ten, when she submitted a poem about rain rushing down the gutter to the Saturday Evening Post (it was rejected). Her interest in the written word facilitated her career in nonprofits where she concentrated on public and community relations and marketing. She's worked for libraries, directed a small arts organization, and managed Denver's beautification program.

Simultaneously, she's been a free lance writer with articles in local, regional, and specialty publications. Her civic involvement includes grass-roots organizations, political campaigns, writers' and arts' groups, and children's literacy. For years, she entered recipe contests and was a finalist once in the Pillsbury Bake Off. A special love is live theater. Had she been nine inches taller and thirty pounds lighter, she might have been an actress

Her true passion is fiction, and her stories have won several awards. Never Retreat is her third novel and her fifth book of fiction. She and her husband have two adult children, and three grandchildren. For reasons unknown (an unacknowledged optimism?), she believes one person can make a difference in this world.

Bonnie loves to hear from readers. You can find her contact information, website details and author profile page at https://www.totallybound.com